Peter Watt has spent time as a soldier, articled clerk, prawn trawler deckhand, builder's labourer, pipe layer, real estate salesman, private investigator, police sergeant, surveyor's chainman and advisor to the Royal Papua New Guinea Constabulary. He speaks, reads and writes Vietnamese and Pidgin. He now lives at Maclean on the Clarence River in northern New South Wales. He has volunteered with the Volunteer Rescue Association, Queensland Ambulance Service and currently with the Rural Fire Service. Fishing and the vast open spaces of outback Queensland are his main interests in life.

Peter Watt can be contacted at www.peterwatt.com

Author Photo: Shawn Peene

Also by Peter Watt

The Duffy/Macintosh Series
Cry of the Curlew
Shadow of the Osprey
Flight of the Eagle
To Chase the Storm
To Touch the Clouds
To Ride the Wind
Beyond the Horizon
War Clouds Gather
And Fire Falls
Beneath a Rising Sun
While the Moon Burns
From the Stars Above

The Papua Series
Papua
Eden
The Pacific

The Silent Frontier
The Stone Dragon
The Frozen Circle

The Colonial Series
The Queen's Colonial
The Queen's Tiger
The Queen's Captain
The Colonial's Son

Excerpts from emails sent to Peter Watt

'Hi Cobber, your latest book *The Colonial's Son* was such an enthralling story. It seems your books are getting better and better. My wife said she has never seen me so engrossed in a book as in your last one. Keep up the good work.'

'I have read every book you have written [and] all your series have given me such enjoyment. I enjoy the history which helps make your stories more real. Thank you . . . I look forward to your future books.'

'I have just finished reading *The Queen's Captain* which I thoroughly enjoyed . . . Please keep writing.'

'Peter, I have finished the Curlew series and the Frontier series. I have finished the Queen's and Colonial books and read the Papua series. What is next and when? I need more!'

'I have just finished re-reading your book *Cry of the Curlew* after my first reading about 15 years ago. A lot of books are easily forgotten but the first three books of the Frontier series always stuck with me. I have to say *Cry of the Curlew* was even better than I remembered and I can't wait to go on and keep reading the series . . . It's wonderful to read something so well-written, well-structured about a fascinating and little known period of history with compelling characters. It's a true inspiration and I wanted to pass on my thanks to you for many enjoyable hours of reading. I will be recommending to all I know who love to read. Thank you Peter, and please keep up the writing!'

'Another compelling, page-turning story. Congratulations on a job well done! Perhaps a note for readers might be a good addition to future works, stating: "All housework needs to be up to date and pre-cooked meals on hand in the freezer before starting this tome, because none of the above is possible once you start reading!"'

'I'm writing to compliment you on *The Queen's Colonial* which I've just finished listening to and enjoyed very much. It was both authentic-sounding as a historical novel and fascinating as a human interest story. Luckily *The Queen's Tiger* was available as an ebook in my local library so I'm looking forward to following your characters through further adventures.'

'Peter, greatly anticipating that you're writing again. I know it will be an excellent book to read. Your research, detailed writing and choice of subject matter have always developed into a book that from the first few pages can cause an addictive desire to keep reading. Awesome!!!'

'I am a 91-year-old woman who is housebound and can barely walk. Last year my very kind neighbour introduced me to your books. I have just finished reading the 12th book in your Duffy/ Macintosh series, which I just could not put down . . . Thank you for being a wonderful writer.'

CALL *of* EMPIRE

PETER WATT

MACMILLAN
Pan Macmillan Australia

Pan Macmillan acknowledges the Traditional Custodians of country throughout Australia and their connections to lands, waters and communities. We pay our respect to Elders past and present and extend that respect to all Aboriginal and Torres Strait Islander peoples today. We honour more than sixty thousand years of storytelling, art and culture.

First published 2022 in Macmillan Australia by Pan Macmillan Australia Pty Ltd
1 Market Street, Sydney, New South Wales, Australia, 2000

A catalogue record for this book is available from the National Library of Australia

Typeset in 13/16 pt Bembo by Post Pre-press Group

Printed by IVE

Map on page viii is sourced from KS Inglis, *The Rehearsal: Australians at war in the Sudan, 1885*, Rigby, Adelaide, 1985.
Map on page ix is from the collection of Private Sidney Joseph Cossart, Australian War Memorial, PAIU2011/224.01. Reproduced with permission.

The author and the publisher have made every effort to contact copyright holders for material used in this book. Any person or organisation that may have been overlooked should contact the publisher.

For Cate Paterson
Loyal friend and wonderful woman

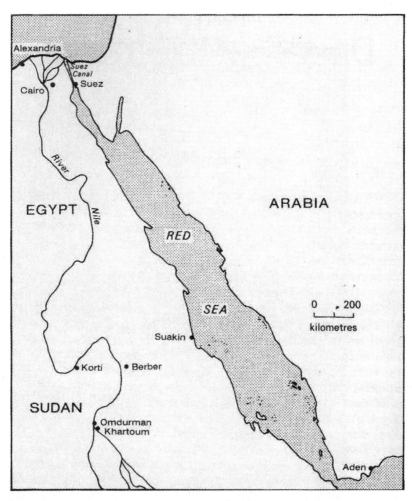

Egypt and the Sudan, circa 1885

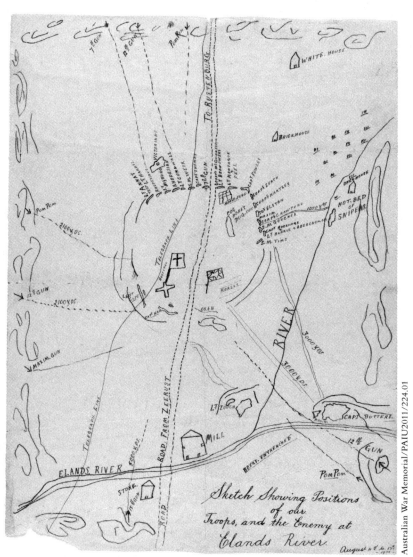

Sketch Showing Positions of our troops and the Enemy
at Elands River August 4th to 17th, 1900

PROLOGUE

It was just before midnight when they splashed across the shallows of the Nile.

Fifty thousand tribal warriors, armed with razor-sharp scimitars, spears and shields, were driven by the religious zeal of a *jihad* against the powers beyond their borders, and led by the charismatic Muhammed Ahmad, self-proclaimed to be the great messianic figure, the Mahdi.

'Allah Akbar!' rose as one sound from their throats as the desert warriors charged the stone city walls of Khartoum, bringing down the main gates and streaming through. Inside, barely eight thousand Egyptian soldiers, led by the legendary imperial soldier General 'Chinese' Gordon, waited. The defenders were starving after the long siege and barely able to stand when the Mahdi's warriors swarmed into the narrow alleyways and through the houses, slaughtering without mercy.

General Gordon would fall to the spears and swords of the Mahdi's men in a futile attempt to rally the soldiers he commanded. A man famed throughout the empire as the epitome of what the British Empire stood for was dead. A war hero whose life had been portrayed as almost saintly to every young English boy and girl, he had been brutally cut down while courageously defending a besieged city against the fanaticism of a tribal chief and his overwhelming army.

The English public cried out for revenge for their fallen martyr. Parliament attempted to resist the outrage but lost against the power of the newspapers supporting the demand for a military response.

Sydney, the British Colony of New South Wales

February 1885

Days later, a telegram arrived in Sydney at the Post and Telegram Office where wires ran into the stone building to enable instant communication with the world through relay stations and local telegraphic services. The dots and dashes of Morse code filling the area around the telegraphic clerk usually spelled out financial reports, death notices and even police communications in the pursuit of intercolonial criminals.

The clerk, a man in his mid-thirties, rolled up his sleeves to give some relief from the stifling summer heat as a report originating in England was clattering away in the confines of his tiny room. He expertly scribbled down the translation and leaned back to read the message. He immediately sat bolt upright when he took in the brief report: *General Gordon has been killed!* The clerk did not know where Khartoum was but, like every young person in the British Empire, he had idolised the British general for many years.

'Mr Todd!' the clerk called to his supervisor. 'I have a message you must read!'

The supervisor shuffled into the tiny office and took the telegram from his subordinate's hand, reading it in disbelief. The arthritis that plagued him temporarily forgotten, he straightened and handed the paper back to his clerk.

'Relay this immediately to the premier's office.'

★

The hundred or so men of Colonel Ian Steele's New South Wales volunteer militia regiment were enjoying a regimental dining night at the town hall on the outskirts of Sydney. Overhead lanterns and tabletop candles illuminated the two rows of citizen soldiers on either side of the long table, with the regimental colonel sitting at the head, wearing his red uniform jacket adorned with the many medals he had earned fighting for the British army in his youth. Although a mere company sat at the table, on paper Ian commanded a regiment, and his hopes were for more volunteers to come forward and fill the vacancies. He knew all these volunteers shared his dream of self-reliance and self-protection for the colony.

At the centre of the table, his son, Captain Josiah Steele, was also resplendent in his dress uniform and campaign medals. Josiah held the role of company commander, and the volunteers – schoolteachers, butchers, bricklayers, bakers, clerks and many other occupations – were like family.

The first course was served, then Ian made the royal toast, with all standing to raise their glasses to the picture of a young Queen Victoria on the wall. As they resumed their chairs, one of the staff hurried to Ian's side, bending to speak in his ear before hastening away again, leaving the colonel in a moment of contemplation. The babble of voices fell silent when the colonel rose and tapped his fork against a crystal wine goblet.

'Gentlemen. I have just been informed that our respected and revered General Gordon has been slain at Khartoum. The city has fallen.'

A murmur of dismay and outrage ran down the length of the table.

Ian continued. 'Our English government may require a volunteer force from its colonies of Canada, New Zealand and Australia. I would hazard a guess that the acting premier will send military assistance to the Sudan. God bless the Queen, and may we answer the call.'

A roar of approval erupted as Ian resumed his seat.

No one noticed the pained look shared by father and son. Unlike the other members of the regiment, they had experienced the realities of war. Both knew that some at the table might also learn of its horrors if the army of New South Wales was invited to travel across the Indian Ocean to Africa.

Part One

Sydney to Suakin 1885

Tommy Cornstalk

ONE

The sun was making its ascent from the ocean in a cloudless blue sky as the British passenger liner approached the mighty sandstone cliffs guarding the entrance to Sydney Harbour.

A tall, broad-shouldered man stood at the bow, gripping the rails like a hunting hound on its leash. He was in his fifties, and his long beard was streaked with grey. Beside him stood a stout, pretty woman wearing a bonnet, and a very attractive, fair-skinned young lady holding a parasol against the biting sun. She was in her early twenties and had caught the eye of every eligible young man on the voyage from England.

'By God, Molly! We will be ashore by mid-morning,' Conan Curry said as if chanting a prayer.

Molly gripped her husband's elbow with an affectionate squeeze. Although she appeared confident, Conan knew that this was not the land of her Welsh roots, all rolling green hills and gentle rivers running to the sea, nor the crowded and smog-infested city where she had spent most of her life building a small financial empire based on her confectionery business. Conan had owned and managed a popular pub there too, where many former military officers and men had been loyal customers. After all, the publican had won the Victoria Cross and was known for his charm and colourful stories of campaigns from the Crimea to New Zealand, in which he'd served as a sergeant major to the mysterious Captain Samuel Forbes who later was exposed as a colonial, Ian Steele.

But now, Conan was returning to the country of his birth. Telegrams had been exchanged between London and Sydney prior to sailing on a course around the southern tip of Africa. The coal-fired steam engines were able to produce electricity for lighting, refrigeration and ventilation, and Conan, Molly and their daughter, Marian, had travelled comfortably in first class. They had departed from a chilly winter into the blazing heat of the southern hemisphere, for which Molly had prepared with lighter but fashionable dresses.

Conan prayed that his closest friend, Colonel Ian Steele, had kept a check on sailing times for the arrival of the passenger liner. As the liner passed through the heads, the harbour seemed much busier than Conan remembered it to be, with some vessels under steam but most still under sail.

Conan had convinced his wife and daughter to sell their assets in England and start a new life in the British colonies, where even more potential lay for capital investment. He had told them stories of how the winters were mild and the air clean, but as they passed close to the southern shore of the harbour, the stench of tanning factories and raw sewage assailed their noses.

Molly cast her husband a quizzical glance.

'It is not as bad as the Thames,' Conan said gruffly.

There was only one thing marring his return home. Conan cast his mind back to the murder of his best friend's mother, far west of Sydney. The matter had long been forgiven by Ian, who accepted that Conan had been a witness and not a participant on that terrible day. Conan knew he had been listed by the colonial police as a wanted man for the murder, and prayed that his name had been forgotten with the long passage of time.

A small tugboat appeared and shepherded the big liner into the Woolloomooloo Wharf, where the three looked down on a crowd of people and a brass band playing tunes to welcome the passengers.

Conan searched the sea of faces for his best friend . . . and there he was! At the same time, Ian saw his former sergeant major beaming down at him. They waved to each other. The disembarkation gangplanks were lowered as the liner was secured to the wharf. Conan bustled his wife and daughter to the exit, and they were soon standing in the packed crowd.

'Sarn't Major Curry,' Ian's distinctive voice called above the din of joyous welcome. Within a moment, they stood face to face, both with tears forming in their eyes. Conan thrust out his hand and the reciprocal strong grasp told a story of too many years apart.

'Damn, it's good to see your face again, Ian,' Conan said.

Behind Ian, Conan spotted Josiah, dressed in a smart suit, like his father. It had been four years since he had last seen Ian's son, after his return to London following the disastrous defeat at Majuba Hill. Conan immediately grasped Josiah in a great bear hug.

'It is grand to see you hale and hearty, my boy,' he said to a startled Josiah. 'I thought this day would never come again in my life, to be with the two men I admire most in the world.'

'Hello, Josiah,' Marian said from behind her father. 'You look well, and a little older than when we last saw each other.'

'Hello, Marian,' Josiah said, disengaging himself from Conan's embrace. 'I might say the same of you.'

Josiah turned to Molly, standing quietly behind her husband, and immediately embraced the woman who had been like a mother to him when he had been living in London. 'I have missed your wonderful meals,' he said as tears ran down her rosy cheeks.

'We have all missed you, my boy,' Molly said.

'I will have your luggage delivered to your new home, which is not far from here. It has a commanding view of the harbour and is only a short distance from our residence,' Ian said. 'I pray that you will like the cottage. It also comes with a maid of impeccable references.'

Ian could see that both Molly and Marian were suffering the effects of the hot summer day, with a sheen of sweat glistening on their faces. 'You will adjust to our climate in no time,' Ian said sympathetically. 'It is not always this hot.' Molly looked doubtful, but nodded.

Ian had two carriages waiting at the entrance to the wharf, and all were bundled in. Their first stop was the Steele mansion on the harbour, where Ian's wife, Isabel, was waiting with his daughter, Becky. Only Ian's younger son, Sam, was absent. At nineteen, he was starting to learn the company business and was currently somewhere at sea in the Pacific islands.

Introductions were made and Ian's guests treated to a lunch of roast lamb and vegetables. The chatter around the great dining room table was almost a din, and Ian was pleased to note that Isabel appeared to have already formed a bond with Molly.

After lunch, the older ladies retired to a large room adjoining the veranda which caught the breeze from the harbour's waters, while Conan and Ian chose to sit in a shaded section of the garden, drinking cold beer from the icebox. Josiah and Marian made their way to another, secluded section of the garden to catch up on the gossip about old friends left in England. Conan and Ian had exchanged a knowing glance; Josiah still carried a flame for the red-headed beauty who had stood on the London docks to farewell him when he'd sailed to war.

'You have certainly made a life away from the army,' Conan commented as he sipped his beer from a pewter tankard. 'We were all devastated when we learned of Ella's passing those years past, but it appears you have been fortunate to find a second opportunity at life with Isabel.'

'She is a fine woman and wonderful wife,' Ian replied. 'My children adore her and have come to accept her as a mother figure. But all my children are of an age where they are starting to pursue their own lives,' he said with a sad smile.

Conan nodded. 'It's the way of things, I suppose.'

'Indeed,' Ian said. 'Did you hear of the death of Gordon?'

'We learned on our arrival in Melbourne,' Conan said, gazing across the manicured green lawns to the rockery, cascading with colourful flowers. 'I always considered Gordon a sanctimonious fool. If the English church hadn't done away with sainthood, he would have been canonised already. The English public will be baying for blood to avenge his demise at the hands of the infidels. A crusade in the Sudan will be messy.' Conan shook his head. 'We're not officially the masters of that region of Africa anyway. The Egyptians are.'

'We both know the English government uses the Egyptians as puppets,' Ian said cynically. 'But I agree that we have no business getting involved in native uprisings in that part of the world.'

Conan stared at his tankard, his expression thoughtful. 'You know my roots are Irish. We fled the old country because of the damned British military occupation of Saint Pat's land, so I am a trifle sympathetic to any people wanting to oust foreign armies.'

'Ah, Conan, did you and I not fight the Queen's imperial wars for over a decade?' Ian asked with a faint smile.

'That was different,' Conan spluttered through his thick beard. 'I was on the run from the English traps and had nowhere else to go.'

'But you rose through the ranks because of your natural ability as a soldier and earned the highest recognition from the Queen herself.'

'It's that damned Celt in our blood. Makes us look for a good donnybrook anywhere we can find it.' Conan's smile faded and he sighed. 'I heard a few former military men discussing on the ship that the colonies might join the English in any expedition to the Sudan.'

'Sir Edward Strickland has already taken the proposal to our acting premier in Macquarie Street,' Ian said. Ian knew the premier, William Bede Dalley, a dapper man in his fifties who always had a flower in his coat lapel. He was liked by all for his bonhomie, and tended to be addressed as 'old boy'. He had only been in his post with the Legislative Assembly for four months. As a Catholic politician in a majority Protestant political system, Ian suspected that the premier might volunteer an expeditionary force to prove to his non-Catholic political colleagues that he was a fervent supporter of the monarchy.

'Is that the same Edward Strickland who was with us on the advance to Sebastopol?' Conan asked.

'He also campaigned in New Zealand when we were there,' Ian replied. 'He now lives in Sydney. From what I know, he is a competent officer. It is interesting that he is also a staunch Catholic who has brought the proposition of sending troops to assist Britain with its campaign in the Sudan to a fellow Catholic. I wonder if this is a conspiracy by Papists to endear themselves to our Queen?' Ian added with a grin. Protestants held deep suspicion of those whose foremost loyalty was to their Pope rather than the British crown.

Conan snorted at Ian's jibe. 'Do you think the premier will volunteer the army of New South Wales to the fight?' Conan asked.

His question was soon answered. On Friday 13 February 1885, without conferring with his government, Premier Dalley, fearing that Canada, New Zealand and the other Australian colonies might beat him to the punch, sent a cable to London, volunteering the services of the armed forces of New South Wales.

★

Josiah Steele was unaware of his government's political manoeuvrings as he sat in the garden with Marian, who had armed herself with a parasol against the biting rays of the Sydney sun. Sweat still glistened on her pale face and the cold glass of freshly made lemonade was little help in the heat of a southern summer in the colonies. Marian had matured into a beautiful young woman who could turn any man's head, with flaming red hair, emerald-green eyes and a trim figure.

'You ceased answering my letters,' Josiah said.

'I saw little point in continuing our correspondence,' Marian replied, sipping her lemonade. 'I did not think we would ever see each other again.'

'But here you are.' Josiah smiled.

'It was my father's choice to return to the colonies,' Marian sniffed. 'From what my friends in London have told me, there is little sophisticated society or any real learning and culture on this side of the world.'

Josiah broke into a broader smile. 'I may be able to change your mind on the matter of us colonials living in a backwater, if you would step out with me. In fact, I promise I will.'

Marian glanced at Josiah from under her colourful parasol with just the slightest hint of interest. 'I will keep you to your promise,' she said playfully.

Josiah experienced a rush of warmth. Ever since his father had told him the Currys would be moving to Sydney, he has been going over the wonderful memories of his time in London, particularly his feelings for Marian. Now a grown woman sitting beside him, so far from the smog and cold of London, he almost felt he was in a wonderful dream.

'Your father told me that you are working with him,' Marian said.

'We are venturing into the Pacific islands to obtain copra contracts and other products,' Josiah said. 'My brother, Sam, is under my wing, learning about trade and transport. He will be a real asset in the future.'

'Your family business sounds fascinating,' Marian said. 'And I am glad you are no longer facing any wars for the Queen,' she added.

Josiah frowned. 'I hold a commission with my father's volunteer regiment, Marian.'

'But the Australian colonies do not supply soldiers to fight England's imperial wars. It has never happened before,'

Marian argued. 'There was discussion on the ship that the Australian colonies should go to assist the British army in Africa, but my friends in London who are with the army and navy say that is a remote chance. They do not consider colonial soldiers as having the same experience or skills as the British.'

Josiah had encountered the snobbish attitudes of the British elite and could not disagree with them more. 'There are many former British soldiers in New South Wales. Myself, for one.'

Marian was silent as she turned to look out at the view of the sparkling harbour. 'You know my feelings about imperial campaigns. They have not changed since we first met,' she said finally. 'This fight is between Sudan and Egypt. Britain has no place there, and the colonies certainly should stay out of it.'

'It's not that simple,' Josiah replied lamely, despite knowing Marian spoke some truth. 'But let us not worry. I am like you, and do not believe we will be called on to assist the British army in avenging General Gordon's death at Khartoum.' He was relieved to see Marian smile slightly as she turned to face him again, and added, 'So I will have the opportunity of showing off some of our wonderful culture when you settle in.'

'Marian,' a voice called.

'My mother,' Marian said. 'I think it is time for us to visit our new home.'

She rose from the stone bench and Josiah followed her to the house. He was torn, as he would dearly love to fight just one more time while in the prime of his manhood. But there was little chance he would march again with men who counted on him to lead and keep them alive. He was destined to live a life contributing to the family enterprises.

Besides, Marian was back in his life and that was just as important as soldiering. He knew he loved her, and that it was a matter of her seeing that.

TWO

This government offers to Her Majesty's government two batteries of our Permanent Field Artillery, with ten sixteen-pound guns, properly horsed; also, an effective and disciplined battalion of infantry, five hundred strong . . . Can undertake to land Force at Suakin within thirty days from embarkation. Reply at once.

'That is a copy of the telegram I had sent to London after a Cabinet meeting and sent to the agent general for New South Wales. I had it sent on behalf of Australia and not simply our colony alone,' William Dalley said, holding a cup of tea in his hand to his esteemed guest, Ian Steele, as they gazed out from the premier's mansion in Manly on the harbour. 'As you are a colonel with your volunteer infantry unit, do you think it is feasible?'

'My unit is under-strength, but I also feel that a call to arms would very quickly provide the numbers required to fully complement an infantry battalion.'

Dalley turned to gaze out the large window that overlooked a lawn browned by the searing summer sun. 'I have also spoken with other esteemed military men, and they echo your thoughts about raising the numbers we need to supply an expeditionary force. My fear is that the British might want our volunteers to be deployed to South Africa on garrison duties, freeing their army. Or even to England for the same purpose. I have forwarded the cablegram to the other colonies, but feel the force would be delayed if we attempted to coordinate an integrated force.'

'A good point, sir,' Ian replied. 'There would be the problem of a standardising of military systems, training and logistics. In my opinion, our colony has the best chance to quickly mobilise the force that you have proposed to assist the British. Because of the vast geography of this continent, we are better able to organise the force required by local telegraph and transport. I know the few of my regiment would jump at the opportunity to employ their military skills in a foreign war. For them it would be a great adventure travelling to another land far from their own.'

'Was that the appeal for you when you were a younger man, Colonel Steele? I know much about your colourful past fighting for the Queen.'

'To an extent, that was the lure of my employment as a commissioned officer with the British army,' Ian replied. 'But after years of exposure to war I am more realistic about what lies ahead for any young man who views the war in the Sudan as an adventure. Sadly, one cannot convince young men that war is hell on earth.'

'I believe your own son Josiah also served as an officer with a Scots regiment on the march to Kandahar back in '80, and was also at Majuba Hill.'

'As you know, Premier, that was a taste of that hell

18

I referred to,' Ian said, placing his empty teacup on a polished cabinet.

'And yet, you and your son continue to wear the uniform of a soldier. Very interesting.'

'We do so because we believe in using our knowledge and experience to defend our shores against any possible enemy invasion.'

'I was informed by a colonial cardinal that you were baptised as a Catholic and yet your son is a Jew.'

'His mother was of the Jewish faith, and before she passed away I promised her that our children would be raised in her faith. I always attempt to keep my promises,' Ian answered.

'You will never be a politician if you stand by the policy of keeping promises.' Dalley grinned. 'I saw your son Samuel play against the Queenslanders at the Sydney Cricket Ground a couple of years ago in the rugby match when we beat them,' Dalley said, gesturing to Ian to take a chair. 'For such a young man, he is a giant. He played in the forwards rather than the backline, with the gentlemen. I have had a few contacts in the newspapers saying rugby should be banned for its brutality. Many are turning to the Victorian game of Australian Rules and soccer because of rugby's inherent violence.'

Ian smiled. 'Sam stands at six feet tall and towers over all the family,' he replied. 'His build made him a perfect selection in the forwards, and he loves the roughness of the game.'

'And you have a daughter, Rebecca?' Dalley continued.

'Yes, my would-be princess is eighteen now and has aspirations to becoming a medical doctor, though we know our medical schools do not admit females.'

'That may be about to change,' Dalley said. 'I know of a young lady, a Miss Georgina Berne, who has been admitted to university. It is rumoured that she also aspires to study medicine in the future and her scholastic grades mean she could easily pass the entrance exams.'

'Becky is also a brilliant student,' Ian said. 'There may one day be an opportunity for her to sit for a university position.'

'This is a country where we all have a chance to better ourselves. Education, ambition and hard work make us all equals. Look at me, of Irish Catholic heritage, now acting premier in a society dominated by the Protestant elite. But back to the business at hand. Do you consider that we have a one hundred per cent chance of assembling a force within the next week or so?'

'I am sure there will be many who will flock to the flag,' Ian replied. 'And many already experienced soldiers will be amongst them.'

'Good to hear, Colonel,' Dalley said with a nod. 'I should at some stage invite you and the family to dine with me when we get this matter behind us. I would be very interested in learning more about your life and military experiences.'

'It would be a pleasure,' Ian said.

The two men shook hands and Ian left to step into a waiting hackney cab that took him to the Manly Wharf for the trip across the harbour. On the ferry, Ian pondered on whether he would be selected to lead the contingent, but had a bad feeling that politics would decide that appointment. He was not well accepted by many in the inner circles of the colonial government. A cloud still hung over his head after the death of a well-known public servant years earlier. Harold Skinner had been ambushed and murdered by bushrangers on the Great Western Road, and many knew that Ian Steele had not liked the man, and had even been questioned by the police. But no one had ever hanged for the crime.

★

Josiah could feel his heart beating hard in his chest. Marian had agreed to accompany him to the National Art Gallery of New South Wales, and it would be his first time alone with her since her arrival in Sydney. This outing was his attempt to display some of the colony's culture, although it was limited to Australian artists as the gallery could not afford overseas masters. Josiah loved the works of the local artists, as they portrayed in lively colours the people and places of his land, but what would Marian think of his love for the local artistry? That thought caused him a shiver of concern. Would she frown on the skills of those who painted in Australia?

He adjusted his tie and reached for a bowler hat. Dressed in his best three-piece suit, he readied himself to depart in the family carriage.

His driver was Will Bowden, a former soldier who was now the family's groundskeeper.

'Mornin', Cap'n,' he greeted cheerfully.

'Good morning, Will. I believe you know where the Currys reside?'

'Certainly do, Cap'n. It was good to see Sarn't Major Curry after all these years.'

'We will be going to the art gallery at the Domain, and I will have Miss Curry home before dark,' Josiah instructed. 'I felt such a long day for you deserved an extra bonus of a crate of beer.'

'Not necessary, but appreciated, Cap'n,' Will replied, urging the light single horse carriage into motion.

It did not take long to reach the cottage overlooking the harbour on the South Head, and Josiah alighted to knock on the door. He was greeted by Marian, dressed in the fashionable bustle dress, pinched at the waist. She also wore a small flower-adorned hat and carried a dainty parasol.

'You are very punctual, Josiah Steele.' She smiled, opening the door wider.

'Good morning, my boy,' Conan greeted, dressed in a shirt and braced trousers. He was holding a copy of the *Herald*. 'It appears that we might get ourselves into this stoush in the Sudan.'

'I do not think that England will heed our cry to assist them,' Josiah replied. 'As someone who served the Queen in many campaigns, you know how well the British army can perform in the field under the worst of conditions.'

'You may have a point, young Josiah, but never under-estimate the fighting prowess of Australian colonials. This will be our chance to show the British that we can fight as good as any one of them.'

Josiah saw Marian frown at the mention of colonial involvement in the Sudan and hastily changed the subject. 'I will ensure Marian will be home for dinner tonight, Sarn't Major,' he said.

'I know you will, on your honour as an officer and a gentleman,' Conan replied, shuffling back into the cottage.

The journey to the Domain, with its leafy trees and gardens, took the carriage close to the crowded inner suburbs of rundown tenements, with many children playing in the narrow streets, wearing ragged clothes. Marian noticed the squalor. 'It is little different from what I witnessed amongst the poor in London,' she commented.

'The wealthier members of our city live in the new suburbs,' Josiah said. 'Those are the homes of labourers and unskilled workers.'

'From what my father told me about colonials, I had imag-ined that food was in abundance and poverty did not exist.'

'Our fathers grew up in a rural region, west of Sydney. Food was adequate and the air clean of the stench we get from our factories in the city. I can promise you that you will be impressed with where we are going. My stepmother is a member of the society behind the establishment of our art gallery.'

They arrived at a stately public building with a wooden annex. Marian seemed to enjoy the display of colonial art, but it was the picnic in the leafy Hyde Park afterwards that impressed her most. She took in the casual strollers, family groups and young couples parading along gravel trails under the shade of the many trees.

Josiah had organised a hamper of lamb tongues, wafers, cheese, fresh strawberries and a bottle of champagne, which Will Bowden produced for them, and they fell into easy conversation on a vast array of subjects. Josiah quickly learned that Marian had not lost her social ideas on equality or Britain's involvement in imperial wars. He was uneasy on the subject, but she conceded that his membership of his citizen militia to defend the colony was admirable.

Before they knew it, hours had passed though they felt like minutes, and it was time to return Marian to her family. Josiah felt emboldened by Marian's crestfallen expression that their time together was over, and invited her to accompany him to dinner at one of the city's best restaurants the following week, which she gladly accepted.

★

The shoreline rose and fell on a gentle sea. A tall, well-built youth stood at the bow of the schooner *Ella,* watching the smoke rise from a campsite in the scrub off the beach. Beside him stood a shorter man in his mid-thirties wearing a sea captain's cap and clean white shirt.

'About time we launched the boat and got our catch ashore,' Captain Ling Lee said to his first mate. 'My people should be ready to take our sea cucumbers and turn them into bêche-de-mer for export to China.'

Sam Steele nodded. 'Hopefully all goes well, and we can prove to my father that your investment into the sea cucumber trade will prove profitable,' Sam mused as the schooner anchor clattered into the crystal-clear waters of the small bay off colonial Queensland's northern coast.

Sam Steele and Ling Lee were an odd couple, but had a mutual respect. Lee was wiry; every part of his body was honed with steel-like muscle, and he kept his head shaved. He was known to be a firm but fair captain. Sam had the hardened body of an older man and was bronzed from the constant tropical sun. He was handsome and carried himself with a new air of maturity, developed aboard the schooner.

Two Chinese men appeared on the coral sand beach and waved to them. The sleek two-masted schooner belonged to the Steele family enterprises, named for Sam's mother, who had passed away from cancer many years earlier. Ling Lee had managed and partly owned the gold ore-crushing machinery on the Palmer River Goldfields and had proved extremely competent in extracting the precious metal. As gold became harder to produce, with the big veins drying up, he could see the writing on the wall and sold off the equipment to an enthusiastic but inexperienced Englishman and his business partners.

While Lee had been born in Parramatta, west of Sydney, he understood much about the country of his parents' birth and knew just how prized slimy sea slugs were to the wealthy of China, and in other parts of Asia. He made the proposal to Ian personally in a meeting in Brisbane and accepted young Sam aboard as his first mate.

The two men had met when the American-built two-masted schooner was delivered to the Brisbane River.

Sam knew that the Chinese man had been his brother's companion on the dangerous Palmer River mission of 1875, and Josiah had told his younger brother that Lee could be a dangerous man when he needed to be, but was a loyal friend of the family. Josiah had hinted that Lee had magical qualities in close combat and Sam had laughed, but he did not laugh after he invited Lee to demonstrate his 'magical combat', finding his strength and size were no match for his new friend's speed and skill, as he flipped Sam on the deck of their new acquisition.

As the schooner's longboat was lowered into the calm seas, the two were joined by a grizzled man in his fifties with a long beard and hair. He had decades of experience doing so in his home waters of the eastern seaboard of the USA. Little was known about the taciturn man, apart from that he could handle a schooner anywhere in the world's seas, and he had fought in the recent American Civil War with the famed Maine Regiment that had held the line at Gettysburg.

To all intents and purposes, Ebenezer Wright was the real captain of the schooner and was paid as such, though he had asked that his name did not appear on any ship's papers. Lee and Sam guessed that he was a man who wished to remain discreetly out of the public eye and they did not ask why.

The valuable cargo of sea slugs was transferred to the longboat in barrels and rowed ashore by the crew, a mix of Chinese and Islanders, and Lee. Sam and Ebenezer waited patiently on the deck of the ship.

After a couple of hours Lee returned and clambered aboard.

'Did all go well?' Sam asked a worried-looking Lee.

'All went well,' Lee replied, gazing east to the calm sea. 'But one of my trusted men ashore has warned a great wind is coming. He has never been wrong before, and says that it will hit in the next couple of hours.'

Ebenezer joined Sam and Lee on deck. 'Mr Steele, I noticed the barometer pressure is falling more than it should,' he said with a frown. 'Looks like we might be in for some bad weather.'

'How bad?' Sam asked, feeling a creeping dread.

Ebenezer looked him dead in the eye. 'It's cyclone season, Mr Steele.'

Cyclone! The dreaded word could mean a death sentence for them all.

THREE

Ebenezer weighed up all options with the imminent storm and chose to remain anchored off the beach, explaining that the outlying reefs would bear the brunt of the high seas. All anchors were lowered and the schooner's hatches battened against the big waves expected to roll in when the cyclone hit.

And then it hit with a ferocity of nature Sam had never before experienced. For two days, they rode out the cyclone, the eerie howling of the wind rocking the schooner, dragging at its anchors and pushing it dangerously towards the shore. A few great waves swamped the sailing ship, but she remained afloat, tossing the crew from one side of the cabins to the other.

On the third day, as if by magic, the winds dropped, the seas abated and the sun shone over a dirty-coloured ocean full of debris.

Staggering onto the deck, Sam marvelled how close they had come to being grounded on the beach. Another day of the battering winds might have seen them blown ashore.

'Thank you, Mother,' Sam whispered as he gazed at the shore. He was sure she had protected her youngest son and namesake vessel from the raging forces of nature.

'It does not look good ashore,' Lee said when he joined Sam at the railings. 'No sign of any life.'

Sam silently agreed. 'We need to launch a boat and survey the damage to the camp,' he suggested. A boat was arranged for him, Lee and two crew members to row to the beach.

When they grounded on the sand, they were met by the bedraggled Chinese supervisor of the camp. He spoke to Lee, who interpreted. 'We have lost our catch,' he said sorrowfully. 'My man said the storm wrecked everything, including the sea cucumbers.'

'Damn!' Sam exploded. 'Our efforts for the last month have come to naught, and your contact from Singapore will probably arrive with the silver and we have nothing in return. My father's company is going to take a big loss.' Even as he bemoaned the financial loss, a sturdy Chinese junk appeared, sailing around a small headland, her sails ripped and showing the wear of passing through the cyclone.

Lee stood on the beach to meet the fierce-looking Chinese sailors manning the longboat from the ship. When it grounded ashore, Lee greeted a well-dressed man in his fifties, the usual buyer of their cargo of sea cucumbers.

'The esteemed ancestors have protected you from the devils of the storm,' the man said.

'But not what you have come for,' Lee responded, causing the older man to frown.

'I have risked my crew and ship to be here,' he said. 'And you did not take precautions to protect our merchandise. This has cost my master much money.'

Lee had met the man's master during his days working the Palmer River Goldfields and knew it was not wise to disappoint the powerful Tong leader, who now lived in Singapore. 'We are just as upset at our financial loss,' Lee answered.

'Master Zhu does not accept excuses, as I believe you know,' the man said with a note of a threat. Lee felt a chill of fear, aware of just how far the dreaded Tong leader could reach to exact retribution.

'I may be able to satisfy Master Zhu in other ways,' Lee responded. 'I am still loyal to his cause to free our people in China from the imperialist grip.'

The captain of the junk paused, seeming to think over Lee's offer. 'Zhu does require the services of a European trading ship to assist him in a venture important to our freedom,' he said finally. 'Your ship would not attract as much attention as a Chinese sailing vessel. I am sure that Zhu would accept the loss of our merchandise and still pay you the silver we would have for the sea cucumbers. I am empowered to even double that payment, if you agree to assist the master's mission.'

Lee listened as the Chinese captain explained the mission before nodding his acceptance. The captain walked back to his boat and spoke to one of his sailors, who hefted out some leather bags filled with silver ingots.

Sam came to stand beside Lee.

'What is happening?' Sam asked as the bags were deposited at Lee's feet. 'Why are they paying us when we lost the catch?'

Lee turned to Sam. 'I have reached an agreement to provide a service for our trading partners,' he said more calmly than he felt. 'We are to smuggle guns for the Chinese. The payment is far beyond that we would have received for the sea cucumbers.'

'What?' Sam exclaimed. 'That sounds dangerous.'

'Disappointing the Tong leader is more dangerous,' Lee said firmly.

'We could lose our lives and the *Ella*,' Sam argued. Smuggling any product was dangerous. If they were caught with guns, it was a death sentence in any country.

'We survived the storm,' Lee said. 'We can weather anything. Think of the profit we can show your father.'

Sam ran his eyes over the bags of silver. As much as he knew the trade-off was risky, the scheme had the smell of adventure.

★

The premier was resting at a pastoral property on his way back to Sydney when a messenger arrived with the cablegram from London. Dalley read it aloud to those around him that fateful Sunday afternoon:

Her Majesty's government accepts with much satisfaction offer of your government upon the understanding the Force must be placed absolutely under General Commanding as to the duties upon which it will be employed. Force of artillery is greater than required; only one battery accepted. Transport should call at Aden for orders. I am to inform you, in strict confidence, that plans of General not fully formed but may probably involve placing troops in summer quarters after short campaign from Suakin; if after this knowledge your government prefer immediate dispatch of contingent, War Office does not desire to delay it. Press comment very favourably upon your splendid offer.

Cheers and backslapping erupted. Finally, the sons of the far-flung colony would have the opportunity to display their patriotic commitment to the Motherland.

Time was short and a force had to be mobilised to meet the deadline. The war, so far away, was drawing the Steele family into the arid lands of the Sudan.

★

On the Tuesday morning following the release of the cablegram news, Ian and Josiah were finishing breakfast and perusing the morning papers. The sun flooded in through the large windows, illuminating the spacious dining room.

'I spoke with Strickland, and he has agreed to accept you for the contingent,' Ian said, sipping the last of his tea. 'But you will have to revert back to a lieutenancy to join them. He is impressed with your service in Afghanistan, and later in South Africa.'

'I would not consider Majuba Hill much of a reference,' Josiah replied bitterly.

'Strickland is aware that the disaster was not the fault of your regiment,' Ian consoled him. 'The commission is yours, if you accept it.'

'I feel it is my duty to serve our colony,' Josiah said. 'This time, I am serving my country and not simply that of my birth.'

Ian folded his paper and placed it down. 'Many young men feel the same way,' he said. 'But I suspect that Marian will not welcome the news. Conan has told me of her strong anti-imperial convictions.'

Josiah glanced at his father with surprise, but then again, there was little that his father did not know. 'That will be a problem,' Josiah admitted. 'We discussed Britain's role in the Sudan, and she is of the opinion that the Mahdi and his warriors are fighting for their independence. She feels that we should stay out of the whole matter.'

'The death of Gordon at Khartoum has sealed England's commitment,' Ian said. 'The newspapers in England and here are clamouring for vengeance, and so are the people. Even our Queen demands justice. And so justice will be had.'

★

The *Ella* was out to sea on a course north along the Queensland coast.

Under the light of a kerosene lantern, Ebenezer, Sam and Lee huddled around a chart, poring over the route they would navigate to Singapore.

Lee had explained how the French were invading the Chinese-controlled Tonkin province of northern Indochina. From the last reports, the Chinese were being beaten back by superior European weapons and technology.

'Zhu has always said that the Chinese people need modern firearms to defend their sovereign territories,' Lee said.

Sam scratched the stubble on his chin. 'From what I have read of geography, the people of Indochina are not really Chinese, but called Vietnamese.'

Lee glanced up at Sam. 'The Vietnamese are subjects of the Chinese Empire, and we must protect them against the imperial forces of France.'

Sam did not argue, but felt Lee was being a bit hypo-critical in his defence of the Chinese army in a place of ethnically different people who he knew from his reading spoke a different language and had a different culture.

'So, how can we help the Chinese against the French?' Sam asked.

'Zhu has arranged for us to take delivery of five hundred Winchester repeating rifles and a substantial quantity of cartridges for the rifles in Singapore, which we will deliver to Tonkin to equip the defenders,' Lee said.

'Do you think that a few repeating rifles will make any difference to the French invasion?' Sam asked.

Lee smiled. 'We have a good example recently, with the Turks and the Russians fighting in the Balkans. The Turkish army were armed with .44-calibre Henry rimfire repeating rifles. They were able to cut the advancing Russian soldiers to pieces when they were within a couple of hundred yards. The future of warfare is no longer the single-shot rifle. Even the meagre numbers we have to take to the army in Tonkin just might turn our fortunes against the French.'

'Do you know how we will get our hands on the cargo?' Ebenezer asked, puffing on his pipe, filling the cabin with grey smoke.

'Zhu has a contact in Singapore who will direct us to the cargo. I know the man who works for Zhu and where I can locate him. He is an American who has lived for many years in China and Singapore.'

Sam frowned, but was prepared to go along with Lee's plan. After all, the silver they had been paid was a considerable amount. Had not his big brother risked his life as an officer for the Queen? This was not much different, in Sam's reasoning, and a lot more lucrative. He now resigned himself to becoming a gun runner rather than a simple island trader.

★

His father had been right about Marian's reaction.

Molly and Conan had invited the Steele family for dinner, and Marian had hardly spoken to Josiah, picking at her meal with a lack of appetite.

Finally, Josiah offered to take her on a post-dinner walk of the garden, and was surprised when she agreed.

It was Marian who opened the first words in the tension existing between the couple. 'I thought that you had put behind you the desire to serve the Queen as an officer in the army,' she snapped.

'This is different,' Josiah defended. 'This time, I will be wearing the uniform of our colony, not of Britain. This campaign is us Australians demonstrating to the Mother Country our ability to stand up to a common enemy.'

'Common enemy!' Marian scoffed as she sat down on a garden bench. 'Since when has a Muslim army so far from your colony been a threat? Josiah Steele, your explanation is hogwash, as well you know. You simply want to dash off and put your life at jeopardy for the sake of soldiering again.'

Josiah hung his head when he sat down beside Marian. He knew that she was telling the truth; he missed the life of being with his men on the battlefield.

'I am sure I am not alone in my resistance to this call to arms,' Marian said. 'For the short time I have been here, I have come to learn one of your esteemed men of politics, Mr Henry Parkes, has expressed his desire to stop the colony sending troops to assist the British army.'

'There are a few who wish to stop us,' Josiah admitted. 'But we have public support. I feel that my presence with the contingent is important, because I have actual experience on the battlefield.'

Marian suddenly stood up and stepped away from the bench to face Josiah.

'Don't expect me to watch you depart. Or to be waiting here to welcome you home, Josiah Steele,' she said angrily. 'I am not going to condone your quest, nor be like my long-suffering mother, who sacrificed her life to a soldier.'

Marian stormed back into the house, leaving Josiah sitting alone in the dark, gazing out at the twinkling lights on the harbour's calm waters. Had some bloody dervish on the other side of the Indian Ocean just cost him any potential future with the woman he most desired in the world?

FOUR

The sounds and sights were so familiar to Ian Steele as he reviewed men recruited for the Sudan contingent. Senior non-commissioned officers barked at recruits attempting to comply with strange words known only to soldiers. The number required to complete a battalion of infantry had been set at five hundred and twenty-two, with a complete artillery battery of two hundred and twelve men in support. Horses were allocated to officers and the premier had cabled London that they would be ready to steam from Circular Quay in early March.

A young man wearing the rank of lieutenant approached and saluted. Ian responded in kind.

'Hello, Father,' Josiah said. 'It is good to see you here to support our lads.'

'We could have provided the British with three battalions,' Ian growled. 'So many men we had to turn away because of the quota restriction, and we have had many from the other colonies express their desire to join the contingent. Ah, but I see that young George is one of the men from our regiment who was successful.'

'I was able to vouch for his skills as a trained member of the regiment,' Josiah said. 'We are whipping the recruits into efficient soldiers, but so many have previously served overseas as members of the British army and navy, and are experienced soldiers.'

'I expect that you will attend dinner tonight. It may be a long time before we see you return to us,' Ian said. 'I only wish I had been able to secure a staff appointment with the contingent, but there was a surplus of senior officers ahead of me.' Ian sighed. 'Maybe just a foolish wish by a father to be with his son on the battlefield.'

'You know that I am capable of looking after myself, Father,' Josiah replied. 'And the family needs you at home. I am sure you promised Isabel that your days of running into danger are past. Besides, Sam is probably in more danger than me, sailing around the Pacific on the *Ella*.'

'I know that you are right,' Ian answered. 'We have a business enterprise that is ever expanding, and it needs a captain to guide it. Speaking of family, Conan informed me that Marian is rather annoyed with you.'

'Marian has always held strong views about what she calls imperialism,' Josiah said. 'But this is different. This is a need to teach the Mahdi that he cannot go about killing such great men as General Gordon.'

Ian smiled. 'You are definitely a son of the Empire. Right or wrong, a soldier marches to the sound of bugles and drums for his Queen. This time we may be New South Welshmen, but you will identify as Australians in the Sudan and represent all of the colonies.'

Both men watched the recruits falling into ranks with a sense of pride. This was the opportunity to express support for the Mother Country, and prove the mettle of the sons of convicts.

★

The *Ella* had smooth sailing past the northern part of New Guinea, newly acquired by the Germans the year before, and set a course for the British port of Singapore.

On the journey, Sam had come to learn more about Lee's passionate support for his desire to see China as a strong and independent nation, free of European dominance. Sam sympathised, possibly because he was aware of the bias of Europeans against his Jewish faith. In Russia, Jewish villages were constantly raided by the Czar's Cossacks, who murdered innocent men, women and children. Sam knew there was injustice in the world and understood Lee's devotion to his cause.

It was early morning when those on the schooner caught sight of the island. Sam gazed at the busy settlement, its waterways filled with a multinational fleet of trading ships. There were European steamers, wind-driven junks, smaller sampans and even a few Arab dhows. The major trading settlement had been established by the English many years earlier, strategically located between the major areas of Asia and connected to Europe by sea. Sam could see a skyline of tall, well-designed stone buildings surrounded by shanty towns of huts, but when the breeze shifted, he caught the scents of the Orient, some pleasant, others odious – whiffs of human waste and rotting food mixed with the pungent aromas of spices.

'We should be ashore by midday,' Lee commented.

'Have you been here before?' Sam asked, marvelling at this alien world off the bow.

'Yes, a couple of years ago, when I was working with Zhu,' Lee replied. 'He has a business here, importing and exporting trade goods which has made him a very wealthy man.'

'What do you know about the man we are to meet and who will organise our cargo?' Sam asked.

'Only that he is an American with a shady past. But that can be expected, considering he was able to acquire so many rifles and ammunition. I think we should always be on our guard dealing with him. One never knows where loyalties truly lie. Hopefully his are to the silver being paid by Zhu.'

Sam felt uneasy, but the schooner anchored, and Ebenezer remained on the ship as a crew member rowed Sam and Lee ashore. Sam was amazed by the bustling streets and brushed past Indians, Chinese, Malays and a few Europeans before they reached the address of the American in a European quarter. They were met at the front entrance of a compound enclosing a small factory. The man who met them was a tough-looking Indian who spoke no English but understood that the big, suntanned European and more slightly built Chinese man were there to visit his boss. He left the front gate and returned some minutes later with a dapper-looking man wearing a white tropical suit and hat.

'I am Haynes. I believe we have a mutual friend.'

'Master Zhu is a friend to many,' Lee replied. 'Our schooner is anchored offshore to take on the cargo.'

'Please, enter,' the American said in his heavy southern accent. 'I have refreshments.'

Lee and Sam followed the American inside a bungalow attached to the factory, which Sam realised was a storage building.

A pretty Chinese woman produced coffee for the three men seated at a low table in a lofty room with a slowly rotating overhead fan. It was hot and humid, and sweat ran down the face of the American, who dabbed it away with a dainty handkerchief.

'I prefer coffee to the insipid English tea here,' Haynes said. 'I hope that you enjoy my coffee.'

Sam was not a coffee drinker, but said nothing. Nor did Lee.

'What are the arrangements for the transfer of our cargo?' Lee asked as Sam sipped the coffee.

'Zhu has paid me, and it will be rowed out to your ship tonight, at which point my part of the deal will be complete. What you do with the guns is your concern, but I am curious as to where you will take them.'

'As you said,' Lee replied, 'your part of the deal finishes with the cargo safely aboard the schooner. That is all you have to know.'

Haynes shrugged. *'C'est la vie,'* he said. 'Something I learned from a Frenchman I once had the misfortune to deal with back in New Orleans. But he no longer has to concern himself with this earthly world.'

Neither Sam nor Lee asked why.

There was little else to discuss after Lee identified the *Ella* to Haynes, so they departed.

What Lee and Sam did not know was that there was another listening in on their meeting with the American. Once they left, a tough-looking Malay man, his face scarred from his brutal life as a Temenggong pirate operating in the waters surrounding Singapore, emerged from a side room.

'You know what to do,' Haynes said.

The man nodded. 'Zhu will know that we have complied with our end of the bargain.'

Haynes had a healthy fear of the Tong leader.

★

Darkness fell over the waters off Singapore. A half-moon cast faint light as Sam, Lee and Ebenezer stood on the deck, nervously awaiting the sampans to transfer their cargo to the schooner. Mid-evening three small sampans hailed the *Ella* and pulled alongside.

All three schooner men were armed with revolvers, wary of their visitors, but the transfer went without incident, and the wooden crates were stowed below deck. The sampans pulled away and Ebenezer had the anchors raised and set course for Cochin China.

The further they got from Singapore, the more relaxed Sam felt. The seas were calm by the time they were out of sight of Singapore, hours later, and Sam was on the deck with a mug of hot tea when he suddenly spotted something on the horizon.

'Lee!' he yelled. 'Get up here quick.'

Within seconds, Lee scrambled to the deck. 'What is it?'

'There,' Sam said, extending his arm beyond their bow.

Lee squinted into the darkness and saw three watercraft that looked very much like Arab dhows.

'And to our port side.'

Lee swivelled his head and saw another boat under sail. Ebenezer joined them and the three men stood watching the four watercraft moving to close with the schooner, approaching fast.

'Fishing boats?' Sam asked Ebenezer.

'I don't think so,' Ebenezer said. 'More like goddamn Malacca pirates.'

'Can we outrun them?' Lee asked.

'Not with the winds as they are,' Ebenezer replied. 'It almost looks like they were lying in wait for us.'

A flash erupted from one of the dhows, followed by the bark of a cannon. Within a second, a waterspout erupted in a column off starboard, uncomfortably close.

Ebenezer called to his frightened crew, who had come above deck to observe the four boats. 'To arms!' he roared. 'Cutlasses and spikes!'

For a moment, the crew members stood petrified with fear at the sight of the boats rapidly approaching before scuttling below to retrieve the weapons required to oppose any boarding of their schooner. Sam had already retrieved the repeating rifle Josiah had gifted him, and Lee had a newly acquired repeating rifle, as well as his sword. Ebenezer stood at the ship's helm, armed with a brace of six-shot revolvers. This was a fight to the death, and as heads started to appear above the deck railings of the dhows, Sam could see that they were heavily outnumbered.

Sam chambered a round and leaned against the mast for a steady shot, but in the dark, it was hard to aim.

'Prepare to repel boarders,' Sam yelled above the soft moan of the breeze washing across the sea. He did not think about this order, used so often in the history of naval warfare. Then he fired and rechambered another round to fire again, as did Lee at the bow of the schooner.

But one of the dhows had already smashed side-on into the *Ella*, and grappling hooks slammed into the deck. The pirates began to scramble aboard, armed with swords, knives and spears.

★

Lieutenant Josiah Steele was poring over the paybooks for his platoon. His men had been stood down for the day and Josiah now worked in the relative peace of his office in the evening oversighting the administrative requirements of his men. His private soldiers were being paid five shillings a day while married men received seven shillings plus sixpence for each child in the family. It was not as much as a civilian bricklayer, who could expect to earn twelve shillings and sixpence a day. Reflecting on this, Josiah concluded that many who had enlisted had done so at a financial loss. The lure of adventure, travel and a good fight for the Mother Country seemed to be their motivation.

The rattle of carriages passing on the road outside the army headquarters was incongruous against the barked orders from experienced NCOs, but the sound of men drilling outside at Victoria Barracks was the background noise of his life now. It was very different from all his years working in an office, but he felt so much at home in uniform. Even now, the better trained men were proudly wearing the red coat, blue trousers and white pith helmets of the British army.

Josiah experienced an inexplicable flash of dread. He paused in his examination of the paybooks and stared into space. Why should he feel this sudden trepidation? His younger brother, Samuel, crossed his mind.

'Sir? Are you ill?' The soldier who knocked on his office door looked concerned. 'You look like you have seen a ghost.'

'Nothing wrong, Private Simpson,' Josiah answered automatically.

'Yes, sir. The company commander wishes to see his platoon commanders at his office in ten minutes.'

'Order received. I will be there. Thank you, Simpson.'

Josiah rose from his desk and retrieved his cap. Was it that Sam was so far from home that he would naturally be concerned for his welfare – or something far worse?

Josiah tried to shake off the irrational sense of unease as he marched to the company commander's office on the other side of the great parade ground, but couldn't quite manage to lose the image of his brother's face.

FIVE

The pirates kept swarming over the sides of the schooner. Sam continued firing rapidly as they loomed in front of him, until he realised he had expended his ammunition with no time to reload. A swarthy, stocky pirate charged at him, swinging a parang, a machete-like weapon that could slice through flesh and bone. In a desperate effort to survive, Sam turned his rifle and swung at the man almost on top of him. The wooden butt slammed into the pirate's head, and he went down.

'Get back to the cabin!' Lee screamed as he scrambled towards Sam. The cabin door was mere feet away, but Sam felt a million miles from safety.

Sam turned on his heel and flung himself towards the small opening. As he did, he noticed from the corner of his eye one of his crew almost decapitated by a parang in the hands of a pirate.

Both men tumbled into the cabin and were met by Ebenezer, armed with two pistols. He fired at a pirate attempting to follow Sam and Lee, hitting the man in the head. Sam quickly reloaded his rifle as Lee and Ebenezer continued to hold off any pirate attempting to enter the cabin, now their small fortress.

The three men could hear the ruckus on the deck, but there were no more attempts by the pirates to storm the cabin. They were now aware that attempting to do so would funnel them into the firepower below.

Sweat rolled down the faces of the men in the cabin as they stood, tensely considering the pirates' next move.

'I had to leave the helm,' Ebenezer said, breaking the silence. 'It was getting a bit hot outside.'

'Our crew?' Lee asked.

Ebenezer shook his head. 'Mostly dead from what I saw,' he replied.

'At least they have desisted in attacking us here,' Sam noted, his rifle now fully loaded.

'You hear that?' Ebenezer queried. 'It sounds like they are opening the hatches to the cargo hold.'

'It sounds that way,' Lee agreed. 'That means they will find the rifles.'

A suspicion grew in Sam's mind. 'The way we were intercepted was an ambush. They knew we had the rifles!'

Lee glanced at Sam. 'That bloody Yank set us up,' Lee snarled. 'He will be able to tell Zhu that he handed over the rifles to us and we lost them to Malay pirates through our own incompetence.'

They waited for a good half-hour in the cabin, expecting another attack, but it did not eventuate. All the time, they could hear the chattering and barked orders in Malay and the sounds of cargo being lowered down the side of the schooner. Finally there were no more sounds from above.

After a short silence, Sam volunteered to open the closed cabin door and see if the pirates had departed. Cautiously, he emerged on deck to find the bloody aftermath of the attack. The pirates had not even bothered to retrieve their own dead, and the crew of the *Ella* lay alongside them in the blood seeping into the slippery deck. The wounds Sam observed inflicted by the parangs were horrific. Sam could also see the pile of dead pirates he had shot near the mast and appreciated the deadly impact of the heavy lead rifle bullets. When he looked out to sea he could see the dhows sailing towards the horizon. He was joined by Lee and Ebenezer.

'Goddamned sons of bitches were after the guns,' Ebenezer growled. 'The crates are gone.'

'What do we do now?' Sam asked Lee.

'If we return to Singapore and tell Zhu what has happened, I doubt that he will be in a very good mood, and that could be fatal for us,' Lee answered. 'I have to think about our options. I guess we clear the decks of the bodies before anything else. At least the *Ella* is still afloat, and the bastards have finished with us.'

Lee was wrong. From the corner of Sam's eye, a flame flashed and a second later, the explosive kinetic force of a heavy, old-fashioned metal cannonball smashed into the upper deck a few feet from where the three men stood. The schooner shuddered under the impact, and Sam experienced a sudden pain rip through his body as he was flung from his feet.

'Sam's down,' Ebenezer shouted.

Sam struggled to sit up, but the timber fragments bit into nerves. Blood oozed from his chest as he fell back to the deck in pain. 'God almighty!'

Lee immediately knelt beside Sam, examining the extent of the wounds. He could see slivers of deck timbers sticking out of Sam's chest when he ripped off his bloody shirt.

Ebenezer left the two to take control of the helm, attempting to swing the schooner nose on to where the firing originated. This would make the schooner a smaller target, just as a second shot boomed out over the water. The cannonball narrowly missed the ship, throwing up a column of water where the schooner had been a moment earlier. Ebenezer braced for another impact, but there were no more shots fired and the dhows disappeared into the darkness.

Two very frightened crew members, Budi and Tono, appeared on deck, Budi with a stab wound to his thigh. Lee and Tono carried Sam to his bunk. Sam had passed out from the pain, and it was a good thing, for the next part would not be pleasant. Lee pulled out the larger timber splinters and was pleased to see they had not penetrated deep. When he was satisfied he had removed the major pieces, he selected a bottle of diluted carbolic acid from the medical supplies. Lee had read that a Dr Lister used the diluted wash to treat wounds and prevent them from becoming infected, and had added the bottle to his medical supplies in case of open wounds. He washed Sam's injuries with the mix and bandaged them. Satisfied that he had done as much as he could, he turned his attention to Budi, washing out the wound that the man said had been inflicted by a spear thrust while he was cornered by a couple of pirates in the hold. Again, diluted carbolic acid was applied and the wound bandaged. The man was grateful and shook Lee's hand with both his own, mumbling thanks in his Indonesian dialect.

By the time Lee returned to Sam, he found him awake and swigging from a whisky bottle. 'For the pain,' Sam said when he noticed the disapproving expression on Lee's face.

'You should not be drinking. Your father would not approve.'

'Father isn't lying in a bunk thousands of miles from Sydney,' Sam responded, 'wondering what the hell I allowed us to get into.'

'The decision to run the guns was mine,' Lee reminded him bitterly. 'I am solely responsible.'

'Risks are necessary,' Sam reassured. 'My father would understand. His whole life at my age was a risk, and look where he is today.'

Lee was not convinced Ian Steele would share Sam's philosophical outlook on the failed venture.

'How have you lived long enough on this earth to be so wise?' Lee commented with a faint smile. 'I am not sure if we should set a course back to Singapore, south back to Queensland, or maybe east into the Pacific, to sail as far as we can from the wrath of Zhu and his Tong.'

'Whatever you decide, you will have my support which, in his absence, is also that of my father,' Sam said.

Lee was warmed by the younger man's faith in him and nodded his thanks before joining Ebenezer at the helm. He knew in those minutes he would have to issue orders for their new course: north, south, east or west? North was out as they no longer had the guns, which left only three options: west to Singapore, east to the Pacific or south to Queensland.

★

It was time for the ladies of the Curry and Steele families to upgrade their wardrobes in anticipation of autumn, so a shopping trip was planned. Becky and Marian had already formed a strong friendship. Becky was fascinated by the sophistication of the red-haired beauty's stories of social life in London, where she yearned to visit.

The journey into the more upper-class shopping of Sydney's King, Pitt and George streets to visit ladies' haberdashery stores in the elaborate glass-ceilinged arcades was also an opportunity for Molly to search out future retail acquisitions for her famed London confectionery enterprises. The four ladies took horse-drawn trams to their destinations in the central business district, and Isabel commented that a new business was to be opened amongst the two- and three-storeyed buildings in George Street, called Grace Brothers. Gas lighting had improved retail businesses by enabling extended hours. On this occasion Isabel had suggested that they first visit David Jones before stopping off at Farmer and Company in Pitt Street.

Early morning turned to mid-afternoon as the four chatted and examined dresses, shoes and hats, selecting purchases to be delivered directly home. Lunch was taken in a teashop before finally exhaustion set in. The last stop was an ornate and elaborate arcade in Pitt Street. Through the glass ceiling, they could see black clouds rolling in for an afternoon storm.

Marian and Becky were trailing behind Molly and Isabel when Marian suddenly stopped at the sound of a voice.

'Good Lord! Miss Curry!'

Marian turned to see a very familiar face from her home in London.

'Mr Anderson! How unexpected,' she replied as a tall, well-dressed man strode towards them.

He stopped a couple of paces away with a bemused smile. 'I never imagined that I would see you on this side of the world. The climate here seems to suit you. You look as beautiful as ever.'

Becky cast Marian a questioning look.

'May I introduce my friend, Miss Rebecca Steele. Becky,

this is Mr Horace Anderson,' Marian said. 'We met when he was living in London.'

'Pleased to meet you, Mr Anderson,' Becky said. 'Are you originally from England?'

'I was in London representing my family's business interests, but I grew up here, Miss Steele,' Horace answered. 'Are you perchance related to Colonel Steele?'

Becky looked surprised. 'Yes, he is my father.'

'Then I went to school with your brother, Josiah,' Horace said. He turned to Marian with a smile. 'As we are in the same place at the same time, we should make an appointment to meet again, and reflect on our old friends we left in London.'

'If you have your card, Mr Anderson, I will consider your offer,' Marian replied. Horace retrieved his silver card holder, passing one of his cards to Marian.

'Until we meet again, ladies, I must bid you a good afternoon. If it was not for a meeting with shareholders, I would have been delighted to offer you afternoon tea.' Anderson left with a smile.

'Who is that man who knows my family?' Becky asked Marian, who was watching Anderson walk away. 'He is very handsome and charming.'

'He is just someone I knew in London,' Marian answered vaguely, turning the card over in her fingers.

The storm hit with a drenching of the hot streets of Sydney, and the four women took refuge in a teahouse until it passed, leaving the air damp and fresh. It was time to return home.

★

It was one of those rare moments Josiah was able to take time off to be with his family at their house on the harbour for dinner. The chatter over the table was of Isabel and Becky's shopping trip.

'Marian and I met a man at the arcade who said he went to school with you, Josiah,' Becky piped up over the roast lamb and vegetables.

'Oh, who was that?' Josiah said, sipping a chilled wine.

'A Mr Horace Anderson. He knew Marian from his time in London. He gave Marian his card.'

Josiah almost spilled his wine. 'Are you sure he said he was Horace Anderson?' he asked.

'Yes. He was a tall and quite handsome man,' Becky replied. 'Do you remember him?'

'Unfortunately, yes,' Josiah growled. 'How did Marian react to you meeting with Anderson?'

Becky looked puzzled. 'She appeared charmed by his appearance. He was rather dashing.'

Josiah frowned. The last he'd heard of his old archrival, he'd been in London, working for the interests of his family enterprises and trying to pursue a relationship with Marian. Now he was back, and just as Josiah was about to be shipped overseas. The timing could not have been worse.

For a brief second Josiah considered resigning his commission to remain in Sydney and fight a different battle: the campaign for Marian's affections. But it was too late for that now, as he was only days away from steaming to the port of Suakin on the coast of the Sudan.

Josiah spent a sleepless night considering the threat Anderson posed. He was aware that Marian harboured some fondness for his bitter enemy, and now he had left the frontlines exposed to the man. Marian had expressed her animosity to Josiah serving in what she called one of Britain's imperial wars and they had not spoken since. Josiah felt her slipping away from him.

SIX

Ebenezer was not sure about the dangerous course Lee had set, but he obeyed regardless.

The *Ella* carried the scars of the battle. Blood still stained the decks, and here and there, damage could be seen to the schooner itself. The bodies had been buried at sea the night of the attack, and now the survivors sailed for Singapore.

Lee was still concerned about Sam's multiple shrapnel wounds from the deck's timbers. A couple of the shards had penetrated deeply into Sam's chest, and he was showing the first signs of fever. It was because of this that Lee had decided to return to port, so that Sam could be taken to a medical doctor as soon as possible.

The settlement was soon in sight and the winds favourable as the sun rose over the tropical island. The anchor was lowered next to a European trading steamer with rust running down its sides. Small sampans pulled aside the schooner and traders offered a variety of fruits and vegetables, but Ebenezer declined their offers and they paddled away.

Below deck, Lee hovered over Sam, who was rapidly settling into a delirium. Sam was strong and fit, but the microscopic bacteria were starting to take hold. Lee knew from his time on the Palmer River Goldfields that infection could be deadly, and he had seen fit men die because of even minor wounds.

He was joined by Ebenezer in the dim light. 'We need to get him ashore as quickly as we can,' the American noted. 'He don't look good.'

'We will take Budi as well,' Lee replied.

'I will get the boat lowered,' Ebenezer said as Lee dragged Sam into a sitting position. In a matter of minutes, Ebenezer returned to assist Lee in dragging Sam above deck. With the help of Tono and a rope harness, they lowered him into the boat below. Tono took the oars while Ebenezer remained on the *Ella*, arming himself with his revolvers to secure the schooner.

Ashore, Lee was able to get information directing him to a German doctor, and hired a couple of Chinese rickshaw drivers to convey Sam and Budi to an address in a predominantly European section of the settlement. A door shingle announced the doctor's name, Hans Schmidt, and credentials in four languages, and Lee had Sam and Budi taken inside to a foyer, where he was met by a short, balding man in his fifties wearing spectacles and a white smock spattered with blood.

'I have two injured men,' Lee said in English, hoping the surgeon would understand.

'*Ja!* You got money?' the doctor asked in heavily accented English.

'I do,' Lee answered, producing a leather pouch of gold

and silver coins. The fee was negotiated, with the German doctor insisting on payment upfront. When Lee helped Sam into the surgery, he could see a European man in his twenties lying on a table with his legs crushed. It was obvious he was dead, which did not reassure Lee.

'Carriage ran over him,' the doctor commented when he saw Lee gazing at the dead man. 'Too late to save him.'

Sam was laid out on another table and the doctor washed his hands in an enamel bowl filled with an antiseptic. He cut away the bandages and probed Sam's numerous wounds. Sam winced under the probing and the doctor frowned. 'He still has wood in a couple of his wounds,' the doctor said. 'I will need to extract the splinters.'

He immediately delved into another enamel bowl and produced a scalpel and tweezers.

'You will have to hold your friend down,' he directed Lee, who gripped Sam's powerful shoulders, hoping that he was strong enough to keep Sam still as the doctor began cutting an incision. Sam strained against Lee's strong grip, but Lee was also strong.

The removal of the timber splinters in the wounds was completed, with the doctor sewing the wounds closed and applying an antiseptic solution before bandaging the wounds again, making Sam look like an Egyptian mummy.

The German doctor stepped back to observe his patient. 'He is young and strong,' he said with a note of satisfaction. 'So long as the infection does not take hold of him, and you change the dressings regularly, he will live.'

Lee felt a rush of relief and thanked the doctor, who waved away the words, turning instead to his second patient's leg wound. 'These people are very resilient,' he said. 'He will also live if his bandage is regularly changed and dilute carbolic is used to rinse the wound.'

In parting, the German said, 'If you have more wounds, you know where to come.'

Lee hoped that would not be necessary, but he could see the fever was still on Sam's brow and knew the young man was far from out of the danger.

Back on the ship and satisfied Sam was resting, Lee went on the deck, staring at the busy settlement. He knew Zhu was out there, and no boat or ship entered the port without the Tong leader's knowledge, so it was only a matter of time before a very angry Zhu knew about the loss of the rifles.

But Lee was not prepared to leave until he was certain that Sam did not require future medical care from a qualified physician. It was time to confront Zhu with all Lee had: the truth.

★

With rifles shouldered, the Sudan contingent marched proudly at Sydney's Moore Park. The Union Jack flew high on the mast and Lieutenant Josiah Steele, wearing the red coat with his medals displayed, marched with his men in the company ranks. It was a splendid martial sight for the proud fifty thousand men, women and children observing the departure. Here was an Australian gesture of solidarity for the Mother Country, and the men on the parade were now representing the continent of Australia in her service.

Josiah knew that one in five of his platoon had served either with the Royal Navy or British Army, and he hoped they would be mentors and an example for the other soldiers who had never been on a battlefield.

George Bowden, son of his father's most trusted employee, had been appointed as Josiah's batman at the young lieutenant's request, so the whole thing had the feeling of a family affair. Another of his soldiers had been a solicitor who now rubbed shoulders with labourers. There was also a former police sergeant and twenty former serving police officers, who were welcomed for their disciplined experience and knowledge of firearms. The majority were single men, and the average age of the volunteers was twenty-six years. In all, the men Josiah commanded were so much different from the soldiers he'd known in the British army, known affectionately by the English public as Tommy Atkins. The Australians would receive their own nickname from the British soldiers they served alongside in the Sudan – Tommy Cornstalks.

The parade over and the men dismissed to their barracks, Josiah could see his father in his old British officer's uniform, waiting with Isabel, his sister, and Conan and Molly Curry. Conan was wearing a civilian suit, and Josiah reflected that had he been in uniform, he would have displayed the Victoria Cross he had been awarded for his campaign in the Crimea.

Josiah saluted his father, who returned the salute. 'Hello, Father, Sarn't Major Curry . . . ladies,' Josiah said. 'How did the parade look?'

'It made our hearts swell,' Isabel replied. 'You all looked so dashing.'

'You look so handsome,' Becky gushed, then her smile faded. 'I cannot bear to think that you are once again going off to war.'

'My duty, little sister,' Josiah replied. 'But I will come home to you all.'

Josiah turned to Conan. 'I thought that Marian might accompany you to see the parade?'

'Marian has gone boating at Lane Cove,' Becky interjected. 'Mr Anderson offered to escort her for a picnic there.'

Josiah did not want to show his disappointment. 'I am sure that she will enjoy herself boating on the river,' he said, but felt a sickness in his stomach. *The bastard Anderson did not wait long.*

'Well, it appears that we have been invited to the officers' mess for afternoon tea,' Ian said cheerily. 'I think that we should not disappoint the PMC.'

During the trip to the barracks, Josiah fumed over Marian being in the company of his worst enemy. At least Josiah could shoot dead the Mahdi if he encountered him on the battlefield, but Anderson would be smug back in Sydney, wooing the woman Josiah most wanted to be with for the rest of his life. That desire was now becoming a mere daydream, as Marian had informed him weeks earlier that it was either her or the Sudan.

★

Lee knew that visiting Zhu armed with a revolver was not a good idea. He would have to pray for his safety and Zhu's rational understanding.

Lee took a rickshaw to a well-established house outside of the main settlement. The high wall had a main entrance surrounded by stone Chinese lions and Lee now felt the apprehension of possibly being able to enter – but not leave – alive. Zhu's reputation was that he did not show mercy to those who let him down.

Taking a breath and attempting to keep his trembling hands under control, he walked up to the main gate and used the big brass knocker to announce his uninvited presence.

A slit slid open in the gate and Lee stared into a face that was familiar to him.

'Kwong!' he exclaimed.

The scarred, broad-faced man blinked. 'Ling Lee,' Kwong replied. 'What are you doing here?'

'I need to speak with Master Zhu,' Lee said. 'It is a matter of great importance.'

The gate opened and the Chinese warrior beckoned Lee to enter. Lee could see gardeners attending to beautifully manicured tropical gardens filled with water fountains and brilliant flowers.

'I am sure Master Zhu will meet with you,' Kwong said, escorting Lee along a paved stone path. Lee could now see another four men armed with swords and pikes near the main door to the bungalow. Kwong also carried a sword in a sash around his waist.

'Wait here,' Kwong commanded Lee once inside a spacious foyer decorated with Chinese prints and small bronze statues of the Buddha. Lee waited apprehensively for a couple of minutes before Kwong returned and gestured to Lee to follow him down a granite-paved corridor to an office with a vast window overlooking the gardens. Zhu sat at a great polished teak desk wearing a white European suit. Zhu was in his late fifties with short, greying hair and spectacles, and very European in his appearance. He could have been an academic in a European university, but Lee knew that this very wealthy and influential man was driven by a passion to free China from those same Europeans he lived alongside.

Lee stood before the desk as Zhu completed paperwork. Kwong stood a short distance away as sweat streamed down Lee's face, fear coursing through his veins.

'Mr Lee,' Zhu finally said when he glanced up. 'My intelligence service has advised that your ship was ambushed at sea and that you have lost your cargo.' His English was perfect from his days working with the British in the financial world.

'Yes, master,' Lee quavered.

'The American, Haynes, betrayed me,' Zhu said mildly.

Lee allowed himself to breathe, feeling a glimmer of hope. Zhu knew that the ambush and loss of the rifles was not his fault. 'I suspected as much,' he tentatively volunteered. 'The ambush on the *Ella* was too well organised for it to be simply a misfortune.'

'I believe that you lost crew members, and Samuel Steele was badly wounded. I hope that he is recovering well?'

'He was injured, master, but appears to be recovering,' Lee answered.

'Good,' Zhu said. He pushed himself away from the desk and stood up, walking to the great window to his garden. 'You and your comrades were very effective in destroying my Tong opponent on the Palmer all those years ago. This has not been forgotten.'

Lee could not detect any threat in the words of the much-feared Tong leader, but knew what was expected of him. 'How can we assist you now, Master Zhu?' Lee asked.

A hint of a smile crossed Zhu's face. 'Before you sail, you are to kill the treacherous American. Kwong will help you.'

Lee felt a flash of trepidation. He had seen how well guarded the American was.

'You were successful in the past and you will be in the present,' Zhu continued. 'Can I offer you tea before you plan with Kwong how you will exact my vengeance?'

Lee wisely accepted the offer and tea was brought to them by a Chinese woman. Zhu's money and power could buy the best in Singapore, and all his female staff were young and pretty. It was almost a social occasion, with Zhu offering his help to recruit new crew for their vessel and chatting about possible financial enterprises that might open in the Pacific region. But Lee knew he had a deadly mission that might cost him his life.

SEVEN

Lee returned to the schooner, where he was met by Ebenezer bearing good news. 'Young Sam seems to be improving. He still has a bit of a fever, but he's awake and lucid.'

'We need to keep him rested and keep a close eye on the wounds,' Lee said, scrambling aboard. 'But I have something else to talk to you about.'

Lee went below to see Sam, who was lying bathed in sweat but coherent. They chatted lightly as Lee changed the wound dressings. Lee did not mention he had visited Zhu, so as not to burden the young man. When he was satisfied, Lee joined Ebenezer on deck to enjoy the slight breeze wafting across the water.

'Goddamned stupid idea,' Ebenezer stated when Lee told him about the meeting with Zhu. 'It's suicide. You sure Zhu is not simply getting you killed for losing his guns?'

'I don't think so,' Lee replied. 'I did something similar for him when I was on the Palmer a few years ago. He wants to send a message to all those he deals with that treachery is answered with death.'

'Do you think you have any chance of carrying out this task?'

'Zhu has provided one of his best men to help,' Lee said. 'He is a capable man with a proven record for getting things done. If I don't carry out the mission, I doubt that Zhu will allow us to leave port. Besides, we need a crew to properly handle the *Ella*, and he has promised that he will supply men to help us.'

Ebenezer gazed at the flotilla of ships anchored off the coast. He shook his head and walked away, leaving Lee pondering the problems that lay ahead. Deep in his gut, Lee knew that the odds were stacked against him being successful. But he also knew he had no other choice.

★

Many opposed the colony's intervention in the Sudan as purely a jingoistic means of supporting imperial Britain and were vocal in the leading newspapers. The community was divided, with some arguing that any foreign deployment of armed forces required consultation with parliament, as it was colonial money being used to support the colonial army. But Premier Dalley knew every day counted if the colony was to provide timely support and fell back on a quote from Shakespeare's *The Merchant of Venice*: *To do a great right, do a little wrong.*

But Dalley had a considerable foe in the political figure of Sir Henry Parkes, who thundered at the illegality of the enterprise and used the *Sydney Morning Herald* to publish his dissent before Dalley's offer of troops had even been accepted. His words echoed of his *'entire dissent from the strange proceedings of the government in offering to send a military force to assist in the lamentable warfare in Egypt'*.

On the eve of embarkation, five thousand people attended a protest rally at a pedestal being built for a statue of Queen Victoria between Macquarie Street and Hyde Park. One attendee was Marian, who had joined a new cause in this land not of her birth to voice her own views on the imperialism of Britain.

She had listened to an orator at Sydney's Domain, who asked the gathered crowd, 'Why are we killing these poor Arabs? For the English government to keep its party contented? Should far-off Australia lend her sanction to the crime?' As she listened to the questions, Marian could only puzzle how an intelligent man such as Josiah could be a party to such a heinous crime. Yet she was torn, because she had loved Josiah from the first moment she had met him when she was just a mere girl in London. How could he be so stupid as not to see her love for him? It seemed that the man she loved was prepared to put himself in danger at the drop of a hat, and to not consider the impact it had on her.

★

Just after midday, Josiah marched in the procession from Victoria Barracks led by mounted police. The streets had been cleared of all traffic for the contingent to travel to the embarkation point at Circular Quay. Dignitaries including the premier and the colonial governor followed in carriages. The procession marched along College Street, swung left around the Captain Cook monument into Park Street, turned right along George Street opposite the town hall, passed the General Post Office before turning into Hunter Street, left into Pitt Street, along Bridge Street to Macquarie Place and finally down to the quay. All the time, the enthusiastic crowds cried out patriotic calls of 'Strike for victory, give it to the Mahdi!', 'Advance Australia!' and 'For England, home and Gordon!' Bouquets of flowers and bags of rice were tossed down on the marching soldiers, and the occasional soldier broke ranks to embrace a loved one amongst the spectators before falling back into line.

Josiah felt proud to be a soldier representing his country, but as he marched, he watched the crowds of civilians either side of the route, looking for that one face . . . but Marian was not to be seen. She was not at the quay, when Josiah finally reached it with his men, but his immediate family were there, standing alongside Conan and Molly Curry.

Will Bowden stood to one side, shaking his son's hand. Josiah remembered how Will had fought alongside his own father years earlier. The significance of their father–son farewell was not lost on Josiah.

The cacophony of sound was almost deafening; ships' whistles, beating drums and the roar of the crowd laughing, crying and shouting best wishes.

Josiah formally shook his father and Conan's hands. Words were not necessary between old and young battle-tested soldiers. Becky, Molly and Isabel tearfully hugged Josiah and then it was time to embark on what was considered a great adventure by many of the soldiers in their red coats, which they would swap for the new khaki uniform the British army had adopted for overseas warfare when they reached the port of Suakin.

The *Iberia* had had her name painted over and was now *NSW 1*. She was pulled stern first away from the wharf by a tugboat at 3.20 pm, and the men lining the rails waved and shouted down to friends and families for a final time.

The troopship was then steered east, accompanying *Australasian*, whose name was also painted over, to become *NSW 2*. The guns of Fort Macquarie and the British warship *HMS Nelson* boomed a salute, almost drowned in the cacophony of small ships' whistles and foghorns as all the pleasure crafts escorted the ships to the headlands. 'Auld Lang Syne' was being played but could barely be heard by those aboard the exiting ships, and the soldiers manning the railings truly realised that there was no turning back now.

They were going to war, and would be in the Sudan within a month.

Very few of the men from the colony had not heard the stories of old soldiers who had fought in such places as India and Afghanistan, of how their Muslim foe did not lack courage or warrior tradition. They all knew that they were going to an uncertain fate on the other side of the Indian Ocean. But they were doing so as Australians.

★

Lee returned to Zhu's compound to confer with Kwong. The solidly built warrior listened to the options presented, grunting occasionally to emphasise his agreement.

'The American has seven armed guards, but they only have swords and spears,' Kwong said.

'How do you know?' Lee queried.

'We have many street people who tell us what we want to know,' Kwong replied. 'He only has two of his guards inside his house, but he is known to have a pistol with him at all times.'

'It is obvious that we will have to make our attack at night,' Lee mused.

'Your father was once a master teacher of our martial arts,' Kwong said. 'Did he teach you the skills of an assassin?'

'He taught me many skills,' Lee said. 'But I was sworn by him to only use them to defend myself.'

'I know that you are capable of killing men, as I saw you do so when we were in the land of the golden mountain,' Kwong reflected. 'This time, you may be required to use your skills to attack and not defend.'

Lee nodded. Although he was reluctant to break his oath to his father, who had once been a Shaolin monk, he justified it to himself because the American had organised the attack against them at sea, and had almost killed young Sam. 'It is a moonless night, and I want to get this over with,' Lee said.

'The master's vengeance must be swift, so none will doubt his power,' Kwong agreed. 'I have clothing we will need, and I can see that you have brought your sword.'

'And I have this.' Lee indicated a Tranter revolver concealed under his shirt.

The two assassins waited until after midnight, then changed into their all-black trousers and smocks, adding hoods and face scarfs. Kwong carried a long, razor-sharp knife and a shorter double-edged blade.

An oxcart driven by one of Zhu's men conveyed them under a tarpaulin along a route with few houses until they were within a block of the American's compound. They slid from the back of the cart and made their way in the shadows of the darkened streets and alleyways until they saw the storage shed adjacent to the residential compound. Lee could feel his heart pounding in his chest, but was reassured Kwong had chosen their entry point well. Only a few lanterns flickered from within the compound, and the alley they travelled in was pitch black.

They found themselves opposite the large storage building, and Kwong indicated that they could enter it through a side door. Kwong had acquired the key earlier in the day from a street urchin who had stolen it from a lazy guard.

Kwong inserted the key and carefully pushed open the door. Weak light illuminated the interior of stacked crates. There was no guard on this door and the Chinese warrior could see one of the guards asleep on a pile of cheap blankets at the furthest end of the shed. Cautiously, both Kwong and Lee entered the shed, moving like stalking cats towards the guard. When they were on the sleeping man, Kwong cut his throat with deadly efficiency.

'There is another man somewhere else in the shed,' Kwong hissed. 'We must find him and silence him.'

Lee nervously glanced around the large interior, but could not see the other man inside the warehouse. He moved forward until he turned the corner around a pile of wooden crates and almost bumped into the second guard, his expression one of utter terror at seeing the black-clad figure holding a sword. Lee struck with an accuracy prac-tised over the years, slicing with all his force through the petrified guard's neck. The body wobbled as the head rolled to one side before falling, a spout of blood drenching the nearby wooden crates.

'You have not forgotten your teachings,' Kwong hissed in Lee's ear. 'Now, we enter the house and find the other enemy.'

Lee followed Kwong to a side door that allowed entry into the residence. Kwong knew there would be three guards in the front courtyard. They would be a problem when they exited the building, but at least the storage shed was cleared as a point of exit.

The door opened to a short, covered pathway with no guard. Both black-clad men could see an open door to the house, which was in darkness. They were careful to remain in the shadows as they moved silently to the house, and towards the main sleeping quarters.

Both men entered the bedroom and waited a moment for their night vision to adjust. They could see the outline of the person they considered must be the target asleep under a mosquito net. Kwong approached the sleeping figure and pulled back the sheet only to step back in confusion as he saw it was not the American but a young woman.

Suddenly, a voice cried out in fear and anger. It was the American, returning to his bed to see the two ominous black-clad figures hovering over the naked woman, who now sat up and screamed.

Lee moved like a striking snake, knocking Haynes down, but the American was stronger than Lee had appreciated and fought to keep Lee off him. Lee was unable to manoeuvre his sword, but Kwong was beside him, stabbing with his short blade through the back of the American's neck, severing his spinal cord. Haynes shuddered before going limp and crumbling to the floor.

The young woman continued to scream, and two men rushed into the darkened residence. This time, Lee resorted to western technology, drawing his Tranter and firing his six rounds point blank at the men, who fell before they made it three steps.

'We have to leave,' Kwong hissed, and Lee followed his comrade along the route they had used to enter the compound. It was a wise choice, as a further three guards entered the residence behind them in a vain attempt to save their boss.

Kwong and Lee exited the shed and escaped into the darkness of the alley.

★

'So, you did not let me down,' Zhu said, standing in his large living room just as the sun was rising on another hot and humid tropical day.

'No, Master Zhu,' Kwong said, still wearing his black uniform but without the hood or face mask. 'I killed the American myself. Lee Ling was very competent in helping me do so.'

Zhu turned to Lee, who was also still wearing his black clothing covered in blood. 'This is the second time that you have carried out a mission for me and have succeeded in ridding me of an enemy. I have learned that Haynes had a change of mind about our deal when he somehow learned the rifles were to be used by our soldiers in Cochin China. I have already made plans to intercept the consignment and have the rifles returned to me as the rightful owner. I am also sure that I will be able to recoup my financial loss.'

'I am pleased, Master Zhu,' Lee said. The adrenaline leaving his body combined with a lack of sleep was making him weary, and it was an effort to stand properly before the Tong leader.

'I am sure that you wish to return to your ship, Master Lee,' Zhu said. Lee blinked, surprised at Zhu addressing him as 'master'. There was a new respect in the Tong leader's tone. 'I have recruited four experienced sailors to assist you. One of them is Kwong's eldest son.'

'Thank you, Master Zhu,' Lee said, turning to Kwong, and was surprised to see the tough warrior bow his head.

'I have asked Master Zhu to allow my eldest son to travel with you, Master Lee,' he said solemnly. 'I know he will benefit from your considerable knowledge and experience in both our world and that of the barbarians. I entrust his life to you.'

Lee was humbled by Kwong's words. 'He will be as my own son,' Lee promised, bowing to the Chinese warrior. 'I pray to our ancestors that he will live and prosper and make you proud.'

Zhu reassured Lee that the local British police would not be concerned over what they would view as a gang clash. There might be alarm that an American national had been murdered, but a telegram to the USA would confirm that Haynes was a dangerous, wanted man in his own country, with a warrant for his arrest on a murder charge.

Lee changed his clothes and collected his new crew members. They all rowed to the schooner to be met by both Ebenezer and Sam on the deck. They were hauled aboard, and Lee smiled at Sam, who was looking just a little pale but obviously recovering well from his wounds. Lee explained that the men he'd brought aboard were sailors Zhu had recruited for them.

'What has happened while I was laid out?' Sam asked Lee. 'Ebenezer has said nothing, but just about chewed off the end of his pipe waiting for you.'

'I had to settle the debt with Zhu,' Lee replied.

'Is everything all right?' Sam asked anxiously, knowing the Tong leader's reputation.

'The debt is settled,' Lee replied. 'I would love a cup of tea and a day of sleep,' he added. Sam could see a trace of blood on the sword Lee carried in his waistbelt, and knew he should not ask any more questions.

EIGHT

Lee was impressed by Kwong's son. He was a man in his early twenties with the solid build of his father and an intelligent aura. As Yuan had a basic knowledge of English, Lee appointed him headman of the newly recruited crew members after quizzing them all about their experience of sailing. Lee had learned that Yuan had crewed Chinese junks and sailed all the waters of the South Asian seas.

'Time we headed south,' Sam said.

Neither Ebenezer nor Lee disagreed with his suggestion, and the sails were unfurled to catch favourable tropical winds. The three men were glad to see Singapore disappear off their stern.

Lee, Ebenezer and Sam were looking forward to returning to Sydney for different reasons. Sam was looking forward to catching up with his family, whom he missed very much. Ebenezer had met a woman in Sydney he was keen to look up when they returned. And for Lee, it was a chance to enquire into his financial investments and be reunited with his aged parents, who lived on their small plot of land outside Sydney.

The *Ella* rose and fell gently on the vast ocean as she cut a course south between the many islands in the straits.

★

Marian stood gazing out into a night sky filled with myriad bright stars.

'Come back to bed,' the male voice requested in the dark bedroom.

'Soon,' she sighed.

It was Josiah's fault, Marian tried to tell herself. He'd chosen soldiering over her, and deserved the consequences. Horace Anderson had wined and dined her, and she had eventually succumbed to his charms. Now she stood in a bedroom in a luxurious house on South Head, where she'd had a view of the troopships departing for the Sudan. The man she'd thought she loved had chosen war over her.

Marian was a realist, and knew it was time to get on with her life. Horace Anderson, with his wealth, charm and aristocratic looks, pleasantly filled the vacuum left in Josiah's wake.

But she had still cried as the ship taking Josiah away from her passed below in the harbour.

★

NSW 1 and *NSW 2* reached Kangaroo Island on a Friday night and were met by many well-wishers from Adelaide. It was an opportunity to post letters to loved ones back in Sydney, and Josiah had a couple of letters to his family as well as one to Conan and Molly. He attempted to compose a separate letter to Marian, sitting at the desk in his cabin with his pen poised over the paper. Was he going to beg for a second chance, or simply write as one would to a friend? Agonising over the choice, he commenced writing:

My dear Marian,

This will probably be my last letter until we reach the next port on our way to Suakin . . .

Josiah paused. This had all happened the last time he had attempted to compose a letter to Marian, when he'd been on the march to Kandahar five years earlier. He had not been able to find the words then, and nor could he now. He took the blotting paper and soaked up the excess ink before folding the letter and putting it aside. He now cursed himself for choosing to join the contingent, knowing that war could mean death, or worse – mutilation. But the call of the Empire's bugle and his brothers-in-arms plucked at his very soul. He was a soldier, but this time a soldier for his own country – Australia. No man felt more torn than Josiah as he listened to the ship's sounds as she came to a halt off Kangaroo Island.

★

Early in the morning, on a balmy autumn day, the *Ella* crossed Moreton Bay and into the Brisbane River, having enjoyed a smooth journey sailing south. They needed to resupply as rations were short, and so was their supply of fresh water. The schooner was moored to a wharf in the busy river of the capital of the colony of Queensland.

One of the first matters to which Sam attended when he and the Yankee captain went ashore was the purchase of a newspaper from a boy selling on the street. Sam was stunned to see that New South Wales had dispatched a contingent of infantry and artillery to the Sudan a week earlier, and strongly suspected that his brother would have been one of the first to step forward for the campaign. Sam wondered if his father was also on a ship steaming to Africa.

'What is it?' Ebenezer asked. 'You seen a ghost?'

'My father and brother,' Sam muttered. 'We need to get to a telegraph office.' They did so, and Sam immediately sent a telegram to his home in Sydney. He was reassured by the post office telegraphist that the cable would reach Sydney that day, and Sam said he would return the following day for any answer.

'Time we went and wetted our whistles,' Ebenezer said, and they went in search of the nearest hotel. It had been a long time since they had done so.

They walked to Charlotte Street where they found the Queen's Hotel. It was a two-storeyed pub with a top veranda. 'Looks as good as any,' Ebenezer remarked, and the two men went inside. There was a scattering of patrons leaning against the bar, and Sam stepped up to order a whisky and one beer. The barmaid pushed the drinks towards Sam and Ebenezer, who raised their glasses to each other.

'To fair winds and a cargo worth the space in the holds,' Ebenezer said, and they took a swallow of their respective drinks. 'What was bothering you when you sent the telegram?'

'The colony has committed a contingent to fight in the Sudan and I fear both my father and brother will be with it,' Sam replied.

'Maybe they are still back in Sydney,' Ebenezer offered.

'Knowing my father and brother, I can bet they are somewhere on the sea steaming to Suakin,' Sam replied gloomily, staring into his beer. 'It's a bastard that we were out of contact with the world when the announcement was made about the colony volunteering troops. I should have been with Josiah and my father if they were sent.'

'I heard what you were sayin' about those bastard New South Walers sending their precious army to fight for England.' Sam turned to see a man as big as himself standing beside them. He was in his mid-twenties, and it was obvious from his solid build that he was physically strong. Sam noticed from the glazed expression that the man confronting him was intoxicated. 'I volunteered from up here, but they knocked me back. Said that preference went to citizens of your bloody colony,' the man said, breathing alcoholic fumes into Sam's face as he swayed provocatively close to him. 'They would rather take sissy boys like you.'

Sam knew that the big man was deliberately provoking him and took a step back. Ebenezer could see the situation developing and reached into the pocket of his trousers for the small but deadly sharp knife he always carried.

'If you had been in Sydney, you might have had a chance to volunteer,' Sam said, attempting to defuse the man's aggressiveness.

It was a move Sam did not expect, but his training with Lee paid off. The man had reached for a whisky bottle near to hand and raised it to bring down on Sam's head. With a lightning-like reaction, Sam raised his left arm to block the descending arm of his enraged opponent, halting the swing. With his right arm wrapped around the arm holding the bottle he snapped it back, pushing the big man down to his knees. Startled, his opponent attempted to force himself to his feet, but Sam delivered a sharp kick into the man's stomach, forcing the wind out of his lungs. The man dropped the bottle and crumpled into a winded state on the floor, gasping for breath. The other patrons in the public bar watched in stunned silence. It had all happened in a split second and the bully was now lying prostrate, writhing in pain.

'Good onya, boy,' someone said. 'He's been deservin' that for a long time.' It was obvious to Sam that the man he had laid out had done this before, and was seen as a bully.

Sam reached for his beer and swallowed it in a few gulps, as did Ebenezer his whisky.

The groaning man remained on the floor, gripping his stomach, as Sam and Ebenezer made a hasty retreat to the street bathed in the warmth of early autumn in the subtropics. It was time to find a friendlier bar.

'Did Lee teach you that trick?' Ebenezer chuckled as they walked.

'That, and a few others.' Sam grinned. 'Those Asians don't fight like us. They use their heads instead of their brawn. I think that we could learn a lot from them.'

They found another hotel and spent the day quietly drinking, discussing future plans for sailing the Pacific islands for trade. After staggering back to the schooner, they collapsed in their bunks and slept off the enjoyable afternoon spent in Brisbane.

The next day Sam returned to the Post and Telegraphic Office in the centre of Brisbane to find a telegram waiting for him. It reassured Sam that only Josiah had joined the expedition to the Sudan, and that his father was looking forward to him returning to Sydney.

Sam sighed in relief. His father was getting too old to be on any battlefield, but Sam was very annoyed his brother had gone to war without him.

★

In a two-storeyed building situated at 109 Phillip Street was the office of the relatively new detective bureau. Detective First Class Andrew Paull sat at his desk amongst other closely packed desks allocated for the others of his branch. Smoke from pipes and cigarettes permeated the air as Detective Paull read one of the newspapers that was routinely delivered to the office each day. Andrew knew that most of his colleagues generally read the sports section or gossip columns, but he recognised that there were other articles of some intelligence importance.

His eye fell on a small article on the third page of the newspaper relating that in this time of public interest in the Sudan contingent leaving Australian shores, a well-known social identity, Josiah Steele, was an officer who was representing his country. Josiah Steele was the son of Colonel Ian Steele . . . Andrew paused at the name. He had always suspected that Ian Steele had been complicit in the murder of a high-ranking senior public servant on the road across the Great Dividing Range years earlier. Although Steele had covered his tracks, Andrew had never given up on his belief that Ian Steele had killed the man.

Andrew continued to read the article and another name cropped up: Conan Curry VC, a family friend of the Steele family. Steele and Curry had served for many years together in the wars for the Queen, and Curry now lived in Sydney after emigrating from England. The irony was that the Victoria Cross winner had been born in the colony and travelled to England to enlist in the British army.

Detective First Class Paull was a highly intelligent man with an excellent reputation for arresting and bringing to justice many classes of criminal. Had it not been for the seniority system of promotion, he would have no doubt been promoted to officer level in the police force. But he loved his work, even though it was badly paid. Conan Curry . . . Andrew mused. Had he heard that name before?

Andrew closed the paper and stood away from his desk to walk over to the rows of wooden filing cabinets. He was not sure where to look, but there was just something strange about the relationship between Steele and Curry. Maybe it was nothing, but Detective Paull did not believe in mere coincidences, nor the fact that the Conan Curry name haunted him. But he would find out.

NINE

The troopships were now steaming in the Indian Ocean, and the fruit taken aboard as a gift from the people of South Australia was a welcome component of the daily diet. The men aboard the ships had no reason to grumble about their rations, and even former members of the British army praised their daily meals. Breakfast at eight in the morning could be hashed meat and potatoes washed down with tea. Lunch comprised soup, roast meat and vegetables, and supper was tea and fruit. Grog and lime juice was served at 1.30 pm and there was wine every Saturday night.

During the day, Josiah supervised his platoon in the routines of military life, caring for issued equipment, oversighting tasks such as pipe claying belts and helmets white or bath bricking rifles to keep them clean. Dress parades were held on deck and uniforms inspected for the tedious sentry duty.

The officers practised with their revolvers, firing at targets held at the end of poles over the side of the ship, and there were always the church parades on Sundays. The Reverend Herbert Rose and Father Edmund Charles Collingridge conducted services, reminding their congregations about the temptations of the flesh and the godliness of sobriety. Many listened as they harboured secret fears that they might lose their lives against the fanatic Islamic warriors of the Sudan. The two padres also acted as entertainment officers, arranging concerts and games.

On one pleasant evening just off the equator, Josiah filled his pipe and went above decks to take in the vast sea of stars overhead and a full moon shining its silvery path across the calm seas. He plugged and lit his pipe to gaze contentedly into the night. War was a long way from his thoughts.

'Evenin', sir.'

Josiah knew the voice well and turned to see his childhood friend, George Bowden. Neither man had disclosed their close relationship outside the army, as they both observed the strict protocols of the military code. But Josiah could see that they were now alone and out of hearing of the nearest soldier on the upper deck.

'George, it has been some time since we were able to chat,' Josiah said.

'Yeah, like you being an officer an' me a private,' George replied, removing his own pipe and plugging it with tobacco from a small leather pouch.

'In this time and place, we are George and Josiah,' Josiah said. 'We shared so much growing up in Sydney together.'

"Cept you went to a posh school and then went off to England to fight in Afghanistan an' Africa. I never dreamed I would get the chance to wear the uniform and fight for

Australia. Me dad's proud of me enlisting, and I know I got in because you put in a word. Got a few mates who failed to get signed up who would have swapped places with me.'

'Not sure I did the right thing, getting you into the contingent, when I look back on my past experiences,' Josiah mused.

'But you came back in one piece,' George said hopefully, and for a moment, Josiah thought about the long scar down his arm from an Afghan warrior at Kandahar, where he had lost a fellow officer who had become like a brother. He also remembered with bitterness the slaughter in Africa at Majuba Hill. 'I always knew you as the most fearless person in Sydney.'

'Not so fearless when it came to fighting,' Josiah countered. 'When the bugles called the advance, I wanted to wet myself. At those very moments, I would have swapped places with anyone in Sydney in the blink of an eye.'

'Truly?' George questioned with a frown. 'You never struck me as a bloke who knew fear. I got to admit that at night in the hammock, I start to see me being killed fighting the Mahdi and his heathens. I guess it is then that, like you, I wish I was home with the other cobbers we knew.'

'Just keep your head when we go into action, and remember all your training and the odds will be in your favour,' Josiah reassured George.

Both men turned to lean on the railing and stare out at the calm seas swishing along the hull of the ship. Now and then, flying fish leapt from the ocean to glide a short distance before disappearing into the head of a wave.

From the corner of his eye, Josiah saw an officer approaching and pushed himself away from the railing. George did the same and saluted the officer he recognised as a lieutenant.

'Evenin', sir,' George said when the officer returned his salute. George turned to Josiah, came to attention and saluted. 'Well, sir, I better join the lads before Last Post,' he said.

Josiah returned the salute. 'I will see you at the morning parade, Private Bowden.'

George marched away, leaving Josiah and Lieutenant Archie Watson alone. Josiah liked his fellow platoon commander, a man in his late twenties with a legal practice in Sydney. He had been a militia officer with another volunteer regiment which was why he'd been able to secure a posting with the contingent. He was prematurely balding, his sandy hair barely covering his early loss of hair, and tall and thin, with an aristocratic and intelligent expression.

'Thought I might take in some of this wonderful evening air before returning to the cabin,' Archie said, turning to gaze across the silver streak on the ocean from the moon's glow. 'Not long now, old chap.'

'Not long,' Josiah echoed, returning to lean on the rail and puff his pipe as the aromatic smoke wisped away on the slight ocean breeze.

'I know that you have seen action from the conversations of our brother officers,' Archie said. 'This will be my first time.'

'Nothing to worry about – except your men,' Josiah replied. 'Firm, fair and friendly is all they expect, if you are to convince them to follow you through the gates of hell in the battles ahead. I always considered that we were made officers to care for them rather than the other way around. My views were not always accepted by the British officers I served with. But I also met British officers who shared my view that class means little when you share the dangers with your men. A bullet or bayonet does not care whether you are gentry or a ruffian from the slums.'

'I heard that your Scots soldiers called you the Colonial,' Archie said.

'I inherited that title from my father, when he was commissioned with the British army.' Josiah smiled. 'I take the English derogatory term as a badge of honour, as did my father.'

'I have read about your father's distinguished career from the Crimea to New Zealand. He was a remarkable soldier.'

'He was. He is a remarkable man still,' Josiah said. 'Given half a chance, he would have volunteered for this contingent.'

'Well, he has you to represent him,' Archie said. 'It seems to be a family tradition for you. Alas, I had a hard time convincing my wife that I had to do my duty for Queen and country. She was somewhat opposed to me signing on.'

'I understand.' Josiah reflected on his last conversation with Marian.

'I was rather surprised that you are not much of a swordsman,' Archie said, changing the subject. 'I was easily able to counter your parry and thrust this afternoon at practice. I would have thought that an officer's symbol of authority would be the weapon he is most skilled in using to defend himself.'

Although Josiah liked the man, he also accepted the fellow officer was rather pompous. 'I prefer to carry a rifle and bayonet when I engage with the enemy,' Josiah said. 'From sage advice and personal experience, carrying a sword into battle instantly marks you as an officer and every enemy targets you. Hence we have a high rate of young officers killed in their first engagement with the enemy. I also find that a long bayonet at the end of the rifle extends my reach at an enemy's throat beyond that of the sword.'

Archie went quiet for a moment, taking in his friend's advice, which he knew was based on practical experience. 'I had never thought of that,' he grudgingly admitted.

'Modern warfare is a high-velocity, long-range rifle bullet fired by a half-trained tribesman who is able to stop you before you can wave your sword over your head at the start line. Worth keeping in mind, old chap. The Boers at Majuba proved to me the deadly effect of a modern rifle in the hands of a trained enemy. Swords are a thing of the past, and will only be good for ceremonial parades in the future. Their day has gone, so I don't bother much about my parry and thrust. Better to concentrate on expertise with both rifle and revolver.'

Archie stared at the ocean rolling by. 'I suppose I should get some kip before morning parade,' he said, and Josiah sensed that his message about the obsolete use of swords might have sunk in.

Alone at the rail, Josiah could not help but think how beautiful Marian might find this night, steaming in the tropics with the great yellow moon lighting the night sky. He sighed and tapped his pipe ash on the rail, where it was swept away. As he turned to walk back to his cabin, he swore he must forget Marian; his first priority at this moment in his life must be the welfare of his men. Marian was but a beautiful dream of paradise found and lost.

★

Eventually, the contingent reached Aden, where it was to receive further orders concerning the deployment. They were met at sea off Aden by a sister ship, *SS Lusitania*, transporting paying passengers and immigrants to Melbourne and Sydney. The ship had changed course to pass by the troopships, and soldiers of the contingent rushed to the railings, as did the passengers on the *Lusitania*, cheering the contingent. 'Auld Lang Syne' drifted across the sea between the ships as a tribute by the passenger ship's band, and semaphore signals wished the contingent well.

Amongst the *Lusitania*'s passengers were two talented artists, Tom Roberts and JF Archibald, who were returning to Australia. Roberts was sketching his fellow passengers for his painting, *Coming South*, which would be exhibited the following year in London.

When the contingent ships arrived in the Aden port, they were met with the news that a major, horrific battle had been fought near Suakin. The commander of the colonials received his orders that they were to proceed at once to land troops and immediately go to the front.

Josiah stood at the railing of the troopship with Archie Watson, watching local boys diving into the sea from tiny boats, fetching coins thrown overboard.

'Curious chaps,' Archie commented.

'No doubt our troops are thinking the same,' Josiah replied. 'But the brown faces will soon become familiar.' Josiah had already heard the term 'fuzzies' being used by the old hands of campaigns in Arab lands, and the inexperienced soldiers had adopted the expression.

Cheering erupted down the deck when one of the Australian soldiers made an unauthorised high dive from the railing into the sea. His friends were aghast as the waters had a fearsome reputation for sharks, but he emerged safely and was hauled aboard to their cheers.

'I was informed that we will be issued with live rounds before we dock at Suakin,' Archie said. 'Just that alone makes it all feel very real.'

Josiah nodded. The almost tourist-like atmosphere aboard his troopship had changed and on Sunday 29 March at noon, the men disembarked to march in their red coats to the cheering of sailors from the ships anchored in the harbour. The city of Suakin was a dazzling white, and its buildings reminded Josiah of small fortresses he had known in the campaign for Kandahar. They marched through streets, passing Greek and English merchants hawking their wares. To the marching men, all the double-storeyed buildings looked alike, the exotic curved architecture of windows and doorways like nothing they had ever seen at home.

After leaving the city, they marched with some difficulty towards their camp two miles away, sand clogging their boots under a blazing sun.

When they reached the camp, they were lined up on the parade ground and the English commander inspected and addressed them.

'Those who are engaged in the present campaign are proud to bear with you the name of Englishman,' their new commander-in-chief, Sir Gerald Graham, said. 'But in welcoming these citizen warriors from a colonial democracy, you are soldiers as well as Englishmen and will cheerfully submit to the privations and severe discipline necessary for the safety of an army in the field. The eyes of all English-speaking races, and indeed those of the whole civilised world, are upon you, and I am certain that you will uphold the honour of the Empire.'

When dismissed, they marched to their quarters to the sound of a Guardsmen regimental band and found themselves shoulder to shoulder with twelve thousand British and Indian troops. Josiah learned that they would be attached to a brigade of Scots, Grenadier and Coldstream Guards under the command of Major General Fremantle. The Scots regiment they were quartered with were from Josiah's old regiment and he would have an opportunity to catch up with former comrades.

Josiah was visited by Archie when the two officers had settled into their tents. 'By Jove, that was a rousing welcoming speech,' Archie said.

'The only trouble is that we were not identified as Australians,' Josiah growled, brushing away sand from his small desk.

'But we are Englishmen,' Archie defended.

Josiah did not answer the statement as there was no sense arguing with a lawyer. As far as Josiah was concerned, he was an Australian who lived in the colony of New South Wales.

TEN

It had been a grand feeling to enter Sydney Harbour under full sail, the *Ella* showing off her prowess as she slid past smaller vessels and one or two British warships.

Docked at the Steele enterprise facilities, leave was granted to a small number of the crew, but Ebenezer remained aboard to supervise any tasks required to outfit the schooner for another venture in the South Pacific.

Lee organised transport to take him to his family's small plot of land in the western reaches of Sydney, where his father and mother grew fresh vegetables for the city's burgeoning population. He and Sam shook hands at the wharf, and Sam knew his first stop would be at the family offices near Circular Quay, where his father would most probably be.

He entered the building and walked up a couple of storeys to his office. Opening the door to the foyer, Sam was met by the man he knew was his father's secretary.

'Welcome home, Samuel,' Tom Porter said, extending his hand. 'I am sure Colonel Steele does not require you to have an appointment.'

Within a minute, Sam stood in his father's office, a tall, broad-shouldered, handsome young man tanned by the tropical sun. Ian immediately went to his son and took his hand in a fierce grip. Sam was sure that he could see a small tear in the corner of his father's eye.

'Sam, there has not been a day go by that I was not worried about your welfare. Welcome home. We will have a truly wonderful meal for you tonight, as it happens to be your favourite, roast lamb. Becky will be delirious with happiness to see her big brother, and I know that all the staff missed you.'

Ian guided his son to a leather couch and pulled over a chair to face the young man.

'I swear you have the look of a man rather than a callow youth,' Ian said, gazing into his son's face. 'Tell me all that has happened since you sailed from Sydney.'

Ian listened in what appeared to be shocked silence as Sam gave an honest report of the events of the last few months: surviving a cyclone only to lose their cargo of bêche-de-mer, taking a Tong leader's payment for a cargo of rifles, then losing them to Malay pirates.

'How badly were you injured?' Ian asked.

'Lee saved my life by getting me to a doctor in Singapore,' Sam answered. 'He did so at great risk to his own life.'

'Lee is a man I would stake my life on,' Ian said. 'He has done much for our business enterprises on the Palmer and since. But we will talk more when you are at home tonight.'

Sam was informed that his brother had taken a reduction in rank to join the contingent that had steamed for the Sudan, and that a letter had arrived posted from

Kangaroo Island days earlier. The newspapers now reported that the Australian contingent had arrived at Suakin and that the New South Welshmen would be sent into the fighting. Sam expressed his annoyance to his father that he had missed the opportunity to join his brother in the campaign, but Ian reassured him he was glad he had missed the action, as it was bad enough for a father to be concerned about one son at war.

And so Sam was joyously welcomed to his family home on the harbour. Dinner was a treat after the rations they had lived on while he was aboard the schooner, and over the meal, Becky prattled on about all the gossip she could think of, even mentioning that many young ladies she knew would give anything to step out with her brother. Sam grinned at his sister's mention of the young ladies' interest in him. It was hard to meet any of them when he had chosen to go to sea, but it was nice to know all the same.

As he lay in his bed that night, he stared up at the ceiling, wondering what was to come next in his life. He had feared his father might force him ashore after the story he had related of the *Ella*'s journey, but his father was a man not like others and seemed to understand that all of life was a risk.

★

Detective Andrew Paull had searched in vain amongst the mountains of police documents for any mention of a Conan Curry. Years earlier he had remembered hearing the name passed between a couple of the older police but had not taken any notice. Both police had since retired, and one had passed away. There was just something that nagged him about Conan Curry's name. He was beginning to think it would forever remain a mystery, but luck was on his side.

One evening, he repaired to a pub not far from CIB headquarters where off-duty (and many times on-duty) police escaped for a cold beer. The bar was crowded, and Andrew noticed that old Herb, a retired police sergeant, was sitting alone in the corner and leaning on his walking stick. All police patrons in the bar knew Herb was dying a slow death from the terrible cancer in his lungs, and when Andrew glanced across at him, he felt pity for a man who had once been awarded a medal for chasing the bushranger scourge of the colony.

Andrew decided to buy him his pot of beer and whisky chaser, which he took over to the table.

'Young Andrew,' Herb said. 'Good to see that you are in good health.' Then Herb began to cough, covering his mouth with the back of his shirt sleeve. When he had finished, he picked up the whisky tumbler and swallowed it down in one gulp. Andrew pulled over a chair and sat down opposite the old policeman.

'How is retirement treating you?' Andrew asked.

'Bloody police pension hardly buys a loaf of bread,' Herb grumbled. 'But all I need is this medicine right here,' he added, lifting his glass of beer with two trembling hands.

'I am sorry to see you in this state,' Andrew said, sipping from his own beer.

'We have seen enough death in our time on the job to know it comes to all men. Dust to dust, ashes to ashes. We just wonder near the end about all the things we never got to do,' Herb said, his eyes running. 'I've got no missus and the kids are down in Victoria, so I will get to think about my regrets when the angel of death comes for me.'

'What is your main regret, Herb?' Andrew asked.

'Not catching the bastards who slew dear Mrs Steele,' Herb said immediately.

At the name of Steele, Andrew became alert. 'What happened?'

'I think it was around '53 or '54. I was called to the scene of a murder of a saintly woman, Mrs Steele, in a little village west of Parramatta. We found her stuffed under a woodpile and after a short time identified two brothers as the main suspects. I've never forgotten the son's look of absolute shock and grief when we informed him of his mother's murder. But those brothers just disappeared, and we never caught up with them.'

'Do you recall the name of those brothers, by any chance?' Andrew asked.

'Yes indeed. Their surname was Curry.'

Andrew leaned forward eagerly. 'Did one of the Curry brothers go by the name of Conan?'

'How did you know?' Herb asked with a puzzled expression.

'Just a copper's guess,' Andrew replied, attempting to keep his excitement under control. 'What was the name of the murdered woman's son?'

'It was a long time ago.' Herb frowned. 'Bill . . . Charlie . . . No! Ian,' he remembered. 'I read about him in the papers a few years back, about his service to the Queen in the army. I was pleased to see that he had made something of himself after that tragedy.'

Andrew could hardly believe what he was hearing. There was no such thing as coincidence in his world of police investigation. Ian Steele and Conan Curry connected by an event over thirty years earlier. And yet, from what he had read, the two men had served together, and Andrew knew that was a bond as strong as any family connection. What were the odds of Conan Curry being the same man still wanted for murder, which had no statute of limitation?

But how could it be possible Steele would be friends

90

with a man who, surely, he must know was linked to his mother's death? It just did not make sense.

Andrew purchased another round of drinks for the deathly ill former policeman before he excused himself.

Andrew knew he would not be going straight home to his wife and children, but would return to the CIB headquarters to undertake another records search. If he could gather the evidence against Conan Curry VC, then Curry would be hanged at Darlinghurst gaol for murder.

★

Lee walked along the dusty dirt track that led to his family shanty. As he approached, he could see an elderly couple with weather-beaten skin bending over between the rows of vegetables, plucking weeds from the earth.

When he was about twenty paces away, the old woman lifted her head, shielding her eyes, and cried out. The old man looked up to see the well-dressed man now striding towards them, carrying a small suitcase.

'Ling Lee! My beloved son!'

Lee felt his mother's feeble but loving embrace and realised he had been away for years. His father stood gazing at his son until Lee walked over to him, bowed and said, 'Hello, honourable father. It has been a long time.'

'You are welcome home, my son,' the older man said formally. 'You have changed. When I saw you approaching, I thought I saw one of those barbarian white people.' Lee could see just the hint of a smile on his father's wrinkled face. He could still see the strength in his father's body had not changed – he was just a little slower in his movements, and his thick hair and beard were now pure white. 'Your mother will prepare us a meal, and you will tell us of your life since you left us so many years past.'

That evening, Lee sat with his parents in their tiny hut, drinking soup and eating a meal of noodles and chicken. His mother never took her eyes off the boy she had watched leave for adventure and who now had returned as a man. Lee hardly spoke during the meal, listening to his mother relate all that she felt was relevant, from the weather and crop failures to people in their tight-knit Chinese community who had been born, married and died in this land so far from China.

Then Lee spoke of his life on the goldfields and how he had been gifted a share in a gold-mining enterprise that had made him a lot of money. Of how he now worked for a large company as a trusted employee, accruing even more wealth, and it was then that Lee opened the small suitcase to reveal the coins and paper money.

'This I have travelled far and worked hard to bring home to you,' he said as his mother and father stared at the small fortune under the dim light of a kerosene lantern. 'I hope that I have been an honourable son and made you proud.'

'My son, you are all that we wished to see before we join the ancestors,' his father said. 'We have been able to save and buy the plot we garden on. Our only wish was that one day you would return to us. I can see that you have lived in the world of the Europeans, but still speak our sacred language well. It is not the money you bring us that causes pride, but that you are able to be a man of the world, mixing with your own people as well as the Europeans. Few who have arrived on these shores have been able to swim in the sea of many different fishes. We do not need the money, which I would hope you use to find a Chinese wife worthy of you, and give us grandchildren.'

Lee's father leaned forward and closed the lid to the small suitcase. 'Please take it with you when I know you will leave us again. I sense that you have not informed us of all that you have done. I sense that death has been a part of your life.'

Lee was startled by his father's perceptiveness. Was it that he could see his soul through his eyes? He hung his head. 'I have used the skills you taught me to save my own life on many occasions,' Lee replied. 'I have not dishonoured the code you taught me.' It was not the full truth, but Lee greatly valued his father's opinion of him.

In the morning, Lee bade farewell to his elderly parents and as he walked back along the dirt track, he realised that the tears welling in his eyes were running down his face. Lee knew that his parents would never see their grandchildren, nor would he ever see them again in this life.

ELEVEN

Josiah made his way into the regimental area of the brigade quarters and was immediately recognised by soldiers who he had served with in Afghanistan and Africa. Beaming smiles, salutes and calls of 'Good to see you, sir,' echoed as he passed. Josiah experienced a warm feeling of being remembered by those he had once led, and stopped to congratulate men who had once been private soldiers and now were wearing the chevrons of corporals and sergeants. One soldier Josiah had recommended for promotion was now a sergeant.

'Sergeant Wilberforce. I see that the regiment had the wisdom to promote you. A finer soldier I have never known.'

Sergeant Wilberforce stood at attention, beaming his gratitude to a man he would have followed into hell. 'Yes, sah. We even have another colonial officer in the regiment whom the men respect, but we don't call him the Colonial as we did you, sah.'

'Who is the man?' Josiah asked, his curiosity piqued.

'Captain Patrick Duffy. I heard he was from New South Wales,' Sergeant Wilberforce replied. 'I last saw him at his tent a few minutes ago. You might catch him. I can see that you are with the Tommy Cornstalks.' Sergeant Wilberforce used the term for the newcomers, as it was noted that they were generally head and shoulders taller than the Tommy Atkins British soldiers, who had been recruited from the slums and impoverished rural regions of Great Britain. Poor diet and starvation had stunted their growth, where the volunteer army had grown with an abundance of meat and vegetables in the colonies.

'Well, here we are, shoulder to shoulder in this campaign, Sergeant. You keep your head down in any future fighting. I expect to see you wearing warrant rank when next we meet.'

Sergeant Wilberforce grinned and snapped off his best salute.

Josiah went in search of this mysterious colonial in his old regiment. He had little trouble finding the officer's tent, and noticed a tall, broad-shouldered young man lounging in a cane chair outside of the tent flap. He was in his shirt-sleeves with his feet up on an empty ammunition crate, and was reading a novel.

'Captain Duffy?' Josiah asked.

The captain barely glanced up. 'Who might you be?'

'Lieutenant Josiah Steele, formerly of this regiment, sir,' Josiah replied.

Immediately, the captain dropped his feet to the ground. Pushing away from the chair, he came to standing before Josiah, his demeanour transformed in an instant. 'I have heard tales about you from my brother officers ever since I was commissioned into the regiment of mad Scots. It is a pleasure to shake the hand of the colonial who blazed the trail for me. I think that calls for a quiet drink, if you will?'

Josiah followed Patrick into the tent, which was furnished with a simple camp stretcher and table constructed from ammunition crates, with a folding canvas field chair. Patrick produced a silver flask of brandy and a couple of battered enamel mugs, gesturing to Josiah to take the folding chair while he sat on the empty ammunition cases.

'I am surprised to see that you have come here to serve as a mere lieutenant,' Patrick said, raising his mug in a toast. 'With your experience, I would have expected you to be a brevet captain at the least.'

'I had to take a reduction in rank as officer field positions were hard to come by, and there was no shortage of experienced British field officers. But I have my platoon and am enjoying being back in this world, which I find much more comfortable than that of our family business.'

'You would not perchance be a member of the Steele family from Sydney, whose patriarch is former Captain Ian Steele?' Patrick asked.

'Now Colonel Steele, with his own militia regiment,' Josiah replied. 'He is my father.'

'Damn in hell!' Patrick exclaimed. 'My adoptive family, the Macintoshes, do a lot of business with your father. I am surprised that you and I have not crossed paths earlier. In these modern times, the world is getting smaller every day.'

An hour went like a minute as the two stumbled across mutual interests and friends back in Sydney until a soldier appeared at the entrance to the tent.

'The commanding officer wishes for his officers to assemble at his tent in ten minutes, sir,' the soldier said to Patrick, who immediately reached for his khaki field jacket.

'Well, old chap, you and I will have to meet up again

in the officers' mess. I am sure that there will be one or two familiar faces who would love to catch up with an old comrade.'

'That would be grand,' Josiah replied, and the two men exited the tent, Josiah to return to his battalion, Patrick to a meeting with his commanding officer.

When Josiah returned to his lines, his men were busy using tea, coffee and tobacco juice to stain once-white helmets a sandy colour to assist with camouflage. The khaki uniforms had arrived from Britain for the colonial contingent, along with goggles to protect their eyes from the desert sand, neck flaps to protect against sunstroke and puttees wrapped around ankles as a protection against nasty creatures such as scorpions. And then it was time to engage in their first battle with the Mahdi's army.

★

Detective Andrew Paull had done as much research as he could on the former British army warrant officer Conan Curry. Andrew knew that it was a very sensitive matter to be developing a case to arrest a man who held the highest military award for bravery. In his research, Andrew had located a wanted poster with a sketch of two men – one being a young Conan. The detective stared at the face on the poster, then at a sketch of Conan taken from a Sydney newspaper, when he had been interviewed after winning the VC. There were similarities in the two pictures, but it was not definitive.

'You goin' to sleep on the job?' Andrew's partner, Detective Grahame White, asked as he stood by Andrew's desk.

Andrew opened his eyes, looking up at his partner. 'What do you think about the poster here of this man and the picture in the newspaper?' he asked. His partner leaned over and squinted at the comparison.

'Yeah, there's a likeness,' he said. 'Is this about the old case from thirty years ago you've been chasin'?'

'Yes. I think that the former British warrant officer is one and the same man as the fellow who is wanted for the slaying of a Mrs Steele, but has eluded justice for all those years.'

Detective White whistled. 'Good luck with that.'

'You are with me on this one,' Andrew said. 'We will be going to visit the gentleman tomorrow at his home to ask some questions and confirm a few facts about his life. I have approval from upstairs.' What Andrew did not tell his partner was that the approval came with the warning to be discreet and to tread very lightly. If Andrew brought down a scandal on the CIB with his investigation, he was on his own.

★

Reveille was called at 1 am, breakfast of coffee at 1.30 am and the men from New South Wales assembled for a parade under a starry desert sky at 2 am. Josiah had received orders that his platoon was to march to a place called Tamai, where they were to attack the Mahdi's army.

By 3 am, they had joined with the ten thousand soldiers of the British army to form a giant square, with the logistics needed on the backs of camels, horses and mules in the centre for protection.

Josiah could sense the excitement and nervousness of his men when two companies of the volunteer infantry took up their place. For the majority of his platoon, this was the first time that they had been called on to kill other men.

The giant square advanced like a great fortress of human bodies. The men from the colonies were awed by the sheer size of the formation, which had more soldiers than all the colonial armies of Australia combined. It was the massive fist of imperial England sent out to crush the rebels who dared challenge the Queen of the British Empire.

When the sun arose as a searing ball of fire, they had reached their first objective, a place known as McNeill's Zareeba, a small defensive area that had been the site of a bloody and vicious battle between British soldiers and the Mahdi's army eleven days earlier. Vultures circled in the blue sky above over the rotting bodies of dead British soldiers and Sudanese rebels, as well as camels. It was here amidst the stench of decomposition that they were to have breakfast of tinned meat, bread and water.

Josiah surveyed the bloody ground, where the legs and arms of the dead stuck out of the sand. The stench of rotting bodies was almost unbearable and when Josiah glanced at his men, he could see that the sights and putrid smells had disturbed them. As unpleasant as their breakfast location was, it did not disturb him much. This was the real face of war, and he suspected one or two of his soldiers were only just coming to grips with the knowledge that the adventure was well and truly over. He could hear a couple of his men vomiting. They must have revised their first ideals of war for the Queen, and if they could have returned to Suakin and hopped a ride on a ship returning to civilisation, perhaps they would have done.

Then it was time to continue the advance. The regiments fell back into their square formation to continue the attack on the Mahdi's army. Rifles at the shoulder with bayonets fixed, they trudged forward under the searing sun. The terrain was rough and during halts, men chose to stand. By 1 pm, water canteens had been emptied, such was the thirst of the army marching in a hot and arid landscape. By late afternoon, two colonial soldiers had to be transported in ambulance wagons when they collapsed.

As the sun began to sink on the horizon, the formation was ordered to build a zareeba of stones and rocks as a defensive measure against a surprise attack. A hot-air balloon was sent aloft with an observer who reported that he could see the Arab army retreating to the hills beyond. It was time to rest, and campfires were lit against the chill of the night. It was such a contrast to bake during the day and suffer the chill of the desert by night.

Josiah went amongst his men, enquiring as to their health and inspecting the blistered feet of many. He joked with them, but could still see the haunted look of men who could not stop thinking about the sights and stench left behind at McNeill's Zareeba. He reassured them that they would not share the same fate as they were safe in the square of so many well-trained and disciplined British regiments who had already fought many battles.

Josiah established his campsite and lit his fire from a scarce selection of dried mimosa scrub twigs. The land around them had barely any vegetation except for a few clumps of dried tussock grasses and stunted, spindly bushes. It was as harsh a place as any Josiah remembered from his time in Afghanistan. When he looked up from his campfire, he could see the silhouettes of sentries on the heights around them against the beautiful desert sky awash with twinkling stars.

He was joined by his fellow platoon commander, Archie.

'I have something to ward off the night chills,' Archie said, offering Josiah a flask of gin, which he gratefully accepted, swigging a good gulp of the fiery liquid. 'Bad show back at McNeill's today,' Archie said, taking his own gulp of the alcohol before screwing the lid back on. 'It put the wind up a few of my lads.'

'They were not alone,' Josiah said, poking his sparse flickering flames with a stick. 'A few of my men were a bit affected, but I think they are coming to grips with the reality that war is not an adventure but a tough slog to stay alive and kill the enemy before he kills you.'

'I must admit, old chap, I have never seen anything like it,' Archie said, staring into the flames of Josiah's fire. 'It was awful. Those fine young British soldiers' bodies being torn apart by vultures when we arrived. Not even a decent Christian burial.'

'I suspect that when the army withdrew, there was no time for the niceties of burials,' Josiah said, staring up at the stars. 'You quickly learn to save your own skin.'

'God help me,' Archie said. 'I hope I don't end up like them if I am killed. My family would expect that I received a full military burial service on the battlefield.'

'I promise you if we end up in the same situation and I survive, I will tell your family that you were buried with full military honours six foot under and that the drums and bugles sounded.'

Archie glanced at Josiah with a sharp look. 'What if I survive and it is you who dies like those poor chaps?'

'I am not a Christian and don't expect any army chaplain to say any words over me,' Josiah answered with a grim smile. 'And we don't have any rabbis with us, so just leave my body for the vultures.'

A few hours later, shots were fired into the bivouacked soldiers from the enemy, who had crept in close to the perimeter of the camp using the darkness of the night as cover. Return fire from the sentries armed with hard-hitting breech-loading Martini Henry single-shot rifles drove them off. The artillery added to the gunfire with a few rounds of high explosive, and then little else was heard through the night.

By 6 am, the army had rested and the previous day's events were behind the men as they drank coffee and ate biscuits for breakfast. It was Good Friday, but no hot cross buns were served before the regiments fell into place in the monolithic square to continue the advance. Josiah was aware that it was Passover in his own religion, but none of it mattered unless he survived to see another Passover back home.

It was on Good Friday that the men from New South Wales would suffer their first battle casualties in the colonial war.

★

So, it had started, Marian reflected, reading the headlines in the *Sydney Morning Herald*:

The Soudan Campaign

The Advance on Tamai

Skirmishes with the enemy

The New South Wales Contingent in Action

Three of the Contingent Wounded

'I have secured tickets for the Theatre Royal tonight,' Horace Anderson said, knotting his tie in front of a mirror. 'I have been told that Mrs Armstrong will be singing, and some say she has the potential to rise to international recognition. It was too good an opportunity to allow to go to waste. What do you think, my darling girl?'

Marian put down the paper she had been reading. 'I think I would like that,' she replied. 'The days can be so boring.'

'You know that you can have anything your heart desires,' Anderson said, crossing to the bed and kissing Marian on the forehead. 'I have opened accounts at the best stores in town for your use.'

'I know.' Marian sighed, leaning back against the pillows of the bed. As each day passed in Horace's company, Marian felt more and more like a kept woman, although she had enjoyed the pampering at first. She was tinged with guilt for being away from her parents, but they had long given up trying to persuade her to leave the wealthy businessman. Unlike Josiah, who put his soldiers before her, Horace was devoted to her needs and had proven to be an intelligent and suave man.

'After the theatre, we will dine at the best restaurant in Sydney,' Horace said. 'I have a very special surprise for you when we do so.'

'What surprise?' Marian asked, sitting up, holding the sheet to her breasts with her long red hair flowing over her shoulders.

'It would not be a surprise if I told you now.' He grinned back at her before departing, leaving Marian curious as to his plan. But Marian was just a little unsettled in her feelings for the handsome and charming man who now dominated her life. Admittedly, she had anything she desired, but she could not completely dismiss her feelings for the soldier on the other side of the Indian Ocean.

A maid brought her a tray for breakfast, returning minutes later with a worried expression. 'Madam, I have received a letter for you from a messenger.'

Marian accepted the letter and could see that it was from her mother. Marian read the contents and immediately flung herself from the bed. Her beloved father, the rock of her existence, had been arrested for murder!

TWELVE

Ian Steele was at his desk, poring over company reports and thinking about lunch. He had commenced his day early but had been delayed en route to the office as a big cart carrying beer kegs had run over a pedestrian, bringing traffic to a halt. By the time the man's body had been retrieved by the police, Ian was an hour behind with the paperwork required for the large enterprise he ruled over. It was near midday when his secretary knocked on his door.

'Colonel, Mrs Curry is here and wishes to speak to you,' Tom said. 'She is rather distraught.'

'Send her in immediately,' Ian said. Within a minute, Molly was escorted into Ian's office. He could see she had been crying and he immediately rose from his desk.

'Molly, what has upset you?' he asked, standing near her as Tom quietly retreated, closing the door discreetly behind him.

'It's Conan. The police have arrested him for murder,' she sobbed.

Ian did not hesitate to embrace her as one would a family member. 'What do you mean, arrested for murder?' Ian asked. 'What murder?'

'They said it was a matter that happened over thirty years ago, and their records show that he is still wanted.'

Immediately, Ian knew what the police were referring to and his mind flashed back to the death of his mother at the hands of Conan's brother in a botched robbery at his family home west of Sydney. Ian knew that Conan had attempted to prevent her assault by his out-of-control brother, who was later murdered himself on a ship to England.

Ian knew that by law, Conan was guilty of the murder for acting in a common purpose and any conviction would inevitably lead him to the gallows in Darlinghurst gaol.

Ian experienced a chill run through his body like never before. This was a desperate situation.

'Did the police say where they were taking Conan?' Ian asked, disengaging himself from the embrace as tears ran down Molly's cheeks. He retrieved a clean handkerchief and passed it to Molly.

'They said they were taking him to Darlinghurst to formally charge him.' Molly sobbed again. 'Oh, what can we do?'

'I will go immediately to the police at Darlinghurst and sort out this mistake,' Ian replied. 'I will have one of my staff take you home, and will inform you of all that I do to get Conan back with you safe and sound.'

Ian's words seemed to calm Molly down, and she nodded her agreement.

Ian's mind was a whirl of thoughts. Technically, the police could obtain a conviction for Conan's part in the murder, but Conan had long paid any debt he owed on the bloody battlefields they had shared as close as brothers. There was nothing Ian would not do to save Conan – including perjuring himself. Conan was his brother, if not by birth, then by life itself.

★

The great square reached Tamai village and found it deserted. So they marched through it to the hills beyond, where they could see the Mahdi's men filling in wells to deny water to the advancing British force. Josiah and his men were now at the rear of the great square, and just behind his platoon, he noticed his fellow colonial Captain Patrick Duffy strolling along beside his men. The two men waved cheerily to each other.

The rebel army was taking cover behind rocks and in the sparse scrub, pouring small arms fire into the square, with the bullets reaching as far as the position the Australians held. Suddenly, one of Josiah's men yelped, turning angrily to the man behind him, who he clearly thought had punched him, only to realise that a bullet had gone through his shoulder. Two more Australians were hit by snipers, more through bad luck than accurate fire. By the time the bullets and musket balls reached the rear of the square, they were almost spent, with one of the wounded colonials taking a bullet in his foot.

Orders were shouted for the wounded soldiers to be taken to the ambulance wagons travelling at the centre of the square, as more incoming fire could be heard. For Josiah, it was an all-too-familiar sound.

The enemy fell back, and the British square chose not to pursue them into the arid lands beyond but to maintain their valuable supplies of rations, water and ammunition. A march back to the Suakin port was ordered, and as they passed back through the Tamai village, all buildings were put to the torch to deny the Mahdi's army from using the village in the future. They then marched to McNeill's Zareeba for the first night of the withdrawal.

Josiah went amongst his men with reassuring words. He could see the expressions of shock in some of the men who had never before been fired upon, realising that the invisible whip-like buzzing around their heads had the ability to kill them. But already, many of the Australian soldiers sought out souvenirs, finding sun-dried skulls and other bits and pieces of the battle.

As usual, Archie joined Josiah under a sky of twinkling stars, where they sat staring into the heavens.

'How did you find your first action?' Josiah asked his fellow officer, who had produced his silver hip flask and handed it to Josiah.

'Damned frightening – and exciting at the same time,' Archie replied, accepting the flask back. 'For a moment, I felt helpless to protect my men as the bullets came in amongst our ranks, fearing that I would lose men, but it seems we were damned lucky to only have three wounded. I must say, I felt a long way from home and the safety of my life there. I think I appreciate your service a lot more after having today's fright thrust upon me.'

'Only a soldier who has been where we are can appreciate what we go through,' Josiah said. 'The continual thirst for water, the ache of the long marches in this terrible heat, the sleepless nights of guard duty and the outright fear of what lies ahead when the sun rises. You will find when you return home, your friends will have little interest in attempting to understand the harsh conditions you lived through. Only another soldier who has faced combat would understand.' As Josiah was reflecting on the life of a soldier, sporadic firing broke out, shattering the quiet. Bullets fell but did little damage. 'Ah, I suspect a few of our men will have a sleepless night,' he said, accepting the flask again. 'But our sentries will keep the enemy at bay.'

Just before he retired for the night, Josiah saw Captain Patrick Duffy a short distance away in conversation with a private soldier from his Scottish regiment. He could see that they were deep in conversation, and Josiah sensed that he should not disturb his colonial counterpart.

Josiah slept soundly until the sun rose, and thought that the previous day had been but a minor nuisance and nothing like he had experienced in the past. He hoped that the three wounded men – whose injuries weren't serious – would be the total extent of war injuries for the campaign.

★

Ian Steele went directly to the foreboding Darlinghurst gaol. The large sandstone building had first begun construction in 1821 but was only finished the year Ian dismounted from his carriage to seek entry. At first he was denied by a guard, but when he declared his position in colonial society, he was granted entrance.

Ian sought out the most senior administrator, who knew of his prestigious place in the colony and reluctantly agreed that Ian could visit their newest prisoner. He was led along corridors and eventually to a dismal cell, which was unlocked for Ian to step in and see Conan sitting on a hard bunk. Conan blinked when light flooded in, standing to extend his hand to Ian.

'My God!' Ian said. 'How could this happen after such a long time, my old friend?'

'It seems the sins of my brother have come to haunt me,' Conan responded wearily.

'You have naturally denied being involved in the murder of my mother by your brother?' Ian asked quietly, lest the guards outside overheard him.

'Yes,' Conan answered. 'I was taken to the detectives' office and interviewed before they brought me here. Molly was present when the detectives and a couple of uniformed officers came to our house, and I hardly had time to reassure her I would be all right. They at least had the courtesy to inform Molly where I would be imprisoned. I knew that you would not let me rot here.'

'You will continue to plead innocent. I am sure that our government does not want to see the recipient of the Victoria Cross convicted for murder when the Queen personally awarded you the medal. And as my mother's son, I will vouch for you in any court and support your innocence. I feel that after thirty years, the prosecution will have a hard time producing witnesses and it will be clear that the accusation is purely speculative. If I remember rightly, it was only hearsay that you were present at the scene because you and your brother were known always to be together.'

A slight smile appeared on Conan's weary face. 'I hope what you say will help, or I will surely be hanged here.'

'I am going to seek out those responsible for your arrest and talk to them,' Ian said, placing his hand on his friend's shoulder.

'I have followed you through some of the worst battles the Queen asked us to fight and we survived. I trust in you, old friend,' Conan said in a choked voice.

They shook hands and Conan slumped down on his bed as Ian departed for another visit, one that he sensed would be critical to saving Conan's life.

★

After the advance to Tamai, the Australian contingent found themselves acting as guards against attacks from roving enemy forces for a vital railway to transport military supplies that was being built towards Berber. At night, they slept in tents but were always aware that the Mahdi's warriors could slip into the British lines and cut their throats. Josiah found an officer from his old Scottish regiment after their return from Tamai and asked if Captain Duffy was around the lines. The officer, a young lieutenant, shook his head. 'He seems to have disappeared. Our staff have not said a thing. It is rather puzzling.'

Josiah walked away, wondering how a British officer could simply disappear.

By day, the colonial soldiers worked in pairs; one holding a rifle while the second man used an axe to clear scrub for the line to be laid. Many of Josiah's men grumbled about becoming little more than navvies, but he half-heartedly attempted to convince them that they were carrying out a vital task that would eventually help destroy the enemy.

It was only the sound of the bugle calling the men to arms that broke the monotony. The colonial soldiers would fall into their squares, bayonets fixed and ready to repel any attack. Although they were aware the drills were simply that, it did give them some reprieve from wielding an axe to clear the path of the railway line, as this was not what they'd signed up for.

It was Archie who brought the good news to Josiah, who was with his platoon working on laying the railway line.

'Old chap, I have just got the news. We are being sent on a reconnaissance mission to Debberet.'

When the word spread down the line, the men were cheered and laid down their axes to pick up their rifles.

THIRTEEN

The cable to the British war office read:

> *NSW Contingent under Colonel Richardson accomplished march of 14 miles from Handoub. Route lay through difficult pass and occupied nine hours. Their retirement was excellent.*

But when the men returned to their lines, all they had to show for their march through rocky ravines and over very rugged mountains was blistered feet, heat exhaustion and frustration. No enemy were sighted – with the exception of dead ones – and all they had to show for the arduous trek was a captured goat.

They had spent the night at Handoub, where the stench of rotting bodies made sleep almost impossible, and they were forced to bury the corpses before they departed. Rumours were rife that the Mahdi's army was planning to attack the railway, but that did not eventuate. For the Australians, war came down to the occasional sniper shot through their tents, and Josiah heard the grumbling of homesick soldiers complaining that they would be better off being sent home.

It became their habit for Archie and Josiah to meet to discuss the campaign after the men of their platoons had finished their tasks for the day, and the two officers would share Archie's flask of strong alcohol.

'My lads are ready to go home,' Archie said as the two men stared up at the night sky. 'This is not what we expected. One or two have expressed the opinion that they would make more money at home clearing scrub and complain that they signed on to fight, not work as navvies for the British army. It is even worse for our gunners back at Suakin, who simply drill every day without much chance to fire their guns at the enemy.'

'Be happy that we have not had to face a situation like McNeill's Zareeba, when they slaughtered so many British troops,' Josiah replied. 'Had we reached Suakin a couple of weeks earlier, the newspapers back home would have been publishing a lengthy list of dead and wounded. I wonder then if the good people of home would have been so enthusiastic in their support.'

'I can see your point, old chap.' Archie sighed. 'But this is not what we foresaw as our participation in this war. I have heard that the staff are considering forming a camel corps.'

'That should be amusing to witness,' Josiah chuckled. 'Bushmen used to riding horses learning to ride camels. But at least the camel has the ability to take us further into the arid lands in pursuit of our enemy.'

A meteorite flashed across the sky and burned out below a ridge of hills. The war dragged on, and so too the frustration of working under a blazing summer sun as little more than uniformed labourers.

★

Ian Steele was admitted to the CIB headquarters by a uniformed police sergeant who also happened to be one of his militia volunteers.

'Thought it might help to know that our boss has a nephew serving with the contingent over in the Sudan, sir,' he said as he escorted Ian to the head of the CIB's office. He knocked and explained who the visitor was, which duly impressed the CIB head officer.

'Come in, Colonel Steele,' he said, and Ian walked into the office with the bearing of an officer of the Queen. Ian had the impression from the demeanour of the inspector that he was not a man to be underestimated. 'I presume that you are here to discuss the arrest of Mr Curry.'

Ian pulled up a chair on the opposite side of the senior police officer's desk. 'You are correct, Inspector,' Ian replied. 'You have arrested an innocent man.'

The policeman glanced down at a file on his desk. 'According to Detective Paull's investigation, we have the right man for the murder of your mother,' he said.

Ian well knew the name Detective Paull. He had always respected the man's integrity for the law when Ian himself had been investigated for a murder which he had actually committed years earlier. But at the time the police detective had been unable to provide enough evidence to arrest Ian.

'With all respect, Detective Paull is wrong.'

'And what of the witness who will give evidence in this matter, Colonel Steele?'

Ian felt a chill. He was not aware that there were any

witnesses. 'I would suggest that the witness is either lying or mistaken,' Ian countered.

'That may be your opinion, Colonel Steele. But a preliminary hearing will decide the veracity of his testimony. I know that the arrest of Mr Curry will bring some embarrassment to many in government circles, as he is a decorated war hero, and many will not wish to see his Victoria Cross besmirched with the charge of murder. It will bring shame to the reputation of such a great honour and if you have any further evidence, we would appreciate your assistance in this matter.'

'I will be seeking out evidence to prove that Mr Curry was not responsible for the murder of my mother. You must see the rationale that if I had even the slightest inkling that he was guilty, I would throw my full force behind seeing him hang. But I know he is innocent.'

'I have been briefed that you served together for many years and that bond has blinded you to his guilt,' the inspector countered. 'It is a failing of human nature. If there is anything else I can help you with, I will do so, Colonel.'

Ian rose from the chair. 'Have you released news of the arrest to the newspapers?' he asked.

'Not at his stage,' the policeman answered, shifting just a little uncomfortably in his chair. Ian suspected that the police were reluctant to release the information until after a preliminary hearing. Then the colony would know that a winner of the Victoria Cross was on trial for his life. Until then, they were aware that if the news leaked out, a public uproar might descend upon them, especially in this time of public support for the New South Wales contingent fighting overseas.

Ian left the building for his carriage. His next stop would have to be to employ the best criminal lawyers that money could buy.

The existence of an alleged witness to the crime was his main concern. Would Conan's life hang on the words of a single individual?

★

Marian was met by the maid, Lucy, at the cottage owned by her parents, and was ushered inside to see her mother sitting on a divan that faced a large French window overlooking the harbour.

'Mother, please, tell me what has happened,' she said, rushing to sit beside Molly, who turned to her with reddened eyes.

'The police took him away and said he was being arrested for murder. They said he was being charged with slaying Colonel Steele's own mother,' Molly said. 'But the colonel has reassured me that this is not true and that your father is innocent. He is doing everything to help your father.'

Marian was stunned. It was something that simply could not be true, and the fact that Colonel Steele had repudiated the police claim only proved it. What man would vehemently deny the accusation if he had even the slightest hesitation?

'I am sure this allegation against my father will be proven to have no substance,' Marian attempted to reassure her mother as she wrapped her arms around her. 'I also know that the colonel will do everything in his power to see to that.'

Molly glanced at her daughter. 'He has so much to be concerned about, with Josiah in a war overseas,' she said. 'I know he will stand by your father, but the fact my husband languishes in a prison cell makes my heart ache. I remember how many times I waited for him to return from some battle or another, and he always did. Now, he is in a situation that he seems powerless to fight alone.'

'He is not alone in this battle,' Marian soothed. 'He has the colonel fighting by his side, just as Father and he did in far more dangerous situations.'

Molly attempted to smile for her daughter's sake as Lucy set down a tea tray.

'I thought this might be a suitable time for afternoon tea,' she said, retreating to the kitchen to prepare the evening meal.

Marian poured the tea for herself and her mother, adding milk from the jug and stirring in the sugar. Molly lifted her cup and took a sip. 'You have not been home in weeks. The talk is that you have been under Mr Anderson's roof for all that time,' Molly said.

Marian experienced a twinge of guilt that she had not been with her mother when the police came. 'I do not deny that,' she replied defensively. 'Horace is a wonderful man who I suspect would like to marry me.'

'What about Josiah?' her mother asked. 'Your father and I always thought that you and he were destined to be together. Josiah is away in the service of his colony, and you flounce around with this other man whom you know Josiah despises.'

'Mother, Josiah chose his duty over love for me by joining the contingent for the Sudan. What man would do such a thing if he truly loved me?'

'I was heartbroken every time your father steamed away for war, but he always came back – just as Josiah will also return to you,' Molly said, turning to stare out through the large French doors.

Marian frowned. 'What guarantee do I have of that?'

'Your love for him, and prayer,' Molly replied.

'And what about the next time the bugles call and the drums beat, calling him back to the army?' Marian retorted. 'What then for me? More hope and prayer that he returns?'

Molly did not reply, but took another sip of her tea. It was balmy outside, but the weather was beginning to change as winter approached. Molly was counting the days until she could feel the cold winds on her face, relieving her of the infernal heat.

'Will you remain with me tonight?' Molly asked.

'I will,' Marian answered, reflecting that the message she had left with Horace's staff would explain why she could not attend the theatre or discover his surprise. Marian understood that her mother needed her now as never before.

She hugged her mother again, whispering, 'Father will be home with us before you know it.' But Marian was not as sure as her spoken words.

★

Ian Steele sat in the office of a man who was infamous for getting criminal cases thrown out of court. Just off to Ian's left sat the solicitor who had made the preliminary approaches to the courts for the paperwork required to brief the barrister, a Mr Humphrey Gooding. The man was very overweight and wheezed when he talked. Ian wondered if he would even live long enough to make it to the court procedures.

'I have gone through the paperwork my learned friend has delivered,' Gooding said. 'I must say, this is all rushed.'

'Sergeant Major Curry VC is currently rotting in a cell at Darlinghurst, and I wish to see this matter dealt with as fast as possible,' Ian snapped.

'It takes time to prepare a defence, Colonel,' Gooding shot back, looking over his reading spectacles at Ian. 'The man's life is at stake if the jury finds him guilty. But first, we have the committal hearing before a magistrate to determine whether the police case can go forward. The magistrate will report his findings to the attorney-general for adjudication. This all takes time. I know that you are impatient to secure the man's release, but the law grinds slowly.'

Ian frowned. He was used to making decisions with a quick outcome, but acknowledged that the barrister who would defend the case in court knew his business.

Never before had Ian felt so helpless. The vagaries of the legal system were a world far from what he knew.

Sam was waiting for him when he returned home.

'Is there any good news for the sergeant major?' Sam asked.

'The bloody system will hold Conan until he goes before a magistrate to determine whether he has a case to answer,' Ian replied wearily. 'Until then, he will remain in Darlinghurst and there is nothing I can do to help him.'

'I think that you are doing all that can be done,' Sam reassured. 'I just know that eventually the sergeant major will be released.'

'Eventually,' Ian repeated bitterly. 'He has given a great part of his life to serving our Empire, yet all that means nothing to those who would see him hang.'

'Maybe we should go to your library and share a stiff drink?' Sam suggested. 'You look like you could do with one.'

Ian glanced at his son with the faintest of smiles. 'When did you start partaking of alcoholic beverages?'

Sam looked sheepish. 'Since I took to sea and had to prove I could drink with the best of sailors,' he defended. 'It *is* a maritime tradition.'

Ian shook his head, but smiled. 'I keep forgetting that my sons are grown men. Time has passed far too quickly.'

Father and son retired to the library, where a bottle of single malt scotch was retrieved to fill two crystal tumblers. Ice was secured from a small ice chest in the library for such occasions. They stood side by side by a window overlooking the harbour.

'To Josiah and Conan,' Ian said, raising his glass, and the toast was repeated by Sam before they both drank. 'I must apologise, son, for neglecting your future plans. I know that you are eager to return to the *Ella* and set sail for the South Pacific with Lee and Ebenezer. I shake my head as to why, when I consider all that you three and your crew have gone through in the recent past. You know I have a position for you here in Sydney – or even managing one of our larger properties out west.'

'When you were my age, would you have chosen a boring office job?' Sam said, taking a sip from his tumbler.

Ian shrugged; his son knew him well. The blood that flowed in his veins also flowed in those of his sons. The Steele men were not fated to be pen-pushing managers but men of action – and always yearning to travel to the far horizon.

'Well, tomorrow at my office, you and I will work out a strategy to make our South Pacific trade lucrative.'

This time, Sam raised his scotch to his father. 'To better times ahead for all of us, and that Conan secures his freedom . . . and Josiah returns in one piece.'

In the distance, they could hear the very faint sounds across the water of ships hooting horns and the rattle of anchor chains.

FOURTEEN

In the month of May, death came to the New South Wales contingent.

He did not know it, but on 1 May 1885, Private Robert Weir became the first official Australian to die on active service for his country. It came by way of an invisible enemy that stalked the soldiers: dysentery.

Josiah had strictly enforced the rule ensuring his men only drank the water transported from Suakin, as the wells could not be trusted because they may have been poisoned by the enemy. The foul-tasting water his men were forced to drink had been desalinated at Suakin, then carried by rail or on camels to the forward lines.

A white clay-like substance called kaolin was dispensed for dysentery and Enos Fruit Salts at the first sign of stomach pains. The hospital ship *Ganges* was anchored offshore to receive patients, but more of the colonial contingent would die as a result of the diseases that had haunted armies ever since the dawn of warfare in massed formations. Life was miserable, with continual thirst, temperatures of 105 degrees Fahrenheit, sunstroke and enteric fever.

Josiah knew from his past experience that such outbreaks seemed to be associated with soldiers living in camps, and wished that they could be deployed on long-range patrols in search of the elusive warriors of the Mahdi to escape the cramped conditions. Even he now dreamed of being sent home; this was not the kind of war he had expected.

There was never a day that passed when he did not think about Marian and, as he had done five years earlier, wondered whether he should finish the letter he had commenced writing to her. He continued to write to his family and was shocked to read in a letter from Sam that Conan had been arrested on a charge of murder. Even more gut-wrenching was that the murder had been of his father's mother. How could this be? Josiah questioned himself and felt helpless that he was not home to provide support for Marian's father.

When Archie turned up at Josiah's tent, pale and weak, to complain of having the backdoor trots, Josiah said what the bulk of the New South Wales contingent felt: 'It's bloody time the British sent us home. We are doing nothing useful over here.'

★

Ian had been able to bribe the guards to smuggle food into Conan's cell as the rations provided were so meagre and of such poor quality. In later years, famous poet Henry Lawson, who had been imprisoned in the gaol for drunkenness and failing to pay alimony, would write a poem in which he used the term *starvinghurst* to describe the conditions. At least with Ian's name and money, Conan was able to get sufficient food. Each time he visited, Ian assured his friend that he was working to have him released.

After one such visit, Ian attended the barrister's office to ascertain any developments and finally had something to proceed on.

'Do you know a Mr James Courtney?' Humphrey Gooding asked, peering at Ian over his spectacles. 'A gentleman in his mid-seventies and, from what my investigator has told me, he has advanced consumption. The police have his written statement that he witnessed the Curry brothers together in the vicinity of your mother's house on the night of her slaying.'

Ian struggled to remember the residents of his village all those years ago, but the name was vaguely familiar. 'I think I knew the man,' Ian said. 'At the time I was a blacksmith, I sold him a shovel he promised to pay me for, but failed to do so. If I remember correctly, he was always suspected of stealing from neighbours and was in trouble with the magistrate. So, he is the prosecution witness?'

'Yes, and the prosecution are determined to have him appear before the court and repeat his statement. It is a rather damning account, but if what you say is true and I can verify his nefarious conduct, it will go to his lack of credibility, which is something I can use to further our case for Mr Curry's innocence. He admits in his statement that he did not witness the murder of your mother.'

'We have the problem that both Conan and his brother fled the village the day after,' Ian added. 'Their disappearance looked suspicious, and that is why the police undertook to hunt them down.'

'Circumstantial, old chap,' Humphrey said. 'Simply coincidental timing that they chose to search for work elsewhere that same night.'

Ian glanced at the man opposite him with a frown. Circumstantial or not, he expected any jury could draw their own conclusion when it was linked with evidence provided by the witness, even one whose credibility would be brought into question. This was a game where a man's life was on the line, and it could easily go either way with a jury. Ian knew that he would kill to defend his best friend, but also knew if the witness met a violent end, it would be blamed on Conan.

But there were other ways to prevent the witness from testifying.

'If the main witness against Conan could not appear in court, what do you think the odds would be for a not guilty verdict?'

Humphrey looked sharply at Ian. 'Colonel Steele, I hope you are not thinking about doing something nefarious?'

'Something nefarious? Yes,' Ian replied. 'But not what you think.'

Humphrey shook his head. 'I don't think I wish to know what you are thinking, and will deny forever your statement here today.'

Ian rose from his chair with a mysterious smile. 'There are many ways to skin a cat,' he said and bade a good afternoon to the barrister, who was frowning as Ian left the office.

Ian returned to his house on the harbour where he was met by his wife, Isabel.

'How is Conan bearing up?' she asked.

'As expected,' Ian replied, giving her a peck on the cheek. 'I must apologise, but I have to pack for a short visit to our old village.'

Isabel cast her husband a questioning look. 'Why do you need to return there?' she asked.

He smiled grimly. 'The solution to one of Conan's problems still lives there. James Courtney.'

'I remember him,' Isabel said. 'A rather nasty man, if I remember correctly.' Then she looked at her husband with an expression of horror, remembering how Ian had handled the man who had bashed and raped her years earlier.

When Ian noticed his wife's concerned expression, he said quickly, 'Nothing untoward is going to happen to Courtney. But I have a plan.'

Isabel relaxed, knowing that Ian's word was his bond. 'Just be careful, my love,' she said, reaching out to touch his cheek.

'There is nothing to fear. I'm still held in high regard by those who knew me as the village blacksmith.'

Isabel accepted his reassurance and assisted him to pack a few items for his visit to the little village at the foot of the Great Dividing Range west of Sydney. He intended to take his coach, so his next stop was to find Will Bowden.

Will was sitting in the shade of one of the imported trees, smoking his pipe and gazing out at the harbour. He stood immediately at Ian's approach.

'A good afternoon to you, boss,' he said.

'Will, you and I are going on a trip west of Sydney to carry out a vital task that could mean the difference between life or death.'

'Who we goin' to dispose of?' Will asked, remembering that their 'task' years earlier had been to track down and kill the senior public servant who had violated Mrs Steele. The job had paid well, and Will had no regrets.

Ian grinned. 'No, Will, not dispose of. A friendly talk only. We will stop over at that inn on the outskirts of Parramatta and in the morning, we should arrive at the village. All going well, we should be home late tomorrow night.'

Will looked visibly relieved and hurried away to prepare their one-horse gig for the journey. When he had done so, the two men commenced the trip to Parramatta.

124

Ian said little of what he had planned, but the two men discussed their sons in the Sudan. Will said that George had written regularly and was well, having recovered from a bout of fever. He had also mentioned that Josiah was a grand officer, liked and respected by the soldiers of his platoon. But George had also said the men were keen to return home, as they felt they were contributing little in the war. Ian spoke of how Josiah had expressed the same sentiments and that he felt the campaign had turned into a job for navvies, not soldiers.

They passed by big wagons bringing bales of wool from out west, and other multi-horse-drawn wagons with other agricultural goods to supply the growing city. By nightfall, they had reached the inn at Parramatta and Ian's money secured them good lodgings.

After a hearty breakfast, they set out on the final leg to Ian's home village, which he was surprised to see had grown and now showed signs of prosperity. There were new shops, and on the streets he saw only the faces of strangers. He passed by his old blacksmith shop, which had been expanded into a wagon-building enterprise.

'Where to, boss?' Will asked, and Ian directed him outside of the village. Ian had been given Courtney's address by the barrister, and prayed that his trip would be worth it.

Blowflies swarmed around the ramshackle bark hut and when Ian and Will approached through the overgrown garden, they could see the hut had its wooden door hanging half off its hinges. Ian stepped inside to see the ghostly figure of a scarecrow-like man lying on a straw mattress. At Ian's intrusion, the pale man with red-rimmed eyes struggled to sit up and rasped, 'Who's there? You gonna rob me?'

'You have nothing to fear, Mr Courtney,' Ian replied.

'My name is Colonel Ian Steele. I remember you from when I used to own the blacksmith shop here.'

The sickly man was able to struggle into a sitting position, but immediately fell into a severe coughing fit. Ian kept his distance, using a handkerchief to cover his face, while Will remained well back in the doorway.

'Ian Steele,' Courtney finally said in a weak voice. 'Youse the blacksmith who got famous. Me mates told me all about youse. They was proud that youse came from 'ere. Whaddaya doin' 'ere?'

'I returned home to look up some old friends and I heard you were not well,' Ian lied. 'Now I can see you need help.'

Courtney tried to scoff, but that set off another coughing episode. Ian was patient and when the coughing subsided, he continued. 'As a valued member of the village, I thought that I might be able to help one of my previous customers.' Ian did not add that Courtney had never paid him for the shovel purchased so long ago, doubting that the dying man would even remember. 'I can arrange to have a doctor tend to you on a regular basis and food delivered every other day.'

Courtney started to laugh, but checked himself. 'Hell will freeze over first,' he said. 'I'd rather have a bottle of rum an' kill meself.'

'I will fetch you a bottle of rum today,' Ian replied, 'and I am sure that a doctor would prescribe strong painkillers for your suffering.'

'Why would youse do that?' Courtney asked suspiciously.

'Because I heard that the traps want to drag you into Sydney to give evidence in a court case against Conan Curry, and that would cause you considerable suffering. The police are not interested in your welfare. All they care about is that you give your evidence,' Ian said. 'I remember well how there was a time you hated the police and here

126

you are, in your last days, helping them against the Curry boys, who never did you any harm.'

'The traps, they came weeks ago and threatened me,' Courtney said, his eyes still bright enough to show his shrewdness. 'But if youse bring that bottle of rum, maybe I won't be remembering what happened all those years ago.'

'I will not lie to you, Mr Courtney. I can see the consumption has taken its toll and I have seen the last signs of death in a man's face many times. But I will ensure you are comfortable in your last days on this earth,' Ian swore.

With a shallow sigh, Courtney fell back against the filthy pillow, cradling his head. 'Just get me the rum,' he said.

Ian nodded before stepping into the morning sunshine. A crow cawed its lazy song in the distance and Ian could hear the occasional barking of a dog drifting from the nearby village that had once been his home. For a moment, he was transported to the days of wielding a hammer in the blacksmith's forge.

'Time to return to the village and satisfy a promise,' he said to Will.

Within minutes of arriving, Ian had purchased a bottle of good rum and then stopped off at his old blacksmith shop.

A solidly built man around his own age was hammering out a wagon rim. He glanced up and blinked as if attempting to focus on the man wearing a good suit standing in the doorway. Then, suddenly, he recognised Ian.

'Cap'n Steele! What are you doing here?'

'Francis Sweeney. It appears that you have extended the shop,' Ian said warmly to his former apprentice whom he had turned over the business to years earlier.

Frank brushed his hands on his leather apron and Ian accepted the firm, calloused handshake. 'It has been a while since you were last around the district. How is your family?'

The reunion was warm and the questions genuine. Ian introduced Will to Frank and gave a brief report of his family. Frank in turn informed Ian that his family had grown to seven children, a mix of boys and girls ranging from twenty-two to five.

'Are you staying for a while?' Frank asked.

Ian shook his head. 'I have pressing business back in Sydney, but hope to visit again and meet your family. But I have a favour to ask before I leave,' Ian continued, and laid out how he wanted Frank to organise a food delivery to Courtney, and also a doctor to drop in occasionally to look to the man's failing health. Ian produced a wad of notes, handing it to Frank. 'This will cover the services and you for your trouble.'

'You don't need to pay me,' Frank said, but still accepted the money for expenses. 'One of my boys will look after Mr Courtney.'

'You were the only man here who I trusted to help me out,' Ian replied.

Will and Ian returned to the bark hut and handed over the bottle of rum to Courtney, whose shaking hands were still strong enough to lift the bottle to his lips. He took a gulp and looked up at Ian. 'I'd be thankin' youse, boss,' he said.

Ian bade him a good morning, departing with Will for their journey back to Sydney.

Within the week, Ian received a letter from Frank, who regretted to say that after a couple of days, Mr Courtney had passed away. The doctor gave his verdict that the man had drunk himself to death.

'There are worse ways to die,' Ian muttered, folding the letter.

FIFTEEN

Detective Paull was called to his inspector's office at CIB headquarters and already knew it had to be about his arrest of Conan Curry VC. He had already been informed that his prime witness had died from tuberculosis, considerably weakening his case, but was determined to proceed with the prosecution.

When he entered the office, he noticed a well-dressed middle-aged man he vaguely remembered seeing at the attorney-general's office once. He was sitting in a chair adjacent to the inspector's desk with his hat in his lap.

'Detective Paull, this is Mr Egbert Conway, representing the attorney-general. He has something to tell us regarding your case against Curry.'

'Yes,' the man said. 'After our office reviewed your case, and with your prime witness now unable to attend court, we feel that there is not enough evidence to mount a reasonable prosecution against Mr Curry.'

Andrew frowned. 'Sir, with all due respect, I feel that the circumstantial evidence I have been able to gather is strong enough to continue. I –'

The attorney-general's man raised his hand and leaned forward. 'You have to understand. At this stage, the newspapers have not got wind of his arrest, but their crime reporters are getting suspicious. It would not bode well if they learned we have a man of Mr Curry's high esteem being held at Darlinghurst in these rather patriotic times. It is not in the political interests of the government to pursue the prosecution of this man based on such a flimsy amount of evidence, especially with Mr Humphrey Gooding as his defence barrister.'

Andrew very well knew of the barrister's reputation for getting the most apparently guilty of men off charges in court. He was a man with a sharp intelligence and winning manner before a jury.

'Mr Curry may or may not be guilty of the charge of murder, but it is not in the interest of justice to attempt to prosecute.'

Andrew knew that politics trumped justice in the colony, and realised he was not going to win this argument. He turned to his boss. 'Sir, if you order me to drop the investigation, I will,' he said bitterly.

'Then I am directing you to drop the investigation, Detective Paull. Mr Curry will be freed forthwith,' the inspector said. 'I know that you have been diligent in all that you have done. This will not be any black mark on your service record and I am sure you have other cases to pursue. If there is nothing else, you are dismissed back to your duties.'

Andrew felt as if he had been delivered a kick in the stomach, and left the office with a sour taste in his mouth.

So close to closing a case of murder, yet time had beaten him with the gap of thirty years.

Andrew knew that Colonel Steele had visited his prime witness only days before he had died. Had Steele somehow arranged the witness's death? Two men linked to the case, and two men the intelligent and dogged detective knew in his gut were guilty of dodging the long arm of the law. But there was no statute of limitation on murder and one day, they just might slip up. When they did, he would be there to arrest them.

★

It was a joyous moment when Conan returned home. Molly wept with happiness, as did Marian. Even Ian wiped at the tears forming in the corners of his eyes. Bottles of beer were opened and the celebrating quartet were quickly joined by Isabel and Becky.

'I know that it was you who had me freed,' Conan said to Ian when they were alone in the garden, admiring the view of the harbour below. 'I heard that you went to see Courtney in our old village.'

'I was just there to help a local who was already dying and provide him with some comfort in his last days.'

'I heard they found him with his hand wrapped around an empty rum bottle and a smile on his face,' Conan said with a chuckle.

'I don't know about the smile on his face, but the consumption finally caught up with him – according to the official medical report,' Ian said, keeping a poker face. 'The heavy consumption of strong beverages may have hastened his death. But I am not a medical practitioner.'

'Do you know, I have never felt so helpless as I did in that bloody prison cell. When we faced what seemed to be a hopeless situation at the Ambelya Pass those many years ago, at least we could fight back. But there I was, four walls and a locked door and no way out.'

'You had me on your side,' Ian said. 'That is all we ever need, my dear brother.'

'I do not see Sam here today,' Conan commented, breathing in the fresh, salty air of freedom.

'Sam, Lee and Ebenezer sailed a few days ago north to Townsville where one of our depots has goods for trade in the Pacific islands.'

'Have you heard from Josiah lately?'

Ian nodded. 'He wrote that he thinks it is time the contingent returns to us. The campaign has drawn to a stalemate and his men are tired of working as labourers. He said he would never go to the beach again when he returns, because the sand would remind him of what they live with every day.'

Conan laughed softly. 'The burden of a soldier fighting for the Queen,' he said.

'But this time, fighting on behalf of the colony and representing all Australia.'

'To their safe return from the Sudan, and to fair winds for the *Ella*,' Conan said.

Both men raised their glasses of beer.

★

The Russian army had invaded Afghanistan and defeated the Afghan army.

Rumours swirled around the Furphy-manufactured water carts that they were to be withdrawn from the misery of the Sudan to confront the Russians. Because the world was now linked by telegraph, the news was already being trumpeted in Sydney newspapers such as the *Daily Telegraph*:

Quick as a flash from the cannon's mouth may come the electric spark which tells us that the two great military Powers have abandoned diplomacy for war.

Grasping and insidious, Russia has again jumped at the opportunity of making a further stride in the direction of Britain's possessions in India. If the storm was to burst over Afghanistan, so be it.

Josiah had been briefed with the other officers of the brigade as to the critical situation developing in Afghanistan, and groaned inwardly at the thought that the men from New South Wales might find themselves being redeployed to a place Josiah knew well and did not wish to return to.

'It all sounds grim,' Archie said as he and Josiah watched the sun go down over the low hills surrounding their encampment. 'I was hoping that we might be on the boats back to Sydney in the next few weeks, and now the damned Russian bear has gone and invaded Afghanistan. Well, at least any place has to be better than this miserable country.'

Josiah passed their now traditional flask to his friend. 'You wouldn't say that if you had been there,' he replied. 'Its bloody mountains reach to the sky, and ravines to the centre of the earth. It's about as arid as the Sudan and its summers and winters are worse. But despite that, there is a kind of rugged beauty to the country. The only consolation is that the Russkies will have a hard time subduing the fiercely stubborn tribesmen if they attempt to occupy the land.'

Archie watched the horizon glow as a dust haze gave colour to the sunset. 'I don't think I am cut out to be a soldier,' he sighed. 'I keep remembering the wonderful comforts of home and the more I do, the more I cannot understand men like you. Before we came here, you at least knew how uncomfortable it is to be a soldier in these harsh lands. I take my hat off to you and pray something is worked out between the Russkies and the British government that does not see us reassigned to fight there.'

What neither man knew was that the premier of New South Wales was already sending cables to London, volunteering the Sudan colonial contingent to be sent to India in the event of a confrontation with the Russians. As each man had signed on for a two-year term, Dalley was able to do so, and Cabinet unanimously agreed. The Australian colonies of the east coast feared that the Russians would invade, and militias were recruiting members to defend the country. Across the Tasman Sea, the same fear of invasion swept New Zealand. No longer was the attention on the country's assistance to Britain, but on self-defence at home against a possible Russian peril.

But the majority of the men dared receipt of a white feather, proclaiming they would rather be sent home. However, if ordered to go to India they would do so. After all, it would be an opportunity for the men from Australia to truly see action against an enemy who would stand and fight.

★

Marian followed the alarming reports of the potential war between the British and Russians. She knew about the premier's desire to see the colonial contingent engage in a real war, and show the Mother Country they were equal to any in the British army.

Since the release of her father from Darlinghurst gaol, she had remained at home and only met with Horace Anderson for afternoon tea in the little cafes in the city's arcades, where he had expressed his desire for her to return to his house at South Head.

Marian still felt guilty for being away from home at the time her father was incarcerated and vowed to herself that she would be there for her mother and father. Besides, absence from Horace had given her an opportunity to reflect on Josiah and her continuing feelings for him, which she could not squash as easily as she once thought. He was more and more in her thoughts – and dreams.

'I have missed you very much, my dear lady,' Horace said to Marian as he stirred sugar into his teacup. 'I heard the rumours that your father was arrested by the police on a dodgy murder charge. I just want you to know that whether he was guilty or not, it does not matter to me.'

Marian frowned and snapped, 'My father is the most honourable man I know and if he said that he was innocent of the charge, then that is so.'

Horace leaned back in his chair, casually waving a hand. 'Of course, of course,' he countered with little conviction. 'I have never met a woman I like as much as I do you, Marian.'

'Like?' Marian echoed. 'Not love?'

'It means the same to me,' Horace said with a shrug. 'Like, love. I just want to have you forever in my life, and I know that you want to be with me too.'

Marian did not reply. She well knew that Horace Anderson was one of the most eligible bachelors in the colony, with his aristocratic good looks, charm and enormous personal wealth. She also knew that she had him captivated with her beauty and poise, and he enjoyed being the envy of every man when she was in his company. He promised a life of financial security and acceptance to the most prestigious levels of society.

But as she sat opposite him, there was something that nagged at Conan Curry's daughter. Horace Anderson

135

had no social conscience, or concern for anyone but himself. He was self-centred, vain and, she was learning, insincere. He had already hinted that he would like to wed her, but Marian was beginning to dread that he might make a proposal, as she was now sure she would reject it.

Her thoughts always seemed to come back to her dismissal of Josiah on the grounds of him dashing off to war when he could have easily remained with his family enterprises – and her. Now the chances of him returning were fading, with the headlines concerning a looming war with the Russians. Marian hardly heard Anderson's chatter about his love for her as she retreated to a world that seemed long ago, when Josiah's troopship returned to London after his campaign in Africa. She did not want to remember how her emotions had soared when she saw him step off the gangway.

Horace's next words penetrated Marian's consciousness and forced her out of her reverie. 'Will you marry me?' Anderson held up an open jewellery box displaying a magnificent diamond-encrusted ring.

SIXTEEN

The feeling amongst Josiah's men was that they should return to Sydney to defend the colony against a potential armed threat from Russia rather than continue serving Britain's interests in Afghanistan. Josiah had already heard the talk by the soldiers of their contingent that they were not satisfied with the treatment meted out by their own officers, but that he was not included in that blacklist. It was said that his previous experience in the British army had equipped him to lead men in a military campaign.

The railway from Suakin to Berber was cancelled, then the news so many men had eagerly awaited was broadcast – they would be steaming back to Australia on 17 May!

Three wounded and four dead from disease was the casualty list for the short military campaign, and Josiah was pleased. He had not lost any of his men and they were going home, leaving behind the oppressive heat, sand and boredom.

Now he could see Marian and attempt to re-establish their relationship. This was his last war, he swore as he listened to the sound of very happy soldiers around him.

'Do we get a medal, sir?' one of his men asked.

'I have heard that you might get two medals,' Josiah replied with a grin. 'One from the British government and another from the Egyptian government. Something you can hand down to your kids one day to show you were prepared to face a fearsome enemy.'

The soldier's face beamed with happiness. 'We might not have done much fightin', but we were ready to.'

'I know each and every man who volunteered accepted he was putting his life on the line for the reputation of Australia. Despite the fact it was our New South Wales own army that was sent here, we came to represent the country as a whole.'

'That we did, sir,' the private soldier said, saluting Josiah, who returned the salute before the soldier ambled away to tell his platoon comrades the news about the medals.

Josiah sighed. That was about all they would get out of their short service in the Sudan.

★

Ebenezer was at the helm of the *Ella*, only hours from docking at the northern Queensland port of Townsville. His new crew of mostly Chinese sailors had proved competent, and sailing north from Sydney had been uneventful. Ebenezer was looking forward to finding a pub and spending some recreational time ashore.

Sam, Lee and Ebenezer had been tasked by Colonel Ian Steele to carry out a reconnaissance mission to gauge the potential for trade in New Guinea and the many Pacific islands.

At the moment, blackbirding was proving to be a very profitable business for ships such as the *Ella*, but Sam's father had instructed that they were to stay away from the trade, as there was a sniff of darkness over the so-called 'indentured labourers' taken from the islands to cater to the cane fields of colonial Queensland. Ian felt that it had all the hallmarks of slavery and did not wish to support the cruel trade in human bodies. He had strong views on human exploitation, remembering how his friend Samuel Forbes had died with the Union army in the US, fighting the slave states in the American Civil War.

He had instructed his schooner crew to stop at Townsville and investigate the enterprise of a couple of Scots, James Burns and Robert Philp, who had formed a company to run tourist excursions out of Thursday Island to New Guinea. The shipping company was also involved in the blackbirding trade and had a depot not far from the Steele Enterprises depot in Townsville. It would be their main competitor if Ian chose to pursue a more vigorous expansion campaign of his Pacific fleet in the years ahead.

Sam joined Ebenezer at the helm and gazed across the almost placid blue sea at the buildings now visible on the shore. He could see two islands, one larger than the other; Ebenezer used these as his landmarks for entry to the wharfs jutting into the bay, which were occupied by a few small coastal traders. Ebenezer realised that he would need to drop anchor offshore and await a chance to manoeuvre to a wharf once it was vacated.

'We will anchor,' Ebenezer said to Sam, who turned to Yuan, standing a short distance away on the deck. Sam was impressed by the young man, whose grasp of the English language improved with each passing day.

'Get the crew to prepare to drop anchor,' he ordered,

and Yuan bellowed the order in Cantonese. The well-drilled crew followed the command with an expertise born of experience, and the schooner was promptly anchored.

They were joined on deck by Lee, dressed in a white shirt and trousers and wearing a wide-brimmed straw hat. At a distance, he might have been taken for a European.

'We will make contact with our depot for supplies and have a look around the town,' Sam said. 'Maybe our man at the depot will be able to give us a bit of intelligence on the Burns Philp mob. Ebenezer, you may be forced to find a pub and engage in a bit of conversation with any locals you think might know the goings-on around here. I know it will be an onerous task, but someone has to do it,' Sam added with a wide grin, knowing that their navigator was itching to find a pub.

'Will do,' Ebenezer replied with a straight face. 'But it goes against my morals to consume strong liquors.'

Sam slapped him on the back. 'Just do your best and try to return without falling in the water. I heard that there are big Yankee-eating crocs around here.'

Ebenezer's face broke into a grin. 'Nothing a good Maine man can't handle.'

'Lee and I will organise supplies and trade stores at the depot, and we will meet up back on the ship tonight,' Sam continued. 'Depending on how things go, we might raise the anchor and sail as soon as the stores are aboard. Our next stop will be Thursday Island before we have a look around the New Guinea coast.'

A place became vacant at the wharfs and they docked near midday. Supplies and stores were carried down from the Steele depot under the supervision of Lee and Sam, while Ebenezer found a cool, shady hotel in which to mix with the local residents and a few Burns Philp employees.

The work was completed near dusk, with Ebenezer returning relatively sober to resume command.

It was then that Lee noticed a woman he guessed was in her mid-twenties standing at the end of the wharf, staring forlornly out to the sea. He could see tears running down her cheeks and sensed that she was distressed.

He walked down the gangplank and made his way to her. She had her back to him and was oblivious to her surroundings.

'Are you all right?' Lee asked, and the woman turned to face him. She was not beautiful in the traditional sense, but had a pixie-like prettiness. She only came up to Lee's shoulder in height and her brown hair was tied in a bun.

'You speak English!' the woman said in a surprised voice.

'I hope so,' Lee replied. 'I was born in New South Wales.'

'My condition is not a matter for you to be concerned about,' she said sadly as she turned to stare across the tropical waters.

Lee sensed that she might be considering drowning herself. 'You must be careful that you don't fall in the water around here,' he said. 'It is not a pretty death if one of the crocs gets hold of you.'

The woman turned back to Lee. 'Is it true there are crocodiles in these waters?' she asked with just a hint of alarm.

'Yes, and a lot of sharks. The locals say the crocs eat the sharks,' he said. 'My name is Lee. May I ask your name?'

'I am Mary O'Lachlan. I do not wish to bother you with my situation,' she said, wiping the tears from her cheeks.

'It is not a bother,' Lee said, retrieving a cheroot from his trouser pocket and lighting it. 'I presume that you are from Ireland from your accent,' he said, taking a puff, the smoke curling into the early evening air.

'Yes, Dublin,' she replied. 'I was a schoolteacher, but came to the Queensland colony because a man wrote to me, promising that he would marry me.'

'Did you know the man before you came all the way to the Australian colonies?' Lee asked.

'We wrote for many months, and he eventually made his proposal, but when I arrived this morning, I was informed that he was already married and did not wish to have anything to do with me. Now I am alone and destitute,' Mary said, breaking down into racking sobs. Lee had a desire to place his arms around her as a gesture of sympathy, but did not do so. The sight of a Chinese man embracing a European woman would have provoked outrage amongst the dock workers.

'Do you have somewhere to stay tonight?' Lee asked, and she shook her head. 'We have a spare cabin aboard my schooner over there,' he said, pointing to the *Ella*. 'You are welcome to stay the night, and I can promise as part owner of the *Ella*, you will not be harmed in any way.'

Mary looked up at Lee with an expression of surprise. 'Is it true that you are part owner of such a grand ship?'

Lee nodded his head and reached out to pick up her small suitcase. Mary followed him to the gangplank, where Sam was standing.

'We have a guest for the night,' Lee said to Sam. 'Miss Mary O'Lachlan. She has nowhere else to go.'

'Miss O'Lachlan is welcome as an honoured guest,' Sam said diplomatically. 'I doubt that Ebenezer is sober enough to navigate tonight. Maybe we will leave on the tide tomorrow.'

Mary was escorted by Lee to a spare cabin, which at least had clean sheets on the bunk and a porthole for ventilation. He gave her a tour of the schooner, pointing out those facilities she may require, and eventually took her to the area they used for meals, inviting her to join them for a late supper. She sat at the table with the three men, who were all courteous to her as they shared a beef stew, tea and a bottle of port with cigars. Mary did not drink and tolerated the thick smoke of the cigars as the men discussed the events of the day, accepting her presence as they would a member of the crew. Eventually, Mary excused herself to go to her cabin.

'What is the story of Miss O'Lachlan?' Ebenezer asked when she had left.

'She arrived in Townsville to meet her prospective husband but learned he was already married. He did not care that she had spent her last money to be here and is now destitute. I felt that we could at least give her accommodation for the night before we sail,' Lee explained. 'She said that she was a schoolteacher in Dublin, so she must be literate.'

'Well, it is not possible for her to remain aboard when we sail,' Sam said. 'We can put off leaving for another forty-eight hours at the most to help her situation.'

Lee frowned. What could he do, other than provide her with money to return to Ireland? 'You know, I have been interested in looking at real estate around here,' he said, rotating his tumbler of port wine. 'It is not essential that I sail on this voyage. You and Ebenezer are more than capable of carrying out the mission. You have a good man in Yuan as leading hand, and I feel it is time I had a break from being at sea.'

Both Ebenezer and Sam looked at Lee with utter surprise.

'You've known the woman a matter of hours, Lee,' Sam said.

'It's not entirely about the woman,' Lee replied. 'I am looking to my future. I have always dreamed of owning my own land to run cattle. Up here, there are many of my people from the days when we prospected on the Palmer, and I hope to establish business links with the Chinese community in Queensland.'

Sam listened to his friend's explanation, but instinctively knew the Irish schoolteacher had somehow had a hand in this change of heart. Was it what some called love at first sight? Sam was sympathetic to Lee, as he knew he had led a hard life, rising above all to be a highly valued member of the inner circle of the Steele Enterprises. He had the utter respect of Sam, his brother and his father.

It was Ebenezer who unexpectedly supported Lee's intention to remain in Townsville. 'About time Lee settled down,' he mumbled. 'Seems whenever he is aboard, all we do is run into pirates and cyclones.' Ebenezer held out his hand to Lee. 'Goddamn! We will miss you, but all the best of luck to you, old friend.'

Sam also held out his hand. 'We will catch up with you when we return to port here,' he said with a firm hand-shake. 'By then, I expect you will own half of Townsville.' Sam raised his port wine tumbler. 'To the good fortunes of our sailing mate Lee, and a grand future.'

Ebenezer also raised his glass to Lee but added to the toast, 'And Mary.'

★

Thousands of miles away, in an office in Westminster adorned with paintings of eighteenth-century sea battles and shipwrecks, a young man with flaming red hair sat in a comfortable leather chair. Lush carpet and teak furniture overseen by a portrait of Queen Victoria gave the final touch to the office of the high-ranking government official.

Douglas Wade had come a long way via rapid promotion for his sterling service in India, where his father's advice to invest had paid off in the accumulation of a small fortune. His promotion in the civil service had recalled him to London, but he had welcomed the transfer as he had missed the social life of London, and had now reacquainted himself with his friends from his days at university, many of whom also worked for the civil service.

The stern man sitting behind the desk was well known to him. A former British officer who had once been the commanding officer of Captain Ian Steele, General Neill Thompson now wore a Savile Row suit and had the ear of the Queen herself.

'The German government annexed part of the island of New Guinea last year, and are rapidly occupying other islands in the Pacific,' General Thompson said. 'But I know you would have read all that in the report I circulated to a few selected civil servants, Mr Wade.'

'I did, sir,' Douglas replied. He had carefully studied the folder containing maps and reports of the unexpected move by the German government to establish an empire in the southern hemisphere.

'Fortunately, we received intelligence that a coastal steamer departing Sydney was crewed by German marines posing as common sailors. Their destination was Port Moresby, and we passed on what we knew to the premier of the Queensland colony. The premier was able to have the police magistrate on Thursday Island dispatched to Port Moresby and annex the southern portion of New Guinea on behalf of the British crown. Unfortunately, our government has yet to legitimise the annexation, but we have been informed the other Australian colonies have promised financial support to the Queensland government. I suspect we will follow suit in the near future to thwart the Germans owning all of that island. There are a few in parliament with peanut-sized brains, unable to comprehend how important it is to keep the Germans in check – which brings me to why you are here. We remember well how your man Captain Josiah Steele befriended Major Maximillian von Kellermann, now a colonel equivalent in the Kaiser's army.'

Douglas had recruited his old friend Josiah for a sensitive political mission in the now united Germany only five years earlier. He had carried it out successfully, as Douglas had known he would.

Thompson continued, 'We have been informed that von Kellermann is currently in German New Guinea, surveying suitable sites for future settlement. I am sure he will be pleased to make acquaintance with his old friend Captain Steele, and I am also sure that Josiah Steele is patriotic enough to carry out an intelligence mission for us to ascertain German intentions in the Pacific.'

'The last I heard, Josiah was serving in the Sudan with the colonial contingent,' Douglas said.

'He and the contingent are currently returning to Sydney. By the time you take a ship to your old home, he will be there for you to secure on our behalf for this mission,' Thompson said. 'I am sure that it would be a feather in your cap to do so.'

Douglas glanced down at the manila folders in his lap, appreciating the importance of the mission assigned to him. It would be strange returning to the country of his birth after the intrigues of London politics, but he would also have the opportunity of catching up with his lifelong best friend.

'When do I depart, sir?' Douglas asked, and he was briefed on all that lay ahead of him.

As Douglas left the office, he wondered how Josiah would react to his plea for assistance. No doubt he would be pleased to be back on an important mission for Queen and country. At least, Douglas hoped so.

SEVENTEEN

Lee watched the *Ella* sail away from Townsville, passing Magnetic Island and continuing out to sea. Mary stood beside him, and Lee's first order of business was to secure lodgings for her. They found a boarding house that predominantly rented to women.

Lee was given a sideways look from the dour landlady as he doled out pound notes to pay three months' rent in advance. The sight of a well-dressed Chinese man and a white woman was highly unusual, and the Asian man who spoke fluent English looking after the interests of this shy, mousy woman was obviously proving to her the evils of the Yellow Peril.

'I will not abide any gentleman visitors to your room, Miss O'Lachlan. This is not a house of ill-repute,' the landlady snorted. 'Mealtimes are posted on the noticeboard, and I expect all lights out no later than ten o'clock. I also have a list of church services, and I need not say that I will not tolerate any alcoholic beverages upon my premises.'

Mary agreed to all the conditions and Lee made payment.

He waited outside the boarding house, a two-storeyed timber-built house with six rooms and a small dining room downstairs, as Mary was shown her room. Mary eventually emerged with a small parasol against bright sunshine.

'Thank you, Mr Lee,' she said with a sad smile. 'I don't know where I would have been if you had not come to my aid.'

'It was a gesture of your Christian charity, Miss O'Lachlan,' Lee responded. 'It will give you the opportunity to consider your future in the colonies. As it is, I will be exploring possibilities to invest here. I will seek accommodation at one of the public houses for the moment.'

'I don't know how I will ever be able to thank you for your kindness,' Mary said, tears forming in her eyes. 'I hope to secure a teaching appointment here until I decide whether I should return to Dublin.'

'I am sure that you will be successful,' Lee said. 'The government needs qualified teachers for these remote areas. You may secure a position as governess on one of the outlying cattle properties, teaching the squatters' children – or even at a school in Townsville. This country offers opportunities to those with a spirit of adventure, and that you came so far from your home in Ireland proves you have such a spirit.'

'Will I be seeing you in the future?' Mary asked with an expression of concern.

'You will,' Lee replied. 'It is my duty to ensure that you are protected and find that which you seek in life. I will bid you a good day and will make contact tomorrow to find out how you are settling in.'

With that, Lee strode away down the dusty street to a hotel he knew about from previous brief visits. The publican cared little that he was taking in a Chinese man, particularly one who was polite, spoke fluent English and paid more than the required fare.

Then it was time for Lee to look into investments, and for that, he had access through the banks for all the finance he desired.

★

'This will be your new home,' Lee said as he and Mary stood before a newly constructed timber cottage with an adjoining annex comprising a spacious room. They were on the outskirts of Townsville with the dry bush and scrub bordering a schoolhouse and residence. There was a tank stand towering beside the residence and a dusty yard with a pole holding a small bell. It had taken Lee a couple of weeks to locate a building suitable for a small schoolhouse, and he had spent many hours in Mary's company on walks in the surrounding countryside. In that time, Lee had come to admire Mary's spirit, intelligence, charm and gentleness.

Mary stood gazing at the surprise Lee had promised her, holding a parasol against the tropical sun while the horse harnessed to the cart grazed on the dry grass.

''Tis a dream!' Mary said. 'Mr Lee, is it really true?'

'Education is very important to the future of the young men and women on this frontier,' Lee replied. 'I feel that with what I have seen of the references you have shown me, you are well placed to deliver reading, writing and arithmetic to the children of the outlying district.'

'But I will never be able to raise the money to repay you,' Mary said.

'There is no need,' Lee replied. 'I like to consider this as a way of repaying the land that has provided me with all the opportunities to make a comfortable life for myself.'

Tears welled in Mary's eyes. 'Mr Lee, that is such a Christian act,' she said and paused. 'Are you a Christian, Me Lee?'

Lee bowed his head before he answered. 'I am not a baptised Christian, Miss O'Lachlan, but I believe all men have a moral view of the world if they follow whatever god they should choose.'

Mary decided that she should not pursue any further questions on Lee's religious views. From what she had observed in the five weeks she had known him, she could see that he was a man of temperance as well as being intelligent, gentle and caring. Sometimes she was oblivious to his racial heritage when she was in his company on a picnic or simply walking the beaches around Townsville. But the stares of passing people quickly reminded her that she was in the company of a man not of European descent. Her previous vague views about Chinese people being an inferior and devious race faded quickly. This man was not only the equal of any other man she knew, but better – much better.

The urge to throw away restraint and impulsively embrace Lee was given free rein, and Lee suddenly found himself gripped by the young Irishwoman.

'Thank you, Mr Lee,' she said, tears rolling down her cheeks. 'No man has ever been so wonderful to me.'

'There are people in this world who should be given an opportunity to prove themselves,' Lee said, gently prying her away. 'I was once offered an opportunity by men I would never have expected to help the son of a Shaolin monk – but they did. Today, I have prosperity. I offer the same to you.'

Mary stepped back to gaze upon the architect of her unexpected good fortune. She knew that she would be able to establish a life in this new world, so foreign to what she had left behind on the other side of the world. None of this would have been possible if it had not been for the enigmatic Chinese man standing beside her. The more she grew to know Lee, the more she felt a great warmth – even a desire for him to always be with her. But by his own admission, he was not a Christian and she had been raised with a strict Catholic upbringing.

'Well, it is time to look inside,' Lee said, and he led Mary to the house and classroom. Mary could see when she stepped inside that the house was already furnished with a wood stove, table and chairs as well as storage cupboards, crockery and cutlery. There were even curtains on the windows, but Mary had the sense not to comment that the curtains must have been chosen by a man. She could learn to live with them. Mary knew she had not known such happiness in her life as she did now. She turned to look at Lee and the thought raced through her mind of how noble and even handsome he was. It was a forbidden thought and yet one she did not want to dismiss.

Lee left her for a moment and returned with a double-barrelled shotgun and box of shells. 'This is your housewarming gift,' he said. Mary looked aghast at the sight of the weapon. 'I will show you how to use it. Around here, you may need it to remove the threat of snakes or anything else that might cause you to have any fears.'

Lee did not need to spell out that the shotgun was also a means of defending herself against unwanted intruders taking advantage of a woman isolated from immediate help.

He passed the shotgun to Mary, who took it tentatively. It was certainly a strange housewarming gift. But then, Lee was not an ordinary man.

★

The troopship returning the contingent to Sydney was the *Arab*. It steamed into Colombo Harbour, where cheers were exchanged with the troops on a French man-of-war, returning from 'protecting' the Vietnamese people in Tonkin. The Chinese had lost the war, and the French were now the masters of northern Vietnam.

Small watercraft swarmed the *Arab*, selling bananas, pineapples and mangoes. The fruit was a welcome addition to their diet, and some of the soldiers were given leave to go ashore, most returning in a highly intoxicated state.

When the troopship departed Colombo, one in ten soldiers was reporting sick, and even the veterinary surgeon died of his illness and was buried at sea.

Eventually, the *Arab* reached Albany to take on coal. None of the soldiers were allowed ashore, but sailors on two nearby British warships gave rousing cheers to the returning contingent.

It was late at night on Friday 19 June when the troopship passed through the great sandstone heads of Sydney Harbour. Josiah and his men had stood at the ship's railings to see the lights of Port Jackson and know they were almost home. It was not as expected, though, as the ship anchored off Manly and the soldiers were taken to the quarantine station. Typhoid fever was the concern, and Private Richard Perry died of the dreaded disease in the quarantine station's hospital. At least he was home.

It would not be until the following Tuesday that the soldiers would be allowed to step ashore in Sydney. This did not deter the many small watercraft and ferries from sitting off the quarantine station, waving to the soldiers, or letters and telegrams arriving for the quarantined men.

Early on Tuesday 23 June, cannon fire, foghorns and whistles heralded the troopship to Circular Quay, where dignitaries awaited to greet the returning soldiers. A special guard of red-coated volunteers recently raised to defend against the Russian threat was formed, and rain belted down hard and cold, almost drowning out all other sounds.

From the troopship came the faint sound of the contingent's band playing 'Home, sweet home' and the men disembarked wearing the khaki battledress they had worn in the Sudan. It was the first time such uniforms had been seen in the colonies, and they impressed all that the army was changing with the times.

Josiah cursed the quarantine station for the fact no breakfast had been provided. Cold, wet and hungry, Josiah led his men in the march to Victoria Barracks at Paddington. There were few to welcome them home due to the fact it was a working day and the weather dismal. The soldiers' uniforms were soaked and their boots muddied as they marched to few cheers from the handful of spectators lining the route. Josiah found himself glancing at every pretty face sheltered under an umbrella along the way. He knew which face he wanted to see.

Eventually, they reached the barracks, where they were forced to stand at attention in the driving rain while government officials and politicians protected by umbrellas delivered long oratories welcoming them home. Representatives of the other colonies also delivered their long-winded speeches without any regard for the men shivering under the continuous rain. Only the colony of Tasmania spared the men a long speech by delivering it to the parade commander. The soldiers truly appreciated the thoughtful gesture by the Tasmanians.

Finally, the parade was dismissed, and a tot of medicinal alcohol issued to each and every soldier in an attempt to ward off the chills they had experienced for the politicians big-noting themselves for political gain.

Josiah shook hands with his friend and fellow officer, Archie, whose family awaited in a closed carriage.

'Well, old chap,' Archie said. 'I see that you have family here to welcome you home.'

Josiah turned, noticing his father and Conan striding towards him through the rain, holding umbrellas.

'We will have to catch up sometime and reminisce on our wartime experiences,' Archie continued. 'Albeit short and relatively uneventful.'

Josiah agreed just as his father and Conan reached him with broad smiles and extended hands. 'It is good to see that you have returned to us safely and in one piece,' Conan said, firmly gripping Josiah's hand.

'Welcome home, son,' Ian said, grasping Josiah in a short but strong embrace. 'There was not a night that passed we did not think about you over the ocean. Our family and friends are at our home to show their thanks for your safe return.'

Josiah was still convincing himself that he was actually back in the city he had so often taken for granted. He had tasks to perform before he was able to seek leave to join his family as his men sought him out to thank him for his leadership. Archie did not receive the same reaction from his men, and while Josiah felt sorry for Archie, he also knew he had not earned the respect of his soldiers. Archie was not alone in this, as other regimental officers were shunned by their men, too.

It was early evening by the time Josiah was able to make his way home to the house on the harbour, where he was met by Isabel at the front entrance. She threw her arms around him and cried with joy. Josiah could see the rest of his family standing behind her and when Isabel released him, he was mobbed.

When Josiah looked over his sister's shoulder, he saw a face he had dreamed of for the weeks he had steamed the Indian Ocean and lain under the stars of the Sudanese night.

'Marian,' he said softly as she approached. Josiah could not read the strained, sad expression on her face, and felt a pang of fear.

★

Lee had suspected that being in Mary's company in the streets of Townsville would eventually draw unwanted attention.

He had taken a horse to her cottage as Mary had promised a wonderful Irish lamb stew to share with him. It was simply a friendly dinner invitation to share company and conversation, but he had an uneasy feeling that he was being followed. When he swivelled in his saddle, he could see the faint cloud of dust in the still air beyond a copse of gum trees, as if raised by the hooves of horses. Lee was not armed, but decided to continue to Mary's cottage just as the sun descended below the horizon.

When he arrived, he secured his horse to a railing built for such a purpose outside Mary's front entrance. A lantern was already lit.

It was then that the trouble he had feared arrived on horseback. There were two big, bearded men wearing the rough clothing of labourers, while the third was dressed in clothing more suited to a clerical occupation.

Lee moved away from his horse to face the men astride their mounts.

The man in the clerical clothing leaned forward in his saddle.

'Hey, Chinaman!' he called. 'It's not right that a Chink be seen with a fine young lady. We're here to teach you a lesson you will never forget.'

Lee felt a sickening fear and wished that he had a weapon to defend himself.

The three men slowly dismounted, and Lee could see that one had a revolver thrust into his belt. The odds were bad, but Lee knew that he must stand his ground if he was to survive.

EIGHTEEN

Lee had the dim light from the lantern inside Mary's residence behind him, but his senses, honed by years of rigorous martial training, gave him a clear picture of the threat approaching. He could see that one of the big, bearded men held a short, wooden club while the other large man had now retrieved the revolver from his belt and dangled it in his hand by his side. The third, better-dressed opponent did not appear to be armed and hung back, allowing his two henchmen to do the dirty work.

Lee had a fleeting thought that Mary was also vulnerable to the trio if he could not stop them, and felt his blood run cold. He realised that he was prepared to die for the Irishwoman.

He could see the man with the club grinning as he approached and could almost smell the liquor on his breath. Lee assumed the demeanour of a frightened man when the stranger was only a few feet away, while waiting for him to come within striking distance.

'Please, sir, I beg that you do not harm me,' Lee pleaded convincingly, lowering his head, but he held every nerve and muscle taut like a finely tuned violin.

The thug paused and Lee could see that his act had worked.

Sneering, Lee's attacker spat on the ground at his feet. 'Youse yellow bastards ain't got no guts,' he snarled. 'Youse vermin deserve to be wiped off the face of the good earth here and –' The man did not even have time to finish his declaration of racial hatred. Lee struck with all the strength and fury he could muster. In the dark, the bearded man did not see the swirl of motion as Lee used his skills to spin and deliver his boot to the man's head. Lee's assailant crumpled into the dust of the yard with a fractured jaw, blood gushing from his nose. Stunned by the impact, he lay moaning in a semiconscious state.

Lee quickly recovered and could see that the remaining two men were also frozen by what they saw. Without hesitating, Lee charged the second man, who had recovered enough to raise his revolver, pointed directly at Lee, who knew that if he fired at such short range, he could not miss.

The blast took Lee by surprise, especially when he realised he was not hit. It also stopped the man with the revolver short.

'Go near Mr Lee and I will shoot you, Mr Rice,' boomed Mary O'Lachlan, standing in the doorway of her cottage. She was silhouetted by the lantern light and holding the shotgun to her shoulder. 'I would strongly suggest that you and your hooligans get on your horses and ride away, never to return, or I will be forced to defend my honour.'

There was no reply from the well-dressed man, who

nodded to the thug with the revolver. 'C'mon, Ron. Get Kurt on his horse and we'll go back to the pub.'

Obeying, the bearded man slipped the revolver into his belt and bent to help the man moaning on the ground to his feet and onto his horse, with Mary still holding the shotgun levelled on the man she recognised in the trio. They rode away into the night.

Lee approached Mary, who he could see was trembling uncontrollably, and gently removed the shotgun from her hands.

'Thank you,' Lee said. 'If you had not intervened, I am sure I would be dead.'

Mary looked at Lee and burst into tears. 'I could not have lived with myself if anything had happened to you,' she sobbed, falling against his chest. 'I think I love you, Mr Lee.'

Lee held her with his free arm. 'I know that I love you, Mary O'Lachlan,' he said, and gently guided her inside the cottage.

Lee later learned that the man Mary had referred to in the confrontation was the same man who had lured her to the colony. He hoped that they would not have to deal with the man ever again.

★

The sight of Marian caused Josiah to falter as she approached. Everything inside the room seemed to fade away.

'Hello, Josiah,' Marian said. 'I am pleased that your war was over in such a short time and that you have returned to us safe and well.'

'I wrote to you,' Josiah said lamely. 'But I was unable to find any words that would make sense.'

'I remember you did the same when you were away in Afghanistan those years ago.' Marian smiled. 'It is as if history was repeating itself. Do you still have the unfinished letter to me?'

'I have,' Josiah replied. 'I kind of carried it as a good luck token.'

'How sweet,' Marian said. 'My thoughts were with you from time to time. We have much to speak of.'

Josiah knew they needed privacy and excused himself from his family and friends to walk outside to the darkened garden. The rain had broken, and clouds scudded across the face of the stars. It was still chilly, but Josiah had his greatcoat over his damp khaki uniform while Marian was wrapped in an expensive fur coat – a gift from her late lover.

They stood face to face in the dark.

'Horace has asked for my hand in marriage,' Marian said seriously without any preamble, shocking Josiah.

'That bastard,' Josiah spat. 'What was your answer?' he added with a note of anger in his voice.

'I said I would consider his proposal,' Marian answered defiantly. 'A life with Horace promises to be stable and comfortable.'

Her support of Josiah's archenemy was almost a taunt. He realised that he had little knowledge of the mind of a woman and was well out of his depth in this exchange of life-changing statements.

'It is your decision and I respect that,' Josiah said with little conviction. 'I am sure he can shower you with worldly treasures beyond any woman's dreams. But . . . do you love him?'

Marian turned to gaze at a small cluster of stars peeking between dark clouds. 'Love is not enough, Josiah. A woman has the desire for her husband to come home every night to his family and share a life. I do not apologise if I seek a comfortable life with the man I love.'

'You could consider marrying me,' Josiah said, and felt how lame his suggestion seemed under the circumstances.

Marian turned to face him. 'If I said that I have always loved you and probably still do, would you be the man who would come to my bed every night of our life together as a husband for a wife? Or, like your father, would you find excuses to dash off to whatever war comes along, in the name of Queen and country? Isabel has told me that she held the same fears concerning marriage to your father. She practically had to make him sign a written contract to remain in Sydney. Would I need to do the same for you?'

Josiah felt a lump in his throat, considering that he had already decided the deployment with the New South Wales contingent was going to be his last military venture. He was ready to be with the woman he had loved from the moment he first set eyes on her in London. She had been too young then, but had blossomed into a beautiful woman with a demonstrated passion and intelligence.

'My days of soldiering are over,' Josiah said quietly. 'I can promise that I will be putting all my time into office hours with the family enterprises, and the most dangerous thing I will face will be falling down the stairs.'

Marian frowned. 'If that is true, I will reconsider Horace's proposal,' she said. 'But, like Isabel, I will need to be convinced that you will actually settle down to a life in the business world and be there for me.'

'It is said that actions speak louder than words,' Josiah replied. 'Just give me the chance to prove I am worthy of you.'

Marian smiled and kissed Josiah on the lips with the passion he craved. 'I think you should return to your party,' Marian said, drawing away. 'Otherwise, tongues will be wagging.'

Josiah followed her back to the warmth of the mansion where alcohol flowed, and guests slapped Josiah on the back. But all the time, his eyes were on Marian, and he vowed that he would prove that he could be a stable and reliable man in her life.

★

Douglas Wade was impressed when he was taken by carriage to Government House. The massive building, with its castellated, crenellated and turreted architecture, was surrounded by acres of manicured gardens and was the home and official headquarters of Queen Victoria's colonial representative in the colony of New South Wales, where he was referred to as the governor-general.

When Douglas was ushered inside, he was impressed by the cedar and teak wood structure, and the walls adorned with expensive artwork. Lord Carrington, also known as Charles Robert Wynn-Carrington, was a high-ranking member of Britain's aristocracy and his appointment was meant to further his colourful political career. But it was not Lord Carrington who met Douglas but a lowly official in his early thirties, balding and pale-skinned with snobbish airs.

'Mr Wade, we would prefer that you do not make any direct contact with Lord Carrington,' he said by way of introduction. 'Your mission to the colonies smacks of political intrigue and his lordship does not wish to know. You will have a visitor tonight who has come out from London, and your quarters have been prepared. You may take meals in the kitchen, and I need not impress on you the importance of your stay here being kept a secret. If you have any questions, seek me out. I have an office on the second floor which you are free to visit. My name is on the door, Mr Charles Pickworth ESQ.'

Douglas thanked the government civil servant and a valet escorted him to his room. It was small and better suited to a servant, but Douglas did not complain as he knew that any discomfort would be rewarded when the mission was completed. Tonight, he would meet with his colonial contact and, all going well, seek out his old friend, Josiah Steele.

★

Josiah was informed by his father that he had recommissioned Josiah into his militia unit as a captain, and that there might be a position coming up for promotion to major. Marian accepted the compromise once he had promised he would not entertain any idea of ever again fighting in a foreign war for Britain.

Josiah now found himself back in his old office with a view over the harbour, and it was not easy shedding the khaki for an expensive suit as he stood by the window gazing at the ships below. Amongst them was a British man-of-war, and Josiah cast his thoughts back to the short-lived Sudan campaign. There were to be dinners for the returning soldiers in the city, complete with long-winded speeches praising Australia's first official call to arms, but at least Josiah would catch up with old friends and his soldiers.

A knock at the office door broke Josiah's thoughtful reminiscences.

'Mr Steele, I have a gentleman by the name of Mr Wade who wishes to see you. He has informed me that you know him,' said Maurice, his secretary.

'Of course, let him enter,' Josiah answered, a little taken aback that Douglas should be in Sydney. When Josiah had last heard of him, his schoolfriend had a position in a prestigious Westminster department in London.

Douglas entered the office wearing a well-tailored suit and holding a furled umbrella and a bowler hat. 'Josiah, old chap. Thank you for taking the time to see me when I know you have barely stepped off the ship from the Sudanese campaign.'

Josiah broke into a broad smile. 'Douglas, what the devil are you doing on this side of the world?' he replied, extending his hand to his old friend. 'I never thought that I would see you home again. Take a seat and I will order tea for us.'

'Thank you, Josh,' Douglas said, using the pet name he had used when they were at school together. He sat down on a comfortable leather chair opposite a small wooden table. Josiah also pulled up a chair to face Douglas.

'The last time we met in Bombay, you shanghaied me into a mission in Bavaria,' Josiah said with a grin. 'I hope you are here to catch up on old friends.'

'You know, seeing you alive and well pleases me more than you can realise,' Douglas said with a frown. 'But my transfer to Sydney is not simply a social visit.'

Josiah's smile began to fade. 'What do you mean?'

'The Queen once again calls on your unique services to assist the future of the empire on a vital mission,' Douglas said, toying with the hat in his lap. 'Your loyalty to the crown is beyond question and the mission is as much a concern for the Australian colonies as for the foreign interests of Britain.'

Josiah stood up and walked over to the window of his office to stare at the ships on the harbour. 'I made an oath that I would remain here, running our enterprises with my father,' Josiah answered. 'The oath was made to the woman I love more than my own life.'

'This mission would take only a few weeks and not put you in any dire circumstances. We are only asking you to make contact with an old friend in German New Guinea,

Maximillian von Kellermann, who is currently undertaking a survey mission for the Kaiser. We know that you have the resources to do so, and it will be very much like your mission to Bavaria.'

'Intelligence gathering,' Josiah said, turning to his friend. 'It is almost like you wish me to turn to the life of a spy.'

'No, not I, but there are people in the British government who keep you in a special file for important matters of state,' Douglas countered. 'I am in that same file as your trusted contact.'

Josiah slumped back into his chair. He was torn over his promise to Marian, but he had to admit to himself that it would be good to catch up with the husband of a woman he once had a crush on but who was now a dear friend. He stared at Douglas, who he could see was feeling some guilt for the meeting. 'You said the mission is only for a few weeks?'

'At tops, old chap,' Douglas replied, his face now showing relief. 'Nothing could really go wrong. Just a meeting between old friends, like you and me, and home again with a report. I have been authorised to compensate all expenses and it will be seen on your company books as a genuine business enterprise to German New Guinea. View it as a paid holiday to an exotic land.'

Josiah shook his head. 'I hope your optimism is justified,' he said with the faintest of smiles. At least he would be able to point out to Marian that he was simply taking a business trip. Both men rose and shook hands.

'You have an invitation to Government House tonight, but not to meet with the governor-general. There is another man from London who will brief you on the mission. After that, we can open the bottle of good champagne I purchased in France before leaving to return to Sydney,' Douglas said.

When he was gone, Josiah gazed once again out onto the harbour, where he knew he would be departing on a trip to the mysterious island to Australia's north.

★

Lee was roughly awakened in the early hours of the morning in his room at his hotel in Townsville. Three burly uniformed police constables shook him out of a deep sleep with the words, 'Get up, Chinaman. You are under arrest for the attempted murder of a white man.'

Lee knew he was in deep trouble.

NINETEEN

Lee was shackled and taken to the relatively new prison in the north ward of the rapidly growing town. The discovery of gold west of Townsville had increased the population, along with the crimes of drunkenness, vagrancy and violence. The gaol was of the latest design, set out in the shape of a semicircle with cells for both men and women, but had quickly proved to be too small for the rapidly growing population.

Lee was flung into a small cell with three other prisoners. He could smell the stench of urine, faeces and sweat.

'A bloody Chinaman,' one of his cellmates said. 'He should be anywhere else but with us white men.'

'Shut up, Pete,' another prisoner said as Lee's shackles were removed by one of the guards. 'Poor bastard is gettin' the same treatment as us.'

Lee nodded his thanks to the speaker, the largest man

in the cell, who had a full beard and scarred forehead. Lee guessed that he was in his mid-thirties, but his weather-ravaged face hid his true age.

'What you in for?' the big man asked.

'They have informed me that I tried to kill a white man,' Lee answered, rubbing his wrists against where the shackles had chafed him. 'I broke his jaw, and would have done the same to his two mates if I'd had the chance.'

Immediately, the smaller man known as Pete shuffled away from Lee. 'How could you do that?' he asked with a note of disbelief.

Lee turned to him with a defiant expression. 'Do you want me to demonstrate how I broke his jaw?' he asked.

Pete quickly shook his head.

'I seen some of you Chinamen demonstrate your way of fightin' when I was a sailor on leave in Hong Kong,' the big man said. 'It was bloody impressive. My name is Griffin. My cobbers call me Shorty.'

'Ling Lee,' Lee responded. Neither man shook hands, but a tacit understanding had been reached.

'You speak English like us,' Shorty said. 'How come?'

'Because I was born in New South Wales, outside of Sydney, and went to a school run by a former Methodist missionary. He was a good man,' Lee answered.

A pack of soiled and tattered playing cards was produced and the prisoners squatted to play in the stifling confines of the prison. Lee stood by the door, hoping to catch the attention of a passing guard through the slit in the door and ask to see someone in a supervisory role. The guard simply ignored him and continued on his sentry duty along the rows of other overcrowded cells.

As far as Lee knew, no one would know of his incarceration on the most serious charge of attempted murder.

He wished that he had remained with Sam and Ebenezer aboard the *Ella*, but she was at sea and could be anywhere in the Pacific.

Lee eventually slumped to the floor to reflect on his dire situation. From the little he had been able to glean from the police who had arrested him, Rice and his two thugs claimed that on a friendly visit to Mary's cottage, Lee had attacked them with a wooden club, causing serious facial injury to one of their number. Had they not been armed, they claimed he might have done the same to them all.

Lee knew the European bias against the Chinese population in the colony would mean that he would be considered guilty before a European jury even heard any evidence.

For the first time in his life, he experienced despair. Hope was just a four-letter word, like love.

★

The storm had hit southwest of Cape York with little warning. For a time, none expected to live. Two of the crew were swept overboard and one of the masts snapped halfway, bringing down the sheeting on the deck and entangling ropes and sails. Tossed like a cork and pounded by massive waves, the schooner was swept dangerously close to the jagged coral reefs when, just as suddenly, the pressure in the barometer had fallen as the storm dissipated. The decision was made for the *Ella* to return to Townsville for essential repairs and Ebenezer was able to steer a course south to the sanctuary of the harbour, where arrangements were made to restore the schooner with a new mast and general clean-up with local shipwrights. While this was under way, there was little for either Ebenezer or Sam to do except take turns supervising the work being carried out.

Sam went ashore to arrange by telegram the transfer of money for repairs, and notify that he would send a written report to the main offices in Sydney. When this was done, Sam set out to find Lee.

His first stop was the Steele depot where Lee kept the Steele Enterprises apprised of his dealings. It was there that Sam received the shocking news of Lee's arrest for attempted murder from an employee who knew of Lee's association with the *Ella*. In disbelief, Sam strode to the police station, where he was met by a sergeant at the front counter.

'Your Chinaman friend was arrested a few days ago on the statements made by Mr Rice and his two cobbers,' the sergeant said, eyeing the well-built and heavily tanned young man. What would someone like Mr Samuel Steele have to do with the likes of a dangerous Chinese man?

'Where is he now?' Sam asked in a firm voice.

'He is being incarcerated until his trial, but he is not to have any visitors except a legal representative. I am sorry, Mr Steele, but those are the rules.'

Fuming, Sam stamped out of the police station to take the news to Ebenezer. There was no way they would allow Lee to remain in the gaol. He would now have a telegram sent to Sydney to inform his father, who Sam trusted would be able to resolve a situation Sam had no real influence on. What the hell had happened? Whatever the answer, Sam knew that Lee could not be guilty of what he had been accused of.

★

The telegram describing Lee's plight arrived at Ian's office.

Ian took a deep breath as he left his desk to stand by the great window in his office, gazing out at the harbour below. He had a habit of considering problems while contemplating

170

the vista below, where he could see ships and the water. Ian understood Lee's position as he had seen the prejudice against the Chinese on the Palmer River Goldfields years earlier. Lee had been made a part of the Steele Enterprises when an old friend of Ian's, Major Hamish MacDonald, had willed his share in their mining operations to the young Chinese man he had also befriended before his own violent death.

Lee had proved his astute judgement many times in the industry of ore crushing, and provided generous profits for the Steele Enterprises. Ian knew that Josiah and Lee were close friends, and Ian had also taken a strong personal liking to the enigmatic Chinese man.

It was obvious that he could do little while in Sydney and as he gazed at the shipping below, he was already formulating a plan to take a fare north to Townsville on the very first coastal steamer he could find.

'Tom,' he called, and a man answered immediately from the office next door.

'Yes, Colonel?' Tom replied, stepping inside Ian's office.

'I need you to transmit a telegram to Townsville addressed to the schooner *Ella*. And also enquire for me to take a passage to the same place as soon as possible. Time is of the essence.'

Ian passed the hastily scribbled message to his secretary, who read it out aloud to ensure that he had understood the text. Ian nodded and Tom hurried away to carry out his employer's orders.

Now all Ian had to do was convince his wife that this was simply a hasty business trip to their Townsville depot. Somehow, he already knew she would raise her eyebrows and frown but remain silent on what her husband was really doing steaming north.

By well-timed happenstance, Ian's next visitor was his eldest son, who tapped on the open door.

'I saw Tom in a hurry; did you just sack him?' Josiah asked with a wry smile.

Ian turned to his son. 'He is carrying out a rather urgent mission for me. I will be travelling north to catch up with your brother and the *Ella* as soon as possible to sort out some trouble with Lee.'

'What trouble?' Josiah asked with a frown, and his father explained as much as he knew from the brief words of the telegram sent by Sam. Josiah was shocked to hear that his close friend of many years was accused of attempted murder.

'I will arrange to accompany you, Father,' Josiah said. 'If Lee is in trouble, he will need all the big guns in support. Besides, I was going to talk to you about seconding our schooner for a mission to German New Guinea. I will explain everything once we get the immediate matters sorted.'

At least now Josiah had a better cover story for his mission. He would explain to Marian that he was required to go north to help a family friend in trouble in Townsville. He knew that if she learned the truth, there was a strong possibility that the woman he loved above all might walk away, seeing his mission as a betrayal of his promise to settle down to a normal life in Sydney. It was not the risk of putting his life on the line again but the thought that he might lose Marian which was the greater fear.

★

At the post office, Sam was handed the telegram and breathed a sigh of relief. His father was taking a coastal steamer to Townsville. Sam had great faith in his father's considerable power and influence to free Lee. After all,

172

had he not rescued Uncle Conan from the hangman's noose? That was for a murder charge – and this was a mere attempted murder!

Sam stepped onto the streets of the booming town and was making his way back to the schooner when he heard a female voice call. 'Mr Steele?'

Sam stopped and turned to see Mary hurrying towards him. 'Miss O'Lachlan. It is a pleasure to see you again,' Sam said when she stopped a pace away.

'Have you heard of Mr Lee's terrible fate?' Mary asked breathlessly.

'I have been informed that Lee is in the local gaol, charged with attempted murder. Why, has something else happened I do not know about?'

'No, Mr Lee is still incarcerated, but he may be transferred down to Brisbane to face court on the ridiculous false charge. I was witness to all that happened the night Mr Rice and his hooligans came out to my place armed with weapons. They confronted Mr Lee with threats of physical violence towards him. It should be they who are charged with attempted murder.' Mary went on to explain all that had happened that evening.

As Sam listened, his anger rose. 'The bastards!' Sam swore and quickly apologised for the use of his ill-chosen words in front of a lady. 'Have you given the police a statement to all that happened?'

'I tried to, but the police explained that Mr Rice is a well-respected married man with a prosperous business in Townsville and said that my statement must be a lie to protect Mr Lee. I am afraid that because of our friendship, I have been branded a fallen woman.'

Sam shook his head in disgust, as there was no finer man on earth than Lee.

'If you have any fears, we still have your cabin on the *Ella*,' he offered.

She shook her head. 'I am able to defend myself,' Mary said defiantly. 'Mr Rice is nothing but a bloody adulterer and liar, and one day I hope he burns in hell for what he has done to me and Mr Lee.'

Sam grinned at her use of the swear word describing this Mr Rice – whoever he was. He sensed that, despite her small stature, Mary's Irish blood was aflame with a desire to find justice for a man even Sam sensed was more than just a 'good friend'.

TWENTY

The hellish days passed slowly for Lee. Strangely, his cellmates became his friends as they shared the same conditions of bad food, stifling heat and the stench. It was always noisy, day and night, as men yelled and screamed, ranting at their confinement.

When Lee and his cellmates were allowed in the exercise yard, a large prisoner sharing the space walked up to Lee with the obvious intent of picking a fight. Lee sized up the man and knew that he would be able to cause him a lot of damage with his martial skills, but it was Pete and Shorty who stepped in to warn off the aggressor. Lee appreciated the gesture as he knew that had he done any physical damage to the prisoner, it would be held against him in his upcoming appearance before the court.

The worst part of the incarceration was that he was

denied any opportunity to meet with visitors, and as each day and night passed, Lee despaired more and more.

★

The coastal steamer conveying Ian and Josiah Steele arrived in Townsville on a bright sunny day. They were met by Sam, who hugged his smaller older brother in a bear hug. They had not seen each other in almost a year, but the bond between the two brothers had not been diminished by time or space.

'I heard you were back, big brother,' Sam said, disengaging from the embrace. 'It is wonderful that here you are with Father.'

Ian realised that this was the first occasion in a long time that he had his sons together in the same place at once.

'Father, I am very pleased to see you,' Sam said, accepting Ian's handshake. 'If anyone can have Lee freed, it is you.'

'Thank you for your faith in my abilities,' Ian replied. 'But my influence may not extend to Queensland. How is Ebenezer faring?'

'He is at the schooner, and we will go there now,' Sam answered. 'I am sure he will be pleased to see you.'

The three men walked along the wharf to where the *Ella* was secured and were met by the American sea captain. They went below and the four men sat around the chart table to discuss their plan to free Lee. Ian listened as various options were suggested, and he was not surprised when Sam even proposed that they conduct a military-style operation to free Lee, but his brother immediately scoffed at the idea.

'That would only make the situation worse for Lee, because he would become a fugitive for life. It would jeopardise us as well,' Josiah said.

'The first matter I will attend to,' Ian said, leaning towards his two sons as Ebenezer just sat back smoking his pipe and listening, 'is to seek permission to speak with Lee and get his side of the story.'

'We already know what happened,' Sam said. 'I was told by a witness, a Miss Mary O'Lachlan, who was at the scene.'

Ian turned to Sam. 'Who is this Miss O'Lachlan?' he asked.

'An Irish schoolteacher who recently arrived on our shores in terrible circumstances. It was the man who accused Lee, a Mr Rice, who promised to marry her when she arrived but failed to mention that he already had a wife and children. He took a dislike to the fact that she and Lee had a friendship. That may have prompted him to visit her and do mischief to Lee,' Sam added. 'I know where she lives. Lee purchased her a cottage with attached room for teaching, but from what I have heard around the pubs, she is viewed as a fallen woman for her connection to Lee and no one will send their children to her school. From what she has told me, the police are not interested in her version of events as they consider this Mr Rice a righteous pillar of the town.'

'I will speak with Miss O'Lachlan,' Ian said. 'For now, I need to send some telegrams south to my friends in politics, starting with the new premier, and the former premier too. We just need to be patient, and I am asking that you forget any rash ideas of a breakout.'

The Steele boys and Ebenezer fell silent, nodding their heads in agreement, tacitly accepting the leadership of Colonel Ian Steele.

When Ian glanced at his two boys, he could not help comparing his sons; Sam was young and headstrong, and had inherited the size and strength of distant Russian ancestors on his mother's side. Josiah was smaller, and more rational and wise. He felt a surge of warmth for the two boys, who were a formidable team. His pride was more than he could express and he knew Ella, their mother who had died from cancer, would have been proud.

★

Two days passed before Ian was able to ride out to speak with Mary. Already there was a murmur in Townsville about the crew of the New South Wales schooner. They were somewhat of a mystery, but information leaked from the telegram operator at the post office that they had powerful connections down south. Those rumours even reached the Townsville gaol and when Ian arrived at the gates, demanding to speak with the gaol governor, he was admitted immediately.

'I will not waste your time, Colonel Steele,' the prison commander said. 'I have been informed that you have a personal interest in one of my incarcerated criminals, Ling Lee.'

'His criminality has yet to be decided, sir,' Ian replied. 'And he is a trusted and very competent employee of my companies. Naturally, I stand by the people I employ.'

'He is here because of his assault on a friend of Mr Rice, who you may not be aware is a fine and upstanding Christian gentleman,' the prison warder offered. 'His reputation is beyond repute, and he is a loyal member of my church congregation.'

Ian smiled grimly, reaching into his trouser pocket and producing a sheaf of folded letters. He handed them to the warden. 'If he is such an upstanding Christian citizen, I wonder why he would lure a poor, honest Irish girl to your colony on the promise of marriage. Before you are his letters to her.'

The warden glanced down at the papers, picked one up and began to read. Ian watched as the man's face reddened with embarrassment. He did not consider reading the rest, pushing them back to Ian. 'I was not aware of this situation.' The warden coughed. 'I must say, I am at a loss for words. But this changes nothing in the situation of the Chinaman.'

Ian had come prepared. 'I have a telegram from the premier of New South Wales requesting that I be given all assistance into Mr Lee's case,' he said, offering the paper before adding a second telegram. 'And another from your premier, corroborating my premier's request. I am sure that even if you may dislike us from down south, you will respect your own premier's orders.'

The warden glared at Ian. Given half the chance, the warden would no doubt have him join Lee. 'What is your wish, Colonel Steele?' the warden asked.

'It is grand to see that our two colonies can work together in harmony,' Ian replied pleasantly. 'I wish to speak with Mr Lee in private.'

'I will arrange that,' the warden replied. 'But remember, he is here on the charge of attempted murder and that is a police matter.'

'I fully understand,' Ian replied. 'We will not be long.'

Reluctantly, the warden issued orders that the prisoner known as Lee be escorted to an office not far from his own.

Lee was surprised when the guards came for him and ordered him shackled to be taken to meet a visitor. With the shackles on he shuffled along the corridor, up a set of stairs and along another corridor to a small room. When the door opened, he saw Ian's face and fought back tears.

'Colonel. I thought I would never see you again,' Lee said.

'Have faith.' Ian smiled, leaning over the small table between them. 'Sam was able to send me a telegram and

Miss O'Lachlan provided me with an eyewitness account of the events that have brought you to this dismal place. I cannot see how any court could convict you, even with their prejudice against you for being Chinese. As far as the family is concerned, you are one of us.'

The warmth in Ian's voice and his demeanour washed over Lee. 'Thank you,' Lee said simply, the word 'family' echoing in his mind.

'This is only the first stage to freeing you,' Ian said. 'You are fortunate to have such a fine lady as your primary witness. I strongly suspect that Miss O'Lachlan must be a special woman in your life.'

'I would wish to propose marriage to her, if I am ever free,' Lee replied, bowing his head and wiping away the trickle of tears. 'I have never met a woman with so much courage and intelligence, and she truly accepts me for who I am.'

'You are a fortunate man to have made the acquaintance of Miss O'Lachlan,' Ian said. 'I was very impressed from the moment I met her, and all that matters to her is that you are set free.'

'Has there been any change in my situation?' Lee asked.

Ian shook his head. 'It is early days and all I can ask is that you remain patient,' he replied.

A guard stepped inside the cell and notified Ian that their meeting time was over. Ian extended his hand to Lee. 'Have faith,' were his final words as Lee was led away in shackles.

★

'I have faith in Father's ability to manipulate the system here, but we also need a back-up plan to ensure the odds are in our favour,' Sam said to Josiah across the chart table. 'I say we pay Mr Edward Rice a visit in some dark alley when he leaves the pub one night. I know where he drinks with his mates and I have learned from a few of the chaps around here that the pious Mr Rice recently had a visit from the elders of his church, who stripped him of his senior position in the congregation. Something about him lacking morals. A visit from us might be the final straw which breaks his resolve to prosecute Lee.'

Josiah reflected on his brother's rash suggestion. Josiah and Lee had been like brothers on the terrible tracks of the Palmer River Goldfields, and he knew sometimes brutal action was required to gain a righteous outcome. 'We do not use violence of any sort,' he said finally.

Sam's expression was smug. 'Just a friendly chat with a hint of violence,' he said cheerfully.

★

Edward Rice had drunk more than he normally did. He was still smarting from his demotion in his staunchly conservative church which did not abide its members drinking, smoking, gambling or womanising. His own family knew that he broke the rule of drinking and gambling, but turned a blind eye to his transgressions. Rice had been able to keep from his wife the correspondence he had conducted with Mary, and had fantasised that he would keep her as a mistress when she arrived in Townsville. He had known that she would be destitute and need to rely on him providing essential items, but it had all gone wrong when the proud Irish lass immediately expressed her moral outrage at his proposition. And then of all people, who should come to her aid but a Chinaman! His drinking companions had smirked about him being second to a Chinaman, but at least the community was on his side in this matter of the uppity Chinaman facing justice.

Rice and his two henchmen spilled out of the hotel in the late hours of the night, stumbling down the deserted, dimly lit street, past dark alleyways. It was from one of these alleys that the ambush was sprung with speed and surprise.

Before the three drunken men knew what had transpired, they were set upon by Sam and Josiah, who were armed with revolvers and supported by Yuan who held a razor-sharp sword. Small hessian bags were thrown over the heads of their captives before they could focus on their ambushers.

The three targets struggled as they were dragged down a darkened alley and into the Steele depot. Ropes were used to secure them hand and foot, and one of the two companions of Edward Rice urinated in his pants in his sudden terror. The three were thrown unceremoniously against a timber wall, and Josiah could see that they were shaking in fear. Yuan ran his sword blade so lightly across the three men's throats that they felt the scrape but it drew no blood.

'What do you want?' Rice croaked. 'If you want to rob us, we have little money on us, but you can have it.'

'I would prefer to take your life, Mr Rice,' Josiah said calmly, 'for being the lying bastard you are. If I order my man to cut your throats now, you cannot give false witness against Mr Ling Lee. I can promise you that the police would never find your bodies.'

'Who are you?' one of the other prisoners asked, his voice filled with terror.

'No one you have ever met,' Sam replied. 'Nor anyone you'll ever wish to meet again.'

'What do you want from us?' Rice asked, his voice trembling.

'Just one simple thing,' Josiah said. 'That you go to the police and withdraw your complaint against Mr Lee in your most convincing manner. And that you never approach him or Miss O'Lachlan again.'

'And if I allow the law to take its course?' Rice questioned, possibly thinking this was all a bluff.

'Cut his throat,' Josiah growled.

Rice felt the razor-sharp steel of the sword blade across his larynx. 'No!' he screamed his desperate protest. 'We will do as you say.'

The blade came away, but blood had been drawn and ran in a trickle down his chest.

Josiah spoke again. 'Remember, you don't know who we are, and thus we are able to take you out whenever we wish. The police will not be able to protect you.'

'Yes, yes! I swear on the lives of my children, we will go to the police at first light and withdraw our statements,' Rice said, trembling uncontrollably.

'Just be pleased that you will see the sun come up tomorrow. We are going to escort you to the edge of the town and tie you up to a tree. You will be able to free yourselves, but we will be gone – for the moment.'

It was a traveller on the track to Townsville who spotted the three hooded men tied to a tree beside the dirt track, and freed them as the sun rose.

'Bushrangers?' he asked, and Rice nodded. 'Bastards! Yer probably lucky to be alive.'

All three men eagerly agreed. They were sure that the mysterious men had meant what they'd said, and must also be friends of the Chinaman. The blood had dried on Rice's throat, leaving him a small scar as a reminder of the all-too-real threat they had experienced.

Their first stop when they returned to Townsville was at the police station.

TWENTY-ONE

'Were you really going to let Yuan cut the man's throat?' Sam asked as he sat sharing a bottle of rum with his brother in the cabin of the schooner.

'In my experience, a man will do anything for just another second of life,' Josiah replied. 'Let alone the promise of a long life. I knew Rice would relent as soon as he felt the sword bite into his throat.'

Sam shook his head and took a long swig of the rum in the tin mug. 'Now all Rice has to do is honour his word to withdraw his evidence, and we will see Lee back in our ranks.'

'What's this talk about Lee?' the voice of their father asked from the narrow doorway to the main cabin. Their father was staying as a guest of the manager of the company depot in Townsville. Both Steele boys had known their father would not have approved of their operation.

'Good morning, Father,' Sam replied.

'We were just saying that we hoped your efforts with the authorities have borne fruit,' Josiah added.

'I need a tot of what you are drinking,' Ian said wearily, slumping down on the fixed bench beside Sam at the table. 'So far, all that I have been able to do is visit him at the prison and provide him with promises of hope. I am afraid my influence in this colony is a bit stretched. Townsville is a long way from Brisbane and Sydney.'

Sam passed his father a spare tin cup containing the dark liquid. Ian took a swig, glancing at Josiah. 'What occupied you two last night?' Ian asked. 'Ebenezer informed me that you both left the schooner for a night on the town.'

'We chose to return early to the schooner,' Josiah lied. 'Not much to do in town once the pubs close.'

'Well, I will make another visit to the gaol today to ensure that Lee is being treated fairly,' Ian said. 'First, I will put together a few food supplies that Lee requested for his cellmates. He informed me that, despite their crimes, he has come to befriend them.'

'That sounds like a good idea,' Sam said, glancing at Josiah, who retained a poker face. Both men were hoping that Rice had honoured his word and withdrawn his complaint. The next few hours would decide the outcome of their ambush.

★

Ian Steele could hardly believe what he was hearing. The gaol governor had informed him that the prisoner Lee was to be released as soon as the signed papers were delivered. For some reason, the complainant had not wished to proceed with the charge and flatly refused to provide any form of evidence.

Ian waited outside the gaol until after midday, when Lee was brought to the front gate. With a broad smile, Ian shook Lee's hand, ushering him into the carriage.

'It is hard to believe,' Lee said, taking in the fresh air away from the stench of the prison. 'I am free.'

'Where can I take you?' Ian asked. 'The *Ella*?'

'I would like to visit Miss O'Lachlan first,' Lee responded.

Ian understood and drove them to the schoolhouse at the edge of the town.

Mary noticed the carriage approaching and recognised Lee in the passenger seat. She brushed down her dress and stepped out onto the veranda with a joyous expression. She could see that her beloved was free, but was confused as to how that could be.

Lee leapt from the carriage, walking rapidly to the veranda to take Mary in his arms.

'I am free of the charges,' he whispered as he held her in his embrace.

Tears flowed down the Irish girl's face. 'My love, I feared for your life,' Mary replied. 'But all that matters now is that you are here.'

Ian watched from the seat of the carriage, and could see that his friend might need more time with Mary.

'I will come back for you tomorrow morning,' Ian called out and Lee turned, nodding his agreement.

With a broad grin, Ian turned back towards the Townsville wharf, pondering how the complaint against Lee could be dropped so suddenly by Mr Rice. He could not help but think that his sons had something to do with this reversal of Lee's bad luck.

'What did you do?' Ian challenged them as soon as he arrived on the deck of the schooner.

'Do, Father?' Sam countered innocently.

'What did you do to make Rice change his mind?' Ian asked sternly.

'We may have visited Mr Rice and his friends for a friendly chat, to advise them why their evidence against Lee might prove disastrous for them,' Josiah said.

Ian shook his head and chuckled. 'So, you abducted them and threatened them with violence if they proceeded with their false testimony?' he said. 'I pray that you took precautions to not be recognised.'

'We did,' Josiah said. 'Desperate times require desperate actions.'

'And who planned your covert operation?'

'Sam made the suggestion,' Josiah answered. 'I planned the mission.'

'Thank God you did,' Ian commented with the slightest of smiles. 'I would hate to think your brother might attempt to plan such an operation without your skills.'

'I would have conducted the mission in the same manner as Josiah,' Sam said defensively.

Ian did not comment but wrapped his arms around both their shoulders. 'You are a good team, and I am proud that you succeeded,' he said, hugging his sons. 'Lee is currently with his lady. I am sure they have much catching up to do. In the meantime, Josiah will be seconding the *Ella* for another important mission in the waters around German New Guinea and I have decided that I need a sea trip while I am still able to. We will rely on your seamanship,' Ian added, turning to Sam. 'And Ebenezer's navigational skills.'

Does that mean I am appointed captain of the *Ella*?' Sam asked eagerly.

'You are, but Josiah is commander of the mission, and you will do as he says when it comes to such matters,' Ian cautioned. 'And we will heed all advice from Ebenezer as regards sailing.'

With the situation clarified, the three men went to Ebenezer, briefing him on the schooner's new mission in the Pacific. Ebenezer pulled out his pipe and nodded. It mattered little to the man from Maine where and when he went, as everyone well knew that no matter what title Ian Steele's sons had, he was the true master of the schooner.

★

That evening, Lee rode back to the wharf and met with Sam, Josiah and Ebenezer on the deck of the schooner, where backslapping and vigorous handshakes greeted him. They went below and Ian proposed a toast to having their friend free and back in their company.

Now they were all eager for him to join the schooner for the venture north into German waters off New Guinea.

'I would dearly wish to be with you all,' Lee said sadly. 'But Mary and I have spoken of leaving Townsville to seek our future elsewhere. The scandal of my arrest has thrown a dark cloud over us.'

His statement was met with a solemn nodding of heads. 'Can we help in any way?' Ian offered.

Lee knew that he had a foot in two worlds that would benefit him in the future. 'I feel that we would be better off moving further north to Cairns, where I have a stronger chance of business opportunities amongst the Chinese community.'

Ian nodded. 'As far as I am concerned, you are welcome in our company at any time.'

'Thank you, Colonel,' Lee responded. 'I may call on your generosity in the future.'

'Then it is done. I now call on all to raise a glass to the future of Lee and Mary,' Ian said, and Josiah, Sam and

Ebenezer raised their glasses. 'To Lee and Mary. May their troubles be little ones.'

The next morning, Lee left his home at sea and rode back to Mary, who was waiting for him. The past was a ghost and the future uncertain. The present was that he loved Mary and she him. That was all that mattered.

★

'Maximillian von Kellermann is aboard the German steamship *Samoa*,' Josiah said as he, Ebenezer, Sam and Ian gathered around the chart table once they had sailed out of Cleveland Bay and were tacking north past Cooktown, carefully avoiding the deadly reefs. The weather was fair, and they had made good time.

'From the last report sent from Sydney, it appears that they are exploring the coast from north to south for the newly established *Neuguinea Compagnie*. It is a private concern, but the fact von Kellermann is aboard could mean it's in truth a military expedition to identify suitable harbours and places for fortifications. From what I was briefed, the German company has a charter from the Kaiser to permit them any land they should claim. My task is to make contact with von Kellermann and renew an old friendship. He might just hint to a man he trusts what the *Samoa's* mission really is.'

'The Germans originally stated that they had no imperial ambitions, but they are certainly active in our part of the British Empire,' Ian said, gazing at the charts of what the Germans called *Kaiser-Wilhelmsland*. 'If we ever go to war with the German Empire, our first troop casualties will be in this part of the world.'

'It is not probable,' Sam interjected cheerfully. 'It will more likely be the Russkies.'

'Today a friend, tomorrow an enemy,' Josiah said. 'Who knows the machinations of politicians?'

Ebenezer and Sam went above deck to take in the sights of the sea while Yuan proudly controlled the helm. Sam could see how much he had learned from Ebenezer. They may have lost Lee from the crew, but he had mentored Yuan well and the young man was proving himself invaluable to the operation of the schooner.

Below deck, Ian packed his pipe and sat down on a bench as Josiah hovered, something obviously on his mind.

'How does Isabel accept your absence on this mission?' Josiah finally asked as grey, pungent smoke filled the cabin.

'I sent a telegram before we left Townsville, explaining that our business trip would mean being away a few weeks longer, but I doubt that Isabel truly believes it is a simple business trip. She will not be very happy.'

'I also sent a telegram for Marian to say that we have been delayed for a few more weeks, but to not worry,' Josiah reflected. 'Do you think that Marian will believe my excuse?'

'No more than Isabel will believe mine,' Ian chuckled. 'But I think both women understand that there is a restless nature in the Steele men. All we can hope for is that when we return, the anger will eventually dissipate. After all, there is no real danger in what we are doing. As you said, our excuse is that we are interested in trade in the German part of New Guinea, and how fortunate the coincidence of meeting an old friend.'

Josiah nodded at his father's words. It was not as if he was back in his army uniform, going into battle. He was simply a businessman on a cruise to reconnoitre for new markets.

TWENTY-TWO

A week later, one of the crew called down that a ship had been sighted steaming south towards them. Ebenezer quickly glanced at his charts and ascertained that they would meet approximately 147 degrees east and 7 degrees south of the German New Guinea coastline, in the Huon Gulf.

Josiah strained to see through the telescope while Sam and Ian stood impatiently behind him on the deck.

'Is it the Germans?' Ian asked.

'Just making out the name now,' Josiah replied. 'She looks a bit like our schooner, but I can see she is steam-powered . . . Yes! It's the *Samoa*!'

Ebenezer steered a course towards the German ship. The tropical azure-blue sea was now a muddy brown from the outflow of a river on the coast bordered by swamps and lush tropical forests. Already those on the *Ella* could see men scrambling to the railings to observe the schooner approaching them.

Josiah held the telescope to his eye again. 'I can see a couple of German sailors. They are armed with Mausers,' Josiah said. 'Ah! I can see a German officer giving them orders. He is not a sailor, but wears a German army uniform.' His father and brother stood at his shoulder.

'Is it Kellermann?' Ian asked.

'Not close enough to make out yet,' Josiah replied before suddenly exclaiming, 'Wait . . . Yes! I am sure it's Maximillian.'

'Thank God!' Ian said. 'We have had luck on our side.'

'I'm not so sure,' Sam interjected. 'Those sailors are pointing their rifles at us.'

Sam was correct, and Josiah felt a twinge of apprehension as they closed the distance until they came aside, within speaking range. A voice projected through a megaphone drifted across the muddy water between the two ships.

'You are in German waters,' a familiar voice called in German, a language Josiah understood.

'We are the *Ella* out of Sydney, and we are a commercial vessel,' he replied in German.

'You are to immediately leave our waters if you do not have a permit from the German New Guinea Company.'

'My name is Josiah Steele, former servant of Queen Victoria in the British army.' Josiah was now certain he was talking to his old friend from Bavaria, who had not changed much in the short years since they had last met. There was a pause, and he could see that the German officer had turned to a naval officer standing beside him.

'Are you one hundred per cent sure that you are exchanging words with Kellermann?' his father asked.

Josiah turned to him with a grin. 'I am sure. It is just taking a little time for him to get it through his thick Prussian skull.'

The German officer broke off his conversation with the naval officer and turned his attention to the intruding schooner in German territorial waters off German New Guinea.

'I am Colonel von Kellermann of the Kaiser's army. If you are who I suspect you are, you can answer this question. When did we first meet?'

'Max, it was on a dock in London when you first met me. I was also your guest in Bavaria, and we had a small adventure together on your private shooting range.'

'Josiah!' came an almost joyous voice across the water separating them. 'God in heaven. Is it really you?'

'Damned right, you Prussian warrior,' Josiah said. 'I cannot believe that we should meet in this far-flung part of the world. I thought you were at least the general of the Kaiser's army by now. I invite you and your executive crew to row over and join us in a celebratory drink to toast the Queen and the Kaiser.'

'We will do so,' Kellermann answered. The rifles pointed at them were quickly withdrawn and a dinghy was lowered from the *Samoa* and filled with four men, two in uniform. When they reached the *Ella*, they were assisted aboard and the first man on deck was Maximillian von Kellermann.

The two men stood staring at each other before the Prussian officer clicked his heels and bowed and Josiah thrust out his hand. The grip between the two men was strong as they smiled at one another. 'Welcome aboard, old friend,' Josiah said in German, and he could see the twinkle in Max's eye.

'It is also good to see you, old friend,' Max replied in

English. 'We have much to catch up on. But I feel that I should speak English, as I am aboard an English ship.'

Introductions were made and there was no further feeling of hostility for the *Ella* in German-claimed waters. Yuan had directed the cook to prepare a lunch of recently caught fish, wine and the few fresh vegetables they still had in the schooner's pantry. It was ascertained that the German naval officer also spoke excellent English, but the two civilians did not. It was explained that one of them was a cartographer mapping the coastline and the other a land surveyor. The *Samoa*'s captain had remained with his ship, but Max explained that he was to relay his cordial greetings to the captain of the *Ella*.

Lunch was surprisingly good and followed by port wine and cigars. The Kaiser and Queen were toasted, then they all went above to take in the fresh air. Max and Josiah retreated to the stern for some privacy.

'I have two sons,' Max said, producing a photograph of his infant sons being held by Elise. 'Are you married, with children?'

'I'm trying to convince a young lady in Sydney to accept a proposal of marriage,' Josiah replied. 'But she feels that I am too restless to settle down.'

Max grinned and slapped Josiah on the back. 'She is a wise woman,' he laughed. 'Look at you now, sailing the oceans of the world. Not something I would have expected from a soldier.'

'I promised when I went with the colonial contingent to the Sudan that I would no longer seek adventure, but my father's companies are looking for business opportunities in this part of the world,' Josiah said. 'I still cannot get over how we could meet by such luck off this coastline.'

'You do realise that you require permission from our

administrator to be here.' Max frowned. 'However, I am sure I will be able to convince him that you do not have any devious intentions, and that you simply got blown here by accident.'

'Thank you, Max. I must confess, we were about to turn about until we saw your ship and curiosity got the better of us,' Josiah replied, trying to lead the conversation in a direction where Max might reveal some information. 'One does not expect to encounter other vessels in this part of the world.'

'I will put it down to your sense of adventure,' Max said, taking a puff on his cigar followed by a swig of the port wine. 'Will you be returning to Sydney? I have always had a desire to visit the Australian colonies.'

'If you and the duchess ever do, be assured you will be greeted as esteemed guests by myself, and I am sure by the colony.'

'Thank you, Josiah,' Max replied.

'I presume that from the guests you brought aboard you are carrying out a mission to find suitable ports for shipping?' Josiah said casually, gazing back at the shoreline bordered by dense scrub and trees.

'Yes, purely for commercial reasons,' Max answered. 'There are those in Germany who desire to seek a life in the tropics, but so far it has not gone well. Fever rages through many who come with high hopes of a new life away from the cold winters of Europe. Personally, I doubt that New Guinea will be a great success for colonisation. Many of the natives here are warlike and that would require strict methods of punishment. You English may protest our system of justice, and we are aware that the Australian colonies are putting pressure on the English government to prevent us claiming any further parts of the island. As it is, the Dutch have the western part of the island and nothing has been raised to protest their move. After all, Britain and Germany are friends.'

'Have you established an administrative harbour yet?' Josiah queried.

'Why do you ask, my friend?' Max countered.

Josiah smiled. 'So that we may have an identifiable destination, should we be granted permission to trade in your part of New Guinea.'

'A good harbour has been located and named on our maps as *Deutschlandhafen*,' Max replied. 'It is able to accommodate many ships.'

And German warships, Josiah thought.

'I will be able to show you its location on your charts,' Max added.

Josiah nodded. 'It will be good to know for the future of our trading links.'

'It is both beautiful and mysterious, this new land,' Max mused. 'We know more about the inland of Africa than anything beyond the coastal strip of this island. What may this land have that is valuable to Europe?'

The two men chatted for another hour until Max looked across at the *Samoa* and saw a signal to return to the ship. Josiah and Max shook hands and the dinghy with the Germans returned to their vessel.

Waving to each other, the *Samoa* and *Ella* pulled away, the schooner sailing north and the *Samoa* continuing to steam south along the coast.

It was that evening, with the *Ella* anchored offshore, that Ebenezer came to Ian and his two boys sitting on a hatch, drinking tea and enjoying the tropical night alive with the twinkling of stars. The serenity added to the ambience of the night as a cool breeze took away the heat of the day.

'All going well?' Sam asked.

'All well,' Ebenezer answered, sitting and taking his pipe from his trousers and plugging it. When it was alight, he blew a wisp of smoke that was caught by the breeze. 'I've just heard the darndest story from Yuan. I think that you should know about it.' The three men knew that Ebenezer had picked up a good grasp of Mandarin Chinese and Yuan English. Between them they were able to communicate effectively.

'What do you think we should know?' Ian asked.

'Yuan told me his father was once with a junk off the place where we met up with the Germans. He said they anchored and went up that river we saw back there to try and get fresh water, which they were low on. While they were drawing water, a couple of the crew found small gold nuggets. They looked around and found even more evidence of alluvial gold. It was their intention to go back to their boat and get some shovels and picks, but near dusk they were attacked by the local natives. As they had few weapons and were heavily outnumbered, they retreated. They lost a few of the crew to the native arrows and were overdue reaching Cooktown, where they knew gold was to be found on the Palmer. His father gave his son a good description of the region, identifying a small peninsula south of the main peninsula in the Huon Gulf. Yuan only remembered the story his father told him when we were anchored off that river mouth.'

The story caught the interest of father and sons.

'If what Yuan said is true, then there might be a mother lode beyond the coast,' Josiah said. 'Maybe this land has gold deposits beyond that of even the Palmer. It would be grand to be the first to stake a claim if gold is here.'

'Do I need to remind you that if there is gold, it is within the territory the Germans have already claimed?' Ian asked.

'I doubt they are going to recognise any claim we might make on their land to prospect or mine.'

Josiah accepted his father's pessimistic advice, knowing that if there was a goldfield out there, the Germans would eventually learn about it and take steps to prevent anyone but themselves claiming rights.

'Why don't we turn about and go back to launch a small boat up the river, just to either verify or dismiss the idea of a possible new goldfield?' Sam said optimistically. 'No harm in having a look.'

'You heard what Yuan said about the natives,' Josiah interjected. 'They don't seem to welcome strangers on their lands.'

'Maybe we could go as traders and befriend them?' Sam continued. 'A handful of beads and a couple of iron axes should get a bit of hospitality.'

'We don't speak their language,' Josiah countered. 'What if they decide to shoot first and just take what we have?'

'We go heavily armed with our Colts and Winchester rifles,' Sam said.

'What do you think, Father?' Josiah asked, turning to Ian, who had remained silent during the conversation.

Ian took a puff on his pipe as he contemplated the situation. 'Why not?' he finally replied. 'We may be lucky and pick up a nugget or two. The Germans don't have to know. There is always risk in life, but only the bold are successful.'

Josiah shrugged. 'I respect your decision, but I'm not sure it is a good idea to row into the unknown, even if we have the arms to do so. We will be in unknown and unmapped territory, which is something a military man might advise against.'

Sam slapped him on the shoulder. 'Big brother, I hope you pick up a nugget big enough to make a hundred gold rings for your beloved.'

Josiah had a bad feeling about the idea. It was bad enough that he had broken his promise to Marian to settle down to a stable life as a businessman, but here he was plotting an adventure into a dark, mysterious land that threatened fever and probably hostile native warriors. But gold fever is a universal state of mind, and after he and his father had spent time on the Palmer, Josiah knew his fever had not gone away.

In the distance, Josiah heard the splash of something very big in the mouth of the muddy river and remembered that the giant saltwater crocodiles ruled the river and its adjoining banks. He gazed into the foreboding darkness of the shoreline and experienced a sinister feeling of dread.

TWENTY-THREE

The schooner's rowboat was lowered into the sea at first light.

'We plan to be away no more than two days,' Ian said to Ebenezer. 'Yuan has recommended one of his better boys, Chen, to go with us.'

'You look to be well prepared, Colonel,' Ebenezer noted as Ian slung a Winchester repeating rifle over his shoulder and checked the big Colt revolver in his ammunition belt. It was no longer a cap-and-ball pistol, as Ian had updated to a newer model that was loaded with fixed cartridges. They had packed enough food, tents and arms to be fairly comfortable, while Sam and Josiah had also brought a couple of shovels and picks as well as three sluicing pans. Chen was armed with a machete.

The *Ella* drifted on a gentle sea at anchor and there was very little chance that she would be seen by any passing sea-going vessels – especially any German ships – as they were well away from the shipping lanes.

The boat was ready and the four-man team scrambled in to row towards the mouth of the river. They had waited until the tide turned in their favour and made good time to the mouth of the muddy waterway. Sweat poured down their bodies and fresh, clean water was in high demand. Now and then, they spotted big crocodiles on the overgrown banks which slithered into the water. Josiah shuddered and the memory of his first sighting of one of the primitive reptiles returned to him.

As if reading his thoughts, Ian smiled. 'I know,' he said. 'They are crocs and not 'gators. I was told that by someone when we were entering the Endeavour River at Cooktown many years ago.'

'And I was left at home,' Sam said.

'You were a bit young to be with us,' Josiah replied. 'But from what I have heard, you've made up for it lately. This might be your chance to experience the thrill of finding gold, as we did.'

At that moment Chen issued what was clearly a warning in Chinese.

'What is it?' Ian asked. They had turned a bend in the river and the men could now see a village on their starboard side. They could also see many dugout canoes and that the scatter of wood and thatch huts was inhabited by a large population. Men, women and children gaped at the alien beings approaching their village in a strange canoe.

Josiah could see that the men were all armed with long bows and, after the initial shock of the unexpected sight, the men began to string up long, reed-like arrows that did not appear to have the traditional flight feathers attached. They could hear shouting from the warriors and wailing coming from the women at the ghost-like aliens intruding into their land.

They ceased rowing and Josiah immediately reached for the rifle at his feet.

'We don't make any hostile moves,' Ian cautioned. 'I doubt that we are within range of their arrows.'

'What if they take to their canoes?' Sam asked.

'I don't think they will,' his father replied. 'They look to me as if they have never had contact with a European before. It seems our German friends have not as yet penetrated this section of the river.'

Despite Ian's reassurance, Josiah gripped the rifle on his lap and noticed that Sam was doing the same. The sun beat down on the men in the boat, and under their broad-brimmed floppy hats they could still feel the humid heat of the tropics.

'What do we do?' Sam asked, and Josiah could hear the tension in his brother's question.

'I think the best course of action is to row away from the village and pass it by,' Ian answered. 'They will see that we have not taken any hostile action towards them and leave us alone.'

Sam was not so sure. There were at least fifty warriors armed with bows, and they did not look happy as they strung their arrows. But within minutes, the longboat pulled out of sight of the village without any further incident, and the yells and cries faded into silence over the muddy waters.

As they rowed, Ian and Josiah scanned the riverbanks for any stream feeding the main river course. Around mid-afternoon, they sighted one. It was narrow and almost unseen because of the heavy jungle foliage of smaller trees under the canopy of the forest giants. Here was a potential place to investigate for signs of gold. They steered the boat towards the creek and secured it to the bank, and all were cautious of the presence of crocodiles as they scrambled ashore.

'We set up camp before night arrives,' Ian ordered, and they used the machetes they all carried to clear a space in the thick brush where they laid out their tents and established a campfire. It was not easy as the timber was sodden with the ever-present humidity, but Josiah was able to start a fire for cooking. The first thing they did was brew a strong tea. Tins of canned meat were mixed with tins of vegetables and curry powder to make something resembling a stew, and it was set to simmer for the evening meal over the small, smoky fire.

Sam and Chen remained guarding the campsite while Ian and Josiah took the prospecting pans to the edge of the clear creek running into the main river. They squatted on the bank, panning gravel and sand for any sign of gold and after an hour, Josiah could see just the tiniest trace of gold flecks in his pan. He called his father over to examine his find.

'There are certainly good signs,' Ian sighed. 'But I suspect the mother lode is at the source of the river, in the mountains beyond. It is not likely we will be able to reach much further with our limited resources.'

Josiah agreed, but felt it was worth panning until the sun went down. In the tropics, night came quickly and always at around the same time. They panned for another hour, recovering a few more flecks of the precious metal, which they placed in a tiny medical phial, and then made their way back to the camp a hundred yards away, hacking through the dense undergrowth to get there.

Grinning, Josiah held up the quarter-filled glass phial to Sam, who was stirring the stew in the pot suspended over the fire. 'I think that we have the fare to pay for our meal tonight,' he said, handing the gold container to Sam, who stared with his mouth agape.

'So that's what gold looks like in its natural state,' he remarked in awe.

'Sadly, not enough for us all to retire on,' Josiah replied. 'But I think it is a good indication that there may be very lucrative goldfields not far from here. I wonder if the Germans will discover them?'

'Not with our help,' Ian said, sitting down and placing his rifle over his knees. 'We should have kept the Kaiser and his dreams of empire a bit further north of here, but the English government did not display much interest and for now, more important than that is a pannikin of stew and a slice of the damper out of the coals. I am sure that this calls for a round of drinks to celebrate that we may be the first Europeans to explore this part of the river.'

Chen joined them in a circle around the cooking pot and appeared to enjoy his pannikin of stew, helped down by the damper bread. Ian passed him a tin mug of hot, sweet tea to wash down the meal.

A kerosene lantern threw eerie shadows around the enclosed campsite as father and sons enjoyed the moment under the brilliant display of stars peeking through a gap in the forest canopy above. Ian watched the banter between his sons and reflected that in this wild and unexplored part of the mysterious island known as New Guinea, he was truly at peace.

They would return home after visiting the port Max had described as a potential settlement area for German immigrants, civil servants and possibly the German navy with its supporting army. Josiah's report to his masters might provide valuable information about the intentions of the Kaiser in the Pacific. It was not that Germany was considered a future enemy, but nothing was certain in the century ahead, Ian reflected as the dancing flames mesmerised with their twists and contortions.

'I think that we should mount a guard tonight,' Josiah suggested. 'Just an old military thing,' he explained to Sam.

'A good idea,' Ian agreed. 'I will take the first watch. Sam, you take the second and Josiah can watch the sun come up. We will spend the morning searching the creek until midday, then return to the *Ella* warm in the knowledge that we at least found some gold.'

★

It was in the very early hours of the morning that Sam was startled to hear loud noises around the camp. Immediately, he had his rifle in his hands and his finger on the trigger, peering into the dark as if he could see through it. There was a squealing noise he knew was that of an animal and not a human – at least he hoped. Then the forest fell silent except for the continuous irritating high-pitched buzzing of the clouds of mosquitoes. Sam did not have any desire to doze off and was pleased to see his brother groping towards him along a rope line that had been laid out between the campsite and the sentry position behind a great tree trunk fallen in some violent storm. He reported to Josiah the only alarming incident during his shift.

'I swear, it sounded like one of our kangaroos, but it came from a tree, and I have never heard of any roos that can climb trees,' Sam whispered. 'This is a strange world.'

The sun rose on another hot and humid day without incident. The coals of the campfire were stoked until they came alive and a billy of tea brewed to wash down cans of fruit. So far, it had almost been like a tropical holiday,

Ian thought. He sipped his tea by the fire and sighed. It was as if there was no other world than that he shared with Sam and Josiah.

Josiah was leaning over to pick up a small spade with his rifle slung over his shoulder and Sam was pulling down the tents when a cry of pain caused a sudden stop to all activity. Ian swung around to see Chen staggering towards him, gripping a long arrow that had pierced his throat, leaving the long shaft sticking out of his neck. He fell to his knees just as Ian recovered his revolver from its holster and desperately sought about for the enemy. The swishing sound in the air heralded a dozen other arrows falling amongst Ian, Sam and Josiah, who by now had their rifles gripped in their hands as they also tried to determine the source of the threat.

Ian thought he saw movement in the dark early-morning shadows and fired twice. Sam and Josiah were already firing into the surrounding scrub, reloading as quickly as they could.

'Father!' Sam screamed when he saw Ian stagger, an arrow protruding from his chest. Ian still gripped his revolver but slumped to his knees, gripping the shaft of the arrow buried in his upper right-side chest.

The yelps from the surrounding bush appeared to indicate one or two unaimed shots had found a mark, and there was the rustling sound of warriors retreating deeper into the rainforest, away from the camp.

Josiah fell to his knees beside his father while Sam kept the campsite protected, casting looks all around. Keeping one eye on the jungle, Sam knelt beside Chen, who lay unmoving. 'He's gone,' Sam said quietly as Josiah snapped off the end of the arrow in his father's chest, leaving the stub protruding from the deep wound. 'We'll have to leave him. But we need to get Father out of here now, before they return to finish us off.'

Josiah placed his arm under his father's shoulder and helped him to his feet, half-dragging, half-walking him down to their longboat, where he placed him as gently as he could into the bottom. When Josiah glanced over his shoulder, he could see his brother withdrawing down to the boat while covering their retreat. He leapt into the boat after untying it from a tree and both brothers immediately commenced rowing as fast as they could to the central channel, away from either bank. When they glanced at the place they had left, they saw the nearly naked warriors emerge to shout at them, stringing their bows and firing at the disappearing longboat. The arrows fell short, splashing into the water as Josiah and Sam rowed around the river bend.

*

'Savages,' Sam snarled as Ebenezer arranged to lift Ian as gently as he could from the bottom of the dinghy. 'We got attacked at first light. Chen is dead, and we had to leave him behind to save our own lives.'

'I can do it,' Ian protested, attempting to stand, which he eventually did. He was lifted onto the deck, where Ebenezer could see a short section of the arrow shaft embedded in Ian's chest.

'We must get your father below,' Ebenezer commanded. 'We have to remove the head of the arrow without causing too much blood loss.'

Ian was assisted below, still walking but in obvious pain, and laid on a bunk. Sam rifled through their medicine cabinet for whatever he thought might help, but it was Ebenezer and Josiah who knew more about such wounds.

Ian looked up at three very worried expressions. 'It will take more than a primitive arrow to kill me,' he said weakly. 'Now, just get it out of me.'

Josiah had separated forceps and a small, sharp knife. He also had a bottle of strong antiseptic, but no kind of anaesthetic to ease the pain. He poured half the bottle of antiseptic over the wound.

'I'm sorry, Father. This is going to cause some discomfort,' Josiah said. With trembling hands, he slit the skin either side of the shaft. His father did not make a sound but arced up before slumping back on the bunk, sweat rolling down his ashen face. As quickly as he could, Josiah reached for the forceps lying in an enamel basin Sam had filled with more antiseptic. He leaned over and pressed the forceps into the wound he had widened for the retrievers, gripping the end of the shaft near the arrowhead point. It was then that he realised what he was dealing with and experienced the deepest despair.

'The bloody arrowhead is barbed,' he muttered loudly enough for Sam and Ebenezer to hear. 'We can neither push nor pull it out with further serious damage. All we can do is keep the wound clean and bandage it until we are able to get to the nearest surgeon.'

'There still might be a doctor at Cooktown,' Ebenezer said. 'Failing that, Cairns.'

'Every hour counts,' Josiah said, straightening his back and dropping the forceps into the enamel basin. 'We up anchor and leave immediately for a course south.'

'What can I do?' Sam asked, feeling helpless as his father lay semiconscious on the bunk.

'You remain by his bedside and provide him with water,' Josiah said, placing a hand on his younger brother's shoulder. 'He needs to know we are with him. Keep his forehead cool with damp clothes to help with any fever he might develop.'

Sam nodded and knelt down beside the bunk to take his beloved father's limp hand. Josiah went above deck, where

Ebenezer was already giving Yuan directions to lift the anchor and set the sails. All the crew had gathered when Ian was brought aboard, and Josiah told Yuan that Chen lay dead in the jungle. It was a blow to the crew to lose a comrade.

As if understanding the dire situation, the *Ella* was able to tack with good ocean winds and cut through the tropical waters on a course to the colony of Queensland.

TWENTY-FOUR

With each passing nautical mile, Josiah felt growing frustration. They could see the vague outline of the Queensland coast off their starboard bow, but he knew from consulting the charts that they were still twenty-four hours from Cooktown.

His father's condition had deteriorated. Ian was still lucid at times, but the infection around the wound was obvious, and in his lowest state, he would fall into a fevered ranting of a man calling out orders on a battlefield. Both Sam and Josiah knew that their father had seen so much on the many battlefields where he had served for the Queen. Many times, he would call for Sergeant Major Curry to bring up more troops. In turn, his sons held his hand, calling soothing words in an attempt to penetrate those terrible battlefields he was once again upon.

Twenty-four hours earlier, Josiah had been beside his

father when Ian seemed to almost recover. Josiah fed him a thin fish soup and Ian had thanked him. A lantern swung from the cabin ceiling, casting a sickly yellow glow.

'Do you know, with all our wealth, the only true thing in life is the family around you,' Ian said in a hoarse voice. 'My time has come. I want to pass knowing that you will give me your promise to steer the companies into the future and be there for your family. So many good people rely on us for their bread and butter, and I have complete faith that you have the ability to take command of the helm of the Steele Enterprises.'

'What of Sam?' Josiah asked.

'Sam and Becky will have equal shares in the family enterprises,' Ian replied. 'But Sam has much to learn and experience before he stands beside you. He is not you, but he will find his path in life beside you. My darling women, Isabel and Becky, will be the responsibility of my boys to care for. You will take my place to ensure they are looked after for life. Swear to me you will assume the helm of our enterprises and steer a safe passage through troubled waters when I am gone. But I also have a final wish that you and Marian find a life together. I know that you are so much unalike in many ways. However, she complements your nature.'

Josiah squeezed his father's hand. 'I swear to honour your wishes,' he said with tears in his eyes. 'But we are almost at Cooktown and a surgeon will tend to your wound, and you will be back on deck before you know it.'

Ian smiled. It was the weak smile of the mortally injured, but he returned the grip. 'We will see.' He sighed, lying back against the sweat-stained sheets of his bunk. Already, the stench of putrefaction could be smelled in the almost airless cabin. Ian's eyes closed and his breathing continued in shallow gasps.

Behind him, Josiah could hear footsteps on the ladder and turned to see Sam coming to relieve Josiah's watch by his father's bunk.

'How is he, brother?' Sam asked when he stood beside Josiah.

'He is sleeping for the moment,' Josiah replied. 'But I fear time is our enemy.'

'Ebenezer says that at the good rate we are sailing, we might strike Cooktown before first light tomorrow,' Sam said, kneeling beside his father's bunk and taking his hand. 'Has he said anything?'

'Not much, but he's started talking like a dead man. I reassured him we were almost at Cooktown.'

Sam nodded. 'It is impossible to believe that our father is not immortal,' he said. 'He has lived a life so full of danger only to suffer a grievous wound at the hand of a primitive savage in a place very few people know exists.'

'He will live,' Josiah said, but knew he also had to face the reality this might not be so.

Ian regained consciousness in the early hours of the morning when he heard Ebenezer call from the helm that he had Cooktown in sight. Josiah was dozing by his side and Ian reached out to grasp his hand. Josiah immediately shrugged off his weariness and leaned over to his father.

'What is it, Father?' he asked.

'We have reached Cooktown,' Ian answered in a weak voice. 'I heard Ebenezer call out.'

Josiah made a move to stand, but Ian continued his feeble grip on his sleeve. 'There is something I must tell you,' Ian said in a trembling voice. 'When you return to Sydney, there is a small box in my desk. In that box is a letter that you must deliver. You must promise me that. It is good that you and I share this moment in a place I truly learned to

212

understand your true and wonderful character. You, Sam and Becky . . . your mother and Isabel and my old comrade Conan have given me the best times of my life. Tell Conan I will miss him. I wish to be buried at Cooktown, so that I can be in a place with old friends.'

'I will ensure your wish is satisfied,' Josiah said. 'But we can get you proper medical treatment as soon as we dock and have you back in Sydney with all those who truly love you.'

Ian's hand fell away and he closed his eyes. Josiah suddenly noticed that his father's breathing had ceased, and placed his cheek against his father's face. Josiah did not want to believe that his father had finally passed from this earthly world.

Sam was already scrambling down the stairs and excitedly exclaimed, 'We have arrived!' He went silent when he saw the tears pouring down his brother's face.

'Just a little too late,' Josiah said. 'Father has passed from us. The world has lost one of its best.'

★

Josiah made the funeral arrangements for a cemetery in Cooktown. He also had a telegram sent to Sydney announcing Ian's death, dreading the reaction it would receive amongst family and friends. He simply wrote that Ian had passed away and little else. The news of the circumstances of his death would come when he and Sam returned to Sydney.

Now, they stood by the gravesite as a storm brewed in the skies above. It was a herald of the imminent wet season and there were few to say last words as the coffin was lowered into the earth.

One mourner attending was an old friend of Josiah and Ian, Mexican Jack, now sole owner of Hamish MacDonald's hotel in Charlotte Street. His business partner,

Frank McNeil, had died peacefully in his sleep a year earlier, and when Josiah shook the hand of the former American, he was saddened to see his long grey beard was now snow white, and the man seemed to have aged beyond his years.

'The old town's not the same since the gold started dryin' up,' Jack bemoaned. 'Not like the old days, when you were here last with your pa, young fella. Now we are putting in the ground one of the finest men I ever knew – along with the major. I am sorry for your loss.'

Josiah thanked the Texan and introduced him to his brother and Ebenezer. The two Americans soon discovered that they had fought on opposite sides in the American Civil War, but appeared to have also buried their old animosities as they swapped stories of their military campaigns over drinks back at the hotel after the service.

'We need to have a headstone made and sent up here to mark Father's final resting place,' Sam said just as fat droplets fell on the small huddle around the gravesite yet to be filled with the earth alongside the grave.

Ebenezer called to Josiah and Sam. 'Jack has suggested that we return to his pub and raise a glass or two to the memory of your pa.'

Josiah nodded and the men filed out of the cemetery to allow the gravediggers to complete their work before the storm broke. As they reached the hotel, lightning rent the sky and crashing thunder caused the buildings in the sedate frontier town to shake. When they entered, Josiah immediately noticed how few patrons there were compared to the boom days of the Palmer goldrush.

Mexican Jack produced a bottle of his finest whisky and filled tumblers to the top. The four men stood in a circle, facing each other. It was Mexican Jack who proposed the toast, 'To a goddamned fine man, taken from us too early.'

The others echoed his words, and the storm broke as a raging torrent on the corrugated-tin roof of the hotel in Charlotte Street, Cooktown.

Josiah reflected that it was as if God had shown his grief at the loss of his father.

★

Short weeks later, both Sam and Josiah stood in the dining room of the Steele mansion on the harbour. Josiah thought that the house had an air of waiting – waiting for the master to return. He had already told the truth to Isabel and Becky concerning the death of Ian, and their grief seemed to have no end. Will Bowden and his son, George, were also told of Ian's tragic demise and Will had muttered, 'The colonel was never fated to die in his bed, a dribbling, imbecilic old man.' Josiah and Sam took a strange comfort from his statement.

Conan, Molly and Marian stopped by to pay their respects and Josiah could see that the burly former sergeant major looked a shattered man.

'My father made me promise on his deathbed to tell you that his thoughts were with you at the end,' Josiah said gently.

The tough former soldier nodded his head, tears streaming into his greying beard. Molly was being comforted by Becky in the corner of the dining room as Josiah glanced at Marian, whose expression was that of sadness and even a hint of anger. Josiah thought he knew why. He just needed to get her alone and face her wrath, but was at a loss as to how to defend himself.

The opportunity came when he saw her step into the garden. Josiah excused himself as the gathered crowd of close friends and family conversed in subdued tones in the dining room, which had been transformed into a wake for the former British officer.

It was a warm summer day and the shrill cacophony of cicadas could be heard, almost drowning out any other sounds drifting from the harbour below.

'Marian, I know I might have to explain a –'

Marian turned on Josiah with an expression of fury. 'You lied to me,' she spat with venom. 'You said that you were simply on a business trip to north Queensland. But now I learn your father was killed by natives somewhere in New Guinea. Does that sound like a simple business trip?'

'We were exploring future trading opportunities in that part of the world,' Josiah replied lamely, praying that Marian would accept his explanation.

'Josiah Steele, you made an oath to me that your days of attracting perilous situations were over. Now it appears it is just in your blood to run away and seek excitement at every opportunity you get. I don't think I can be with a man like that.'

Josiah stood, oblivious to everything except his ill-fated love for the beautiful red-haired girl standing in the garden. He desperately wanted to tell her the real reason he, his brother and father had found themselves in the waters of New Guinea, but knew he could not as he had sworn an oath to his Queen and country.

'When my father was dying on the *Ella*, he made me promise him that you and I would spend the rest of our lives together,' Josiah quietly said. 'A promise to a dying man cannot be broken and I swear on his grave that my days of seeking any kind of danger are over. It is now my responsibility to manage our estates, and that means a normal life with a wife and family by my side. I love you, Marian Curry, with my whole heart and soul.'

Marian stared into his eyes for a brief moment, her expression softening. 'I have always loved you, Josiah Steele, even when I tried not to. I accept that conditions are different now and that you are obliged by blood to continue your father's work. I desperately want to believe you have changed.'

'I beg that you consider the change of situation and understand that all in my past is now just a ghost. All I wish is to honour my father's last wishes and to honour you, as my wife. I can also promise you that I will be the most boring man you ever met.'

Josiah was surprised when Marian laughed softly. 'That is one thing you could never be,' she said. 'Horace Anderson is boring, but I sense that you will discover a passion for something else, and do great things.'

Josiah reached out for Marian's hand and she did not resist his touch. 'Will you forgive me and consider marriage?'

With a smile, Marian nodded. 'If you ever stray from your promise to me to settle down, my father has taught me how to inflict great physical damage with a sword. Yes, I will become your wife. But this is not the right time to make any announcements.'

Death had touched the Steele family, but now there was also a promise of life ahead. How strange that he could feel so happy and sad at the same time.

★

Detective Sergeant Andrew Paull arrived at the CIB office to find a uniformed constable waiting to pass him a thick envelope. 'Delivered this morning, sir,' the man said.

Andrew took the envelope with his name on it to his desk and opened it. He could see that it had been handwritten, and as he read the contents, he almost fell off his chair.

It was from an old suspect he had never forgotten, a confession to the slaying of one Harold Skinner years earlier. The statement also went on to explain the reason Skinner was killed, and that Conan Curry had never been guilty of the death of Ian's mother. Ian explained that he had the greatest respect for the police detective and wanted him to know the truth in the event of his death.

Andrew already knew of Ian Steele's passing from the many newspapers reporting the untimely death of the well-known Sydney businessman and former military hero for Queen Victoria.

'You look like you've seen a ghost,' Andrew's partner commented as he brought two mugs of tea to the desk. 'Got one for yer before we go out on a tip about a burglary. Something in that wad of papers you got there of any importance?'

Andrew looked up at his partner. 'No, nothing of any importance,' he replied, shoving the statement back in the envelope. The former army officer, had done the honourable thing. And Andrew could be satisfied that his police instincts had been right all along.

He considered the circumstances that had caused Ian to kill the senior public servant. What would he have done under the same conditions? Andrew knew that he should hand over the letter to his senior officer, but what good would that do? It would only stain the good name of a man who had a proven record for generous charitable works in the colony and had served his Queen with courage and distinction. Andrew picked up his mug of tea and took a sip.

Some matters needed consigning to the fire, and this was one of them. The good name of Ian Steele would remain just that.

PART TWO

1900

A New Century, a New War

TWENTY-FIVE

Josiah Steele stood by his office window overlooking the harbour below, reflecting on his life. He and Marian had married, and it had been she who insisted that they do so in a synagogue after she converted to Josiah's religion, and was now raising their four children in the Jewish faith.

Sam was somewhere in South Africa as a sergeant with a New South Wales mounted infantry unit, as was Corporal George Bowden. Josiah sighed. He was now the patriarch of the Steele family, and had proven extremely competent at managing the vast array of industries his father had developed. But Josiah still secretly wished that he was back in uniform, serving across the Indian Ocean on the African veldt.

Marian was currently in Victoria on a committee for the eventual federation of the nation as the Steele fortune gave her the means to pursue political issues concerning the emancipation of women. Josiah often thought how different they were, he, a conservative, and Marian, a political fire-brand. But they clung to each other with a real love that strengthened with time, and Josiah smiled when he remembered how she would tease him for his 'stuffy ways' but also acknowledged that he was not so with his children. There was David, now fourteen years old, Benjamin, thirteen, Judith, twelve, and finally Rose, eleven. In many ways, his children saw more of their father than their mother, with Marian forever travelling the colonies to meet with the women with like minds for equal rights.

The families of Conan Curry and Josiah Steele remained very close. Molly had secured financial success with her confectionary shops established across Sydney and had plans to expand her product into the other colonies. Conan spent long hours at his desk writing his memoirs of his service to the Queen, with most of his story highlighting the career of his best friend – Ian Steele. But he always found time to hobble down to the local pub, leaning on a walking stick, to share his stories with the many friends he had made since returning to the colony of his birth. Life was good for the two families that were now connected by marriage.

The new century had opened with natural disasters. An ongoing drought had seen catastrophic fires in the colonies of Western Australia, Victoria and Tasmania. Up north, cyclones ravaged coastal towns and Josiah was informed that Cooktown hardly existed as a result of a terrible cyclone. It was currently summer in the southern hemisphere, with the high temperatures searing the countryside and city equally. The land was arid and the constant conversation was of the war against the Boers and the coming federation of the colonies under one flag as a single nation.

At least the war had proven good for the Steele Enterprises, with their military contracts to supply the

British army in Africa. Josiah had read that the British had underestimated the Dutch farmers and their commandoes, as the mounted enemy militia units were known. In the initial stages of the war, the Boers had smashed the regulars of the British army with modern artillery and firearms purchased from German factories. The deadly accuracy of the German Mauser rifle had played a big role in defeating the British troops sent against the irregulars of the Boer republics. Josiah was very familiar with the Boers; his Scots regiment had been slaughtered at Majuba Hill years before.

'Mr Steele,' the voice of his secretary interrupted Josiah's reflections.

'Yes, Tom?' Josiah asked, turning.

'You asked me to remind you that you are to have lunch with the premier today,' Tom said from the doorway.

'Thank you,' Josiah replied. He had forgotten that he was to go to Macquarie Street to meet with the premier of the colony and some of his advisers.

He walked away from the window and took his tall black hat from the rack. He hated the hat, but it denoted his place in the upper ranks of colonial society. He would have preferred the slouch hat of his colonial volunteer militia, of which he was now the commanding officer, with the rank of colonel.

★

Thousands of miles away on the other side of the Indian Ocean, a well-built man in his thirties sat astride his mount with a telescope up to his eye, surveying the plain before him from atop a small, stony mound the local Boers called a *kopje*. Samuel Steele wore the rank of a sergeant on his sleeve and his tanned face still bore the small scars from his years of getting into trouble in bar-room brawls from Sydney to the Rand. His impressive size and tough nature coupled with his leadership made him popular with the colonial mounted infantry he rode with. As a member of the mounted infantry, his role was to ride to battle, dismount and fight on foot, whereas cavalry and lancers charged into the enemy ranks on horseback. But Sam had seen soldiers of the cavalry and lancers armed with swords and spears mown down by the deadly accurate fire from concealed marksmen, whose 'one shot, one kill' reputation had proved warfare was changing from the traditional nineteenth-century tactics of massed infantry attacks. Artillery had become more sophisticated, and the Boers had a weapon known as a pom-pom, which fired explosive one-pound shells like a machine gun spewed out bullets.

Beside Sam was Corporal George Bowden, a veteran of the Sudan campaign now in his early forties. Sam knew of other colonial soldiers who were even older than George serving in the war at the front. The third man was Smith, a young man in his late teens who had been a baker's apprentice in Goulburn, a large rural town west of the Great Dividing Range.

'See anything?' George asked.

They had traversed a landscape of low hillocks that were either covered in stunted, tough grasses or stones. Sam's troop of mounted infantry had been seared by a hot sun and occasionally blasted by savage winds. There was little water, and any found was usually a mere trickle in the earth. The country was tough on the horses, and many had died under their riders during the pursuit of the elusive Boer commandoes, men who knew the land and were armed with the magazine-fed Mauser rifle, which fired a smoke-less cartridge.

They were now pitted against men not unlike themselves. Many of the troopers with Sam's squadron were farmers used to a tough life in the country. Sam knew Africa as Josiah had sent him to the goldfields to manage a mine they owned. He had been in the country five years earlier when the ongoing trouble between the Dutch-governed states and British interests brought matters to a head at the Rand mines. War between the Dutch citizens and the British Empire was always simmering under the surface, and when it appeared it might break out, Sam had joined the local militia of Australian miners under the title of the Australian Corps. He did so because of the Boer attitude towards anyone who was Jewish or Catholic, as neither religion was allowed rights in the Boer republics. This bias had got under Sam's skin, although he could not boast of being a devout Jew. But it was still his heritage.

The incident of the Jameson Raid, intended to create a rebellion in the Boer republics, fizzled out and the miners who were on strike went back to work.

Sam had returned to Sydney a year earlier to consult with the board members on their small share of the goldfields of the Rand. It was while he was home that all-out war was declared, and Sam enlisted in a colonial mounted infantry unit. It had been declared that in the confrontation with the Dutch farmers, only white men would participate, so volunteers were called from Canada, the Australian colonies, and New Zealand. They came with colourful titles such as the New Zealand Rough Riders, the Queensland Mounted Infantry and even a contingent of Irishmen from New South Wales. But old rivalries existed when the hodgepodge of colonial units arrived to form brigades, and New South Welshmen refused to have Victorian officers command them – and vice versa.

Across Sam's chest was a bandolier containing the .303 cartridges for his Lee Enfield bolt action rifle. The magazine on the rifle contained ten rounds and his bandolier pouches the five-round clips to charge the rifle's magazine. It was an accurate weapon and a match for the German Mauser of his enemy.

'Still can't see anything?' George asked again as Sam swept the veldt to his front.

'Wait . . . I see dust, but just on the horizon. It must be the party we are tracking.'

No sooner had Sam announced his discovery than he thought he heard a faint popping sound. A second and a half later, Smith suddenly let out a surprised yelp and toppled from his horse. Sam's mount reared up, almost felling him, and when he swung around, he could see the young trooper on the dusty ground, gripping his right arm at the elbow. Sam immediately swung himself off his horse and knelt by the trooper. A marksman must have been left behind somewhere on the plain, and had scored a hit. Sam could see that the high-velocity bullet had smashed Smith's elbow, leaving the bottom half of his arm useless. The pain was setting in and the young colonial trooper had tears in his eyes as he gritted his teeth. Sam quickly bound the elbow with an army-issued bandage just as George shouted a warning followed by the scream of the trooper's horse as it was hit in the chest, crashing into the rocky ground, thrashing its hooves in its death throes.

'The bastard's got our range,' George shouted, grabbing hold of the reins of Sam's mount and swinging around to get out of the line of fire. Sam placed his arm under Smith's shoulder to lead him to the far side of the *kopje*.

Sam could see that the bullet wound had pulverised flesh and bone, and the young soldier was losing blood at a dangerous rate. George dismounted and assisted Sam to get the trooper onto Sam's horse before he flung himself into the saddle. Two horses and three men returned to their regiment, and Smith was immediately taken to the aid post for treatment.

'I should have known better,' Sam said bitterly. 'The bastards have a habit of leaving a sniper behind to pick us off if we follow. And there I was with us sitting on a high point, just asking to get shot at.'

'Not your fault, Sam,' George soothed. 'None of us spotted him out there in the glare of the sun.'

Sam did not answer. His thoughts were with the young trooper in the medical tent. Sam knew from experience that the only choice the army surgeons had was to amputate the arm, and he doubted that there was much of a future back in Goulburn for a one-armed baker.

★

The following day, Sam and George found themselves once again on horseback, advancing with their squadron as a protection detail for British artillery guns being repositioned to fire into a line of Boer defenders. The guns were unlimbered and provided supporting fire for the infantry to assault a position known as Diamond Hill, which they did as the Boer defenders fell back to other defence positions at Rhinoceros Spring Hill. From there, they poured small arms fire into the attacking forces. Sam could hear the gunfire coming from the south and knew that his squadron would soon join the fight.

The order came and Sam retrieved his rifle from the leather bucket at his knee. When he glanced to one side, he saw the West Australians astride their mounts and recognised that there was going to be colonial cooperation for the attack. They advanced to a farm where the artillery set up two pom-pom guns in support. The one-pound fused shells exploded on impact, throwing steel in all directions to tear and shred flesh concealed on the high ground. Sam recognised the gum trees growing around the farmhouse and for a second reflected how this could be any farmstead in Australia. The moment of reflection reminded him of the orders to burn Boer farms in an attempt to deny their enemy sustenance. Like Sam, most of the colonial volunteers were angry and bitter at the sight of Boer women and children sobbing as they witnessed everything they owned on this earth go up in flames before they were herded to rail heads to be transported to concentration camps deeper in the country. At those times, Sam felt more sympathy for the Dutch farmers than he did for the officers who gave the orders to destroy Boer farms. It haunted him and always would.

'Trot!'

The order was called down the line and the extended column of troopers advanced across an open plain in parade-ground formation towards the hill occupied by the Boer defenders. As the small arms fire from the Boers grew more intense, the order was issued to break from a trot into a charge.

Sam leaned across the neck of his horse, gripping his rifle in one hand and listening to the crack of Mauser rounds snap past his head. He felt no real fear as the hill grew ever larger until they were at its base, where Sam and George flung themselves from their mounts and quickly fixed bayonets for the assault amongst the rocks. It was a difficult climb and bullets continued to fall around them, but none of the colonial troopers hesitated. They eventually reached the flat top covered with boulders, and all Sam could think of was the tiny piece of ground directly to his front as he advanced from boulder to boulder. He was vaguely aware of the two troopers advancing with him, brothers from New Zealand who had been living in Sydney when they'd enlisted in Sam's regiment. Brendan and Nate Welsh were excellent soldiers who had grown up on a sheep farm on the South Island.

A chip of flying stone cut Sam's face, drawing blood. Ignoring the wound, Sam realised how thirsty he was but dared not stop, fully aware that death could be waiting for him around the next boulder.

'Forward New South Wales!' an officer yelled above the constant sound of rifle fire and screamed curses from both sides.

Sam was on his feet and rushing forward with the rest of his squadron, who were now all yelling to discourage the defenders. In a split second, a Boer defender rose up from the ground to fire point-blank at Sam, but fell sharply after two shots were fired, one by Trooper Brendan Welsh, the other by George. Sam could not be sure who had saved his life.

The rush by the colonial troopers cleared the top of the hill of the Boer defenders more through bluff than numbers. Now the British artillery could bring up their guns to sweep the retreating enemy on the plain below.

Sam sat back against one of the boulders, drinking from his canteen, and was joined by George.

'We bloody well did it,' George said, retrieving his own canteen. 'But I will be glad to get home and head for the nearest pub for a cold beer and a counter lunch.'

'We're a long way from home, cobber.' Sam sighed with tiredness, the adrenaline now drained from his body. 'Thanks for doing that Boer. If you hadn't spotted him, I doubt that I would be thinking about home right now.'

'What are cobbers for?' George said, and the matter was forgotten as both men knew their war was far from over. This was a war that Sam knew could drag on for years, as the Dutch farmers and their town counterparts bravely showed no signs of admitting defeat against the numerically larger and better-equipped British enemy.

TWENTY-SIX

Sergeant Sam Steele and Corporal George Bowden sat on empty wooden ration boxes by their tents, enjoying a quiet moment to smoke their tobacco pipes. It was a cold, windy day on the veldt, with the southern winter temperatures turning even more bitterly cold at night.

A new officer had joined the squadron, but his reputation for drunkenness and abuse of his soldiers had preceded him. However, Lieutenant Cecil Anderson was from a well-known family in Sydney, so the colonial army superiors turned a blind eye to any criticism of a fellow officer and gentleman. He had only been with Sam's unit for two days and was already despised by the men he commanded for his incompetence and lack of leadership. As far as Sam had heard, the man had not seen any action in the six months he had been posted to South Africa.

'You!'

Sam turned his head to see the newly transferred officer striding towards him and George.

'Yes, you two!'

Sam slowly rose to his feet. As he was not wearing a hat, he simply came to attention as army protocol dictated.

'What are you and the corporal doing lazing about when there is work to be done?' The lieutenant was a mere pace away from Sam. George had also risen to his feet. 'What is your name, Sergeant?'

'Sergeant Samuel Steele . . . sir.' Sam delivered the last word of his reply in a recognisable sneer.

The lieutenant blinked. 'You would not happen to be related to that infamous Jew Colonel Ian Steele of Sydney, perhaps?'

'My father was a Christian. I am a Jew,' Sam replied calmly.

'My Uncle Horace has told me many stories about your family – none of them good,' the officer said disdainfully. 'My uncle is probably known to you, Sergeant. Mr Horace Anderson.'

'I do recall the name,' Sam replied. 'My brother married the woman he had unsuccessfully attempted to woo. I believe my sister-in-law said your uncle had bad breath.'

Sam's attempt at humour caused Anderson's eyes to almost roll into his head. 'I could have you on a charge for insubordination for that remark, Sergeant. As a matter of fact, I think I will, and see how you like field punishment.'

'That might not be wise,' George said. 'I heard your disparaging remarks about Sergeant Steele's family, and I would give evidence to those remarks.'

Anderson turned on George. 'You address me with the proper term of sir,' he snarled, 'or you will be joining Sergeant Steele on a charge for insubordination.'

By this time, a small gaggle of Sam and George's squadron

troopers had ambled over to witness the tense exchange. Anderson could see them out of the corner of his eye and realised that they would be witnesses to any further conversation. 'I will give you a warning just this once, Sergeant, but only once. I do not want to see you lounging around the lines again.'

'With all respect, *sir*, our squadron commander stood us down for the day as we have attended our mounts, weapons and kit to his satisfaction,' Sam said, realising that the uncalled-for attack on him and George had run out of steam.

Anderson turned on his heel and stormed away.

'Good onya, Sarge,' one of the troopers said. 'You're lucky he's not your direct OIC, like we have to suffer.'

Sam nodded to the trooper. 'With any luck, he might come face to face with a big, bearded Boer in a bad mood.'

The small crowd dispersed and Sam resumed his seat on the wooden crate, relit his pipe and turned to George. 'Where were we?' he asked.

George chuckled. 'Maybe considering how we keep out of that bastard's sights in the future?'

'Or maybe in my rifle sights,' Sam said, his rage slowly abating. Sam could even feel his hands trembling as he attempted to relight his pipe. No one slurred his family and walked away. There would be a time and place for the matter to be settled – one way or another.

A call went out that mail had arrived, and the camp came to life as the soldiers immediately made their way to a trooper dispensing the most valued gift from home. Sam and George were amongst the eager crowd waiting for their names to be called, and Sam was not disappointed when he received three letters from Sydney, and George two.

Both men marched back to the improvised chairs outside their tents and slit open the envelopes. Sam was impatient to open one letter in particular, recognising the dainty hand-writing on the front of the envelope.

George glanced across at his friend. 'I would guess from your panting and sweating that you have a letter from Miss Gladys Entwhistle?'

Sam nodded with a broad smile. Gladys was a young lady from a well-to-do family in Sydney whom Sam had met at an afternoon tea party almost a year earlier. She was very pretty and had been pursued by all the eligible men on the day, but it was the tall and broad-shouldered Samuel Steele who attracted her interest. For months, they had engaged in a racy dialogue in their letter exchanges and Sam felt that he had met the woman he would marry when he returned from the war.

George was enjoying the news from his father and feeling the pang of wishing he was once again back at the house on the harbour when he sensed something was wrong. He turned to Sam, who was staring blankly at the flat horizon dotted with small scrub trees.

'Is everything all right?' George asked, concerned.

'Gladys has met someone else and feels that she and I never really had a future together,' Sam answered in a flat voice. 'Apparently the new man in her life is wonderful and gentle and she has accepted his proposal of marriage.'

George shook his head in sympathy. 'Sorry, cobber.' Sam was not the first man in a campaign of war to receive such a letter, and George suspected that he would not be the last.

'Gladys is right about one thing, though; you are not exactly the gentle kind,' George added, attempting to cheer up his friend.

Sam looked down at the dry earth. 'Maybe she is right to find someone else,' he sighed. 'I'm not a sure bet, the way things are going in this war. Who knows if I will survive it? And even if I survive the Boers, bloody illness or disease can take us as quickly as a Mauser round.'

'You don't think like that, Sam, or it might come true,' George said. 'Besides, from what the papers are saying, the Dutchmen are on the run and it will only be a matter of time before we beat them and go home. You'll see.'

Sam rose to his feet, screwed up the letter and walked away. So much for love and war.

★

Josiah had his second cablegram from Bavaria in three years. The first had arrived from Duke Maximillian von Kellermann bearing the tragic news that his beloved wife, Duchess Elise, had died in childbirth with their daughter, leaving Josiah's friend with four motherless children.

This cablegram bore the happier news that von Kellermann would be visiting Sydney with his eldest son, Hermann, aged fifteen years. The German government had sent him on a goodwill visit as a way to quell the animosity towards the Kaiser for his open support of the Boer rebels in South Africa. It was hoped that men who had a link to the Pacific islands colonised by the Germans under the Kaiser might sway some public sympathy towards better relations with the Australian colonies. After all, the German government now had a geographical closeness to the Australian colonies with German New Guinea and other Pacific islands they had annexed.

Josiah was pleased to have the opportunity to once again meet the man he had last spoken to on the deck of the *Ella* in the Huon Gulf fifteen years earlier.

Today was the day Maximillian's ship was due to arrive in Sydney Harbour, and Josiah made arrangements to meet him and his son. No doubt the German army officer would have official meetings with the German Consul General's staff in Sydney before he was free to be a guest of the Steele mansion, but Josiah wanted his old friend to see him on the wharf.

It was a cold and blustery day of showers when Josiah stood with his umbrella on the dock near Circular Quay to watch the European ocean liner steam in and tie up. It was met by a brass band playing welcoming tunes as the passengers came down the gangplanks. Josiah immediately recognised Maximillian in his fine tailored suit. Beside him was a tall young man with the blond hair of his mother and the military bearing of his father. Josiah waved, pushing his way through the crowd that had gathered to welcome friends and family home and European visitors new to the shores.

Maximillian spotted Josiah and waved back. He and his son stepped ashore, but were immediately met by three men Josiah guessed were from the German Consul General. After a few minutes, the welcoming party moved off and Maximillian turned to Josiah, waiting patiently a few yards away.

'My dear friend. It is good to see you,' he said, stepping forward to grip Josiah's extended hand.

'The last time we met was at sea,' Josiah replied.

'And I suspect that you were not there by coincidence,' the German officer said with a faint smile, causing Josiah to squirm.

'We both know how we play by the rules,' Josiah answered honestly. 'All that aside, I was deeply saddened to learn of Elise's passing. I know how much she loved you.'

'I still mourn her death,' Maximillian said, the sadness in his voice a testament to his loss. 'But life goes on, regardless. This is my eldest son, Hermann.' Maximillian turned to his son, who was standing quietly beside him. 'Hermann, this is Captain Steele, who is a dear friend of the family.'

'It is an honour to meet you, Captain Steele,' the boy said in stilted English, clicking his heels in the traditional Prussian salute.

'It is a pleasure meeting you, Master von Kellermann. Your English is very good.'

'My mother insisted that we learn English as she did,' the boy replied. 'It is good I will have the opportunity to practise *mein* English while we are here.'

Closer now, Josiah could see Elise in the boy. Josiah too missed the young girl he had saved on the Palmer River Track so many years earlier.

'I know you will be involved in the protocol of your government with your welcome to Sydney, but hopefully you have time to be my guest at our home. We have guest rooms and I know my family would dearly love to meet you both. My eldest son is fourteen and I am sure will find ways to entertain Hermann.'

'We will be honoured to accept the invitation,' Maximillian said. 'It will be a time to reminisce on the past and talk of the future between the German and British empires in the Pacific.'

After arrangements were made, Maximillian ushered his son to a waiting coach from the German consulate just as the rain grew heavier. Josiah turned, making his way back to his office to confront yet another day of business meetings, reports and decisions on financial prospects. Federation loomed and the customs and excise duties imposed on crossing colonial borders would be abolished. This would have a dramatic impact on a new nation's economy, although the former colonies would retain the right to seek taxation from their state's citizens.

Josiah did not notice a red-haired man standing a short distance away under the protection of an umbrella, observing the meeting of Josiah and Maximillian. Douglas Wade expected his responsibilities would be enhanced to cover all the new states when Federation came in the following year. After all, matters of the nation's defence had been a priority in the agreement for unification under one flag.

★

The order was given that Sam and his men were to carry three days' rations and as much ammunition for their rifles. They were to be part of a force of mounted men pursuing the Boer commanders De Wet and Steyn's convoy of four hundred wagons across the veldt.

It was bitterly cold, and Sam hunched against the cutting wind as they plodded across the vast veldt, but the discomfort was quickly forgotten when the great parade of wagons was sighted on the horizon.

The British artillery guns were brought forward and began shelling the convoy, scattering the armed escort. Upon seeing their enemy flee, the pursuing British and colonials split their force to seize the convoy from the flanks, but one group of twenty-five West Australians chose to intercept a group of Boers by galloping up a small ridge. They had almost reached the summit when the men they were pursuing chose to stand and fight, firing down on the exposed West Australians. The colonial soldiers realised they were very vulnerable and dismounted to seek cover in an old cattle pen nearby, while the rest chose a solid wall of termite nests for protection. Within fifteen minutes, the withering fire from the Boer guerrillas tore into the pinned-down West Australians, wounding seven severely and killing another three.

On the plain below, the Boers chose to defend the wagons and their fierce reputation as tough and courageous fighters deterred one British commander from charging them with the excuse that his horses were exhausted and not capable of an attack. The duty instead fell to the New South Wales colonial soldiers.

Sam glanced at George, whose face was a grim mask as he slid his bayonet onto his rifle.

'Into the fray once more, lads,' Sam yelled with a broad grin to his friend. It was something Sam vaguely remembered from some play he had to read at school.

Already they could hear the crack of Mauser rounds, and even a captured Lee Enfield rifle, as many of the Boers wore captured British khaki uniforms and hats. Their own normal supplies of food, clothing and weapons had been cut off by British operations.

'Charge!'

Sam leaned forward, kicking his mount into a gallop as the colonials advanced into a hail of well-aimed bullets. Three men went down dead in the charge and the Boers expertly fled their defence.

Sam's squadron continued to pursue the fleeing Boers, but the enemy's horses were better rested, and the day came down to being cautious of the Dutch farmers' tactic to use snipers against any pursuers. The tactics worked and the pursuit was called off. The men of the mounted infantry returned to the wagons where talented New South Wales surgeon Captain Bernard Newmarch had improvised a field hospital for the wounded.

After the skirmish, there were rumours in the commanding staff that the colonials had put the regular British cavalry to shame with their aggressive tactics under fire. But that was quickly and conveniently forgotten by the British command.

Sam and George had survived another day and shared their campfire as comrades do. It was then that George pointed out to Sam that a Boer bullet must have nicked his neck, leaving a nasty welt. Sam shrugged and passed George a mug of hot tea he had brewed over the flames. The sky turned dark and the few stars fought to break through between scudding clouds.

'It's funny,' George sighed, the hot tea warming him as they ate the last of their rations. 'I did not see Lieutenant Anderson at all when we were in the thick of it.'

'You didn't hear?' Sam grinned, the flickering flames of the fire revealing his expression. 'He suddenly fell sick before we went into action and reported to the medical officer, regretting fiercely that he would not be able to take part in the squadron's charge on the Boers. The surgeon said he could if he wished, but the gutless bastard insisted his illness would not allow him to do so. What a shame, he might have covered himself in glory.'

George chuckled. No doubt the cowardly officer would one day tell stories of how he was at a place called Palmietfontein where he charged with his men into the jaws of hell.

TWENTY-SEVEN

Rebecca Steele was a spinster in her early thirties. She had the dark beauty of her mother, Ella, inherited from a Russian ancestry. She was intelligent, lively and kind, and many who knew Rebecca – or Becky, as she was affectionately known to family and friends – wondered why she had discounted the many men who attempted to woo her over the years.

There had been times when one or two had come close to winning her heart, but something caused her to shy away when she unconsciously weighed their characters against that of the man she idolised, her father. After a time, she found those rich men with impeccable pedigrees shallow and boring compared to the legendary Colonel Ian Steele.

Becky had resigned herself to life as a matriarch of the Steele family. With Marian away so often, Becky was in charge of the family home. She had a life filled with the love of her brothers, sister-in-law, nieces, nephews and step-mother. What more could she want?

Becky was pleased to welcome Duke Maximillian von Kellermann and his son to stay in the Steele family mansion, regarding it as her duty to ensure their guests received every comfort. The duke captured her attention immediately with his warm smile and charming manners. She knew a little about him from Josiah, who said that he was now a widower, an aristocrat, a serving soldier who had fought the French in the Franco–Prussian war as a young officer with great courage. This handsome man with an aristocratic bearing had much in common with her deceased father, but time would confirm her female instincts.

Hermann opted to dine with Josiah's children early in the evening, where they did not have to be on their best behaviour and could eat as much as they liked. Becky checked in on the children and found they were enjoying a raucous meal. By the end, Hermann had bonded with David over common interests and annoying younger siblings.

As the adults sat down to dinner, she overheard the count say quietly to Josiah, 'I was not aware that you had such a beautiful sister.' Her heart fluttered. Was it that there was such a thing as love at first sight?

★

Later that evening, Josiah and their guest retired to the library to share a bottle of fine port wine and cigars.

'You have a fine house and family,' Maximillian said as he sipped his port and puffed on his cigar. The room was already filling with the sweet scent of the smoke drifting away on a gentle breeze from an open window. Although it was chilly outside, the warmth from a log fire warded off the cold.

'Thank you,' Josiah replied. 'I must compliment your son for his manners. I believe he and my oldest son, David, have become instant friends.'

'That is not like Hermann,' Maximillian said. 'He is usually a reserved boy who has aspirations to entering a military college, following in my footsteps.'

'As I cannot see any future wars ahead of us, you can rest in the knowledge that he will not experience those horrors I know you and I have. A career – even in a peacetime army – has its merits.'

'I am pleased that you think that way, my friend,' Maximillian said. 'The current bad relations between our people are not good, yet the Kaiser insists on supporting the Dutch cause in Africa.'

'Why would he jeopardise the long friendship we have with the German people?' Josiah asked.

Maximillian frowned. 'The Kaiser has a deep hatred for England,' he sighed. 'The last time I was in his court, he expressed this publicly to his officers.'

Josiah was shocked. 'But his mother was our Queen's daughter! From what I know, the Kaiser is very fond of our Queen, as she is of her grandson.'

'I think Willie is envious of the British Empire and wants to show the world that he is an equal,' Maximillian replied. 'He is even throwing his support behind our navy to build dreadnoughts, similar to those Britain possesses. Rule of the sea is rule of the world.'

'Do you believe that Britain and Germany may ever go to war against each other in the future?' Josiah asked, leaning forward to his friend.

'Sadly, with Willie as the Kaiser, there will always be that dreadful possibility,' Maximillian said. 'Europe is a powder keg of nationalist and anarchist zealots, and we cannot predict who will light the fuse to another European conflict not seen since Napoleon swept across the continent. But then, Blucher and Wellington stood shoulder to shoulder to prevent the French dominance of Europe.'

Josiah leaned back in his big leather chair and stared at the dancing flames. 'I pray that there will never be such a war between our two empires,' Josiah said.

Maximillian raised his glass. 'To peace between Germany and England,' he said, and Josiah responded to the toast.

But it had a hollow ring to it.

★

It was a cold day of drizzling rain when the men of Sam's squadron came upon the Boer farm. Led by Lieutenant Anderson, George and Sam knew what the mission was, and it left a bitter taste in their mouths.

Surrounded by Australian gum trees, it could have been any farm in western New South Wales, and this was not lost on the mounted infantry of the squadron. Wispy smoke rose from the stone chimney of the small cottage as half the men dismounted while the rest stood alert to any Boer fighters in the district.

'You, Sergeant, and the corporal with you, follow me,' Anderson barked when he had dismounted.

Sam slid from his horse as did George, rifles in hand. They reluctantly followed the officer to the front door, where Anderson hammered, demanding entry. After a short time, a middle-aged woman wearing a bonnet answered, fear written across her features.

'You speak English?' Anderson demanded, thrusting forward into the terrified woman's face. She shook her head and turned to call something into the cottage.

'You have ten minutes to pack your belongings and get out of this house, which we will burn, along with any other outbuildings. Do you understand, woman?'

Again, she shook her head and retreated into the house.

'You two. Search for any signs of complicity with the enemy,' Anderson commanded. 'See if you can find any small arms or ammunition.'

Anderson stepped into the house. A photo of two proud men sporting thick beards and displaying their Mauser rifles with ammunition bandoliers slung across their chests was on display. Anderson ripped it off the wall, smashing it to the ground, splintering the glass from the frame.

The woman shrieked in despair and scrambled for the remnants. It had been a photo of her husband and son, now long dead after battling the invaders of their independent republic.

Anderson kicked her as she was on her knees sobbing.

Instantly, Sam stepped protectively forward. 'No need for that, sir,' he said, holding his rifle across his chest. 'Bad enough that the woman is about to lose every worldly possession she owns in the middle of winter.'

Anderson looked into Sam's eyes and blinked. 'Be careful, Sergeant Steele. You are facing disciplinary charges if you dare interfere with a commissioned officer of the Queen.' But Anderson took a step back when he saw the smouldering menace in the big sergeant's eyes and turned to George, who had emerged from a side room, ushering four children ranging in age from three to fourteen. The eldest was a blonde-haired girl whose terror-stricken look did not hide her beauty. Sam could see a strange expression on Cecil Anderson's face that he did not like.

'No sign of any weapons or ammo, sir,' George said. 'Just another poor Dutchie family tryin' to eke out a living here.' George's sarcasm was lost on Anderson, who was still fixated on the pretty blonde girl.

'I think this family has had enough time to get their belongings together, Sergeant. Get them out of the house before we torch it,' Anderson demanded.

'Sir, with all due respect, they do not understand anything we have told them. I think they should be given the chance to gather up personal belongings of a valuable nature to them,' Sam countered.

'You saw the photograph on the wall, Sergeant. It demonstrates to me that they are in league with the enemy and have most probably been giving them succour.'

'It looked like a photograph of her husband and son,' Sam challenged. 'Who knows if they are still alive?'

'Just get the family out – but leave the girl,' Anderson said with a glazed look. 'I wish to interrogate her away from her mother.'

'She does not speak English,' Sam countered. 'She is better off accompanying her mother in these traumatic moments.'

'You heard me, Sergeant. Leave now and close the door after you. You are forbidden to re-enter unless on my explicit orders.'

Sam turned to George and both soldiers ushered the terrified woman and her children into the wet, cold front yard, where they looked up at the mounted soldiers with their rifles on their hips wearing the slouch hat popular with their own men in the field.

They were hardly out in the yard when Sam heard a scream from the girl they had left with the despised officer. Without hesitating, Sam turned and smashed his shoulder into the door, flinging it open, where he saw that the front of the young girl's dress had been ripped down, revealing her small breasts. Anderson was attempting to force her down on the rough wooden dining table, but she was fighting back with all her strength.

Sam brought up his rifle and levelled it at Anderson. 'Let the girl go or I swear I will put a bullet in your head,' he snarled.

Anderson immediately let her go and stood up defiantly, adjusting his uniform. 'You have gone too far this time, Sergeant Steele. I will see you arrested immediately.'

'I don't think so . . . sir,' Sam sneered. 'Rape – or attempted rape – is an offence punishable by death under military regulations, even for officers.'

For a moment, Anderson appeared confused, then the realisation dawned on him that there were two of his troopers standing in the doorway, observing the scene. Troopers Brendan and Nate Welsh held their rifles in a threatening way that made it plain they would not hesitate to shoot if ordered by Sergeant Steele. Anderson knew his threat was useless with so many witnesses.

'She attacked me, and I was forced to restrain her,' he replied weakly. 'Thank God you came in when you did.'

Sam glanced at the girl, who had retreated to a corner, where she crouched, attempting to cover her breasts with the ripped dress. In the little of the Boer language he had learned from his years on the African goldfields before the war, he asked, 'Did this man try to have his way with you?'

The girl nodded vigorously, and Anderson appeared stunned that his sergeant was speaking in the enemy's language.

'She agreed that you attempted to molest her,' Sam said. 'I am sure that she would give evidence to the fact in any court of law. But we can let the matter stay here and proceed with real soldiering and not your idea of fighting the Boer.

I know it has been you who has volunteered us for all the farm burnings.'

Anderson knew he was cornered and nodded his head. 'I will not volunteer the section for any more farm raids,' he replied, walking stiffly past Sam to his horse.

The farmhouse was conveniently overlooked and was not put to the torch. The woman and her family were left alone to gather the remnants of their life in the harsh land they had fought for long ago.

At least Anderson was true to his word and Sam had burned his last farm.

★

The day cruising the harbour on the Steele motor launch was only dampened by scudding showers, but Becky conveniently found that the enclosed cabin gave her the opportunity to converse with Maximillian. Becky impressed him with her grasp of German, which she explained was one of the languages she spoke, along with French and Italian.

Josiah noticed the warm exchange between his sister and his German friend and was surprised. It was obvious while they cruised the harbour that Maximillian hardly took notice of the tree-lined foreshores and cottages on the northern side. Becky and Maximillian were deep in conversation, switching from German to English and back. She was laughing at things Maximillian said, and Josiah swore that he saw his sister touch the usually reserved Prussian on the hand.

Josiah shook his head; who would have known?

★

It was just another routine day scouting the veldt for retreating Boer commandoes. The icy-cold barbs of rain bit through the khaki uniforms of the patrol, under the orders of the squadron commander and led by a sullen Lieutenant Cecil Anderson.

George and Sam rode side by side, always scanning the flat land studded by low, rocky outcrops that formed a perfect position for enemy snipers. The troopers of the mounted infantry scouting party of ten men remained silent, hunched against the wet and cold conditions, wishing they could return to camp and indulge in a mug of hot tea and shelter from the rain.

In the distance was one *kopje* that was larger than the surrounding outcrops. The rain had brought some green to the African grasses but made the footing slippery for the mounts.

'Halt,' Anderson said, holding up his hand and surveying the *kopje*, which Sam calculated was about five hundred yards away. Anderson took a set of binoculars from a leather case at his waist and peered through them. He sat back in the saddle, looking around at his small scouting party.

'Corporal Bowden, I want you to ride directly to the high ground to our front and see if there are any enemy located there.'

'Sir?' Sam said. 'It might be wiser to flank the *kopje*.'

Anderson turned to Sam with anger in his eyes. 'I gave an order, and it will be obeyed.'

George glanced at Sam and shrugged, withdrawing his rifle from the leather bucket and spurring his horse into a gallop. Sam watched his friend with a feeling of dread. If there was anyone on the high ground, they had a perfect shot at the horseman riding directly towards them.

'Sir, we could still provide cover for Corporal Bowden if we advance out to one side on a flank,' Sam protested, but was met with a steely stare by the junior officer.

'Corporal Bowden knows his job, which is more than I can say for you, Sergeant Steele.'

Sam felt rage boiling up. How the man had ever been commissioned struck Sam as ludicrous. The decision to send a lone man against a potentially lethal position was akin to murder.

They saw George fall before the gunshot was heard.

'Withdraw!' Anderson screamed in a shrill, terrified voice. Sam sat stunned by the sight of George lying under his badly wounded horse, and could see that George was struggling to pull himself away from the mount, which was thrashing in its death throes.

Sam did not turn about with the rapidly retreating troop, noticing that Anderson was well and truly galloping in front of the troopers, heading back to the main body of the advancing mounted infantry regiment. Only the two recruited Kiwi troopers remained with Sam.

'We can go out and get him back,' Brendan said, rifle in hand.

'Just give me covering fire,' Sam answered, galloping at breakneck speed towards George's position. As Sam lay low over the neck of his panting horse, he could hear the crack of Mauser rounds around his head. He slid the horse to a halt beside George, who had been able to extract himself from under the dead animal.

'Sam! Get away from here!' George yelled up at his friend as Sam leapt from his mount. 'I'm done for. My legs are broken!'

'I'll get you out of here,' Sam yelled, slinging his rifle over his shoulder and leaning down to grip George under the armpits and pull him to his own mount nearby. But the hail of bullets from the high ground continued, and Sam felt the sting of one grazing his shoulder.

George grunted and went limp in Sam's grip. Horrified, Sam could see that half George's head had exploded from one of the high-velocity rifle rounds, splattering Sam's face with bone, brain and blood. It was obvious the wound was fatal, and Sam dropped George to the wet earth.

The heavy rain now falling must have spoiled the accuracy of the incoming rifle rounds. Sam guessed that there was a small party on the high ground, and he was now alone.

Sam dragged George's lifeless body onto his shoulders and staggered to his mount, throwing him over the front of the saddle and taking hold of the reins to walk his mount away.

Sam could not know that the Boers firing upon him had seen the courageous act and ceased shooting at the man walking beside the horse with the body of his fallen comrade slung over it. They, too, understood the meaning of courage.

Sam trudged in the rain towards the main column, hardly aware that the bullets had stopped. He reached the Kiwi brothers, who were waiting for him out of range of any accurate sniping.

'It was bloody murder to send George out there,' Nate growled. 'That bastard deserves to be court-martialled.'

Sam silently agreed, and gave the order for them to return to the squadron commander's position. The rain concealed the tears streaming down his face as they withdrew. All the time, Sam swore that there would be a reckoning.

TWENTY-EIGHT

Sam reached the main column of his regiment in the rain. Two troopers met him and the Kiwi brothers.

'Bloody hell!' one of the troopers swore. 'They got old George.'

Sam glanced up at the squadron commander sitting astride his horse, watching Sam. Beside the squadron commander sat Anderson.

'That bastard Anderson got George killed,' Sam snarled quietly. 'He and I are going to square off over this.'

Sam let go of the reins of the horse he was leading and strode towards his squadron commander.

'Sir, I wish to speak with you privately,' he said, gazing up at a man he respected for his leadership.

'Over there, Sergeant Steele,' the major said, pointing to a single scrubby tree. 'There we will talk.'

Sam followed the mounted infantry major to the tree,

where he dismounted. 'I am sorry to see Corporal Bowden dead,' the major said wearily, wiping the rain from his face with his gloved hand. 'I know he was a personal friend of you and your family.'

'He was murdered,' Sam responded savagely. 'He should never have been sent forward without us covering the flanks.'

'Mr Anderson made the decision, and I have to respect that of one of my officers, Sergeant Steele,' the major replied calmly. 'These unfortunate things happen in war.'

'Not when we are being led by competent men, sir,' Sam replied. 'Anderson should not even be in charge of a dunny wagon, let alone some of the finest men from the colony.'

'That is for me to decide, Sergeant,' the major snapped back. 'I will call for a report from Mr Anderson as to the incident and make any decisions based on my findings. In the meantime, you have a duty to your section, which will need your guidance in the aftermath of Corporal Bowden's death.' He stared thoughtfully at Sam. 'I have always wondered why you did not take a commission when I know about the fine service your father and brother have given for the Queen and Empire. You have all the credentials for a commission in my regiment, and I know that you are one of the finest non-commissioned officers I have.'

Sam reflected on the words of his respected commanding officer, who had been a successful grazier and militia officer in Bathurst before enlisting to serve in the South African campaign. 'Sir, I considered taking a commission, but felt that I would have to live up to the high standard set by my father and brother. It was easier to just be in the fight without proving myself.'

'Well, Sergeant Steele,' the major said. 'You have done that many times. The fact that you refused to leave Corporal

Bowden behind merits official recognition. I will be recommending you for a military decoration for your courageous act. For now, we need to carry on the advance.'

With these parting words, he walked back to his horse and rode back to the head of the column to consult with his subordinate officer, leaving Sam alone to ponder the commanding officer's parting words. It was not the mention of official recognition for his act of bravery but the implied message that it should have been he and not Anderson in command. If it had been so, George might still be alive. A sergeant must follow an officer's orders – even the hated Lieutenant Anderson – whom all the troopers of the squadron despised for his incompetence and cowardice.

★

Josiah met regularly with his old schoolboy friend Douglas Wade at the exclusive Australia Club. For the last fifteen years, Douglas Wade had been posted as a permanent staff member to the Queen's colonial representative, known in New South Wales as the governor-general. He had married and had two children, and lived a comfortable life in one of the harbour city's better suburbs. Josiah had noticed that his old friend was always vague about his exact role in the office he held with the colonial government.

At this meeting, Douglas gave away a little of his real role. 'We have observed that your Prussian friend appears to be more in your sister's company than your own,' he said casually, but Josiah could read between the words.

'There is not much that the duke has exposed to me of any strategic value, and it appears that my sister and Max enjoy each other's company,' Josiah answered, leaning back into his leather armchair. 'One might even suspect that my sister is smitten by his charm.'

'We do know that your friend is making contact with a lot of influential Germans living in Sydney,' Douglas said, sipping his gin and tonic. 'Merchants and leading members of the colonial government. International relations are a little strained between Britain and the German Empire at the moment, so it seems queer that the duke should suddenly visit our shores.'

'Are you implying that he is involved in espionage?' Josiah asked, and knew he sounded annoyed at the insinuation.

'No . . . no! But it is our duty to be ever vigilant in these troubled times. I would request that you report any suspicions to the governor-general's office.'

Josiah swished his scotch around the ice cubes before answering. 'I think that goes without saying, old chap.'

'I thought as much,' Douglas replied. 'Old friend, I must excuse myself for a meeting this afternoon, but look forward to having the wife and kids over at your place soon for dinner.'

Josiah nodded as Douglas excused himself and walked away. Josiah remained, deep in thought, pondering the point that Douglas had made about the timing of Maximillian's visit to Australia. Maximillian had once said during a casual conversation that he had been chosen by the Kaiser because he had experience in the Pacific, spoke English and was thus the appropriate person for the goodwill mission. Now Josiah had his doubts, as he also had been assigned a similar mission in the past to learn about German intentions. However, it seemed that if Maximillian was on a covert mission, Becky was sabotaging his efforts with the time she spent with him on picnics, boat cruises and dinners. Her German had improved considerably and when she was at home, she wandered around the sprawling mansion like a lovesick girl.

He stared at his remaining scotch, wondering how his beloved brother Sam was faring across the Indian Ocean in Africa. With a touch of guilt, Josiah wished he was with Sam, but he had long promised Marian that his days of dangerous adventure were over, and now he had a family that needed him.

Marian had sent a telegram to say she would return within the week, and even though Josiah knew she would have to leave again soon for South Australia, he had begun to count down the days until he could hold her again in his arms.

★

Corporal George Bowden was buried in the earth of Africa with full military protocols. Sam stood with the honour guard, remembering the man who had served alongside his brother in the Sudan and now with him in the Transvaal. Sam had already written a letter to George's father, who still worked at the Steele residence. It was the hardest letter Sam had ever written.

A newly appointed corporal was assigned to Sam's section of the squadron. He was a man Sam knew well, and was pleased to see him promoted. Corporal Nate Welsh had a fine reputation as a reliable trooper and an instinct in understanding horses, which Sam thought was amusing because he had been forced to learn to ride after a stint with a foot infantry battalion. Nate was a quick learner, but he was not George Bowden. However, Sam warmed to him as Nate was prepared to listen and learn. In the meantime, Nate's brother, Brendan, was promoted to lance corporal. Sam hoped the promotions would not cause any family friction between the two Kiwi brothers.

Sam walked away from the grave when they were dismissed and knew he would go to his tent, find the hidden bottle of rum and drink in private to George's memory. The tears were gone and only the war ahead mattered as George joined the long list of battle casualties in this never-ending conflict.

Alone in his tent, Sam found that he was homesick and now knew what Josiah had warned him about when he had volunteered to fight. This war had cost him the girl he thought loved him, his freedom to simply go where he wanted, and now his best friend. He shuddered when he remembered how he had been splattered with George's brains, blood and skull fragments and felt guilty that it was George and not he who now lay under the African earth, so far from friends, family and home. For a moment, Sam considered that he might be joining George soon and experienced the darkness of despair.

'Sarge, just got told we are moving out in a couple of hours.' It was the voice of his new corporal through the tent flap.

'Okay, Corp,' Sam answered. 'I'll get my kit together and join the squadron assembly.'

Sam snapped out of his melancholy, knowing that there was a small band of men who needed him to keep them alive as best as he could. No doubt another patrol – but to where?

When briefed, a few groaned as their duty was revealed: to guard a great pile of supplies.

'Why not the infantry?' someone asked.

'Because we have the duty,' was the simple reply.

Sam did not care. At least sitting around the supplies meant a chance to get at the rum inevitably in the depot. Besides, it got the men away from the dangers of patrolling after the elusive and dangerous Boer commandoes.

'Where are we going, sir?' Sam asked his squadron commander.

'Some place called Elands River, Sergeant,' he answered.
'The rest of the squadron has orders to join a British column.
Sorry it had to be your section, but that's the army for you.
From what I've heard, you will be joined with our brother
contingents from the other colonies.'

Before they reached the depot, Anderson had disappeared from the squadron. The rumour was that he was to
be shipped back to Sydney on medical grounds.

Sam smiled grimly to himself. The squadron commander
had obviously taken Anderson's report and made a decision.
That left Sam temporarily in charge of his section of troops.
At least their task of guarding a great pile of bully beef tins,
bags of flour and even bottles of rum at some out-of-the-
way British supply depot meant seeing little action until a
new officer was appointed to lead them.

★

The change in Becky was obvious. She was happier than
Josiah had ever seen her, but this day Josiah noticed that
a different mood had come over his sister at the breakfast
table. She spoke little and appeared nervous. Josiah did not
ask if anything was upsetting her as he had the feeling things
had gone awry between her and Max, and he had enough
sense to let his sister come to him when she felt she needed
a shoulder to cry on.

Josiah reached his office and was met by his secretary.

'Sir, you have a visitor waiting for you in your office,'
Tom said. 'It is the duke. I ensured that he was given a coffee
while he waited.'

Josiah thanked his personal assistant, took a deep breath
and walked into his office to see Maximillian standing by
his window, gazing down at the shipping on the harbour.

Josiah greeted his friend with as much cheerfulness as he

could muster, as he had a feeling he was about to hear bad news concerning Becky and Maximillian.

'It is a fine harbour,' Maximillian said, turning to greet Josiah. 'I can see why the British navy use it as a port base.'

'It's also good for fishing and simply sailing the waters,' Josiah replied.

Maximillian placed his cup and saucer on a small table and Josiah could feel the tension between them.

'Josiah, my friend, I have something of extreme importance to speak with you about. It concerns Rebecca,' Maximillian said.

'I think I know what you wish to discuss,' Josiah said, walking to the window to stand beside the Prussian army officer.

'Has Rebecca already said something?' Maximillian asked with a note of surprise. 'She said it was my duty to speak with you.'

Josiah shook his head. 'No, but I did notice this morning at the breakfast table she was very silent for a woman who likes to talk.'

Maximillian appeared to relax, and even smiled. 'Ah, but the duty has been left with me,' he replied. 'I know this might be a shock to you, but I have come here this morning to ask for your sister's hand in marriage.'

Josiah gasped. 'You wish to marry my sister?'

'Only with your permission,' Maximillian replied. 'I did not think I would ever find love again, but the time I have spent in Rebecca's company has proved me wrong. She is a truly remarkable woman who even my son likes, just as I hope all my children would accept her as my wife and their stepmother.'

Josiah was still in shock. Such a marriage would make the Bavarian duke his brother-in-law. For a moment, he remained silent, mulling over the request, and he could see the tension in the Prussian's demeanour.

'You know we are of the Jewish faith,' Josiah finally said. 'And I believe that you are a Catholic.'

'No, I am a Lutheran by faith, and was required to promise to Elise's priests that our children would be raised as Catholics.'

Josiah chuckled. 'Your family is not unlike my own. But you would be marrying a Jewess.'

'Many in the new Germany have such marriages. Religion is not a bar to love.'

Josiah held out his hand to his friend and future brother-in-law. 'Then you have my blessings on the union.'

Maximillian took the strong grip and broke into a broad smile. 'I promise that I will love, cherish and care for Rebecca for the rest of our lives. I swear that she will never want for anything.'

'I think I will be telling my staff I will not be at my desk today,' Josiah said. 'We have a tradition in the colonies that such an announcement requires a celebration. Time for us to find a good hotel and uncork a bottle of champagne to celebrate a union of our two families. Now we will both have nephews and nieces on the other side of the world.'

It was a rather inebriated Josiah who passed on the news to his nervously waiting sister that she was to marry the prince of her dreams. Becky almost broke her brother's neck when she hugged him, crying as she did so.

Josiah had never understood why women cried when they were happy.

TWENTY-NINE

Sam reported to the senior officer of the New South Wales contingent and was welcomed to the squadron at Elands River, albeit on detachment from his own regiment of mounted infantry. Sam was briefed that they were guarding around a hundred thousand pounds' worth of stores, but none thought there would be any trouble.

'The bloody British ride off to gather glory and leave us sons of convicts to guard the stores,' Sam said to the commanding officer, Major Thomas, a solicitor from Tenterfield who was also a journalist and had held a commission with a militia unit before the current campaign. He struck Sam as being competent and saw the slight smile on the officer's face.

'Some of my men have said that this is a good break from chasing the Dutchmen from hilltop to hilltop and burning farms,' Thomas replied.

Sam saluted and returned to his huddle of men preparing their camp and looking amongst the New South Wales troopers for anyone they might know. In all, Sam begrudgingly agreed with the commanding officer's summation that the protection of the mountain of stores was a break from watching farmhouses burn under General Kitchener's scorched earth policy.

'What's for dinner, lads?' Sam asked.

One of his men grinned as he dragged a wooden crate marked as tinned meat from his tent, and Lance Corporal Welsh produced a bottle of rum. Sam had heard rumours that the Kiwi brothers had enlisted to stay one step ahead of the law; Sam did not ask how he had obtained the meat or rum, knowing how grateful his detachment was for the lance corporal's dubious skills.

That evening, they sat around a campfire, eating bully beef with hardtack biscuits and sharing the bottle of rum.

'Promise I'll do better tomorrow,' Lance Corporal Welsh said when the rum was gone and again, Sam did not ask how.

★

Like all good soldiers, Sam attempted to keep a low profile for his section and avoid the tedious tasks of sentry duty and camp chores, but this did not work and for the next couple of days his troop was engaged in the mundane tasks of manhandling wooden crates, sacks of flour and ammunition. But it gave his men an opportunity to pilfer a couple of bottles of rum and Sam found himself supervising the labour around the camp.

He had just given his section a rest from the backbreaking work to have a mug of tea and a smoke when a column rode in led by a senior officer Sam recognised from previous operations as Lieutenant Colonel Hore, a commander of the Queensland Mounted Infantry. His men looked weary and had the air of soldiers who had been in constant fighting. As for their leader, he appeared to be suffering a fever and was weakened with what seemed to be malaria. Sam learned from one of the Queensland troopers that they had been in a running fight with a strong Boer commando.

'I think the Dutchies are a bit closer than we thought,' Corporal Welsh said.

Sam nodded. 'Boys, I think your job has changed. Find shovels and picks.'

The men knew that such items were in short supply and guessed that Sam had sensed something only an experienced soldier would. They were right.

The depot broke into a new atmosphere of frantic fortification, using the bags of flour, crates of tinned foods and wagons to build a defensive perimeter around the relatively small, stony, flat-topped hill, surrounded by high ground on all sides. Sam could see that the defence was puny and gazed at the surrounding hills, knowing that an enemy would occupy them and be able to besiege the depot.

Sam also knew that the Boer commandoes were very low on supplies, and here was a goldmine of food, clothing and ammunition to take.

'Sergeant Steele,' a voice called as his men went about their task of building improvised defensive works. Sam turned to see a young lieutenant striding towards him.

'Sir,' Sam replied, standing to attention.

The officer was from the Queensland Mounted Infantry unit that had just joined them, bringing their complement to around five hundred defenders. 'I have been informed that your New South Wales troopers are experienced men. We need someone to ride to a farmhouse to deliver a message for HQ. Get your men into battle kit and report to Colonel Hore's HQ.'

'Yes, sir,' Sam replied, and turned to his men, who were sweating as they attempted to dig away at the rocky ground. 'Hand over the shovels and pick up your kit for a ride out of here,' he said. The troopers gladly ceased their attempts to penetrate the solid earth and quickly returned to their lines to retrieve all they would need for a patrol.

Sam was briefed by a junior officer with an envelope and map. 'You are to ride to this farmhouse,' he said, pointing to a place on the map. 'You are to hand over the envelope to the farmer and return to the depot. Do you have any questions, Sergeant?'

'No, sir,' Sam replied. 'I know the place. We passed it on our way in.'

'Good,' the young officer said. 'It is vital that HQ learn that we may be in a bit of a sticky spot. We have uncon-firmed reports that a strong Boer force under de la Rey of possibly three thousand or more men is making its way to us. As you can see, the odds are not in our favour.'

Sam accepted the envelope and made his way back to his troop. Corporal Welsh had already prepared Sam's steed and he swung himself into the saddle.

'Our mission is simple,' Sam said to his mounted men. 'We are now glorified postmen.'

The small troop departed the depot as feverish activity went on to fortify it.

They reached the farmhouse an hour later without inci-dent and were met by a young Englishwoman, to whom Sam passed the envelope as instructed. She read the contents and tore up the letter. Sam knew that she could not be intercepted by Boer scouts with the dispatch on her.

'Good luck,' Sam said to her as she rode off to deliver the vital intelligence. He turned his patrol around to return to the Elands River depot. On the way back, Sam noticed movement up towards the hills and used his binoculars to survey the scene.

'Boers!' he said aloud. 'A bloody lot of the buggers.' Even as a mere senior non-commissioned officer, he could surmise that they were now being enveloped by the Boer commandoes. Using his spurs, Sam kicked his mount into a gallop, making haste with his small patrol to provide a report on what he and his troop had observed. If what the Queensland officer had told him was correct, they were vastly outnumbered and in a dire situation.

What Sam did not know was that Colonel Hore already knew that the Boers were armed with field artillery, and all they had to respond with was an obsolete artillery gun of dubious reliability and two Maxim machine guns. At least they had an army surgeon from Queensland, who had a crude form of aid post constructed of crates of tinned jam and flour bags daubed with mud in an attempt to disguise them from any enemy observers.

Sam informed his commanding officer of his men's readiness to take their place in the defences under his command. He was not about to allow his troop to be dispersed to other units; they were as close as his own family.

Nothing happened for the first day. Some soldiers questioned if all the frantic work had been for naught. It was the last day of July, and a patrol that had been sent out to reconnoitre the area around Elands River returned with two badly wounded troopers. The patrol reported that the Boer commandoes were commandeering cattle from surrounding farms and burning the grasslands to deprive stock of feed around the British outpost. The appearance of the two wounded troopers returning to the depot camp silenced any doubters of a possible major attack on them.

Stone fortifications had now been constructed in a crescent shape facing outward with barbed wire to their front. The impromptu stone walls had been named after the officers responsible for their defence. The two main sangers came to be called Butters after the tough Rhodesian officer and his battle-hardened men, and the second after their commander, Richard Zouch, who had been a grazier in his fifties from Bungendore. Each small fortress had been chosen for a good field of fire at the surrounding hills overlooking the depot.

They reached the third day of August with still no sign of an attack. That night, a singalong was held in the ten hectares of improvised defences of the depot.

Sam retired with his troop to their tiny camp set amongst the larger camp of New South Wales mounted infantry to enjoy their now traditional tot of rum with coffee they had also purloined. They sat in a circle around the small campfire under constellations that the bushmen of his troop knew well from riding the plains of the colony.

'I heard that Colonel Hore has a reputation for cowardice from the siege of Mafeking,' Corporal Welsh said to Sam sitting beside him. 'Not the best man to command us.'

'I wouldn't take much notice of rumours,' Sam replied. 'He is not the only officer we have here if things go wrong.'

Nate nodded. He had come to learn that Sam was not a man who put much stock in rumours but judged a man on what he personally observed. 'I reckon we can hold off any attacks they try to make on our defences with our rifles and bayonets.'

'From what I have seen the boys constructing, I reckon you are right,' Nate said, finishing his coffee and rum. 'We might even die of boredom.'

Sam hoped so, because from all that he had been able to glean from different sources of intelligence, their chances of survival were extremely poor if the Boers attacked in force. So long as they did not have artillery, there was the chance they might – just might – hold out if quickly relieved. Sam sat on his empty crate as his men retired to their tents to snatch as much sleep as they could after the long, physically exhausting day of hard labour.

Sam's thoughts wandered to home, and he hoped that mail might be sent to the depot. It did not matter how old the news was; simply being able to look at the handwriting and see the personal touch from so far away raised his spirits.

Sam sighed, rose from the crate and disappeared into the tent he shared with his corporal, who was already deep in sleep and snoring softly.

★

The sun rose and Sam organised his section to fetch breakfast after the predawn stand-to had been stood down. Sam was shaving with his cutthroat razor and a small mirror attached to a tent pole when he heard the crack of rifle fire.

Sam quickly wiped his face and snatched up his rifle, chambered a round and cast about for his troop. Men stood looking around with confused expressions until an explosion erupted on the hilltop, soon followed by many others. What Sam had dreaded had materialised; high-explosive artillery shells rained down on the small hilltop, spraying men and animals with red-hot shrapnel and concussive blasts of air that could smash a man's internal organs. The hard rock also became lethal when it erupted from the artillery explosions, and soldiers scrambled for the nearest trench or barricade of boxes.

Sam lay flat on the earth, clutching his rifle. It was chaos as the ground around him was littered with smashed wagons, broken shale and pieces of the animals blown apart by the deadly barrage. His ears were ringing and from where he lay, Sam could see the puffs from the barrels of the Boer artillery guns and counted a six-second delay before the shells slammed down on their woefully exposed position. The word *hopeless* seemed to define the present moment, and Sam realised that his main duty was to the safety of his men.

Despite the hilltop being swept by artillery and the rapid-firing pom-poms, he needed to locate his troop and ensure they were safe. It was then that a one-pound pom-pom shell exploded near him, and he felt the red–hot metal slash fragments into his lower leg. Sam cried out in pain as he realised that the depot was now being swept with machine gun and rifle fire from the Boers on the surrounding hilltops.

THIRTY

Sam felt his leg give way and fell heavily onto the rocky earth. Small arms fire and high explosive continued to be dropped on the improvised fortified hilltop as he lay on the ground, observing one of the artillery shells explode a few yards away. When the dust settled, Sam could see that it had torn the leg off a trooper, the severed limb slamming into a nearby defender. Sam could hear the plaintive cries of another trooper who'd had his arm ripped off and was rocking back and forth, begging for someone to put him out of his agonising misery.

Sam could taste dirt and acrid smoke.

'Over here, Sarge!'

Sam recognised the voice of Corporal Welsh calling to him from a shallow trench a few yards away, and dragged himself to the opening on the hilltop where hands grabbed him, pulling him to relative safety. He fell and the pain in his leg caused him to yelp like a whipped dog.

'You look like you copped a bad wound, Sarge,' Lance Corporal Brendan Welsh observed. 'We need to get you to the aid post.' But the artillery barrage continued unabated, spraying deadly jagged shards of red-hot metal across the colonial defences. Sam gritted his teeth and was surprised to find that he was still gripping his rifle in his hand.

'Do you think the Dutchies will make an attack when the shelling lifts?' Brendan asked.

'We have to presume that they will,' Sam answered, but the shelling continued all day, with around a thousand explosive shells, rifle and pom-pom fire falling on the outnumbered defenders, tearing into flour bags, stacks of tinned goods and wooden crates used to fortify the defences and scattering the contents.

*

The Boer commander's aim was simple. Koos de la Rey had the numbers and firepower to overwhelm the few defenders of the well-stocked British depot. He would simply bombard the outpost and cut the defenders off from their water supply, located below the hill, and force them to surrender. On the first day, this seemed feasible.

His best marksmen had taken up well-concealed sniping positions around the depot. The Mauser rifle had a reputation for long-range, accurate shots using smokeless powder, and so didn't give away their positions. Added to the small arms fire was the chatter of his Maxim machine guns raking the hilltop.

The colonial Australians had provided the Boer artillery men with their targets the night before by the location of their campfires, and the five modern artillery guns rained hell on them. From his considerable experience fighting the British, de la Rey believed it was merely a couple of days before he would see the white flag fluttering on the hill. He had observed one of the exploding shells destroy the telegraph line, which meant all communications with the outside world were now destroyed, and the Boer commander had a plan to ambush any possible reinforcements or relieving force sent to raise the siege.

★

From the relative safety of the trench, Sam observed that the Boer gunners had concentrated a lot of their targeting on the horses and cattle, guessing that the Boers were attempting to deny any mobility to escape the outpost. But a small party of Queenslanders under the command of their officer, Lieutenant Annat, crawled forward while the shells were falling, and took aim at a Boer crew manning a rapid-firing pom-pom, forcing the enemy crew to take cover. The only response to the Boer artillery was from the single, outdated gun in the possession of the Australians, which fired just two rounds before malfunctioning. Sam was surprised to note that the Boers had not mounted an assault when they could see they vastly outnumbered the defenders.

When night fell, the troopers used their bayonets to dig and extend their trench fortifications. Sam used the cloaking darkness to crawl to the aid post for medical assistance for his badly lacerated leg. When he reached the makeshift post, he saw the Queensland army surgeon working on a soldier with shrapnel wounds to his back, the feeble light of kerosene lamps the only illumination for his delicate work of removing pieces of metal. When he had finished, he turned to Sam, who was leaning against the wall of crates, and examined his leg.

'You are lucky,' the surgeon said. 'The shrapnel does not appear to have made contact with any bones. I can cleanse the wound and remove any shrapnel I find. After that, all I can do is dress the wound. No sense telling you to go home and get plenty of bed rest,' he added with a touch of black humour. 'I had a trooper in early this afternoon who had the bottom half of his leg sheared off, and all I could do was seal off the stump. When I had stitched him up, he had immediately crawled back to his post to continue his duties.'

'Thanks, sir,' Sam said, and reflected how he was indeed lucky as he still had his leg.

Using his rifle as a crutch, Sam hobbled back to the trench to find that his section had already prepared a meal, using candles under the cover of planks to illuminate a repast of bully beef and biscuits. Sam gratefully accepted a mug of tea, attempting to ignore the throbbing pain in his leg, which was now wrapped with blood-soaked bandages.

'They never came,' Nate said, sipping his tea. 'Maybe tomorrow at first light, they might come.'

'Why should they risk their troops when all they have to do is sit back and blast us off the hill with their bloody artillery guns?' Sam said. 'I think that their plan is to continue shelling us to force a surrender.'

'Sarge, how do you feel?' Brendan Welsh asked. 'We were a bit worried that the doc might amputate your leg.'

'No, it seems that all I have is a few deep cuts. It's not as bad as it looks.'

'Sergeant Steele.'

'Here,' he answered the call of his name from the edge of the trench, and a burly figure crawled into the opening in the earth. Sam saw it was a warrant officer from HQ.

'Heard you copped a wound today,' the sergeant major said, eyeing the blood-soaked bandages around Sam's leg.

'Nothing to put me out of action, sir,' Sam replied.

'Good. We have a job for you and your boys,' the warrant officer grunted. 'We need to use the night to go down to the river and fill up as many canteens as we can, and as I heard you boast that you have the best section in the post, I figured you would be just the men for the job.'

'You heard right, sir.' Sam grinned. 'We will save the depot from the Boers.'

The sergeant major returned the grin, slapping Sam on the shoulder. 'Good show, Sergeant Steele,' he said. 'The canteens will be dropped off here in a few minutes, when the passwords for the night's challenge will be given to you and your route of exit and entry also provided. Sergeant Steele, with your current medical condition, you will not be a part of the water supply patrol. Any questions?' There were none and the warrant officer departed the trench, leaving Sam with his men.

Sam swallowed down his disappointment at not being the one to lead his men out into the night, then turned to Nate. 'Corporal Welsh, you will pick two volunteers to go with you. I presume that your brother will be one of the volunteers.'

The water canteens were delivered, and the water patrol disappeared into the darkness, leaving Sam to fret about their safety on such a dangerous mission. Hours later, in the early morning before sunrise, his men returned safely.

'The Dutchies were not down on our side of the river,' Nate reported, and only then was Sam able to snatch some sleep.

When the sun rose, the intensive shelling recommenced, turning the overcast day into hell as the ground shook and shrapnel sought out exposed flesh, while acrid smoke wafted over the earth and into the trenches.

★

273

When Josiah met with his friend Douglas Wade at the Australia Club, he noticed his friend's sombre expression. Over a rack of lamb and fresh vegetables, Douglas said very little, with conversation mainly about the Australian colonies accepting Britain's request to send armed forces to China in an attempt to quell the Boxer Uprising. Already the colony of South Australia had sent its gunboat *Protector* as the Australian colonies now found themselves involved in two British wars.

'The China campaign is for our blue jackets,' Douglas said, sipping an excellent locally made wine. 'Something to keep the navy boys busy after their complaints of not seeing much action in South Africa. By the way, have you heard from Sam over there?'

'The last letter we received was after George was tragically killed in action,' Josiah replied. 'A dear friend from my boyhood and from our service in the Sudan. I am just glad that my father is not here to learn of George's loss. Sam also wrote to say that he and his section of men were being detached for guard duties at a supply depot at some place called Elands River. He thinks the posting was his commander's idea of letting him have a break from chasing the Boers across the veldt. At least he will be safe on what we called garrison duties out of the frontlines.'

'That is good news,' Douglas said, but the strained expression had not left him, and Josiah had known his old friend a long time.

'I can see something is bothering you, old chap,' Josiah said. 'What have you really on your mind?'

Douglas placed his glass of wine on the table, picked up his linen napkin and wiped his mouth.

'I do have something on my mind,' he said. 'We have been keeping track of the duke's movements while he has been here, and noted that he has made contact with some Boer-friendly Germans in Sydney. We suspect that he may be raising money for the Boer cause. As you know, there are many other Boer sympathisers in our colonies, especially amongst the Irish.'

Josiah was shocked by the allegation against his sister's fiancé. 'Do you have any proof?'

Douglas shrugged. 'We know enough to fear that the duke might possibly be fomenting subversive trouble here. We consider him a persona non grata, but his close links to the Kaiser make it hard to express our suspicions. It would cause a diplomatic furore.'

'You do know that he intends to marry my sister?' Josiah queried.

Douglas nodded. 'That is why I am telling you, Josiah, so you may be prepared,' he said, leaning forward across the table and speaking in a near whisper. 'I still remember when we were at school, how you stood up for me against the bullies like Anderson. It is for our friendship that I am warning you. I know that you are a true and loyal patriot for the Queen, and no suspicion falls on you. I would not see you or your family embarrassed.'

Josiah appreciated the efforts of his old friend to protect the Steele name. 'So what happens now?'

'We will have discreet meetings with our German counterparts and lay out all our evidence. I have no doubt that the German government does not wish for a whiff of scandal when anti-German sentiment is being expressed all around the British Empire. I am sure that the duke will cut his visit to Sydney short and return home to Bavaria, solving the problem for us.'

Josiah lifted his glass of wine. 'I am only concerned for my sister. They are to be married here in a couple of weeks' time.'

Douglas looked uncomfortable. 'That is not something I can answer to,' he said with a grimace. 'Is it possible for the marriage to be postponed to Bavaria?'

'It is possible,' Josiah sighed. 'But how do I explain why they should marry away from her friends and family?'

'As a last resort, you might inform the duke that you know of his unlawful activities in Sydney and suggest it is in his and your sister's interests that they wed on the soil of his own country,' Douglas said.

Josiah realised that this was the only real option he had, but dreaded the moment of confrontation. Becky's happiness meant everything to Josiah. Not to mention that Maximillian was a dear friend and his son Hermann and Josiah's son David had formed what appeared to be a lifelong bond of close friendship. The matter was bound to cause a rift between the two families just as they were supposed to be uniting in marriage.

Now Josiah wished that he had volunteered to serve in South Africa; facing bullets and bombs seemed like the easier option.

THIRTY-ONE

The shelling continued for two days, coupled with accurate sniping from Boer marksmen firing into the shattered remains of the defences. But under cover of darkness, the colonial troops would slip out of their trenches and repair the damage wrought by the artillery and rapid-firing pom-poms.

Sam felt the pain in his bandaged lower leg, where fragments of the small artillery round had penetrated his flesh. Although it throbbed, Sam forced himself to stand, ignoring the searing agony. The carrier parties continued to sneak down to the river to fetch water at night, and with the supplies of tinned meat and jam, they were in no way subject to starvation. The dead animals, horses and mules were dragged away from the main body of defence as the stench of their decomposing bodies wafted over the men on the hilltop. This work was also carried out at night, and snatches of sleep were still possible for the exhausted men deep under cover during the day, even as the explosive crashing of Boer artillery shells and small arms fire swept the small plateau.

The commanders of the defence realised that something had to be done to push back the Boer encirclement, deny them the proximity of their field pieces and force any snipers out of accurate range.

Sam was invited to attend a briefing at the HQ, where some of the officers from the different colonial contingents suggested that armed parties go out at night and attack the enemy lines. It was a dangerous mission, but all agreed this was the tactic to use.

Sam returned to inform his small section of what was going to occur, and every man begged to be allowed to join one of the raiding parties.

'I will go this time,' Sam said, ignoring his injured leg. 'Corporal Welsh, you will take command back here. I will volunteer three men to come with me on the raid. We have identified a couple of troublesome Boer snipers well concealed on the side of the hill to our front, while other raiding parties are going to attempt to attack artillery positions.'

'If it is that bastard sniper causing the mischief to our section,' Nate growled, 'I hope you get him.'

Sam selected the men he would take with him, including Lance Corporal Brendan Welsh, and saw the disappointment on the faces of those being left behind. Kit was checked to ensure nothing made a noise in the night operation, and Sam led his men over the top of the trench.

They were vaguely aware of the movement of other such raiding parties moving silently to their left and right, knowing that the element of surprise was on their side and the night dark enough to conceal them. All raiders' nerves were still as tight as piano strings as they moved stealthily off the hill and began climbing the high ground before them. Slithering on their bellies, stopping often to look and listen, they came close enough to hear the distant voices of their enemy talking and laughing.

Sam ignored the pain he was experiencing, gritting his teeth. A tug on his trouser leg caused him to turn his head to see one of his troopers pointing to their left. Sam could hear soft snoring and just make out the slight mound of something in the dark. Carefully, he withdrew his long bayonet from its scabbard and crawled on his elbows in the direction of the snoring until he came across a pile of tree branches partially covering the body of a sleeping Boer, a Mauser rifle beside him. He was no doubt one of the snipers who had caused casualties amongst the colonial defenders of the depot.

Sam slipped his hand over the mouth of the sleeping man, who immediately came awake, but too late. The long blade penetrated his back through to his heart. It was a deadly assault carried out with precision, and the body under Sam went limp. Death had been mercifully quick when the bayonet had ruptured his heart, Sam attempted to reason to himself as the warm blood of the enemy soldier soaked his hands and shirt. Only for a brief moment had the body twitched before going limp, and Sam quickly went through the Boer's pockets for anything that might be of intelligence value. He was stunned to retrieve a sizeable pile of gold coins in a leather pouch. Sam looked closely into the dead man's face in the dark to see that he was a mere boy, around fifteen to sixteen. The only other items were a pocketknife and a letter.

A voice called out ten paces away in the Boer dialect. 'Who is there?'

In the dark, Sam could see two figures rushing the location of the suspicious Boer sentry and heard a desperate scuffle. Sam instinctively knew that one of the troopers accompanying him had bayoneted the Boer who had challenged their presence. The man was most certainly dead, and Sam knew that they had accomplished their mission.

'C'mon, boys!' Sam called softly. 'Time to get back for our tot of rum and some sleep.'

Sam and his small raiding party slithered down the slope until they came upon their own lines, marked by barbed wire and wooden crates, and when challenged Sam responded with the password for the night, allowing them past.

Exhausted and with the adrenaline receding, Sam made himself comfortable in the trench now covered with a ceiling of planks made from the wooden crates, where a lantern cast a sickly yellow light.

'You been wounded again, Sarge?' a trooper questioned, seeing the front of Sam's shirt soaked in blood.

'Not my blood,' he answered wearily, the face of the young Boer soldier still burning in his mind. 'I brought you each a present from the Boers.' Sam retrieved the pile of gold coins and handed them out to each of his stunned men, keeping a couple for himself.

'Bloody hell!' Nate exclaimed, staring at the Dutch gold coin. 'Are they all as well-off as the man you took these from?'

'He was a boy,' Sam admitted, choking back his words lest he show his emotional pain at killing a young man who would never have the chance to experience a full life with a wife and family. Sam was disgusted with himself for the life he had taken so easily, even as he reminded himself that it had been essential.

'A Boer boy with a rifle can do as much harm as any grown man,' Nate said, sensing his sergeant's distress.

'I know,' Sam answered, steeling himself to the fact that removing the boy could save the lives of those in the depot lines.

When the sun rose, the Boer besiegers would discover that they were not safe in the cloaking darkness, and in the following days the Boers chose to withdraw to a greater distance from the depot to ensure their own safety, which lessened the accuracy of their small arms and artillery.

Word got out the next day that Sergeant Steele's raiding party had recovered gold coins from a dead Boer, and that night, many more stepped forward to volunteer for raiding party duty. The continuing night raids on the Boer lines worked, as it was noticed that the enemy pulled his siege lines even further back, but the situation was still desperate. The battered defenders continued to face the devastating artillery and small arms fire from the Boer besiegers. Water was always in short supply, and disease was a constant threat for those on the crowded hilltop.

De la Rey was an astute tactical commander and knew that the British would probably send a relief force to rescue the defenders. He was correct. A relief column set out to reconnoitre the depot, but a small force of Boers ambushed it and the British column retreated twenty miles. A report was filed that it appeared the defenders must have surrendered, which was most probable as they were vastly outnumbered and outgunned.

Lord Roberts received the message and decided to investigate himself, but when he was close to Elands River, he did not hear the sound of continuing gunfire and returned to his HQ.

★

'Oh, I wish Father was still with us for the wedding,' Becky sighed as Josiah sat with her at the dinner table. 'Marian has cabled that she will be home in time. I am looking forward to being a spring bride.'

Josiah and his sister were alone for the meal, but neither was eating, with Becky talking a mile a minute and Josiah lacking appetite. He had yet to meet with Maximillian and explain the situation. Would his Prussian friend still wish to marry Becky when Josiah revealed what he knew?

'Have you ever considered perhaps being wed in Bavaria?' Josiah asked quietly, hardly daring to look at his beloved sister.

'Why would I wish that?' Becky countered with a frown.

'Well, Max also has family, and you will be moving to live there. I am sure that he would appreciate the chance to have the wedding at his castle and share it with his children,' Josiah said, adding, 'It might make an easier transition for them, and for you. Remember how Father introduced Isabel to us?' Now that he considered it, this truly might be the best way.

Becky's expression turned thoughtful. 'I do remember,' she said. 'I was so excited to become a wife, I had selfishly forgotten that I am to be a stepmother too.'

'You are not selfish, Becky,' Josiah said hastily.

Becky flashed him a grateful smile. 'I will consider your suggestion, dear brother,' she said, rising from the table. 'First, I must consult with Maximillian.'

Josiah watched his sister hurry out of the room. If she chose to marry in Germany, then Max could depart Sydney immediately, avoiding any possible scandal between the British and German empires.

Josiah had long learned that the world of espionage was not black and white, but a world of grey shadows. After all, had he not twice been tasked to spy on his Prussian friend over the years?

The simple matter of where his sister wed could avoid shaking the ground beneath the feet of two great dynasties: that of Queen Victoria and her grandson, Kaiser Wilhelm.

★

A message was sent down to the colonial defenders to surrender, with the promise that would be granted full military honours if they complied. Under his flag of truce, de la Rey was able to inform Colonel Hore that the relieving force sent to Elands River had been sent reeling back, and it seemed that the British High Command now presumed that the defenders had either surrendered or been killed. It was obvious that the situation was hopeless.

The offer of surrender was politely refused with the return message that if they wished to have the supplies, they were obliged to come and get them. The Boer artillery began once again to pound the defenders.

The siege had now dragged into a second week without any sign of relief. Unshaven, uniforms in tatters, filthy and weak from lack of sleep, Sam worried only for the welfare of his troopers, even as the wound to his leg became infected. He had no time to worry about his own health; the chevrons on his arm made him responsible for that of all his men.

Drunkenness was becoming a poor solution for many of the defenders in the dreary days of avoiding exploding artillery shells and rifle bullets that sought out the unwary or those foolish enough to expose themselves.

A bullet chipped stone from the lip of the trench, striking Sam just below the eye when he chose to have a quick look around using his binoculars.

'Bloody hell!' he swore, ducking down. 'Another bloody sniper is watching our sector.'

'Not worth goin' after, unless he has a pocket full of gold,' Brendan said with weary humour. 'What's goin' to happen to us?'

Sam wished he had an answer. Each day, they would reinforce their position with whatever they could scrounge, and they now had overhead protection against the exploding artillery rounds. Short of a direct hit on their position, they were relatively safe for now.

★

It was a clear and balmy end-of-spring day when Josiah and his children travelled to the harbour to bid farewell to Maximillian, Becky and Hermann, departing for Europe.

The group stood on the wharf as passengers embarked on the grand liner.

'I will miss our conversations, my friend,' Maximillian said. 'I would like to express my heartfelt thanks for convincing Rebecca to hold the wedding in Germany. She told me that it was you who changed her mind.'

Josiah felt a twinge of guilt, as he would have preferred that his sister wed in Sydney. 'I entrust Becky to your care, knowing she will be cared for and loved.'

'Thank you,' Maximillian replied, thrusting out his hand. A few paces away, Hermann and David were deep in boyish conversation, swearing they would keep in contact and be brothers for life, while Becky and Isabel were embracing. 'We both know why I am returning to Germany,' Maximillian said in a low voice, looking Josiah directly in the eye. 'Sadly, I was not as good at my mission as you were when we first became friends in Bavaria, that Christmas so long ago. I know that you had been sent to gather information.'

Josiah was not offended. They had both pretended in the interests of their respective empires. 'What we do for our countries does not diminish our friendship,' Josiah said. 'We will always be friends.'

'I pray so,' Maximillian said, gripping Josiah's hand tightly. 'May our two countries never be at war.'

Josiah glanced at Maximillian's son and his own, deep in discussion. 'May our sons never experience what we have in the past,' he said with conviction. 'May our two countries always be friends in this new century.'

Final farewells were made as the last call came for passengers to board. Becky hugged her beloved brother, crying. 'Promise that you will take time to visit us in Bavaria,' she said. 'I will miss Isabel, you and Marian and the children.'

'You are embarking on a great adventure, and with the modern means of communication, we are only a cablegram away from each other,' Josiah said. He fought back tears as his sister and Maximillian waved from the gangway before disappearing onto the ship.

Josiah waited until the great ship threw off its mooring ropes and a tugboat assisted it away from the wharf. When it disappeared from direct view, Josiah turned and walked away with his children.

★

Small arms ammunition was running low for the colonial defenders, who were into the tenth day of August when de la Rey sent a second envoy to offer the defenders an honourable surrender. The British Colonel Hore gave his answer:

'Even if I wish to surrender to you – and I don't – I am commanding Australians who would cut my throat if I accepted your terms.'

A message was able to be slipped out from the depot for General Baden-Powell at Mafeking. At around the same time, a Boer messenger was captured with a report that the post had not fallen as presumed. With the two sources of information, Kitchener had to accept the impossible, and personally rode with a relief column to the besieged post. There, he was welcomed by filthy, shell-shocked survivors living in what looked like a rubbish heap. Kitchener was overheard to make a remark to his staff: '*Only colonials could have held out and survived in such impossible circumstances.*'

Sam watched the grand British general in his smart uniform riding through the remains of the depot and shook his head. Why had reinforcements not been sent earlier?

'It's all over, Sarge,' Nate said.

'Yeah,' Sam replied, smelling the obnoxious infection from his leg wound. 'For now. I suspected about a day ago when they stopped shelling us that they had withdrawn the siege.'

Sam was medically evacuated by a covered ambulance wagon bearing the sign of the Red Cross to the nearest big town, where a field hospital had been set up. He was taken into the operating room and placed under anaesthetic.

When Sam finally awoke, he was vaguely aware he was lying in a bed of clean sheets with an overhanging mosquito net. His leg throbbed and he struggled to sit up, but a matronly nurse wearing the uniform of the British Nursing Corps was by his side, gently pressing him back onto his pillows. 'You must rest, Sergeant Steele,' she said. 'I'm afraid our doctors had no choice but to amputate your leg from the knee down.'

Sam thought that she must have made a mistake, because he could still feel the pain in his leg. But that night, he was able to struggle into a sitting position and saw that half of his left leg was gone.

He fell back against the pillows and cried like a child. His sobbing went unheard as many of the wounded and sick patients cried out in their pain or shouted strange words in their sleep.

In the dark of the hospital, Sam wished that the Boers had killed him instead of leaving him a cripple.

THIRTY-TWO

In early September, Sam was transferred by train to a military hospital in Cape Town and placed in a ward for wounded soldiers, but was separated from many Empire troops suffering from the old enemy of all armies – typhoid.

Determined to walk again, Sam requested crutches. After a couple of weeks, an interim wooden leg had been tailored to cover his stump and with the help of crutches, Sam was able to force his left leg forward as he hopped along. The nursing staff expressed their admiration for his perseverance and with the help of an African orderly, he was even able to hobble his way out of the hospital, which was in the vicinity of a beach, although the stench of the raw sewage being dumped in the sea nearby made the surroundings not pleasant to see or smell.

It was on one of his daily forced walks that he noticed an officer wearing a military jacket and pyjama pants, who

Sam could see was from a New South Wales infantry regiment. The man was sitting on a driftwood log, smoking a cigar. Sam could see that the officer was around Sam's age, and had lost his left arm from the shoulder down. Sam briefly wondered what would be worse – losing an arm or a leg.

The officer turned to Sam as if he knew he was being watched. 'Good morning, soldier,' he said pleasantly. 'I see that between us we have three legs and three arms.'

Sam smiled at the witty observation. The last time he had smiled was when former Corporal Welsh had visited him up country wearing the stripes of a sergeant. Sam was pleased to see the promotion, and even more pleased to learn Nate Welsh had taken Sam's role in the squadron's troop, while his brother, Brendan, had also moved up, to corporal rank.

'Fortunately, I only lost my left arm, so I can still shake your hand with my right,' the infantry officer said, extending his good arm while clenching the big cigar between his teeth. 'Lieutenant Steve Walton,' he said.

Sam accepted the extended hand. 'Sergeant Sam Steele of the New South Wales Citizen Mounted Infantry, sir,' Sam said, taking a liking to the cheery disposition of the officer. 'Formerly of Sydney. Are you actually a Stephen or a Steven, sir?'

'No need for formalities, Sergeant Steele, for a couple of chaps who will no doubt be discharged to return to civilian life again. It is officially Steve, as the registrar left off the "n" when writing my birth certificate and ever since then I have been known simply as Steve. It sounds a lot less formal than Steven and I like it,' he said thoughtfully. 'Steele . . . you would not happen to be any relative of the Josiah Steele of some financial fame?'

'My brother,' Sam answered. 'Do you know of him?'

'Know of him!' Walton exclaimed. 'He and I have had many business dealings over the past few years. My family are graziers and we have adjoining properties near Goulburn. I am surprised that we have not met before.'

'Probably because I was mostly sailing the Pacific before travelling here back in '95 for gold,' Sam said, sitting down on the log next to the officer. Sam rubbed the area around his stump where it met the prosthetic wooden leg in a futile attempt to rub away the pain.

'Can I offer you one of these superb Cuban cigars?' Steve offered.

'That would be a treat. I lost my pipe somewhere back at Elands River,' Sam replied.

'I heard about the Elands River stoush. You did all Australian colonials proud with your efforts,' Steve commented with genuine feeling. 'I suppose that is where you lost your leg?'

'In a manner of speaking,' Sam said as he bit off the end of the cigar, spitting it to the wind before lighting it. 'A bloody pom-pom shell exploded, causing shrapnel to shred the lower part of my leg. It was all right at first, but the wound became infected, and the rest is history.' Sam took a puff and the sweet smell of the tobacco helped to dampen the odious stench of the nearby sewage.

'Does your brother know about your condition?' Steve asked, watching a flock of seagulls diving into the sea where the outflow met the ocean.

'I was able to send a letter home explaining that I was still alive after our detachment to Elands River. The rest is a bit difficult to explain in a letter.'

Steve nodded. 'My parents in London were told by the army that I had lost my arm. I guess that was because

I am a commissioned officer, and the army gives us special treatment, but I am not looking forward to taking up a job back home as an administrator, although I will be glad to see my family. Oh, come to think of it, old chap,' he exclaimed, 'my little sister is currently in the company of your sister-in-law in South Australia. We live in a small world.'

'What on earth are they doing in South Australia?' Sam asked in surprise.

'Rosemary is a bit of a firecracker,' Steve replied. 'She has a great interest in politics and our up-and-coming Federation next year. Damned if that is not so far away now! Marian took Rosemary under her wing and has been acting as a kind of mentor. My sister and I are at odds about the fight against the Dutchies – she calls it an imperialist plot to subjugate the Boers.'

Sam grinned. 'Sounds like she and Marian would get on well.'

★

It was a hot summer's morning in early December when the ship carrying Sam and Steve steamed into Sydney Harbour. Sam knew that the army had already posted the news to the newspapers of the returning heroes of the South African campaign, and he had been officially listed as wounded in action, but it did not elaborate what his wounds were, nor had Sam been able to bring himself to write home about the loss of his leg. Was it vanity or simply a weak effort to deny that he was a partial cripple?

As he stood with his crutches at the top of the gangplank in a new khaki uniform and slouch hat and gazed down on the waiting crowds below, he knew that the moment of truth had arrived.

Steve stood beside him and assisted Sam with his good arm to slowly make his way down the gangplank. Those who had been severely wounded had already been removed on stretchers, and Sam was glad that was not the way he was returning home. For a moment, he considered that it could be worse.

'Steady, old chap,' Steve said in his ear. 'Take your time.'

But when Sam put pressure on the stump connecting the artificial leg he grimaced, gritting his teeth as the pain racked his body.

'I can see my sister,' Steve said. 'She is waving a handkerchief.'

Sam did not know who in the sea of faces was his friend's sister, but made it to the bottom and onto dry land.

'Thanks, cobber,' Sam said as Steve released him. 'I reckon I will be able to walk with the crutches from here.'

It was then that Sam saw his family, pushing their way towards him. Josiah was first, followed by Marian and his nephews and nieces, who cried shrilly, 'Uncle Sam!'

Josiah's expression of shock greeted Sam. 'Little brother, it is beyond joy to have you back with us,' he said, embracing Sam, crutches and all. 'Were you wounded in the left leg?' Josiah asked, glancing down at Sam's legs.

'I lost my leg below the knee,' Sam replied. Absolute shock was on Josiah's face, followed by tears welling in his eyes. 'No need to worry, I can still walk . . . sort of.'

Marian hugged Sam and the children embraced him around the waist.

'Children, be careful,' Marian warned. 'Uncle Sam has a sore leg.'

'We need to get you off your pegs,' Josiah said. 'I will organise for a wheelchair.'

'No need,' Sam insisted. 'I can walk.'

'Marian,' a female voice called, and a young woman holding her arm under Steve's pushed forward. 'I would like you to meet my brave brother, Lieutenant Steve Walton.'

Sam turned to see a smiling young woman he guessed was in her late twenties. She had titian hair piled under a summer hat, a spray of freckles over her nose and the bluest eyes he had ever seen. Sam was immediately struck by her wholesome beauty. It was not as if she would adorn a postcard, but there was something that he could see behind the smile and deep in her eyes that was beautiful. He became aware that she was also gazing curiously at him.

'You must be the Sergeant Samuel Steele my brother wrote to me about,' she said. 'He did not tell me how handsome you are.'

Sam was taken aback by her forward comment, but felt a warmth he had not experienced in a long time. 'Not so handsome,' he replied with a twisted smile. 'I am a man with only one leg.'

'I know,' Rosemary said. 'Steve informed me that you have a pact to work together so you can share an arm and a leg between you.'

Sam glanced at Steve, who suddenly looked sheepish. 'I figure when we return to being civilians again, we should keep in contact,' Steve said.

'But I do not know what I will do,' Sam said.

Rosemary turned to Josiah and introduced him to her brother, while Sam found his attention fixed on this bubbly young woman. He was deeply attracted to her but sadly reflected that he was not whole, with part of his body gone forever. Such a beautiful young woman could not find a crippled man attractive.

The two families chatted for a short time as the crowd

dispersed, then farewelled each other with promises of catching up.

That afternoon, Sam found himself at the home he knew so well, sitting with his brother in the shade of the trees that had grown over the years he had been gone. He held a cold glass of beer and gazed out on the harbour where life went on far from the semi-arid lands he had ridden as a mounted infantryman.

Marian came to the garden and passed him an official letter embossed with the royal coat of arms. 'This came a couple of days before you reached us,' Marian said. 'It looks important.'

Sam opened the letter, scanned it and handed it to Josiah without comment. Josiah read it with an expression of surprise, then pleasure.

'What is it?' Marian asked. 'I hope it is not bad news?'

'No,' Josiah replied. 'It informs Sergeant Samuel Steele that he has been awarded the Distinguished Conduct Medal for his actions attempting to save the life of a fellow trooper. The medal has already been gazetted in London as the act was witnessed by his commanding officer. Sam is now Samuel Steele, DCM. Congratulations, little brother,' Josiah said, holding out his hand.

'Oh, my goodness!' Marian exclaimed. 'I will inform the children that their uncle is officially a war hero!'

As Marian hurried away, Sam lifted his glass of beer, swallowing the contents. 'The CO did not directly witness the event when I rode out in an attempt to save George and must have extracted the information from Anderson's report.'

'Any relation to Horace Anderson?' Josiah asked.

'His nephew,' Sam said. 'As unsavoury a character as his uncle. The gutless bastard was responsible for getting George killed in the first place, and needs to answer for his actions.'

'Damn!' Josiah exclaimed. 'I heard that the man I knew had a nephew with aspirations of becoming a politician in the new federal government. From what I have heard around town, Anderson's nephew is being proclaimed as a war hero in the newspapers.'

'A what?' Sam exploded. 'Every time the shooting started, he would disappear. We all knew that he was a gutless coward and not fit to lead a dunny man's procession at a funeral.'

'From what I have heard, it appears that there is no one to oppose him when he stands for election.' Josiah shrugged. 'After all, he is being sold to his future electorate as a war hero.'

Sam could feel the bile rising in him. Here was the cowardly man cashing in on a war that had seen him virtually murder Sam and Josiah's best friend. Life was never fair, but this went beyond even that, and Sam experienced a silent rage that overwhelmed even the constant ache of his lost leg.

Then he remembered something from conversations with Steve Walton, who had talked about a political career in the new federal government. When they were on deck enjoying the breezes of the Southern Ocean, Steve had laughed that he only needed one arm to sign bills.

'Brother Josh.' Sam smiled grimly. 'I think I know someone who can bring Anderson to his knees – a *real* war hero.'

Maybe there was something in Steve's offhand statement after all, that civilian life meant that their destinies lay together in a partnership of two men with three legs and three arms between them.

THIRTY-THREE

Josiah and his children had braved a chilly late-winter's day to see the departure of the New South Wales naval contingent to China from the Cowper Wharf at Woolloomooloo. The naval contingent marched from Fort Macquarie, led by an older man in the uniform of a naval captain. Following marched the blue-jacketed band men playing the tune of 'Sons of the Sea'. Behind them marched over two hundred men carrying swords and cutlasses 'at the ready', led by a bulldog pup mascot named Nipper. At the rear of the column was the New South Wales Marine Light Infantry.

It was that contingent that Josiah had come to farewell. Weeks earlier, many of the men of the Marine Light Infantry had been scheduled to steam to South Africa as army infantrymen for the war still dragging on, committing Britain to deploying the bulk of its army to the South

African theatre. Josiah had friends in the third contingent for South Africa who had volunteered to fight in China as infantry. The colonial navy had objected to the former infantrymen being called 'sailors' as the naval men of the expeditionary force did not want men called 'infantry' fighting alongside them. So a compromise was reached and the term 'marines' was applied, creating a part-soldier, part-sailor, and copying the model of the British navy.

The naval contingents from the colonies of South Australia and Victoria were already steaming to the distant war in China, where a rebellion was under way for independence against the European powers dominating its political systems and exploiting its resources. The rebellion had been an uprising inspired by a mystical religious organisation, dubbed Boxers by the western powers. The aim of the Boxers had been to destroy Christian missionaries, whose influence they viewed as corrupting Chinese culture, but they had eventually allied with the Chinese army, and had already defeated a British force sent to quell them.

The city of Pekin was under siege, and many nations had called for help lest they be overrun. Contingents from Germany, Britain, France, Russia, United States of America, Japan and Austria were under steam to provide support in crushing the Chinese rebellion against foreign occupation.

★

Ling Lee staggered through a swamp in the retreat from Pekin. Under a low cloud of bitter rain, he could see all around him the skeletons and decomposing bodies of men, women and children. Their causes of death could have been numerous; in the year preceding the twentieth century, plague, famine and war seemed to shadow the land of Lee's parents. Death was a constant in the vast land of China, and

Lee was a long way from his home in Cairns and his wife, Mary, and his young son and daughter.

Months earlier, he had travelled to China, telling Mary and his friends that he was simply making a business trip for his successful import/export enterprise that was thriving in north Queensland. Chinese friends had warned him of the trouble brewing in northern China, but Lee had simply shrugged off their cautionary tales. In fact, he knew that rebellion was in the air, and that was his real mission: to honour an oath he had taken long ago to do all he could to free China from foreign occupation.

The drizzling rain soaked his clothing. Lee was still very fit for a man in his mid-forties, but hunger gnawed at his body and exhaustion wore him down. Lee knew that he was a fugitive from the European forces that had lifted the months-old siege on the city of Pekin, as the rebellion had its back broken in the battle against the foreign legations adjoining the Forbidden City of the Empress. The Chinese did not have the modern arms to fight the well-equipped European armies, nor did they have a unified leadership.

The Boxers Lee had been able to associate himself with had accepted him for his martial arts skills. But they believed that bullets could not kill them, and as Lee had witnessed in the attempted storming of the defended legation, they fell like rice at harvest to the farmer's scythe, no match for the deadly firepower of modern rifles. Cut off from the coast by the advancing European armies, his chances of escaping back to Queensland were bleak. All he could do for now was flee, as he knew that the pursuing European armies would execute him without recourse simply on the grounds that he was a Chinese man of fighting age.

★

Lee was on his knees, gasping for breath when he became aware of three red-shirted men approaching him. He immediately recognised them as Boxers.

'Who are you?' one of them asked, standing over Lee with his ancient musket pointed at him. The other two Boxer warriors carried battleaxes.

'Ling Lee. I was at Pekin with the Chow Tong, but we were forced to retreat when the British broke through the city walls. We had no other choice because we knew the British were also with the other armies coming up to break the siege.'

'You do not sound like a local peasant,' the man with the musket said. 'Why should I believe your story?'

'I was born in the land of the golden mountain to the south, but my father was a Shaolin monk in this region many years ago. I swore to him that I would devote my life to seeing China a nation free of foreign rule.'

'Ling,' one of the warriors standing behind the man with the musket said thoughtfully. 'My parents told me stories of a famous monk of that name who was forced to flee the district because he opposed the foreign devils. There were rumours that he went to the land of the golden mountain.'

'That was my father,' Lee said, kneeling in the mud, surrounded by the remains of what had once been humans. Lee provided further information on his father's monastery and the musket was lowered. He could see in the three men's expressions that they were convinced of who he was.

'Come, brother,' the man with the musket said, extending his hand to help Lee to his feet. 'We have a fortified position not far from here and we can give you a bowl of rice if you come with us. We have been informed that the Russians are advancing on us, and we will show them how we will not surrender to foreign devils.'

Lee rose to his feet, now covered in yellow mud, and was led to what seemed to be a last and heroic stand. The rebellion was on its last legs, and they all knew it.

★

It had been decided that an attack on the remaining rebel mud forts was to be made. With winter coming in, that would inevitably slow down military operations. A joint force of British, Russian, Austrian and German troops would be ordered out of Pekin to carry out the attacks. Amongst the British force would be three hundred colonials from Australia, half of whom had enlisted in New South Wales.

Lieutenant Edgar Hampton was excited to be given the task of commanding the twenty-five marines of his detachment as it would be an opportunity to blood the sword. The blue jackets had long been swapped for the khaki worn by the men fighting in South Africa, and their rifle was now the Lee Metford .303.

But from the start, things did not go well. The inexperienced colonials were told to travel light and did so without drawing rations. The first leg of the journey to the forts was to be by train on the other side of the river, but when they arrived at the railway station, they were told firmly by the Russians that they were only allowing Russian and German troops to use the railway, which was under Russian control.

So the British commander ordered the contingent to recross the river and use a river boat that was towed from the shore to convey them down the watercourse to a point that was as near as they could get to the enemy forts. This delayed their deployment to the forts, as mules and horses were loaded onto the lighter, and it was midnight before the colonial troops and Sikh soldiers were crammed in with the livestock. It was standing room only, but officers were allowed to go on deck while the men crammed below grumbled about the stifling conditions. Just after midnight, the rain came down, soaking all not under shelter, which gave the other ranks some comfort, knowing the officers had not got off lightly.

But the lighter ran aground on a sandbank well short of the rendezvous point. As the lighter could not be re-floated, all the troops and livestock had to be disembarked with the marines to form up and march as quickly as possible to the railway line, where the Russians had taken their troops the day before.

The marines marched at a gruelling pace, and when they eventually reached the rendezvous point, they collapsed from exhaustion. They had spent too much time aboard the ships conveying them to China and were not fit. Worse, they were now extremely hungry and regretted the decision to leave rations behind.

As they rested under a blazing sun, the men were aware of the sound of distant fighting and could see black smoke on the horizon. With orders to fall in, the Australians continued a forced march of eighteen miles and, just on sunset, reached a Russian field hospital to learn to their fury that the Russians had stormed the forts an hour earlier. The forced delays had denied the colonial troops any chance to prove their mettle.

★

Lee was armed with a pike, standing on the wall of one of the low-set mud forts looking out at a sea of enemy uniforms as artillery shells exploded around him. He had resigned himself to dying, and only regretted that he would never again see the faces of his beloved wife, Mary, and his dear children. Lee's tears were not for his inevitable fate but for his family who would never see him again. But he had always known that travelling to China to realise a dream of freedom for the country of his parents came with the strong possibility of death.

A Russian artillery shell exploded on the parapet, taking off the head of the musketeer standing next to Lee, and the blast wave threw Lee off the wall to the earth below. He landed heavily and was winded, struggling to breathe and vaguely realising that he could hear the Russian war cry of 'Huzzah!' growing closer, mingled with the defiant Boxer war cry of 'Sha! Sha!' – 'Kill! Kill!'

Still aching from the fall, Lee realised that he could hardly feel his arms, and crawled to a small mud-brick shelter. He had just reached the doorway when another shell exploded in the courtyard, knocking him out.

He no longer heard the cries of men spilling over the walls with bayonets, swords and rifles. The killing was now hand-to-hand as the ladders against the walls continued to feed the tough Russian infantry into the melee. The forts had all been captured, and the Russian soldiers went about bayoneting and shooting any wounded Boxer survivors.

★

A bitter row broke out between the British and Russians over the Russian action of attacking the mud forts before the British and the colonial troops had joined them for the planned attack. While the British and Russians squabbled, parties were sent back to find the stragglers along the route used to reach the battle, and the colonial troops found no food nor wood to boil water when they arrived.

Lieutenant Hampton sought permission from his senior officer to visit one of the forts during the night, accompanied by one of his marines, and report back what he observed.

Permission was granted and the young officer set out to locate a fort, passing through Russian lines in doing so. Eventually, he reached the mud walls but did not have to scale them as the Russians had during the day. A gate was open and the Australian officer stepped inside. The weak light from the lanterns they carried cast shadows over the dead and mutilated bodies of the Chinese enemy. The bodies of fallen Russians had already been retrieved for burial. A Russian soldier challenged them, but when Hampton identified himself to the big, bearded Russian, he reluctantly lowered his rifle. Hampton and the marine poked about the scene of carnage, knowing that when the sun rose, the bodies would begin to bloat and fill the air with the stench of decomposition. For the moment, only the lingering coppery smell of blood and gunpowder filled the evening air.

★

Lee was desperately thirsty and still weak from his days of deprivation on the retreat from Pekin as he lay in the dark under the body of a Boxer warrior, now beginning to bloat as he decomposed. From the corner of his eye, Lee could see a flickering lantern and still dared not move lest the Russians remaining in the courtyard realised he was still alive.

He remained deathly still as the flickering light of the lanterns came close.

'Some kind of outbuilding over here, soldier,' the voice said, and Lee could hardly believe what he was hearing. Whoever the speaker was, he was not Russian, and the accent not British. Lee recognised the slight difference that marked the man as a colonial Australian! But was it some kind of hallucination brought on by his desperate thirst? Now the two shadowy figures stood over him with their lanterns.

'Couple more dead 'uns,' the voice said.

It was now or never. Maybe if he was hallucinating, death from a bullet or bayonet would be preferable.

'Help me?' Lee croaked weakly through parched lips.

'Good Lord!' Hampton exclaimed in shock. 'That Chinaman seems to be alive and he speaks English!'

Lee struggled to push off the body over him and sit up. 'I am formerly from New South Wales and currently live in Queensland,' Lee said to the shocked Australian marines. 'I was taken prisoner by the Boxers and imprisoned here while I was on a business venture to China.'

'Help him, soldier,' Hampton said, and the marine bent to drag off the body covering Lee, who struggled into a sitting position.

'Who are you, man?' Hampton asked, bringing his lantern to Lee's face. 'How did you get here?'

Hampton could see that Lee needed water and passed him his water canteen, which Lee gulped from gratefully before answering.

'Thank you,' Lee said, returning the canteen. 'My name is Ling Lee, and I was born near Sydney. I am a merchant. I have a business in Cairns, and I was in China to secure a contract for my import/export business when I was captured near Pekin and brought here as a prisoner. Thank God the angels sent you here to rescue me,' he lied. The desperate will to survive and return to his family made him put on a performance that would have been the envy of any Victorian actor.

'We will need to get you back to our headquarters immediately,' Hampton said, extending his hand to assist Lee to his feet.

'*Stoyte!*'

Hampton saw the big Russian soldier step into the light of their lanterns, his rifle pointed menacingly.

'Prisoner,' Hampton answered, pointing at Lee. 'My prisoner.'

The Russian did not understand, but sensed that the British officer was attempting to indicate that he had personal control of the Chinese man. But he also had his duty, which was to execute any Chinese rebels found alive in the fort.

'Easy, sir,' the marine said. He reached into his trouser pocket, retrieving a handful of the Spanish dollars the Australians had been paid for their service in China, and cautiously extended his hand to the Russian, who looked just a little confused. There was a tense moment before the Russian lowered his rifle, accepted the money, then turned and marched away.

'You owe me five dollars, sir,' the marine said to Hampton with a grin.

That night, Lee told his story convincingly to Hampton's commanding officer and was eventually extended a welcome, with assurances he would be repatriated after being debriefed higher up the chain of command.

Six days later, a telegram from the Queensland government confirmed Lee was a reputable member of the Cairns business community. Two weeks after that, he was able to secure a fare on a ship steaming for the Australian coast with a stop in Townsville. He was going home. As the ship steamed out of the Gulf of Chihli, Lee looked back on the still-occupied land of his ancestors with tears in his eyes. The rebellion had failed and doomed his parents' country to European servitude for the foreseeable future.

THIRTY-FOUR

The ache in Sam's leg returned when he divested himself of the crutches and attempted to move about with a walking cane. Josiah had organised for a better-fitting wooden leg to be made and it eased some of the pain.

Steve Walton visited often, mostly to confer with Marian Steele about the world of politics. Sam had avoided Rosemary, as his vanity would not allow him to see her while confined to crutches or a wheelchair. He accepted that walking with the aid of a cane was a step forward and hoped that one day he would not even need it.

This morning, he had succeeded in walking a good distance around the garden, sweating with the exertion of it, but at least he was independently mobile – although dancing was still out of the question. Not that he was ever much good at dancing, with little opportunity in his past busy life.

'Sam, your friend Steve has arrived. I also invited him to bring Rosemary,' Marian said. 'She and I have a lot of catching up to do on the issue of all women having the right to vote when Federation occurs.'

For a moment, Sam panicked. He was leaning on his cane, sweating profusely under the morning sun, and was contemplating retreating to the house where he could wait in his room until Marian and Rosemary had their heads together before meeting with Steve. But he was too late, as both brother and sister appeared in the garden.

'Hello, old chap,' Steve greeted him breezily. 'Good to see that you are back and ready to mount a steed.'

Sam smiled weakly and noticed that Rosemary was watching him. 'Miss Walton,' he said, leaning heavily on the cane to avoid falling over.

'Please, call me Rosemary,' she said with a sweet smile. 'After all, from what my brother has told me about your support for his aspiration to become a member of the federal parliament, we are practically family. Steve told me that you received a decoration for bravery from the Queen, although I suspect you might have preferred to retain your leg instead of the medal.'

'You are right about that,' Sam said. 'It's put paid to a career as a dancing instructor after my military service, and it would be nice if you called me Sam.'

Rosemary's smile broadened. 'You do not strike me as a man with an interest in dancing, Sam. From what Marian has told me of your time aboard the *Ella,* the wooden leg suits my image of you as one of those old-time pirates,' she said dryly. 'All you need now is a parrot on your shoulder and an eye patch.'

Her humour endeared her even more to Sam and he laughed. 'I think that we should go inside for a cold drink,' he said, taking an awkward step forward. He appeared as though he might fall, and it was Rosemary who came forward.

'Sam, I think that you are attempting to convince the world that you are ready to display your independence despite your war wound,' she said, placing a hand under his shoulder to balance him. 'That is truly not necessary in my company.'

Sam bridled at her offer to help him, until the touch of her gloved hand sent a pleasurable shock through his body.

'Old chap, do not resist Rosemary's aid,' Steve said. 'It is in her nature to help others.'

Sam was able to hobble to the house, where Marian had already given instructions to the staff to prepare a morning tea for their guests.

Sam slumped down in a comfortable leather chair and the three were joined by Marian, who had to excuse herself as she was due to speak at a public meeting on women's voting rights, leaving the three alone in the spacious room that had been added to take in the beauty of the garden. A servant brought scones, cream and jam and pots of tea and coffee.

'I apologise for the unwashed state I am in,' Sam said, leaning forward to pour the tea. 'You caught me before I had the opportunity to bathe.'

'No excuses needed, Sam,' Steve said, reaching for a scone. 'We both experienced real stench back in that Cape Town hospital.'

For a time, the three chattered about trivial matters over a few scones and cups of tea before returning to the subject of politics.

'Anderson has spread stories in the newspapers of his heroic actions in South Africa,' Steve said. 'As you knew him personally over there, can you shed light on whether there would be any grain of truth in his self-aggrandising?'

'Only the fact that he was a commissioned officer serving in the campaign is true,' Sam growled. 'I once stopped him from . . .' Sam hesitated, glancing at Rosemary sitting opposite.

'Once stopped him from what?' Rosemary asked, leaning forward.

Sam took a deep breath before answering the question. 'From raping a very young Dutch girl when we were tasked to burn Boer homes.'

Rosemary did not express any shock. She had contact with the impoverished working girls of the Sydney slums in her work with Marian, and was attempting to improve their miserable lives of beatings from drunken spouses and other men. The only expression Rosemary exhibited was anger.

'Were there witnesses to what you saw?' Steve asked, also leaning forward.

'Yes, the men of my troop saw all,' Sam replied. 'But it was the virtual murder of a very close friend on a mission we had that I know witnesses would vouch was ill-conceived and absolutely incompetent. George Bowden grew up with my brother and served with him in the Sudan. When George was killed, Anderson did not attempt to send aid to rescue or retrieve his body. Instead, he fled, commanding the patrol to do the same. Only two Kiwi brothers of my troop, Brendan and Nate, remained to provide me with covering fire against the express order of Anderson.'

Sam went on to recount the many instances that Anderson had avoided combat by feigning sickness, and it could only be concluded that the man who wished to represent the people was not only incompetent but also a craven coward.

'There are many soldiers returning to our shores from South Africa and all we have to do is keep track of any who may have belonged to your unit who might be prepared to make public statements as to what they observed from their illustrious leader, Lieutenant Cecil Anderson,' Steve said. 'From what you have told us, it appears Anderson would not want what they know becoming public knowledge.'

'When are the elections to be held for seats in the new parliament?' Sam asked.

'It appears that elections will be held in March of next year,' Rosemary said. 'From what Marian and I have learned in our travels, the Protectionist Party led by Mr Barton, who stand for the imposition of tax on any imported goods, universal suffrage, aged pensions, a uniform railway gauge and a transcontinental railway to link the east and west of the country, appear to be the most popular voters' choice. The Labor Party are also popular and have similar policies, but I think Mr Edmund Barton will rise to be our first prime minister.'

Both men listened intently to Rosemary, who they respected for her superior knowledge of political machinations. 'Then we have a few months before Anderson stands for election,' Sam said. 'Is Anderson politically affiliated?'

'Alas, yes,' Rosemary answered. 'He is a Protectionist Party member.'

'Damn!' Steve swore. 'He could just fall into a seat based on the popularity of the party.'

'Then we will have to work hard to expose the bastard as a liar, coward and incompetent,' Sam commented.

They continued to discuss further matters of politics until the hours swept past and it was lunchtime. Rosemary and Steve accepted an invitation to stay for a meal and Sam excused himself to bathe and change clothes while brother and sister strolled in the gardens.

Lunch was a success and Steve was quick to notice the bond between Rosemary and Sam, and he even found himself cut out of the conversations that flowed between his beloved sister and best friend. Steve did not feel offended; when he observed the two, he had to admit that they made a handsome couple. Never before had Steve known his sister to laugh as much as when Sam regaled her with funny stories of his life. She in turn poured out her hopes and dreams for the future ahead for a united nation called Australia.

When Steve and Rosemary left that afternoon, Steve was convinced his sister had met the man she would share her life with. He was secretly pleased, as that would make his best friend also his legal brother-in-law. It was just the matter of Sam being of the Jewish faith that worried him a little, but Steve dismissed this aspect as being of little concern. Catholics and Protestants married in the colony, albeit mostly to unite family wealth. This was not the Mother Country, with its strict sectarian divisions.

★

A day later, an invitation arrived for Sam to attend a tennis party at the Walton residence. A note had been scribbled on the back that Sam was not expected to play, and Sam guessed that the delicate handwriting was Rosemary's. Sam was reluctant to attend, but his brother persuaded him.

'I have a feeling that Rosemary wishes to introduce you to her friends.' Josiah grinned. 'I have noticed that she seems attracted to you.'

'Not bloody likely,' Sam growled. 'What woman would want a man with just one leg when it is obvious that she has the pick of the crop?'

'From what I can see, you are able to walk and appear to improve each day. You have to remember she has a brother who has only one arm. Besides, you're a recognised hero.'

Sam pondered his brother's sage advice and decided to attend Rosemary and Steve's tennis party.

The Walton residence was only slightly less grand than the Steele mansion. It was situated on the southern extremes of the city with unspoiled views of the distant Great Dividing Range and bordered by farming land.

When he arrived in the buggy alone, he was met by a smartly dressed servant and produced his invitation.

'This way, sir,' the valet said, leading Sam towards the double-storeyed sandstone house with its sweeping verandas. Other coaches and guests had already arrived, and Rosemary was at the front entrance to greet them. Her face lit up when Sam walked forward stiffly with the aid of his walking cane.

'Samuel!' she exclaimed. 'I am so pleased that you accepted our invitation. Please, come inside so that I can introduce you to some important political contacts.'

Impressed by her confident manner, Sam followed Rosemary inside, where his eyes fell on some notable persons of the colony. He had learned more about those in the Protectionist Party and quickly realised that this was no ordinary tennis party but a political gathering. However, he could still hear the distant sound of a tennis ball being hit and the cheers of spectators.

'Ida, this is my brother's dear friend, Samuel Steele,' Rosemary said to a pretty young lady of obvious pedigree.

'So, you are the man Rosemary told me lost a leg at the Battle of Elands River and had your courage recognised with a military decoration,' Ida said in cultured tones. 'From what I can see, you have seemed to overcome the loss of your leg. Good show.'

312

Sam was surprised to hear the frank statement as to who he was, but then considered Rosemary would have such friends, given what Marian had told him of her character.

'Do not have any ideas of setting your sights on Samuel. He's mine,' Rosemary said with a laugh, taking Sam's elbow and guiding him away to meet another guest with her words still ringing in Sam's ears. *He's mine.* He was halfway across the room filled with well-dressed men and matronly women when his heart skipped a beat at the sight of none other than Cecil Anderson!

'What in hell is he doing here?' Sam said quietly to Rosemary.

'Oh, he had to be here,' Rosemary replied airily. 'He has put himself forward to stand for a seat in the new federal government next year for our party.' Sam could see that Anderson was in the company of an older man with a striking family resemblance. As if reading his mind Rosemary whispered, 'That's his uncle, Horace Anderson.' Sam knew the man was a cad, and it was clear to him that the apple didn't fall far from the tree.

'So, why are the bastards here?' Sam growled.

'"Know your enemy" is a wise tactic in politics,' Rosemary said. 'At least I do not have to introduce you.'

As Sam leaned on his walking stick, he realised that Cecil Anderson had turned to see him on Rosemary's arm and Sam could see how Anderson's face paled. It was obvious that Sam's presence had shocked him, and he almost spilled his champagne. Sam took pleasure from the fact that he had obviously upset the man he would have gladly killed for the death of George Bowden.

'Ah, old chap,' Steve said, approaching Sam and Rosemary. 'The big moment has arrived for the announcement by our party leader as to who they will be nominating in this electorate for the elections next year.'

Sam was puzzled. Had they not plotted for Steve to stand against Cecil? Had not Rosemary convinced Sam to sign on as a party member to assist?

A spoon was clinked against a glass to request silence and attention fell to a distinguished man with bushy sideburns. 'Ladies and gentlemen, distinguished guests. It is time to announce one of our future representatives for the new federal parliament. It is my honour to announce that Mr Cecil Anderson, a returned hero of the war in South Africa, will be our unopposed representative for the elections next March.'

A polite round of clapping followed the announcement as a smiling Cecil Anderson stepped forward to stand beside the party leader.

'Ladies and gentlemen,' Cecil said. 'It is a great honour to be selected for –'

'Excuse me.' Rosemary's voice cut Anderson short. 'My brother, Mr Steve Walton, will also throw his hat into the ring as one of our nominated representatives for the seat Mr Anderson is vying for.'

A confused hush settled over the room and Sam bit back a smile. Rosemary had set the ambush as well as any soldier on the battlefield. She pushed her way forward to stand beside the party leader and a stunned Anderson.

'Steve, will you please come forward and accept the nomination?' Rosemary continued.

'Who nominated Mr Walton?' Anderson demanded belligerently as Steve stepped forward.

'I did!' Sam called out, knowing now why Rosemary had paid his membership dues. 'You will see that I am an official member of the party.'

'Your name, sir?' someone asked.

Rosemary answered. 'Sergeant Samuel Steele, who was the recipient of the Distinguished Conduct Medal and a man who lost his leg at Elands River. You will find his name on the roll.'

A hush fell over the crowd.

'I accept the nomination,' Steve said, cutting across the silence.

'Well, this is totally unexpected, and we will need to review the candidacy of Mr Walton,' the meeting leader said. 'We will make our decision as to who we will endorse after Christmas. So, ladies and gentlemen, please continue to enjoy the wonderful hospitality of the Walton family.' He stepped away and immediately there was a buzz of voices as the guests discussed the late upset.

Rosemary walked over to Sam, who was unable to control his grin any longer. 'Remind me never to get on your bad side, Miss Walton,' Sam said. 'You are more dangerous than any Boer commando.'

Rosemary took his elbow. 'Never forget that, Sergeant Steele,' she said with a twinkle in her eye.

Sam noticed that the two Anderson men angrily departed the house in a huff. This was the next best thing to actually killing Cecil Anderson for his crimes in Africa, Sam mused. Killing his grandiose ambitions for a political career was a satisfactory outcome.

Now it was time to enjoy the first battle won in the company of the woman Sam knew he was in love with. He even suspected that he might have a slight chance of winning her hand in marriage.

THIRTY-FIVE

Uncle and nephew had left the meeting in a rage.

'Do you know the man who nominated that bastard Walton?' Horace finally asked his nephew when they were settled into his grand coach.

'Sadly, I do,' Cecil answered. 'He was one of my troopers – a sergeant – for whom I inadvertently provided the information that saw him awarded a DCM when his best friend was killed. Samuel Steele is the brother of Josiah Steele, who I know is not exactly a friend of yours.'

'Damn!' Horace swore. 'The world is a bloody small place. Josiah Steele is at the top of my list of people I would like to see burn in hell.'

'Unfortunately, Samuel Steele knows certain things about me that I would not want made public – not that there is any truth in the lies he would spread,' Cecil added quickly, staring out the carriage window at horse-drawn carts they passed.

'What kinds of lies?' Horace asked carefully.

'He . . . he might spread a rumour that I was a coward in the face of the enemy,' Cecil said. 'It would only take one or two of his loyal troopers to support his smear to dash any attempt at my chance of a rightful position in the new parliament.'

'That cannot happen!' Horace said, slamming down his fist on the carriage seat. 'It is vital that you gain a seat in parliament. I need you there to help along some critical future contracts with the government, contracts your position in parliament will afford me.'

'I cannot think of any way I will be able to prevent Steele from spreading malicious lies about my service in South Africa,' Cecil said. 'Short of the man suddenly dying. Besides, there is still Walton. His wound from his service to the colony makes him a sympathetic character to the party leadership.'

'I see your point,' Horace said, staring ahead as they approached the suburbs. 'But it is of the utmost importance that you gain a seat in parliament.'

'I cannot see much hope of that now,' Cecil commented miserably. 'The party will surely believe a decorated war hero over me.'

'But if both men were to meet with a fatal accident . . . then the problem goes away,' Horace said quietly.

Cecil glanced at his uncle with an expression of shock. 'That is not likely to happen.'

'Not unless it is arranged,' Horace replied. 'I will need time to ponder the matter.'

Neither man spoke until they reached Horace Anderson's luxurious home, built on bricks of dishonest dealings.

★

The bar was crowded and filled with tobacco smoke. The patrons were mostly clerks from the nearby office buildings and a few merchant sailors from the ships at the docks, who filled the busy bar, celebrating their paydays.

On this particular late Friday afternoon Sam and Steve were joined by another former soldier, who had contacted Sam only that day. Former Sergeant Nate Welsh had been discharged after his enlistment was over, and Sam was looking forward to introducing him to Steve as one of the witnesses to Cecil Anderson's actions in South Africa.

When Nate pushed his way through the raucous laughter and shouts of the patrons already well on their way to a hangover, he was greeted by Sam with a firm handshake and also received one from Steve. In no time, they were hefting large beer glasses and discussing the war they had left behind.

'So, you have a job as a house painter,' Sam said to the man whose friendship had been forged in the horrors of war.

'Yeah. Not a job I was hoping for,' Nate answered. 'My time travelling to South Africa kind of piqued my interest. I'd like to see more of the world.'

'I might have the solution to your desire to see the world,' Sam said. 'My family owns a schooner that has been in dry dock and is almost ready to sail again. We will need men of adventure to crew the *Ella* on her journey through the Pacific, and I know that you are such a man.'

'Is this fair dinkum?' Nate exclaimed. 'If it is, I'm your man.'

'If it was good enough for our New South Wales infantry to become sea-going marines, I can't think of any reason why a former mounted infantryman can't get used to being at sea,' Sam said with a laugh.

Nate extended his hand. 'Aye, aye, captain,' he said. 'When would I start?'

'How about you report down to the Woolloomooloo docks at ten tomorrow morning? You will be paid at a generous rate, and we hope that the *Ella* will sail next week for Fiji. You will be part of the crew, but I know you have the ability to learn the ropes in no time. The skipper is a crusty old sailor from America, but I know he will take you under his wing when he learns of your record of service in the Transvaal, as he is a veteran from the civil war they had over there a few years ago.'

Nate was almost in a stunned state at how his fortunes had changed in this moment. It was like a dream come true that he would not be reporting to work in the morning but would instead be setting out on his future life of adventure, all because he had the fortune to be a friend of the finest soldier he had ever served with.

Evening turned to night and the three men spilled out of the pub to return home. Sam and Steve looked for Hansom cabs while Nate intended to walk the short distance to his cheap, dingy boarding house.

★

Standing opposite the hotel was Cecil Anderson. His uncle had briefed him on the plot by allocating him the task of signalling to the waiting killers the men he wanted taken care of. It was a safe task, as he knew the odds of being recognised in the crowd coming out of the pub would not be great. Besides, if Steele or Walton did see him on the street, they would be dead within short minutes anyway.

There they were!

Cecil felt his heart pounding. But there was a third man with them. Probably just someone they had met in the pub, and Cecil was relieved when he saw the third man break away to walk in the opposite direction, carrying a bottle of beer. Steele stood out as he was using a walking stick to limp along the street. A one-legged man and a one-armed man would be easy victims.

The targets were walking in the direction Cecil had hoped, and all he had to do was point out the two men to the waiting killers. But then Steele ceased walking, gazing in Cecil's direction before saying something to Walton, who turned to glance across the street now filled with men stumbling home.

Damn! It was obvious that he had been spotted – but that would not matter. Cecil raised his hand and pointed.

*

Sam had no time to consider what the hell Cecil Anderson was doing near the pub they had exited because three hulking figures emerged from an alleyway to fall on him and Steve.

Sam called out to Nate before they were dragged into the dark shadows of the space between the two tall buildings, but couldn't be sure if his friend had heard his cry.

The man who held him from behind brought up a knife, and Sam reacted quickly. With all his strength, he was able to deflect the blade and swivel to face his attacker. But his wooden leg gave way and he fell heavily to the cobblestones. This at least saved him from the long-bladed knife. Without hesitating, Sam grappled for his walking cane, gripping it as the man he was up against looked irritated. His victim's disability meant he would have to bend down and thrust his knife into the man's chest. As he leaned forward, Sam brought up his cane to use the tip as a weapon. His aim was true, and the blunt end of the cane buried itself in the man's eye and into his skull. The man screamed in agony, dropping the knife and throwing his hands up to his shattered eye socket.

Sam was desperate. He knew he would have trouble getting to his feet, and to stay off them surely meant he was a dead man . . . but suddenly, Nate was in the alleyway, holding a broken beer bottle and thrusting it into a man's face, savagely twisting it. The would-be assassin stumbled backwards with his hands over his face. The third assailant, seeing his two comrades badly wounded, hesitated for a moment before turning on his heel to flee down the alleyway, leaving Sam, Nate and Steve alone in the pools of blood. The remaining two wounded attackers also wisely followed their companion, stumbling away from the scene of the crime for safety. The ruckus of the attack had hardly raised any alarm on the street as occasional brawls were par for the course in the inner city.

In the gloom of the blood-spattered cobblestones, Sam was aware that Steve lay on his back without moving. When Sam was helped to his feet by Nate, he stumbled over to Steve and fell to his knees beside his friend's body. It was obvious that Steve was dead from the deep gash from ear to ear, his eyes staring blankly at the night sky. It had taken mere seconds in this seedy alley of the inner city to change all their lives.

'You bastards!' Sam screamed, cradling Steve's head in his lap and remembering Cecil Anderson giving some kind of hand signal just before the assault was launched. Sam knew that it was not a coincidence, and he vowed that Cecil Anderson would pay with his life. First George and now Steve . . .

Cecil Anderson was a self-proclaimed war hero who had powerful and influential friends, and Sam knew there was a good chance he would walk free of any attempts to bring him to justice. After all, he had just happened to be on the street that night and had nothing to do with the sudden ambush, he would argue.

A raging fire seethed in Sam that only Anderson's blood could put out. There was the law and there was justice, and in Sam's experience, they were not always the same thing. Sam would seek his own kind of justice for the murder of his friend – and for Rosemary's loss of her beloved brother.

There was something in the Steele blood that followed a different path to the law and could not be explained in any rational terms. It was a primitive instinct that the Steele men had little control over: the ancient biblical law of an eye for an eye.

THIRTY-SIX

Sam and Nate remained with Steve's body until a couple of uniformed beat police appeared as a result of being called by a member of the public. At first, they treated Nate and Sam as strong suspects until a couple of independent witnesses assured the police that they were also victims of the vicious crime and not the assailants.

Three plainclothes police arrived led by Detective Andrew Paull, who approached Sam, now back on his feet, leaning on his cane.

'Your name and place of residence?' Andrew asked, pulling out a small notebook and pencil from his suit pocket.

'Mr Samuel Steele. I reside with my brother, Mr Josiah Steele,' Sam answered defiantly, knowing that his brother was well known in colonial society.

The police detective paused writing and looked up at Sam, who was covered in Steve's blood. 'I know your family,' he said. 'It seems that such violence follows you all.'

'My friend has been brutally slain, and I hope that all your resources are used to catch his killers,' Sam said, still fighting the rage inside him. 'The man at our feet is Mr Steve Walton, who was to be a candidate for the new federal government. He is also a man who lost his arm in the war in South Africa, serving his country and Queen.'

'I will need a statement as to what occurred here tonight, Mr Steele,' Andrew said, and Sam explained all that had happened but left out the fact that he had seen Cecil Anderson nearby. Anderson would deny all knowledge and anyway, this was a matter Sam intended to settle privately. Sam also had Nate promise not to divulge to the police that he had also witnessed Cecil Anderson near the scene.

Steve's body was taken away and Sam made his way home to deliver the news while Nate returned to his boarding house.

Sam knew that Rosemary was currently a guest of Marian and staying overnight at Josiah's house. It was in the early hours of the morning when Sam arrived at a sleeping household and quietly went to the bathroom to strip off his bloody clothes and wash himself clean of all traces of blood. Sam changed into trousers and a white shirt he fetched from his room. He did not want to disturb anyone and decided he would deliver the sad news when the sun came up.

Sam made his way to his brother's library, where he took a bottle of good scotch from the liquor cabinet and poured himself a large tot. He had hardly taken a swig when he noticed the door open, and Josiah appear in his nightshirt.

'Sorry,' Sam said, slouching in a big leather armchair. 'I did not mean to disturb you.'

In the dim light of a candle Sam had lit, he could see the shadows flicker over the concern on his brother's face.

'I had trouble sleeping,' Josiah said quietly. 'When I went to the bathroom, I saw the pile of bloody clothes. What happened? Have you been injured?'

'Steve Walton was murdered when we left the pub,' Sam replied. 'I have enough evidence to convince me that the low mongrel Cecil Anderson was behind the murder and the attempted murder of myself.'

Josiah didn't respond for a long moment, then finally said, 'I think I need a drink as well.'

Josiah poured himself a scotch before taking a seat in a leather chair opposite his brother. Sam explained in detail what had happened and how he had seen Cecil Anderson appear on the street opposite the pub to signal to the three men who had ambushed them.

'If Anderson was behind the murder, you can bet he was in league with Horace, his uncle,' Josiah commented.

'They both deserve a bloody vengeance, and if the law won't deliver it, maybe I will,' Sam declared.

Josiah regarded him seriously. 'I think it is time that I told you a family secret.'

Josiah explained how, after their father's death, he had located the letter that was to be delivered and read it. It was a confession to killing a man who had avoided justice for a heinous crime; their father's way of settling a debt he felt that he owed society.

'Bloody hell!' Sam swore. 'I would never have thought the old man would do such a thing.'

'It seems that our father respected a police detective by the name of Paull, to whom the letter was delivered. I did not hear anything else about the matter and suspect the detective buried it. After all, he could not arrest Father.'

'A Detective Paull questioned me last night,' Sam said. 'Funny how life and death are linked.'

'From what I have learned, he is a good man and an honest copper with a reputation amongst his peers for solving crime. If you are indeed considering following in Father's footsteps, just remember that you will always have Detective Paull as your dark shadow.'

Sam pondered his brother's words. 'Like you, brother, I have faced possible death on the battlefield, where I probably killed good men who were deemed our enemy,' he said finally. 'In this case, Cecil Anderson is a real enemy deserving of death.'

'You may be right,' Josiah said. 'But who are you to be the one to deliver it?'

Sam didn't answer his brother, saying instead, 'In the morning, I have to face Rosemary and tell her that her beloved brother was murdered.'

'Would you rather I be the bearer of the tragic news?' Josiah asked, leaning forward.

Sam shook his head. 'It must be me,' he replied. 'Steve was my dear friend, and we served our country together. Better that I break the news as gently as possible.'

Josiah leaned back. The sun was rising on another hot summer's day and the household would soon stir.

'Maybe you should have a nap?' Josiah suggested, rising from his armchair and gulping down the last of his scotch.

'No,' Sam answered wearily, rubbing his eyes. 'I think Rosemary needs to know as soon as possible, before someone outside the family leaks the bad news.'

★

It was the hardest task Sam could ever remember doing in his life. He was able to take Marian aside and explain what had happened. She gasped and threw her hands up to her face.

'Please be calm for me,' Sam begged, gripping his

sister-in-law's shoulders. 'I need your strength to help Rosemary through the time ahead. I know she looks up to you as almost a big sister.'

Tears welled in Marian's eyes, but she nodded her understanding of the role she must play in the moments ahead and beyond.

Rosemary was joking with the Steele children at the breakfast table when Marian approached her and gently said that she was needed in the sitting room. Puzzled, Rosemary excused herself and followed Marian.

'Sam!' Rosemary exclaimed with a bright smile when she saw the weary man waiting for her. 'I hope that my brother did not lead you astray last night?'

'It might be better if you sat down, dear Rosemary,' Marian said gently. Rosemary looked from Marian's face to the wrought expression on Sam's. 'Sam has some sad news.'

Rosemary almost collapsed on a couch, still staring at Sam, who approached and knelt in front of her, taking Rosemary's hand.

'Steve was murdered last night,' he said.

Rosemary's face paled. 'How? Who would do such a thing to my beautiful brother?' she asked, her shock evident.

'Three thugs attacked us, and Steve was killed in the melee,' Sam replied. Now the tears welled in Rosemary's eyes, and she fell into a racking fit of sobbing with her head bowed, almost touching Sam's hand.

Marian stepped forward and wrapped her arms around the distraught young woman's shoulders as Sam eased himself to his feet with the aid of his cane.

'I promise you that the men who did this will be punished,' Sam said, not knowing that the three thugs were already aboard a ship due to depart Sydney's shores. Not that they were Sam's primary target.

Sam limped from the room, leaving Marian to comfort Rosemary.

He had a mission to punish the real murderer of his friend.

★

Only miles away, uncle and nephew met at Horace Anderson's extravagant house in one of the new city suburbs for the upper- and middle-class citizens.

'That damned Samuel Steele survived the ambush,' Cecil said, swilling back a badly needed gin and tonic. 'That damned soldier of his came to their aid. From what I could ascertain, they inflicted a lot of injury on the men hired for the job.'

'The incompetent fools allowed a one-legged man to survive,' Horace said angrily. 'Fortunately, they were only paid half up front. I suppose that covers the cost of killing just one man. What are you going to do now?'

Cecil sighed and sat down in a comfortable chair with ornate wooden arms. 'Well, they at least eliminated any opposition to me for the coming elections, so you should be pleased. Steele was really just a bonus. I doubt that he is any longer a threat to me gaining the nomination by the party.'

'Did anyone see you in the city?' Horace asked.

Cecil blanched, as he was afraid of his uncle and his shady criminal contacts. 'Not that I am aware of,' he lied. 'Besides, if Walton saw me, he is in no position to give evidence.'

'What about anyone else?' Horace persisted.

'No. I walked away quickly,' Cecil answered, and that part was the truth, although he had a sick feeling Sam Steele may have seen him.

'Pray that you are right,' Horace growled. 'I do not

want any scandal on my doorstep. If it comes, I will disown you without any hesitation. You are only good to me in parliament.'

'I swear that will not eventuate,' Cecil answered in a desperate tone. 'The police will most probably report that the attack was motivated by an attempt to rob the men.'

Horace nodded and Cecil breathed a sigh of relief. It was unfortunate that Steele had survived, but there was little he could do to the man with only one leg.

★

Many attended Rookwood Cemetery to farewell Steve. Amongst the mourners were men of his infantry company who had returned from South Africa and wanted to pay their respects to an officer they'd liked and respected for his leadership.

Sam stood beside Rosemary at the edge of the grave as Steve was lowered to his last resting place. She was not crying, but had an enigmatic set expression as the mourners dropped flowers and earth into the open grave.

Then Rosemary turned and walked slowly away, Sam accompanying her. It was mid-morning on a hot, sultry day but Sam sensed a southerly buster would arrive before late afternoon, one of those Sydney storms that brought drenching rain, lightning and thunder.

Rosemary had a parasol to provide cover from the hot sun as she walked to the carriage that awaited them. Josiah and the family had their own carriage to convey them to the Steele mansion for the wake for former Lieutenant Walton.

'I suspect that you know who was behind my brother's death,' Rosemary said.

'Why would you say that?' Sam countered.

'Because I can see it in your eyes,' Rosemary replied.

'And I also suspect you think Cecil Anderson is responsible.'

Sam was surprised by her perceptiveness and realised he had no reason to lie to her. 'I know Anderson was the man who organised Steve's death – and mine,' Sam replied. 'And I promise you he will pay.'

'The best way to punish him is to cause him shame in front of the party at our next meeting,' Rosemary said calmly. 'With my brother dead, the party will no doubt endorse Anderson. You will not allow him to profit from Steve's death in this way.' They reached the carriage and driver waiting for them on a roadway running through the cemetery. 'I am going to nominate you in my brother's place after you reveal what kind of hero Anderson really is. The party will have no other choice than to endorse your nomination. Time is running out and the party needs someone in the seat.'

'But I am not a politician,' Sam protested. 'There must be someone else you can nominate.'

'None with your pedigree,' Rosemary replied firmly. 'You are the perfect example of a truly patriotic man who has given his leg for his country, and it helps that you are a member of the well-known and respected Steele family. Besides, I like the idea of being married to a member of parliament.'

Sam stopped in his tracks. Maybe he had misinterpreted Rosemary's last words, but she had a satisfied smile at his confusion.

'We are moving into a new century, and I cannot see why a woman does not have the power to make the decisions about her own future. What is your answer, Samuel Steele?'

Still stunned, Sam stood with his hands dangling at his sides. 'I . . . I am truly honoured, Miss Rosemary Walton, and I accept your proposal.'

Rosemary leaned up to kiss Sam on the lips. 'Then I must commence making marriage arrangements for early next year. I think autumn is a nice time of year for a wedding. Do you agree?'

'Yes, yes. Whatever you say,' he answered quickly. The world had gone mad. A funeral and now a marriage proposal on the same day!

'Then it is settled,' Rosemary said decisively. 'You will be one of our representatives in our first federal parliament.'

His fiancée made it sound easy, but Sam wondered. Would he be a good representative of the people? Then again, Rosemary had confidence in him and that was all that mattered.

THIRTY-SEVEN

Christmas was approaching when a letter posted in Bavaria arrived at the Steele residence. It was from Becky, who now held the title of duchess. Included with the letter was a studio photo taken on their wedding day, with Becky wearing a beautiful wedding dress and standing beside Maximillian, who was wearing the ornate military uniform of a high-ranking German army officer. They both beamed with happiness and Becky explained in her letter that although they had married in a Lutheran church, she had done so for political reasons and remained true to her Jewish faith, attending the local synagogue on a regular basis.

Becky went on to explain that the wedding was a lavish affair, attended by Maximillian's family, friends and military colleagues. Even the Kaiser had sent a generous present with apologies for not being able to attend. She wrote that the children had accepted her on a formal basis, but she hoped that with time they would come to see that she could be a warm and caring person, albeit never one who would attempt to replace their mother.

Joshua read the letter to his family and Isabel cried with happiness.

'Our joy has not abated,' Marian said, wiping away her own tears of joy. 'We will have another wedding early next year, with Sam and Rosemary's wonderful announcement of their engagement.'

'Hear, hear,' Joshua replied with a broad smile. 'My little brother will finally have to give up his wild ways and return to normal life.'

'All going well, your little brother will be a voice in the new federal parliament next year,' Rosemary said, slipping her arm under Sam's. 'Sam will make the family proud.'

'He already has,' Josiah said. 'He has given much for the new Australia on the battlefield. But for now, we need to plan a Christmas Day for the staff and their families.'

Although the Steele family did not celebrate Christmas, Josiah always ensured that his staff were well compensated for their loyal service over the past year. They would have a sumptuous Christmas lunch prepared, not exactly kosher, although Josiah and Sam were also guilty of breaking many of the kosher laws themselves. Gifts would be distributed to the families by Josiah, Marian and Isabel, and to all appearances, the Christmas Day festivities would not appear any different from those of the Christian households of their friends. Then it would be time for his children to engage in the tradition of Hannukah with the Jewish community of Sydney. Josiah had come to accept that he was both an Australian and a Jew.

When only Sam and Josiah remained in the library, Josiah recovered a bottle of his best scotch from the liquor cabinet. He poured two tumblers, handing one to Sam. Both men slumped into comfortable leather chairs opposite each other. Josiah raised his glass in a toast.

'To you and Rosemary and a wonderful future together,' he said.

'Thank you, brother,' Sam responded.

'Where will you take your wedding vows?' Josiah asked, taking a sip of his drink.

'Rosemary has approached me to convert to our religion,' Sam answered. 'I did not ask her to do so, but she said that she had always had an interest in doing so on the basis that Judaism was the first monotheistic religion and that it was linked to Christianity through their bible anyway. So, we will have the traditional Jewish ceremony at the synagogue.'

Josiah raised his eyebrows. 'I wonder how her parents will react to her conversion?' he said. 'I believe they are returning from London very soon.'

Sam chuckled before speaking. 'If I know my future wife, I doubt that they would be brave enough to question her choice. She is one of the most remarkable women I have ever known.'

'If you are elected, I have no doubt that she will become your chief adviser,' Josiah commented. 'And I know she will be a wise one. But for now, it seems all she is interested in is conversing with my wife about the wedding dress she will wear on the day – and the reception to follow. Funny how weddings are so important to brides.'

'It means a lot to me too,' Sam said. 'But all the details of weddings are really the domain of women.'

'We do have another matter to discuss, and that is you stubbornly wishing to pursue Anderson,' Josiah said. 'You have already had your revenge by shaming Anderson and his uncle. Losing his nomination has also disrupted all plans by the Andersons to have the political power to line their pockets.'

'You know, I still remember how light George's body was after half his head was blown off,' Sam said, staring into space. 'For that alone, I want revenge.'

'It is your road to walk, but you must be fully aware that if anything goes wrong in your burning desire for vengeance, you just might make Rosemary a widow,' Josiah cautioned. 'Either from a knife to the ribs or swinging from the Darlinghurst gallows. You must think on that.'

Sam did not reply. In his mind he was back on the veldt, remembering in vivid detail the order given that amounted to murder. The army hierarchy would justify Anderson's order as a sound tactical decision when even the newest trooper in the squadron knew it was virtually suicide to obey such an order. Cecil Anderson must pay in blood for the death of Corporal George Bowden as much as for that of Sam's dear friend Steve Walton, who would have been his brother-in-law.

But Sam would not rush into any plan. No, he would plan the man's death as meticulously as any military operation.

'Dear brother,' Josiah said, breaking Sam's memories of the past. 'Not all military action requires a frontal assault.'

Sam glanced at his brother. 'I'm not sure I follow.'

Josiah rose from his chair to refill his tumbler. 'I have an idea. If it works, justice will come for Cecil Anderson without endangering you. But it is a long shot.'

Sam frowned. 'I am not sure I know what you mean,' he said. 'If you told me what your plan is, I might understand.'

Josiah turned to Sam. 'I will explain everything if my plan eventuates. If not, I swear that I will assist you in any ideas you have to see Anderson suffer the consequences of his evil murders of George and Steve. For now, I simply ask for your patience before you go ahead with any plans you may possibly be harbouring.' Josiah extended his hand to his brother.

Sam stood. 'I trust you, brother. Even with my life,' he said, grasping the proffered hand firmly. 'I will wait until you give the order.'

'For now,' Josiah said, 'the birth of our nation is mere days away and that should be our focus.'

Sam agreed and they raised their glasses to the birth of Australia as a united nation of once-squabbling colonies.

★

Christmas and New Year's Eve had come and gone but a fierce storm in Sydney on the eve of 1901 threatened the official birth of a new nation. However, when the sun rose on 1 January, it was a fine, hot day.

Edmund Barton had formed his Cabinet and Sydney had been chosen to herald a new era on the continent of Australia, despite ongoing legal arguments about what the Federation of Australia meant to all the citizens of the new nation known as the Commonwealth of Australia.

In the morning, a crowd of around a quarter of a million people had roamed the highly decorated streets of Sydney, where the excitement was obvious. The formal declaration of the new nation was to be held in Centennial Park that afternoon, where a huge crowd surged towards the place where the governor-general, Lord Hopetoun, would read from the Queen's text before a white pavilion. As the Queen's representative, he would proclaim the new nation of Australia before the gathered thousands. Amongst the many in that crowd of spectators were the Steele family and others close to them, including their staff, who had been given the day off to celebrate.

In Centennial Park, the colourful uniforms of many nations representing their governments could be seen along with the well-dressed dignitaries. It was a day when the words rang out, '*One people, one flag, one destiny.*'

An impromptu cheer rose, marking the end of the formalities. A bugle call rang out, signalling the gathered troops to march off in their gold-braided silver helmets, khaki and red-jacketed uniforms, and they did so as a single unified military force. No longer were they the armies and navies of separate colonies, but a united armed force for the defence of all Australia. The huge crowd dispersed to take up vantage points for the great parade along the streets of Sydney.

The parade was led by a contingent of shearers, recognising their contribution to the national economy. They were followed by the troops and brass bands under constructed arches displaying words such as *We welcome in unity our comrades from over the seas.* The tune of 'Soldiers of the Queen' was roared out by hundreds of voices as the banners of the armed forces fluttered by, even as the new federal Cabinet was being sworn in by Lord Hopetoun.

Then it was over. A nation called Australia now existed in the Commonwealth of the British Empire. On 2 January 1901, people from one side of the continent to the other woke to welcome a new day under a new nation in a new century.

★

Two weeks later, Sam's ongoing plan to exact justice on Cecil Anderson was interrupted when he read Cecil Anderson's obituary in the morning paper. It disclosed little, merely that he had died in his own residence. Sam was confused, as Anderson had been in good health and only a young man.

It was Nate Welsh who revealed the truth to Sam, gleaned from a constable he knew. Cecil Anderson had shot himself in the head with the service revolver that he had carried in the Boer campaign, leaving a suicide note that stipulated he could no longer bear the shame of the threat of his cowardly military service being revealed to the public.

Something niggled at Sam, and he suspected he might get answers from his brother. Hours after learning of Anderson's suicide, Sam approached Josiah in his library, shutting the door behind him.

Josiah was signing documents and glanced up. 'You have that expression I know well, where something is troubling you,' he said, placing the pen on the blotting paper.

'You do know that Cecil Anderson has shot himself?' Sam questioned, standing before his seated brother.

'Yes, I read that he was dead. Sensible to choose to shoot himself as the alternative to hanging himself, as it is a slow means of dying,' Josiah replied calmly. 'It seems that any plans you had to go after him yourself are now moot.'

'Why is it that I have this irrational thought that you were the cause of his death?' Sam said with a frown.

'Because you are right,' Josiah answered. 'I tipped off a few people in the newspapers about his false claims to heroic deeds in South Africa. I had help from your former corporal, Nate Welsh, and his brother Brendan, who were able to collect statements from a few of your former troopers. Anderson refused to be interviewed. My newspaper reporter friend left Anderson's residence and commented to me that the man appeared extremely distressed. He later learned from the police that Anderson probably shot himself a few hours after his visit. Very unfortunate that your former commanding officer should choose that path, but at least he used his service revolver and did the right thing by not shaming the regiment with his cowardly record. I believe that it is a very British thing to do.'

'You are bloody devious, brother,' Sam sighed with a wry smile. 'Brains before brawn.'

Josiah rose from his desk and walked over to the liquor cabinet, retrieving their favourite bottle of scotch. 'Just Horace Anderson still standing, but I have no desire to kill him,' Josiah said, handing his brother a glass half-filled with the expensive spirit. 'At least you have learned a lesson for your future political career: words have more power than bullets. Here's to the Honourable Samuel Steele, Member of Parliament.'

Josiah raised his glass and Sam responded. He was still leery of a position as a member of parliament, but knew that Rosemary very much desired him to hold the position.

Three months later, after a campaign managed by Rosemary, Sam came very close in the final election results but was narrowly beaten by an opposition candidate. Although Rosemary was bitterly disappointed, secretly Sam was not.

'Do you still wish to marry a man who has failed?' Sam asked Rosemary as they stood in the garden of the Steele mansion one evening. It was a balmy night with just the faintest wisp of an evening breeze, and Sam enjoyed how it tousled the tips of Rosemary's hair.

'Of course I want to be your wife, you silly man,' Rosemary answered without hesitation. 'I think I fell in love with you the day you hobbled off your troopship.'

Sam was surprised at her admission, but dared not ask the beautiful and intelligent woman standing beside him what she could have seen in him. All he knew was that he could breathe again.

★

Rosemary and Sam were married in the city's grandest synagogue, and the wedding was heavily featured in the social columns. It was the happiest day of Sam's life and one he would never forget. All his family were in attendance and a cablegram even arrived from his beloved sister to congratulate the newlywed couple. It was read out by Josiah as being from the duke and duchess, which impressed the newspaper columnists in their reporting of the grand affair.

The following day, Sam had a coach convey them to a wharf at Woolloomooloo on Sydney Harbour. Rosemary was confused because her husband had not told her why he wanted to take her on the coach ride.

Sam helped his bride down and escorted her to the edge, where a schooner with the name *Ella* painted on the bow was secured. Rosemary was impressed by its size and lean, clean looks, and was surprised to be met at the gangplank by Nate and Brendan Welsh.

Sam had signed on Brendan as crew when requested by Nate. It did not bode well to separate brothers who had proved themselves on and off the battlefield.

'Morning, Sam. Congratulations, Mrs Steele,' Nate said cheerily. 'She will be ready to sail first thing tomorrow, when Ebenezer and Yuan join us.'

Rosemary glanced at Sam, who was leaning on his walking stick. 'What is going on, if I may ask?' she said, still confused.

'Tomorrow, Mrs Steele, you and I are departing for a journey around the Pacific Ocean to celebrate our marriage. There will be a little business along the way, but as skipper, I have the final say where we will travel.'

Stunned, Rosemary stared at the schooner rocking gently on the tide. She reached out and took Sam's hand.

'It will be a new adventure,' she said.

And thus it proved to be, in the months and years ahead.

EPILOGUE

The Western Front

Summer 1916

A cting Major David Steele was hardly aware of the stench of rotting flesh anymore. He had first seen action in Rabaul, a part of the German Pacific Empire, a mere few weeks after the declaration of war, fighting the German colonial troops where Australians saw their first casualties of this terrible carnage. Then he'd been sent to the Dardanelles as a lieutenant commanding a platoon of infantry, when he had also been exposed to the sickly sweet smell of death.

Now David lay in a shell crater with five surviving men from the company of which he was now in charge after the death of their appointed commanding officer. David was aware that there were others from his company sheltering in the moonscape of craters who were also alive after the disastrous attack on the German-held ridge that was in all degrees a man-made reinforced concrete fortress of enemy trenches and machine-gun posts. The initial melee had degenerated into primitive close-quarter fighting with bayonets, fists, teeth, homemade clubs and anything else a man could use to kill and maim.

The echoes of this form of warfare rang in David's ears and haunted his mind if he closed his eyes. Men screaming curses in two languages; the awful sounds of others dying and the strong, acrid smell of blood. David knew that his hands trembled uncontrollably, and as the night descended he also knew that the Bavarian regiment would mount a counterattack, as was always their tactic when they lost ground. The order had trickled down to David's level of command that they must hold to cover the withdrawal of other Australian troops after the disaster of the battle of Fleurbaix. Later, it was given another name – Fromelles.

David knew that he must assume command and control of the few of the company still left alive, and would need to gather as many as he could for their defence against the inevitable counterattack. But that meant leaving the relative safety of the shell crater to locate his soldiers across the bloody battlefield. The wounded had to be recovered, but the constant artillery fire made that almost impossible. For a moment, David wished they were still back at Gallipoli, as bad as that had been. The redeployment to France and Belgium had shown the veterans the meaning of industrial mass slaughter, with the artillery shells killing more than the bullets of machine guns or small arms. A soldier was helpless under an artillery barrage, as the exploding shells tore bodies apart with deadly red-hot shards of jagged metal, or by causing trenches to collapse and bury men alive. An unlucky direct hit virtually smashed a body to atoms.

David was aware that his men were looking at him with questioning expressions and tried to hide his trembling hands.

'What is our ammo state, Sergeant?' David asked, the question his way of displaying normalcy in this insane man-made butcher's shop.

'Each of the lads have two bombs and around twenty rounds left, sir,' the sergeant answered, blood running down his sleeve from a shrapnel wound to his arm. 'Private Woods has been gut shot.'

David knew the wound was most probably fatal and that the soldier was in extreme agony, although he refused to admit it. One look at his ashen face twisted into a permanent grimace gave him away. David wished now that he had been smart and enlisted in the mounted infantry, where his younger brother had taken a commission and been posted to Palestine. In his letters, Ben complained of the long days of boredom on the desert patrols, continual lack of water and the searing heat. David would gladly have swapped places.

'I will need to go out after dark and attempt to find the other fellows of the company,' David said. 'When we have enough men gathered, we will organise a defence.'

The sergeant, a man around the same age as David in his early thirties, frowned. 'It's bloody suicide,' he said. 'I reckon we should wait for the brass to send up reinforcements to relieve us.'

'I wish that were possible,' David replied. 'But if I know the Hun, they will mount a counterattack before that occurs.'

The sergeant nodded. He knew the acting major came from the wealthy Steele family in Sydney and was a volunteer like himself. He had proved to be an officer men willingly followed for his leadership and, to an extent, his great luck in keeping his men alive.

But luck was a fleeting spirit.

'I will come with you, boss,' the sergeant said.

★

A mere three hundred yards away, Colonel Hermann von Kellermann was holding a briefing with his junior officers deep in a heavily protected bunker. He informed them that they were to lead their companies in a counterattack to sweep the battlefield clean of any remaining troops from the earlier assault on the ridge. Hermann was acting *Oberst*, which put the Bavarian infantry regiment under his command as the equivalent of a British colonel. When his orders had been delivered to his officers, they withdrew to brief their own soldiers, leaving Hermann with his orderly, an old private soldier who had once been a gamekeeper for Hermann's father on the family duchy in Bavaria.

'The Tommies put up a spirited attack today,' the old man said, preparing a mug of coffee for his commander.

'They were not British troops who attacked us today,' Hermann said. 'They were Australians. A different kind of soldier altogether.'

'I remember when you had a young friend who would stay with us when his family visited,' the old man said, stirring the coffee with the rare ration of sugar. 'You and he were as close as brothers.'

'Yes. David Steele, nephew to my stepmother,' Hermann said with a note of sadness in his voice. 'I will always miss his friendship. One day, when this war is over, we will possibly meet under different circumstances and go hunting again in the forests.' Hermann took a swig of the sweet lukewarm coffee. 'But right now, I must prepare to lead the sweep.'

It was Hermann's way to personally lead his men and they respected him for it. He slipped on his cap rather than a metal helmet so his men could distinguish him in the attack across what was now no-man's-land.

★

David did not have the chance to leave the shell crater.

A flare went up, giving light to the lunar-like landscape. There had been no preliminary bombardment by the German artillery and as the small parachute flare descended, David could see the ominous shadows moving towards him and his few survivors. He could surrender, or die with his remaining men in their forlorn defence.

A Lewis machine gun opened up from an adjoining shell crater on David's left flank, indicating that one of his surviving company members had made the decision not to surrender.

'C'mon, lads! Let's give 'em hell!' David yelled, and those who could fight scrambled to the lip of the bomb crater, opening small arms fire into the dark as another flare lit the sky, illuminating the sea of German soldiers advancing across no-man's-land.

On that summer night, two close friends from opposing armies would meet for the first time in five years. Only one would live to see the sun rise.

AUTHOR'S NOTE

When Australians think about our military history, they might think it commenced on 25 April 1915, but even before we became a united nation in 1901, we had already sent colonial troops and navies to three military campaigns on behalf of Britain. Before even this, thousands of Australian colonials volunteered with the British army in the New Zealand wars of the 1860s.

Our first overseas service was the deployment of the army of New South Wales to the Sudan in 1885. I have a link to one of the military units, a field battery which is the longest-serving army unit in the Australian Army. In 1969, I was posted as a gunner to A Field Battery, which had the honour of wearing the white lanyard on the same side as the infantry battalions because of its unbroken history dating back to 1885. Needless to say, I was often told by members of the Royal Australian Regiment that I had my lanyard on the wrong shoulder!

My second link to the Sudan war is when I joined the Army Reserve unit, 1/19th Royal New South Wales Regiment, after my regular army service. The Ares unit, also known as the Bushman's Rifles, carries the colours of the 1st Battalion and 19th Battalion. It is inscribed on the colours of the 1st Battalion for its service in the Sudan campaign and later all wars up to the end of WWII when the Royal Australian Regiment was formed for all wars since WWII. So, I have had the unique military experience of serving in the two units who trace their origins back to 1885.

A very readable book written on the subject of the Sudan campaign was published by KS Inglis, *The Rehearsal: Australians at war in the Sudan, 1885*. It is detailed with first-hand recollections and the intrigue of colonial politics as well as recollections of the men who served in the Sudan. I thoroughly recommend the publication to anyone who has an interest in military and political history of those times.

Our second military campaign was the Boer War, 1899–1902. It was a war with parallels to the later years of the Vietnam War in the '60s and early '70s. Over six hundred Australians were killed in action, died of disease or accident between 1899 and 1902, which is a higher toll than we lost in Vietnam in ten years. It was a war fought by colonial armies, which became one upon Federation before the campaign ended. An interesting note is that fifty Aboriginal trackers also served in the war under British command and a small number of colonial Australians fought on the Boer side.

A truly detailed coverage of the Australian experience in the Boer War can be found in Craig Wilcox's *Australia's Boer War: The War in South Africa 1899–1902*. I hardly touched on the many actions the colonial troops fought during the campaign, but the siege at Elands River was an example of the character of the digger long before Gallipoli.

In comparative terms it was a greater battle than that fought by the British at Rorke's Drift during the Zulu wars, but did not receive the same recognition by the British government. However, the superb Boer irregulars certainly recognised their enemy on more than one occasion. It was summed up best by the Boer commander, General Smuts, when he reflected later, *Never in the course of this war did a besieged force endure worse sufferings. It had shown magnificent courage, albeit fortified by dugouts and drink and had taught the local Boers a proper appreciation of the Australians that overturned the contempt engendered at Koster River.* Eight soldiers were killed and many wounded by the end of the siege and no battle honours were awarded to the defenders. Craig Wilcox has published a truly interesting story of a forgotten war in our history, and I thoroughly recommend his publication which details the many desperate battles Aussie fought on the veldt of South Africa.

I did not have the scope in this novel to properly cover the third military campaign before Federation, which was our involvement in the Boxer Rebellion of 1900. This time, it was our colonial navies which dominated and the marines who served ashore. For those with an interest in this very important campaign to the future of Sino–Australian relationships, look to Bob Nicholls' book: *Bluejackets & Boxers: Australia's Naval Expedition to the Boxer Uprising* (Allen & Unwin, 1986). Nicholls has written a fascinating account of the politics and life of the participants in that short but violent war.

Before the landings at Gallipoli in 1915, Aussie soldiers died fighting the Germans in the Pacific mere weeks after war was declared. They were engaged in a direct defence of Australia's east coast against the Imperial German navy based in China – another forgotten campaign in our military history.

ACKNOWLEDGEMENTS

A special welcome to Alex Lloyd as my publisher, and acknowledgement to the following wonderful people on this writing project: Bri Collins, my principal editor, Libby Turner, copyeditor, editorial assistant Grace Carter, proofreader Hilary Reynolds, my publicist, Ellen Kirkness, and publicity and marketing director, Tracey Cheetham. Also to the entire team at Pan Macmillan, with a special mention to Marsha Peters who works in the background distributing the books.

My former publisher of over two decades, Cate Paterson, has left Pan Macmillan and it is with my humble thanks I dedicate this book to her. It was Cate who originally commissioned *Call of Empire* for you all to read.

A special thanks to Rod and Brett Hardy, always working on the *Dark Frontier* project for television production.

Others who have influenced my working life are Dr Louis

and Christine Trichard, Pete and Pat Campbell, Pete and
Kaye Lowe, Mick and Andrea Prowse, Kristie Hildebrand
and family, Nerida Marshall, Rod Henshaw and Anna, Rea
Francis, John Wong, Chuck and Jan Digney, Larry Gilles,
Peary Perry and family, Betty Irons, OAM, and in memory
of an old mate, Bob Mansfield and Peter Leslie.

For my extended family of my sister, Lyn and Jock
Barclay, Tom and Colleen Watt and their extended family,
my cousins, Virginia Wolfe, Tim Payne and Dan Payne
and their families. As always the Duffy boys and their
clan members. My daughter, Monique and her wonderful
partner, Nate Welsh and my granddaughters.

A special mention to the executive of our now established legacy for emergency service volunteers – VESL.
Nick Clark, John Riggall, Tania Peene, Geoff Simmons,
Steve Walton and Mark Carr. The mission objective can
be found at veslltd.org.au. It is a registered charity with tax
benefits for donating – just a hint!

Never forgotten are my cobbers-in-prose: Dave Sabben
MG, Tony Park and Simon Higgins.

And above all my beautiful wife, Naomi, who has stood
by me through a rocky road of writing novels for over two
decades. My heartfelt thanks and love forever.

MORE BESTSELLING FICTION FROM PAN MACMILLAN

The Queen's Colonial
Peter Watt

Sometimes the fate for which you are destined is not your own . . .

1845, a village outside Sydney Town. Humble blacksmith Ian Steele struggles to support his widowed mother. All the while he dreams of a life in uniform, serving in Queen Victoria's army.

1845, Puketutu, New Zealand. Second Lieutenant Samuel Forbes, a young poet from an aristocratic English family, wants nothing more than to discard the officer's uniform he never sought.

When the two men cross paths in the colony of New South Wales, they are struck by their brotherly resemblance and quickly hatch a plan for Ian to take Samuel's place in the British army.

Ian must travel to England, fool the treacherous Forbes family and accept a commission into their regiment as a company commander in the bloody Crimean war . . . but he will soon learn that there are even deadlier enemies close to home.

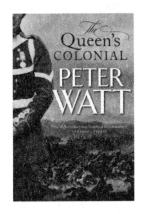

'One of Australia's best historical fiction authors' *Canberra Weekly*

The Queen's Tiger
Peter Watt

Peter Watt brings to the fore all the passion, adventure and white-knuckle battle scenes that made his beloved Duffy and Macintosh novels so popular.

It is 1857. Colonial India is a simmering volcano of nationalism about to erupt. Army surgeon Peter Campbell and his wife Alice, in India on their honeymoon, have no idea that they are about to be swept up in the chaos.

Ian Steele, known to all as Captain Samuel Forbes, is fighting for Queen and country in Persia. A world away, the real Samuel Forbes is planning to return to London – with potentially disastrous consequences for Samuel and Ian both.

Then Ian is posted to India, but not before a brief return to England and a reunion with the woman he loves. In India he renews his friendship with Peter Campbell, and discovers that Alice has taken on a most unlikely role. Together they face the enemy and the terrible deprivations and savagery of war – and then Ian receives news from London that crushes all his hopes . . .

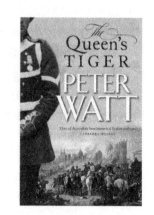

'Watt has a true knack for producing captivating historical adventures filled with action, intrigue and family drama'
Canberra Weekly

The Queen's Captain
Peter Watt

From India to America and New Zealand, action, intrigue and family drama.

In October 1863, Ian Steele, having taken on the identity of Captain Samuel Forbes, is fighting the Pashtun on the north-west frontier in India. Half a world away, the real Samuel Forbes is a lieutenant in the 3rd New York Volunteers and is facing the Confederates at the Battle of Mission Ridge in Tennessee. Neither is aware their lives will change beyond recognition in the year to come.

In London, Ella, the love of Ian's life, is unhappily married to Count Nikolai Kasatkin. As their relationship sours further, she tries to reclaim the son she and Ian share, but Nikolai makes a move that sees the boy sent far from Ella's reach.

As 1864 dawns, Ian is posted to the battlefields of the Waikato in New Zealand, where he comes face to face with an old nemesis. As the ten-year agreement between Steele and Forbes nears its end, their foe is desperate to catch them out and cruel all their hopes for the future . . .

'Australia's master of the historical fiction novel' *Canberra Weekly*

The Colonial's Son
Peter Watt

Danger, passion and bravery in nineteenth-century Australia, Europe and onto the battlefield of Kandahar.

As the son of 'the Colonial', legendary Queen's Captain Ian Steele, Josiah Steele has big shoes to fill. Although his home in the colony of New South Wales is a world away, he dreams of one day travelling to England so he can study to be a commissioned officer in the Scottish Regiment.

After cutting his teeth in business on the rough and ready goldfields of Far North Queensland's Palmer River, he finally realises his dream and travels to England, where he is accepted into the Sandhurst military academy. While in London he makes surprising new acquaintances – and runs into a few old ones he'd rather have left behind.

From the Australian bush to the glittering palaces of London, from the arid lands of Afghanistan to the newly established Germany dominated by Prussian ideas of militarism, Josiah Steele must now forge his own path.

'an adventure reader's delight . . . I was breathless as I read'
Central Western Daily